Changes and Chances

ALSO BY MARY ELMBLAD

All Manner of Riches

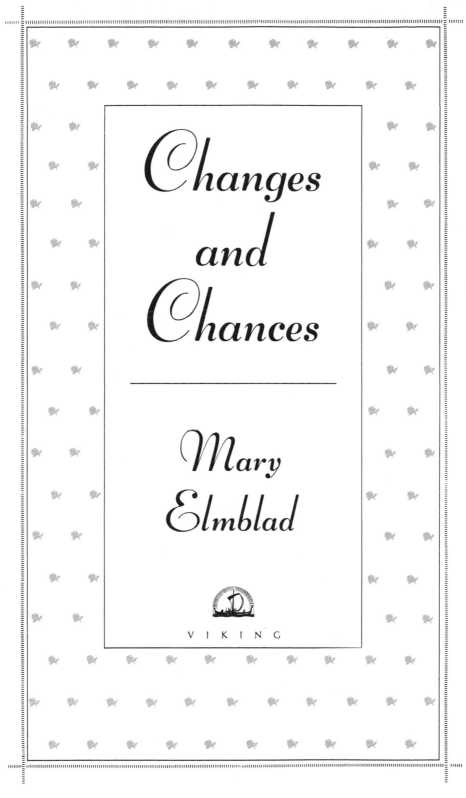

Changes
and
Chances

Mary
Elmblad

VIKING

VIKING

Published by the Penguin Group

Viking Penguin, a division of Penguin Books USA Inc.,

40 West 23rd Street, New York, New York 10010, U.S.A.

Penguin Books Ltd, 27 Wrights Lane, London W8 5TZ, England

Penguin Books Australia Ltd, Ringwood, Victoria, Australia

Penguin Books Canada Ltd, 2801 John Street, Markham, Ontario, Canada, L3R 1B4

Penguin Books (N.Z.) Ltd, 182–190 Wairau Road, Auckland 10, New Zealand

Penguin Books Ltd, Registered Offices: Harmondsworth, Middlesex, England

First published in 1990 by Viking Penguin, a division of Penguin Books USA Inc.

1 3 5 7 9 10 8 6 4 2

Grateful acknowledgment is made for permission to reprint an excerpt from
"The Second Coming" from *The Poems of W. B. Yeats: A New Edition* edited
by Richard J. Finneran. Copyright 1924 by Macmillan Publishing Company,
renewed 1952 by Bertha Georgie Yeats. Reprinted with permission of Macmillan
Publishing Company.

LIBRARY OF CONGRESS CATALOGING IN PUBLICATION DATA

Elmblad, Mary.

Changes and chances / by Mary Elmblad.

p. cm.

ISBN 0–670–82206–X

I. Title.

PS3555.L629C4   1990

813'.54—dc20   89–40656

Printed in the United States of America

Set in Sabon

Designed by Fritz Metsch

For my family and friends—
with love and gratitude.

Dispose the way of thy servants . . . that among all the changes and chances of this mortal life, they may ever be defended by thy help.

—The Book of Common Prayer

Part One

Deliver me from mine enemies, O God . . .

For lo, they lie waiting for my soul.

—Psalm 59, The Book of Common Prayer

Chapter 1

 A squirrel chattered in the oak tree and awakened Cassie Steele from her doze. She raised herself on one elbow and looked down at the naked man lying beside her on the rumpled patchwork quilt. He was all arms and legs, sprawled out like a marionette dropped on the ground. His body was long and thin, an ascetic's body without an ounce of extra flesh. His Indian-straight black hair was tousled on his broad forehead, and even in sleep his high-bridged nose gave him the look of a hunting hawk.

Cassie reached out to touch his hand but hesitated, not wanting to disturb him. The squirrel chattered another complaint, however, and Dixon Steele opened one eye and looked up at it.

"It's okay, squirrel," he said. "We're old married folks."

Cassie laughed and lay back next to him. He pulled her onto his body and their warm sweaty flesh seemed to melt together. Dix put his arms around her and held her close. "Mmmm. I like being old married folks."

"Sticky old married folks," she said. "How hot do you suppose it is, anyway?"

Dix held up an imaginary microphone and imitated Edward R. Murrow's graveled voice. "See it now, folks. High life in eastern Oklahoma, summer of 1956. Sweaty state senator and winsome wife, wily woman attorney, at play on fabled shores of San Bois Creek."

"Idiot!" She kissed him lightly.

"Well, hey, what do you expect? Cool ocean breezes?"

She looked up at the dusty dry oak leaves over them. "Any breeze would help. Any breeze at all." She felt his body stirring beneath her and gathered her clothes and stood up.

"Wait," Dix said. "Don't get dressed yet. Let me look at you."

She stood, as unashamed as Eve, watching him and enjoying his pleasure in her body. She was tall, over five eight, long-legged and slender except for the slight swelling of her abdomen, a leftover from the pregnancy that had ended five months before with the birth of their son Taylor. She was thirty-one that summer, but looked younger with her long blond hair braided into a single plait that trailed down over her shoulder. Her face reflected her inner contentment, and within their fringe of dark eyelashes her deep blue eyes were clear and calm. The yielding look of a woman who loves and is loved, however, did not obscure the strength in her high, prominent cheekbones, her thin straight nose and the stubborn set of her square jaw. She was a woman who was loved, but she was a woman who belonged only to herself. Long walks on the farm and regular exercise had tightened muscles that were slack from pregnancy, and her skin was burnished by the sun and dappled by the shade of the oak tree. She laughed lightly. "Old married folks, sure! Cavorting under an oak tree for all the world to see!"

He laughed, too, and stretched his long arms. "Desire under the oaks? Come here, woman."

"Dix, I must see to Taylor. It's almost time for him to nurse again." She pulled on her clothes, a blue sleeveless blouse, white shorts that enhanced the tan on her long legs and white tennis shoes with no socks. She leaned down to kiss Dix. "Coming to the house with me?"

Dix flopped back on the grass. "One more kiss like that, woman, and I'll really give that moralistic squirrel something to fuss about." Reluctantly he sat up and reached for his clothes. "Not married four months yet and another man is already coming between us."

Cassie laughed. "A five-month-old man? Our son?" She touched her breast, swollen with milk. "He needs me, you know. And if he doesn't get what he wants, he'll scream his little head off."

"Damn it, I should have known I was using the wrong approach." He pushed himself to his feet, favoring the leg where a deep blue scar still marked the shrapnel wound he had suffered in Germany. "I was using the wrong technique. Instead of wooing you with kisses and honeyed words, I should have been screaming my own little head off!" He pulled on khaki pants and a white T-shirt and folded the quilt.

"You idiot!" She took his hand. "Oh, Dix, I do love you so much."

"Wah," he said, and then again, louder: "Wah, wah, waaah!"

"Come on!" Cassie pulled him up the path from the creek. They walked through a grove of dark cedars, and it was there before them, the house that Cassie had bought with the farm.

As always, she stopped to look at her house. It was not a grand place, just a rambling one-story hunting lodge that had been cared for and improved through the years. The walls were covered with brown-stained shingles that made the house blend into the woods behind it, into the oaks and sumacs and the dark shag-barked cedars. Only the windows set it apart from the woods, the glass catching and reflecting the hard glare of the midday sunlight. They were tall narrow windows with sills just above the floor of the veranda that surrounded the house on three sides.

Cassie looked at the lodge and in her mind she saw the people who had lived in the house or had passed through: James Steele and his wife, Amelia, and their two sons, Dix and Jimmy. Cassie hurried past the memories of Jimmy. Her sharecropper father, Howard Taylor, had been in the house, as had her half brother, Bo, and her grandmother, Martha Hendricks. Granny.

"Wah, waaaah!"

Cassie returned to the present instantly because the cry was not

Dix's teasing but a cry of misery and anger from her son. She dropped Dix's hand and hurried toward the house.

"Waaah!" Dix gave a piteous bleat that made her laugh even as she ran to her son.

Ruby Keeler Vance was on the veranda, trying to comfort Taylor. "Reckon he's hungry, Miz Steele."

"Of course!" She took the red-faced crying baby and he immediately began to nuzzle at her blouse. "Give me a minute, Taylor. Just one minute!"

In less time than that, she was seated in a wicker rocking chair and Taylor was at her breast. He sobbed a few times and spluttered, then settled into the serious business of filling himself with warm milk.

Ruby Keeler nodded, satisfied, and went into the house. Cassie smiled at the girl's unspoken criticism. She knew that Ruby Keeler thought Cassie should devote every waking moment to Taylor. Cassie disagreed, which was why she had employed a fifteen-year-old girl to live at the farm and help with the baby. Ruby Keeler came well recommended by her grandfather, Henry Starr, who was Cassie's hired man, but even he had not suspected that Ruby Keeler would love Taylor dearly and would be as fiercely protective of him as a mother tiger of her cub. At first Cassie said the girl's name as if it were in quotation marks, but she soon became accustomed to it. After all, it was not the girl's fault that her mother was addicted to *Modern Screen* and had named her three daughters for movie stars: Ruby Keeler, Shirley Temple and Rita Hayworth. For no discernible reason, Mrs. Vance had named her three boys for lesser-known American Presidents: Millard Fillmore, Franklin Pierce and Andrew Johnson.

Dix went into the house, too, for a shower, and Cassie sat on the veranda feeding her son and looking out over her land. A little breeze came up and stirred the hollyhock blossoms by the veranda.

By August of 1956, the killing drought that had ruined the land and the lives of its people during the 1930s had long since ended, but still the late summer sun scorched the crops in the field while farmers prayed for rain. There was not a cloud in the sky and the sun beat down on the hills of Eastern Oklahoma, the foothills of the Ozark Mountains to the east. Red clay roads cracked in the heat and the roly-polies and dung beetles crept into the shadowed fissures to escape the sun. In the fields, dry corn stalks rattled in the hot breeze.

A lawn sprinkler clicked nervously in the yard of the lodge, spreading a fine spray that glittered in the sunshine but evaporated before it fell to the grass. It added moisture to the dry breeze, however, and softened the air.

Cassie put the baby on her shoulder and burped him. He chortled in her ear. "Oh-ho," she said, "so it's giggle time now. Well, let me put you down in your playpen where you'll be cooler." She put the baby down on the white quilt and he smiled at her toothlessly. "Oh, you darling! You do know your mama, don't you?"

The screen door squeaked behind her. "Does he know his papa, too?" As if to answer, Taylor chortled again and smiled up at Dix. "Hey, buster, that was pretty good. Let me dry off a little and I'll pick you up." Dix flopped down on the porch swing. "Damn it all, Cassie, I just can't imagine being in Oklahoma City without you and Taylor."

"I thought we'd settled that."

"Well, we didn't. We just swept it under the carpet."

Cassie sighed. "I want to be with you, darling. You know that. I just don't see why it has to be in Oklahoma City."

Dix smoothed his damp black hair. "Because that's where the clients are, damn it. Remember what we planned: 'Steele and Steele, Attorneys-at-law.' You can't run a law practice from the farm, for God's sake. And don't forget that my state senate responsibilities are in Oklahoma City, not in Clifton County."

"I know that." Cassie tried to keep her voice level. "But there is so much to do here, changes I want to make on the farm, and—"

"Did you marry me, or did you marry this damned farm?"

*   *   *

Whether it was arguing or bickering or merely dissent, it had gone on for three days, from the minute, almost, of Dix's return from Oklahoma City. He had been away for a week, in their first long separation since the wedding in May, and he had made it clear that on future trips, he wanted Cassie and the baby to be with him. He had big plans for the firm of Steele and Steele. Cassie, however, had some plans of her own.

"Dix, at least let me explain what I have in mind for the farm. I want to—"

"Don't tell me about the farm! I know what you have in mind for us, and I don't like it at all."

Cassie sighed. "Dix, I can't go back to full-time law practice, not now. Taylor needs me. Can't you understand that? If I keep him here, on the farm, I can be with him off and on all day, but in the city I'd have to leave him—"

"So you'd rather leave me?"

"Yes—no! Of course not!" Cassie jumped to her feet. "Look, you could drive to the farm on Thursday nights and back to the city early Monday morning. We would be apart only three nights a week."

"What about the times when the state senate is in session? Or when I have a fund-raiser on a weekend? You know how important it is for us to make political appearances together."

"We can, darling! We'll go from here, or I'll come to Oklahoma City and spend the night."

Dix stood up too. "Damn it all, it just won't wash, Cassie. I don't want a part-time marriage." He grinned at her suddenly. "And remember, you've been living the high life in Dallas, honey. You're accustomed to the excitement of the courtroom and of being a successful litigator. You'd be bored to death as a farmer."

Cassie put her hand on a veranda post as if to touch base. It was true that in Dallas she had practiced oil and gas law, a field that was both lucrative and endlessly fascinating. Would working an Oklahoma dirt farm be as interesting? And the people she had last worked with in Dallas had wildly diverse backgrounds but shared one important characteristic: they were wheeler-dealers. In Oklahoma she would work with her hired man and the owner of the feed store in the little town of San Bois and the semiliterate men she took on to work the land.

"I'll be happy here," she said as much to herself as to Dix. "I love this land."

Dix looked up at her and in spite of her distress about the argument, she felt a surge of love and desire. His face was as dear to her, and as craggy, as the limestone cliffs in the hills behind the lodge. His wide mouth, however, was set and his eyes snapped with anger. "No! I will not approve this half-assed scheme of—"

"Approve!" Cassie drew herself to her full height of five feet and eight inches and gave him the icy glare she had perfected during her early years of practicing divorce law, a look guaranteed to reduce the most recalcitrant husband to tapioca pudding. "Who asked for your approval? I am a grown woman, Dixon Steele, and I will do what I want to do, with or without your approval!"

"You are my wife, and don't forget it! I have a right to—"

The screen door screeched open and Ruby Keeler passed between them, stepping across the veranda as delicately as a soldier crossing a minefield. "Reckon I better change this here baby," she said softly. She gave Cassie a reproachful look and carried the baby into the house.

Her face red with embarrassment, Cassie turned to discover that Dix was watching her speculatively.

"What were we talking about?" she asked.

Dix scowled. "What have we talked about for three straight days? Now, listen to me, will you?"

"No, you listen to me. I love you, Dix. I love you more than life itself."

"But not more than this farm," he said flatly.

"Can't you understand, darling? I have to stay on the land. I need it and it needs me."

"The way I need you, Cassie?"

She saw that need in his eyes, and with it, pain. She wanted to give in, to do everything he asked, but there were too many factors to be considered: Dix's need for her, Taylor's need, the land's need. All of them were valid, but there was one more need that had to be taken into account: her own. She, Cassie, needed to be herself. Still, she hesitated. "Darling, maybe we can find a compromise? Couldn't we just try it, try this weekend commuting thing for, say, a month?"

"Cassie." Dix took her hand and pulled her to him. "God, if you only knew how much I love you. Okay. We'll try it. But if it doesn't work out—"

Cassie lifted her face to kiss him, but she was not thinking of him. It will work out, she thought. I will make it work.

Chapter 2

 Dix left at dawn the next day to drive to Oklahoma City. By the time his car disappeared into the dry woods, Cassie was certain that she had made a terrible mistake. She wanted to be with him, with her husband, but she had stubbornly insisted on staying on the farm. Was the farm that important? Was it important enough to make her settle for a part-time marriage?

Linked with her self-doubt, however, like the blue ribbon woven into her long blond plait, was a strand of excitement. When she had Ruby Keeler and Taylor started on their day, she hunted out the cardboard box that held all the notes she had made long ago, on cattle-ranching and soil conservation. She pulled out a notebook and was startled by the handwriting on the yellowing paper. The notes could have been made by a different hand. But it was a different hand, she realized. A different hand belonging to a different person. Cassandra Steele was her name then, too, but she was married not to Dixon Steele but to his older brother, Jimmy. Older, she thought, but never wiser. She remembered the day Jimmy Steele walked into his father's law office, where Cassie Taylor, age eighteen, worked as a typist. In her eyes he was a prince come to search for his Cinderella. In fact, Jimmy was as close a facsimile to a prince as eastern Oklahoma could produce in 1943. He was a handsome young lawyer, a playboy in terms of the Ballard Country Club, and the son of a rich and powerful lawyer with kingly holdings in land and oil production and the royal prerogative to exact favors from the rulers of the state of Oklahoma. Unfortunately Jimmy, like some other princes, had never grown up. After they were married, she discovered that within his man's body was only a boy, and a destructive boy at that.

Cassie tried to build a life of her own within the marriage, shopping with her friend Fran Jordan, exploring the countryside and reading until late on the nights he was out with other women. While he had affairs with her contemporaries at the Ballard Country Club, she studied books on agriculture and ranching. Her interest in the land stemmed not only from her grandmother's teaching that owning land was the only way to establish oneself, but also because the land existed. It was there, and it would always be there, long after the rulers of the land were gone.

After two years of marriage she had no love left for Jimmy Steele and little respect. Even that disappeared when he infected her with a venereal disease, and at his father's suggestion but without her knowledge arranged for her to undergo a therapeutic abortion. She fled Ballard then for Dallas and a new life. She took little with her: clothes, her car and the money James Steele gave her in return for her promise to tell no one about the disease and the abortion. In the car, however, she had packed a box of notes on her research on farming and soil conservation, and she had kept that box with her through the years as a talisman that might someday work its magic and return her to the land she loved, to the land where she was born.

Shaking her head to clear it of useless memories, Cassie laid out a new legal pad and opened the first of the dusty notebooks.

As she read and jotted notes on her pad, Cassie's heart sank. One month. She had suggested a one-month trial to Dix and it was painfully obvious that one month would not be enough for even a beginning. Moreover, the more she read, the more she realized that farming had something in common with litigation:

all the books in the library would not make up for a lack of experience in court. Her hired man, Henry Starr, was an experienced farmer, but how much he knew about ranching was something she would just have to find out. When Taylor went down for a nap, Cassie sent Ruby Keeler out to find her grandfather. Ruby Keeler slept in the house, but from his first day on the farm Henry had lived in a room he had set up in the toolshed.

Henry came in wiping his forehead with a gnarled hand. He was no taller than she, a wizened man in faded overalls with a tanned, wrinkled face. His hair was black, liberally flecked with white. His eyes were small, almost hidden among the wrinkles, and were a clear pale brown.

"Sit down, Henry," Cassie said. "I need to talk to you."

He shifted a dangling straw from one corner of his mouth to the other and sat down on the very edge of a wooden chair. He watched her like a robin keeping a wary eye on a marauding cat.

Cassie knew it was pointless to ask him to relax. "You've done lots of farming, haven't you, Henry?"

"Been farmin' fifty years, on and off."

"Have you had any experience running cattle? Henry, I want to quit farming this place, to change over from row crops to ranching."

He rubbed his chin. "Ain't no ranchin' around here. Good bit on the Canadian River and on the Illinois, near Tahlequah. Worked up there myself ten, fifteen years ago. Got to have water for cattle."

"There's plenty of water here. The San Bois never did run dry, not even during the drought in the thirties."

"Cost a lot of money, changin' things around that way."

Cassie thought of her profitable investments in Dallas real estate. "Henry, I can come up with the money and the textbook information we need. Can you supply the experience with cattle?"

Henry Starr looked at her closely, as if she herself was the land to be cultivated. He shifted the straw to the other side of his mouth. "Reckon I can do that, Cassie."

She took a deep breath and let it out slowly. She did not know how knowledgeable he was and there was every likelihood that he was descended from the outlaw Belle Starr, possibly even named for Belle's father, Henry, but she trusted him. She sketched in her plans for the changeover, but Henry Starr's taciturn comments did not reveal his opinion of her ideas until she began to lay out a schedule of tasks.

"Then we'll start the plowing this week."

Henry shook his head doubtfully. "Folks don't much plow before late September and this here ain't even the end of August."

"I have to start now, Henry. I want to get the Bermuda drilled in by the end of September."

"That ain't goin' to do you no good, Cassie. You'll get yourself a winter-kill and have the whole thing to do over come April."

"April! I can't wait that long."

Henry shrugged. "Ain't nobody can move the seasons around."

"Damn!" There was no point in arguing, because he was right: she could not change nature to fit her schedule. Winter would follow autumn, and spring would follow winter in the minuet of the seasons that had ruled since the beginning of time. And man— or woman—would have to set his step to that stately dance. "But we can get started on the plowing, can't we?"

He scratched his head. "Reckon we could. Heard of a fellow down Stigler way that likes to plow early. Says he wants to plow the weeds under before they go to seed. Reckon we could give her a shot."

Early the next morning Henry started tuning up the old tractor in the barn. Cassie tried to make herself useful and to speed his work by fetching and carrying for him. When she went to the toolshed for a hammer she saw that he had walled off one end of the shed with rough planks. Justifying her curiosity by the thought that she deserved to know something about her employees' personal lives, she pulled open the door to his room and peeked in to see what he had made of it. He had built a narrow quilt-stacked bunk on one wall and had put in a small window. A naked light bulb hung from the ceiling, with an extension cord dangling down to a little radio on a wooden crate beside the bunk. Lying next to the radio were a worn Bible and a tattered *Farmer's Almanac.*

A small cookstove stood next to the crate, with a saucepan and a black cast-iron skillet hanging on the wall over it, and next to that was a rickety white cabinet with one leg set on a chunk of wood. His shaving gear was on top of the cabinet, and on two nails driven into the wall there were a thin towel and a piece of mirror. The place was clean and tidy and smelled like Henry Starr himself, a slightly musty smell that was not at all unpleasant but that reminded Cassie of the woods on a damp winter day. She pulled the door closed quietly, regretting her invasion of the man's privacy.

Their first clash of wills came the next day. Cassie spent the afternoon tramping around the farm with a soil conservation agent, and after supper she went over her notes with Henry Starr.

"So we'll want to handcast the clover seed as soon as we get each field ready. We'll sow the bottomland first."

"It's too early, Cassie. You got to seed your clover in late November, and it ain't even September yet."

Cassie hesitated. She did not want to tell him that she had to make some sort of showing within a month. "Well, at least we can start preparing the land for Bermuda grass. The soil conservation agent says we can get some federal money if we hire it out."

"They won't pay anything like what it'll cost you. If you're in such a all-fired hurry, you might want to rent another tractor with a plow and harrow and what-not."

Cassie hesitated. "I don't know, Henry. How many men would we have to hire?"

"Me and you could do it, if you ain't scared of work."

She could tell by the way he looked at her that it was a dare. She lifted her chin. "I'm not afraid of work, Henry Starr."

He looked at her as if to measure her against a standard of his own. "Reckon you ain't, Cassie. Reckon you ain't."

Cassie rented a tractor from a neighbor who obviously could

hardly wait to get into San Bois and tell the world about that crazy Miz Steele that was fixing to plow her fields in August. It was a heavier machine than her own, so Henry took it to plow the hard-baked ground of the cornfield that would become the upper pasture, and Cassie drove her own tractor down to work the rich sandy loam of the bottomlands by San Bois Creek.

Cassie had told Henry that she was not afraid of work, but by noon of the first day she had begun to realize that she had never really known what work was. It was cool, that first morning, with the creek mists filtering the sun. Cassie felt strong and powerful, in control, as she drove the tractor in the fresh morning, the deep-set plow blade churning the rich soil of her land. She steered carefully, maintaining straight furrows and swinging in a wide U-turn at the end of the field to retrace her route with the front wheels of the tractor guided by her first cut through the matted weeds. As the sun rose higher it burned away the mists, however, and heat rose in waves from the land, mixing with the fumes of the tractor. Sweat rolled down her body in salty trails through the dust clinging to her skin. The insects attacked then, mosquitoes and flies, until she was covered with stinging, itching bites.

By nine o'clock, she was longing for ten o'clock, when Ruby Keeler would bring Taylor to the field for nursing. Finally they came and Cassie climbed down stiffly and sat in the still, hot shadow under an oak tree to put the baby to her breast. As greedy as her son, she drank big glasses of cold, acid-sweet lemonade, replacing some of the fluids she had sweated out. All too soon, it was time to send Ruby Keeler and Taylor back to the lodge and to clamber up to the steel seat of the tractor.

By nightfall her hands were blistered by gripping the steering wheel, her buttocks were bruised from bouncing on the seat and her muscles ached so that it was all she could do to eat something, take a hot bath and fall into bed. The next morning it started all over again with swallowing a hasty breakfast, nursing Taylor and trudging to the barn to start up the tractor.

On Friday Cassie stopped work early. She took a long soaking bath, washed the sweaty dust from her hair and tried to repair her broken fingernails. At dusk she was rocking on the veranda, wearing a white lawn sundress and sipping at a tall cold gin and tonic. She watched the woods to the east, hoping to see Dix's car lights coming through the woods, coming west toward home.

West. "Go west, young man," Horace Greeley had said. Go west! The young woman named Cassandra Taylor had done just that. The physical distance she had traversed was short: the site of her childhood home lay less than a mile east of the lodge. To travel that mile, however, she had taken giant steps and covered infinite distances. She was a child when she had lived on the farm before, a sharecropper's daughter, until June of 1938 and the terrifying night of fire and murder that drove her from the weathered tenant's shack and a poverty-ridden life with her drunken father, a feral half brother and the grandmother who had loved Cassie and had imbued in her an eagerness to learn and a love for the land, which she came to believe was the only bridge across the great gulf between the haves and the have-nots.

Cassie's journey had taken her to Whitman and her father's cousins and then to Ballard, Oklahoma, and her miserable marriage to Jimmy Steele and, finally, to Dallas where she rose to wealth and power as a successful attorney. She had given all that up to return to Eastern Oklahoma, to buy the land of her roots and to bear an illegitimate child fathered by the one man she had ever truly loved, Dixon Steele. It was there at the lodge that she and Dix were married and it was there, less than a mile west of her starting point, that they gloried in each other and in their child.

Lights flashed in the woods and Cassie sat up straight. Dix, she thought. It was Dix!

The car pulled to a stop by the picket fence, and Dixon Steele got out and strode across the front yard with his seersucker jacket slung over one shoulder. When he saw Cassie sitting there in the dusk, waiting for him, he stopped to sketch a deep bow. "Why, Miz Scarlett, ma'am, I swear you never looked so pretty."

Ignoring her sore muscles, Cassie jumped up from her chair and ran across the veranda. "Rhett, dahlin'! I thought you'd never come!"

Dix took her in his arms. "God, how I've missed you, Cassie." He pushed her away, holding her shoulders. "You look like a million dollars! What a tan—you must have been sunbathing every day."

"Well," she said nervously, "something like that."

"Taylor's asleep, I'll bet. I'd hoped to get away earlier. At least let me get a look at him. Look, I'll change clothes and bring us both a drink. You haven't had dinner yet?"

"No, I waited for you."

He kissed the tip of her nose. "Great! I won't be a minute, darling. I've got so much to tell you."

While he changed, Cassie checked on Taylor, who was sound asleep and snoring lightly. Dix leaned over the side of the crib to kiss his son, then took Cassie's hand. For a moment they stood together, looking down at the baby they had created, and then, holding hands, they tiptoed out of his room. In the kitchen Dix chatted with Ruby Keeler, who was finishing up the dinner, but as he and Cassie walked out to the veranda, he began to tell his news, like a boy with a secret so exciting and so glorious that he can't keep it another minute. "Listen, you aren't going to believe this, but I've been asked to participate in something so wonderful, so great that I—Cassie, there's a new wind blowing through the South."

"That's real romantic, Rhett, honey, but I don't—"

He scowled at her. "I'm not kidding now, Cassie. There are going to be some big changes down there."

"In the South? Okay. So tell me, what does that have to do with Oklahoma? Or with us?"

Dix pulled his wicker chair close to her. "Everything. Do you remember the bus boycott in Montgomery that started last year?"

"Well, yes. When the Negroes refused to ride the segregated buses."

"Before that, had you honestly noticed that Negroes had to ride in the rear of the bus?"

Cassie shifted uncomfortably in her chair. "I don't really ride the bus, Dix. You know that. And in Dallas, I never—"

"But you were aware of the segregation, right? You knew what was going on."

"I guess so, but I—it's not that I'm against the Negroes or—"

"Of course not. You're like the rest of us. You use the Whites Only drinking fountain or restroom, but you'd rather not think about the fact that some American citizens are kept from using them. You studied constitutional law, Cassie. You know that segregation based on skin color is illegal. But let me tell you, darling, the bus boycott is just the beginning. It's a new wind, I tell you. A powerful new movement toward desegregation." He sat back in his chair and took a long drink of his gin and tonic. "And I have met the man who has emerged as a Negro leader." He leaned forward, his eyes glittering with excitement. "I met Martin King today, Cassie, and he asked for my help."

Something in his voice touched Cassie deeply, but at the same time a cold chill moved down her spine. "King? That's his name?"

"Yes. Remember it, Cassie, because it's going to be a big name in our lives, in all our lives. Reverend Martin Luther King, Junior."

Chapter 3

A month went by, and another, and it was November. Dixon, occupied with the state senate and with his new interest in the South, had not asked for a progress report on the farm and Cassie had not volunteered one.

Day after day she worked the fields with Henry Starr. Ruby Keeler was back in school, a high-school sophomore, but Cassie rigged a sling and carried Taylor on her back. At first she felt like a mythic earth mother, keeping her child with her, but starting up the noisy old tractor each morning brought her back to reality. Taylor apparently thrived on the noise, dozing and then waking to try to imitate the clatter. Cassie began to think that he would learn to speak Machine before he learned English.

Night after night she eased herself into an armchair by the limestone fireplace and studied the Oklahoma statutes to prepare herself for practicing law.

Dix came to the farm almost every weekend, and more and more his talk revolved around the strategies of what had come to be called the black movement. Cassie was relieved that he focused on that rather than on her moving to Oklahoma City, but sometimes she felt that their being together was less important to Dix than to her.

At eight months, Taylor showed promise of having Dixon's lanky build. He was shaped more like a little boy than a baby, with a thin wiry body and long arms and legs. He was blond like

Cassie, though, and he had her deep blue eyes and long dark eyelashes. He was beginning to wean himself from the breast. He was crawling, and trying his best to walk. He would stand by the couch, let go of it and sway one way and the other, laughing, until his diapered bottom hit the floor with a thud that always surprised and delighted him.

The day came when Cassie and Ruby Keeler took Taylor to the barber shop in San Bois and wept in each other's arms as the barber trimmed away Taylor's soft baby hair. Together, too, they tucked the clippings into a cellophane envelope to save in his baby book.

Dixon was as dotty about their son as Cassie was. On the weekends he sat on the floor while Taylor used his father as a geologic feature to be climbed on and pushed and gripped with white-knuckled fingers while he took his first tentative steps.

On the morning of Thanksgiving Day, Cassie and Dix bundled Taylor's supplies and Taylor himself into Cassie's 1954 Cadillac convertible and drove to Ballard to spend the day with Dix's parents, James and Amelia Steele.

Ballard had grown in the eleven years since Cassie had left for Dallas. The new buildings downtown dwarfed the one where James Steele's office was located, the six-story edifice that Cassie had once considered the epitome of wealth and commerce.

Dix turned onto the street leading toward Ballard Heights, and Cassie laughed to herself. How old was she when she first saw that building? Seventeen? Yes. Not quite eighteen and newly arrived from a circumscribed life with her father's Pentacostal cousins in Whitman, Oklahoma. She was just twenty years old when she left Ballard but she was far more knowledgeable. Oh, yes, she thought bitterly, when she left Ballard she was no longer an innocent.

She saw the house then, James Steele's house, and was thrown back to the moment she first saw it: the rainy morning when Jimmy Steele had brought his new bride home to his family.

"Cassie?" Dix said. "Cassie, are you all right?"

Cassie put her hand on his leg to connect herself to his solid strength. "Yes, darling. It's just that this house—"

Taylor, who had slept all the way in his car-bed in the back seat, chose that moment to rouse and make questioning sounds.

Cassie got up on her knees to reach back and lift him over the seat. He snuggled into her lap and she smoothed his fair hair.

Dixon drove into the circular driveway. "Hey, son, look at that," he said. "It's your grandpa and grandma's house."

The house loomed over them, a tall two-storied place with attics Cassie had never explored during the time she lived there. The corners of the house were rounded, like turrets of a castle, and the broad front porch was surrounded by a balustrade of sand-stone. With Dix at her side, however, and her son in her lap, Cassie relaxed. It was just a house, after all, and James and Amelia Steele were only Taylor's grandparents. They had nothing to do with her. James Steele no longer had any control over her life.

Amelia Steele must have been watching for them, because she had the big front door open before the Cadillac came to a stop. A small woman with frazzled white hair, she scurried down the front steps like a quick little mouse. "Taylor!" she cried. "Cassie, do give me that baby!" Her voice was firm, unlike that of the Amelia Cassie knew, whose words wandered along in half-sentences that seemed to emerge from misty thoughts.

To Cassie's surprise Taylor beamed at Amelia and reached out for her. "But he never goes to strangers!" Cassie said.

"I'm not a stranger. I'm his grandmother."

Taylor buried his face in Amelia's neck and chortled with pleasure.

"Well, Dixon, Cassandra." James Steele's voice was flat and heavy. He stood over them at the top of the concrete steps. He was a big man, and even now that his shoulders were sloping with age, he had an air of careful control. There was a flabbiness around his jaw that hinted at a gradual deterioration of his body, but there was no apparent deterioration of the power within that body. "We are pleased to see you."

Was that, Cassie wondered, the royal "we," as in "we are not amused"?

James had changed but Amelia had aged markedly. Her face was a mass of tiny wrinkles and her shoulders were rounding into the hump of an elderly woman. Her hands moved as they always had, in small ineffectual gestures, starting and stopping without relation to her words. Cassie remembered when she had first seen the Steeles. James Steele had come to the tenant shack when she was no more than five. He had looked huge to her then, strong and powerful in his city clothes and his fancy automobile. It was a few years later when she first saw Amelia at the lodge: curly brown hair, a red dress, a neat apron, framed in the doorway of the lodge and, in the warm lamplight, looking just the way the motherless Cassie had thought a mother should look. Almost twenty-five years ago, she thought. A quarter century.

"Can I take your wrap, Miz Cassie?" It was Luella, the Steeles' housemaid. Even Luella had a few white hairs, and her dark skin had lost some of its sheen. Cassie flushed, remembering that Luella had immediately pegged her as Poor White Trash, but she saw no hint of that now. In fact, Luella was watching Dix with open admiration. Of course, Cassie thought, Dixon Steele, the supporter of Martin Luther King, Jr., and a white participant in the desegregation movement. Luella looked over at Taylor, happily ensconced in Amelia's arms, and pleasure sparkled in her dark eyes.

Cassie sighed. She herself was still white trash to Luella, but at least her two men gave her some standing. She turned then and saw that James Steele was watching her. Nothing could improve her status with him. She was still the sharecropper's daughter who had invaded his family. He hated her then and he hated her now. But Cassie smiled coolly. She was his son's wife and the mother of his grandson. She had attacked his patrician fortress and his defenses had crumbled. He would never forgive her for it, but neither could she forgive what he and his son Jimmy had done to her. For Dix's sake, though, she would try. She would do her best to keep mutual hatred from disrupting their life, her own hostility as well as James Steele's.

Amelia Steele led the way into the living room and the others trailed after her. Cassie looked around curiously. The room had changed very little in the years since she had lived there. Two of the sofas had been re-upholstered, there were more of Amelia's needlepoint pillows, but the ebony grand piano still gleamed in the light from the leaded glass of the bay window at the front of the room, and the spindly tables and straight chairs still hovered near the couches like courtiers attending their queens. The polished oak floors gleamed as brightly as ever, and the Persian rugs were as rich in color. Amelia settled herself and Taylor on a pale blue brocade sofa and the others pulled up chairs while Dix passed drinks around. Cassie looked into her glass and stifled a laugh. What a happy family group they were! Three generations gathered to give thanks. Was it always so, she wondered? Were all families like the Steeles? Did currents of distrust and hatred run deep beneath the Norman Rockwell illustrations?

Amelia, who did not notice undercurrents, led the conversation to focus on Taylor. Even James unbent enough to offer the baby a large finger. Taylor examined it thoroughly and then used all six of his razor-sharp teeth to bite it hard enough to make his grandfather grunt with pain. They laughed then, everyone but James, who obviously was not amused.

The turkey was carved and served and Luella was passing molded cranberry salad on a silver plate when James brought one of the deep-lying currents to the surface. "Dixon, I can't say that I see any value in your support of those colored rabble-rousers in the South. And this so-called leader of theirs, the self-styled Reverend King—I heard quite a funny joke about him the other day."

The joke was not funny. It was both racist and scurrilous. Dix's face went red with anger and Cassie glanced up at Luella. There was a flash of something in her eyes. Anger? Sorrow? She lowered her head and the look was gone as suddenly as it appeared, leaving Cassie with the memory of another exchange of glances with Luella. On the day of Franklin Roosevelt's death, James and Jimmy were interested only in the politics of his successor, Harry Truman, but Cassie and Luella had for one silent instant shared their sorrow at the passing of the man.

"I will admit, however," James said, "that the position you have taken has brought you a certain amount of attention. I suspect, Dixon, that it is time to cash in on this."

"Cash in on it?" Dix said. "Now, look here, Dad, I support Martin King because he is right, not for the publicity."

"Of course, of course. Everyone knows that you are an idealist, my boy. But we must be practical as well. The statewide, even nationwide, publicity your stand has engendered is invaluable to the state Democratic party. Your name has begun to be mentioned in party discussions."

"In the traditional smoke-filled rooms?" Cassie said. "Among the party bosses?"

James looked grim. "That sort of comment is not called for." He turned back to Dix. "My boy, I believe you will continue to advance in stature, both in the party and with the electorate. I know, Dixon, that we have not always seen eye to eye on the issues, but for the good of the party I will help you in every possible way."

"You, Father?" Dix put his fork down carefully. "I won't make any promises, you know. Whatever office I might be elected to, I must be free to follow my own conscience."

"Of course you must." James smiled. "I would not have it any other way."

Cassie stared at him. Could they believe James Steele? Had the leopard changed its spots? She looked at Dix and was appalled to see him nodding, accepting his father's statement as true.

"Dix," she said, but she stopped. They could discuss it later. They would talk about it later, in private.

*   *   *

After dinner Taylor settled down for a nap and Amelia led Dix into the living room. Cassie would have followed, but James Steele stopped her. "May we talk for a few minutes, alone?" Without waiting for an answer he waved her to his study.

The room was as impressive as Cassie had remembered it: the book-lined walls, the big walnut desk, the view of downtown Ballard softened by the November dusk, and on one wall the map of Clifton County with James Steele's landholdings colored red. Cassie went over to look at the map. In the center of the red was one area of white: the farm she had bought from James through a middleman. She turned away from the map, smiling.

"Yes." James sat down in the swivel chair behind his desk. His voice was heavy. "You own that farm now, the farm that belonged to my family since my father first came to the Indian Territory, before Oklahoma was even a state."

"Wait, James. It's back in the family now, isn't it? I mean, Dix is your son and Taylor, your grandson."

James frowned. "Thank you for pointing it out, but I am well aware that you have my land and my son and my grandson. I remember when I gave you your first job. 'You won't regret this,' you said, but your prophecies, Cassandra, are less reliable than those of your mythological namesake."

Cassie sat down in a leather armchair. "Why do I have the feeling you're leading up to something?"

James laughed shortly. "Your Dallas career sharpened your wits, Cassie. Yes, I am leading up to something, but I believe I can shorten my approach. Ownership, as I'm sure you know, is closely linked with responsibility."

"Yes, I know. What I plan to do with the farm is—"

"I am not talking about land." He put his hands flat on his desk. "Cassie, you must make Dixon drop this foolish alliance with Southern Negroes."

"Make him? Make Dixon Steele do anything he doesn't think is right?"

"As I said at dinner, the publicity has brought his name to the front, but the perception of his political wisdom has already been damaged."

"I'm sure it has, James, among conservative Democrats. Don't you think that I know that, and that Dix knows it, too? And do you really think that he cares?"

James shook his head. "Neither of you knows the extent of the damage. You are too deeply involved with the liberal wing of the party to see the whole picture."

"So what?" Cassie leaned back. "Wasn't it the liberals who elected him to the state senate?"

"Oklahoma is changing, Cassie. You've been away, down in Dallas, and Dix is too blinded by his ideals to take it into account, but you can believe me. The days when winning the Democratic primary was tantamount to winning the general election are passing. The Republicans are growing in strength and are fielding a stronger slate of candidates. If the party takes Dix into consideration as a candidate for a national post, his election would require the support of both conservative and liberal Democrats."

"That may be so, James, but I can't possibly influence Dix's beliefs." Cassie's curiosity got the better of her. "What post? What do they want him to run for?"

"I am not at liberty to discuss the details, but we have received word of a development not yet known to the general public or, thank God, the press. It appears that a certain seat will fall vacant next year. If—a very important 'if'—if Dix does not allow himself to become too vocal on the topic of desegregation, I believe that he can expect support from both wings of the state organization." James sat back, watching her. "With Dixon's war record and the legislative ability he has displayed in the state senate, certain party leaders feel that he would be the strongest candidate we have for a post in Washington."

Cassie was stunned. Washington. Dix would have the opportunity to place his ideas before a national forum. Washington. It would mean changes, huge changes for all of them, but how could she possibly stand in his way? Except that there was James's "if," his big "if." How could Cassie possibly ask Dix to give up his commitment to the black movement in the South?

She shook her head slowly. "No, James," she said. "I can't do it. I can't try to influence Dix in something so important to him."

James's face reddened with anger. "You oppose me in this, then? What a fool you are, Cassie Taylor. You have risen in the world, but when it comes to constructive thought, you are still no more than a sharecropper's daughter."

Cassie rose to her feet. "You can't say that to me! You have no right to talk like that!"

"No right?" He laughed unpleasantly. "And who are you to talk about rights? With a drunken bum for a father and a criminal for a half brother." He smiled. "Have you heard from your brother lately, Cassie?"

"From Bo?" She shook her head, confused by his sudden change in subject. "Why, no. I guess he's still in—"

"In prison at San Quentin? I believe he is, for now, but you know how lenient the California parole system is. I realize that it is a difficult situation for you, just when you are ready to start practicing law in Oklahoma. No matter how impressive your Texas record may be, clients are not likely to flock to a new lawyer whose brother is a convict, especially one guilty of such a heinous crime as child molestation. Not to mention the effect on Dix's campaign."

Cassie covered her face with her hands but she could not hide from the words nor from the flood of memories they evoked: a deputy sheriff coming to the tenant shack with a story of a little girl being dragged into the bushes, Bo's attempt to rape Cassie herself when she was thirteen, and later, his conviction in California.

There was more to it than memory, however difficult it was to admit, even to herself. There was a blending, a confused entanglement of self and other: half brother and half self. It was as if she was part of him and he of her, an evil lurking within her, as deep and as obscure as the dark side of the moon. She could ignore it now, push it down to the bottom of her well of memories, but what if he were paroled? What if he returned to Oklahoma? What then?

She forced herself to put aside emotion and let the facts stand alone. James Steele had a motive in bringing up the subject of Bo, she knew. James always had a motive. "This is blackmail, James, isn't it? You're trying to get me to use my influence on Dix."

"Blackmail?" James laughed. "Let me refresh your memory, Cassie. You are the one who indulges in blackmail, not I."

"I can see why you would do this to me, but Dix is your son!"

"Quid pro quo. I will help Dix, but he must stop these anti-segregation activities." He smiled. "It might be interesting to obtain a transcript of your brother's trial. It might well lead to a resurgence of interest in the case, perhaps even in the national press. In the eyes of the voters, even a tenuous connection with a child molester would cling to Dix like mud to a white picket fence. The party, of course, would immediately lose interest in Dix as a candidate."

Cassie's shoulders sagged. He was right. She knew he was right.

"Well?" he said impatiently.

"I'll think about it," she said helplessly.

He watched her for a minute with narrowed eyes. "You do that, Cassie. You think about it."

Chapter 4

Cassie did think about James's threats, but she said nothing about them to Dix. She knew it was foolish, but she clung to the hope that if she ignored it, it would all go away. At any rate, she had no time to worry with future schemes and plans: she was completely involved in the here and now.

On a bitter cold afternoon the first week in December, Cassie was casting clover seed in the high field. To rest her shoulders and arm, she put down her bag of seed and walked out to the end of the road to get the mail from the RFD box. There, waiting, was a letter that informed her that she was officially a member of the Oklahoma bar. Fingers stiff with cold, she folded the letter back into its envelope. She laughed, but her physical misery turned the chuckle into a sob.

She had walked the upper fields every day for a week, as Henry Starr said, "from cain't see to cain't see," handcasting clover seed mixed with sand while Henry did the same in the bottom by San Bois Creek. During the first few days, her imagination had made the job easier. She had seen not the gray December days, but the sunshine of March. She had envisioned pastures green with the clover that would enrich the soil and hold it against the winter rains until April when the fields could be sprigged with Bermuda grass. After a few days, however, her shoulders ached from the repetitive act of casting seed, and the image faded as she slogged through the cold mist, digging into her bag and throwing the seed, digging and throwing until she moved like an automaton, a dumb thing doing its assigned job day in and day out.

Admitted to the bar, she thought, leaning on the fence post by the mailbox. An attorney. A wealthy attorney at that. Then why was she doing a job that any farm laborer could handle? Why was an attorney doing menial work worth only minimum wage? She raised her head and looked out across fields at a view softened by the mist. She saw the fields and beyond them the winter-bare oaks among the dark branches of cedars, and then the hazy hills rising into the misty Ozarks.

Why? Because they were her fields, because it was her land. She looked at the dirty, blistered palms of her hands, and suddenly she was back on the porch of the tenant shack where she had spent her childhood. She sat on splintered gray boards, playing with Francine, her rag doll, and listened while her grandmother read haltingly from her worn Bible: " 'Give her of the fruit of her hands, and let her own works praise her in the gates.' "

Cassie remembered the divorce suits she had handled in Dallas, when hatred had poisoned the air of the courtroom; and later cases, oil and gas suits in which opponents fought bitterly to take money from each other and liquid black gold from the land. Taking, always taking. She thrust the letter deep into the pocket of her plaid mackinaw and rubbed her rough palms together. Her hands were dirty but it was honest dirt, the result of hard cleansing work that would not take from her land but would enhance it. She walked back to the field with a lighter step.

The seeding was finished, finally, and Cassie could begin to plan for Christmas. Her schedule was interrupted, however, on the evening when Henry Starr came to her with a problem. He sat by the fireplace where oak logs burned with a slow steady flame. He looked at the fire instead of at Cassie.

"Well, I'll tell you. Bubba Vance, he's got hisself in trouble. Wonders can he talk to you, bein' as how it's law trouble."

"Your son-in-law, Henry? Ruby Keeler's father? Of course. I'll do whatever I can to help."

"He ain't got the money to pay no lawyer, Cassie. He ain't nothin' but a sharecropper."

In Cassie's mind, the word conjured up the weathered shack where she had known all about living with no money. "Let's forget about money, Henry. What is his problem?"

Henry grinned. "Reckon he better tell you hisself. He's out in the kitchen."

"Well, for goodness' sake, bring him in here."

Bubba Vance was big, with bulky shoulders under a faded plaid-flannel shirt. Beneath a shock of straw-colored hair his face looked too young for a man who was the father of a high-school girl. After a few minutes of talk with him, Cassie realized that the lack of wrinkles in his face probably matched the lack of memory wrinkles in his brain. Bubba Vance was not very bright.

Cassie heard his confused explanation and then tried to get at the facts of the matter. "So, Bubba, you say the television place is going to take your pickup truck because you haven't paid them for a new TV set. Why not? Is it because you don't have the money?"

Bubba shifted on his chair. "They got it set up so's I can pay a little ever' week, Miz Cassie, and they give me one of them guarantees, so it don't hardly seem right to have to pay for a TV that don't even work."

"You're exactly right, Bubba," Cassie said with some surprise. "They are obligated to keep it in good working order for the warranty period. Do you have the guarantee and the sales contract with you?"

"Yessum." He fished a wad of papers from his shirt pocket. "This here is what they give me."

Cassie unfolded the papers, trying to ignore the odor they released of unwashed sweat and mustiness: the smell of Bubba Vance himself. "Have you talked to the store about your problems with the TV set?"

"Yessum. I called 'em twice and I told 'em how my wife, she

was real upset. She had a lot of hopes for that there TV. She was countin' on watchin' all them movie stars and presidents and the like. Well, they say, plug it in and do this and that, then I say, well, I don't rightly reckon I can do that, and they start yellin' at me how they're fixin' to take away my pickup if I don't pay."

"But have you done what they suggested, Bubba? Have you tried to get the television set to work?"

He shook his head sadly. "I keep tryin' to tell them how Mr. Chandler got the REA to his house, but he didn't hook it up to the cropper's place. So they says, plug her in, but there ain't no way I can do that, not with nothin' to plug her in to."

Cassie took a deep breath. "Bubba, do you mean to tell me you don't have electricity? Then why in God's name did you buy a television set?"

Bubba's chin shook and Cassie was afraid that he was going to cry. "It was that there salesman, Miz Cassie. He never told me it had to have the electricity or nothin'."

"Bubba, surely you knew that—"

Behind Bubba, Henry Starr grimaced at Cassie.

She sighed. "Oh, never mind. You leave these papers with me, and I'll see if I can get this straightened out."

Bubba beamed at her with the wide happy smile of a child without a worry in the world. "Henry, he said you was real smart, Miz Cassie. He said you could make them old boys leave me be."

Through clenched teeth, Cassie said, "Bubba, if you get the urge to buy something else, or decide you want to sign a paper for someone, will you talk to me about it first?"

"Yessum, Miz Cassie. I sure-fire will!" He went to the kitchen to tell Ruby Keeler the good news. Henry Starr would have followed, but Cassie stopped him.

"Henry, why on earth did you bring Bubba to me? You knew what the problem was. You could have handled it yourself."

He obviously felt no remorse. "Well, Cassie, for nigh to twenty years I been tellin' Bubba not to buy anything lessen he checks with me first, but he don't pay me no mind. I just figured he might listen to you." He started toward the kitchen but stopped in the doorway and looked back. "'Sides, with you startin' a law practice and all, I figured you might just as lief have Bubba to practice on." With a cackle of laughter, he left the room.

One telephone call and a few waves of an invisible flag imprinted LAWYER solved Bubba Vance's problems with the television dealer.

Word of Cassie's success flashed through San Bois like wildfire. Before the week was out she had received two calls from prospective clients. One was from the owner of the DX filling station, an octogenarian who had decided the time had come for him to sign a last will and testament, but the other case took Cassie back to her early practice in Dallas: Grace Johnson needed legal protection from threats made by her ex-husband. Cassie immediately went to court to enjoin the man from threatening Mrs. Johnson, from attempting to see her and even from calling her on the phone. She followed up the court appearance with a visit to the local branch of the sheriff's office.

Deputy Skeet Beasley was in charge, the deputy who had in the past linked her irrevocably with her half brother, Bo Taylor. The man was white-haired now, and when he leaned back in his chair his uniform shirt gaped over his paunch.

"Well, well, so Cassie Taylor's got her a fancy ranch and a fine, upstandin' husband and a license to practice law. Never would have thought it, girl, not with a paw like yours and that brother of—"

"Half brother, Deputy. Can we get on with our business? Does this man Johnson have a record?"

Deputy Beasley shuffled the papers on his desk. "Bo Taylor's sis a lawyer. Ain't that somethin'?"

Cassie felt as guilty as if she, not Bo, were the criminal. She stood up and leaned over the desk. "Are there charges out against Bo Taylor, Deputy? Do you have a warrant for his arrest? If not, he can be no more and no less to you than any other citizen. I don't want anything to do with him, but I'll remind you of your responsibilities, since you seem to have forgotten them. Bo Taylor is serving his time and you have no control over him, none at all!" She stood up and looked down at him. "The man you should be interested in is this Ben Johnson. If he lays one hand on his ex-wife, or calls her even once, and you don't pull him in, it will all come down on you like a ton of bricks. I'll have your badge, Deputy, I swear it. I'll be watching you, I promise. I'll have my eye on you!"

Cassie turned away, ignoring his fury, and stomped out of the room. She was angry at him, but she was angry at herself, too, angry that she had let the fool upset her.

Taylor was so full of energy that evening that when Cassie picked him up, his arms and legs kept churning as if even in midair he had to fulfill his quota of miles crawled per day. At nine months he was trying to walk but reverted to crawling when he was in a hurry. When Cassie tucked him into his crib, he went right off to sleep, exhausted by his day. Cassie stood over his bed, awed by the knowledge that she and Dix had produced such a perfect creature. When she went back to the living room, however, her pleasure was replaced by the resentment and shame she had experienced in Deputy Skeet Beasley's office.

She called Dix in Oklahoma City that night, but she did not mention the deputy. Just hearing his voice and knowing that he loved her was enough, or almost enough. She replaced the receiver and poked up the fire in the fieldstone fireplace. She loved Dix and he loved her. She was the mother of a bright, beautiful son. She owned land and a car. She was an attorney with a small but growing practice. She was a member of the establishment, a respected citizen of Clifton County. Why on earth should a conversation with a fat ignorant country deputy throw her into a depression? Consider the source, she reminded herself. Consider the source. She stopped, still holding the poker, because she realized that Deputy Beasley had merely reminded her of what she knew. No matter how successful she was, how loving and how loved, deep down she was still a sharecropper's daughter, the sister of a no-account convict.

She stirred the fire again and sparks flew upward from her angry jabs. It was not fair, she thought, not fair!

She had worked hard, all her life, for her success and now she could not relax and enjoy it. No. She could not relax, because she had to go right on working to convince herself that she deserved what she had earned. Perhaps she had been wrong to come back to Eastern Oklahoma. Even loving Dix and their son was not enough to clear away the miasma of memories that clung to the farm. Bo still haunted her life. Deputy Beasley still watched her with little pug eyes, waiting for her to make a slip. And James Steele still sat in Ballard like a deadly sea-thing, sending tentacles of hatred into her life.

A December snow fell on Friday night and Dix did not get home until after nine. Cassie had kept Taylor up late, but he was so tired that he fell asleep on Dix's shoulder. The firelight flickered on the baby's round, fair head and Dix's haggard face.

"Were the roads terrible?" Cassie asked.

"They were bad, all right. Worse near Oklahoma City. It sleeted late in the afternoon, then changed to snow. The highway was coated with glaze ice."

Cassie took Taylor in and tucked him into bed. Back in the living room, she rubbed Dix's shoulders. "Have a hot shower, darling, while I fix you something to eat. A bowl of soup?"

"Sounds great, but just let me sit here for a while first."

Cassie felt a twinge of fear. "Are you all right? Did something happen?"

He smiled. "I'm fine but, yes, something did happen. Something good, I think. He watched the fire for a few minutes and then looked directly at her. "Cassie, I've been asked to run for the House of Representatives."

"For Congress?"

"They seem to think that I have a pretty good chance at winning the 1960 Democratic primary. I wouldn't be a shoo-in, but the conservative Democrats' candidate is nothing but a party hack."

"He would be your father's candidate."

"Yes. You know, of course, that winning the Democratic primary in this district is tantamount to winning the general election. It would mean—"

"Washington," Cassie whispered. "We would have to live in Washington."

"I know how much the farm means to you, darling, and we could be here part of the time, but since we're already planning to move to Oklahoma City—"

We are? Cassie thought, but she did not say it aloud. "Dix, there is only one thing that matters. How do *you* feel about it?"

He looked at the fire. "It's a temptation. I wouldn't be telling the truth if I said I didn't care about the honor and the position, but there's more to it than that. A U.S. Congressman represents his own constituency first, of course, but he must also consider the national good."

"Desegregation."

He looked at her quickly. "Desegregation, yes. It's more and more obvious that it can't be dealt with on a state-by-state basis. There will have to be federal intervention of some kind."

Cassie rubbed her temples. "Another Civil War."

"A legislative war, honey, not a shooting war. A shouting one, though, when we drag those segregationists kicking and screaming into the twentieth century."

"Oh, come on, Dix. It's still only 1956. Surely by the time you could take a seat in Congress—"

He laughed. "You mean, *if* I take a seat in Congress! Look, Cassie, the siege of the South has just begun. It will take a long time to breach those walls. A hell of a long time."

Cassie saw it then, the excitement lurking at the back of his eyes: the lust for battle. "Dix," she said. "Dix, I think—"

"Yes?" He leaned forward.

"I think you ought to risk it."

"Are you sure, Cassie? I was afraid—leaving the farm, leaving Oklahoma—"

" 'Whither thou goest, I will go.' "

Dix stood up. "Oh, Cassie. My dearest Cassie."

They kissed then, lit by the flames in the fireplace, and there was in that kiss a new commitment that was beyond love and lust, a commitment to their life together. For the first time, Cassie felt that they truly were married.

The dog appeared on the Wednesday before Christmas during a sleet storm. He was small and looked even smaller on the back porch of the lodge, a shivering bundle of wet brown hair, whining and scratching at the back door.

"You, sir! Get away from here!" Ruby Keeler flapped her apron at him. "Scat!"

Taylor toddled across the kitchen floor, laughing with delight.

Cassie wanted to join Ruby Keeler in driving the creature away, but there was something appealing about him. In all his misery, he could still wag his tail. For Taylor, there was no question about it. It was love at first sight.

Henry Starr left his coffee cup on the kitchen table and went to the door. "Poor-looking thing, ain't he?" he said. "Old stray dog like that, he's bound to be full of fleas and ticks."

Cassie drew back. "I didn't think of that. I was just going to let him in and give him something to eat, some table scraps."

Henry wheezed with amusement. "Let that critter come in here once, Cassie, and he'll set up housekeeping."

Taylor scooted between Cassie and Ruby Keeler to grab the dog's head. Cassie reached for him, but the dog immediately sat down and bowed its head to be patted.

"He's not a stray, Henry," she said. "Only lost. You can tell he's lived around children, with a family." Taylor's face was alive with excitement. "Look, can't you clean him up, get rid of the fleas?"

Henry shook his head doubtfully. "Don't know about that. Got some pine tar soap that might do the job." He grinned at her. "Well, I'll do it, Cassie. Reckon you and the boy here, you got yourselves a pup."

After a bath and a rubdown with an old towel the dog looked better, although he smelled strongly of tar. He ate every leftover Cassie could find and then stood at the back door until Ruby Keeler let him out. A short time later he barked once, politely, and waited to be let in. He went to each of them and sniffed and then with Taylor crawling along behind, he marched into the living room and lay down in front of the fireplace. He did not object while Taylor poked and prodded every inch of his body.

Henry winked at Cassie. "Looks like you can send Ruby Keeler on home now."

"Grandad!" Ruby Keeler protested.

"Well, Cassie's got herself a new baby sitter for the boy now, and she don't have to pay him nothing but table scraps."

"Henry," Cassie said, "you leave that girl alone! Just for that, Ruby Keeler, you get to name the dog."

Ruby Keeler blushed. She screwed her mouth in thought and then smiled happily. "Let's call him 'Rags,' Cassie. That's what I thought when I first seen—"

"Saw," Cassie said.

"When I first saw him out there on the porch, I thought he looked like a bundle of old wet rags."

Big snowflakes were drifting down by the time Dixon Steele arrived at the lodge at noon on Christmas Eve. Henry Starr and Ruby Keeler drove off to spend Christmas with the Vances. Cassie held Taylor up to the living room window to wave good-bye, then turned to Dix, who was adding a chunk of split oak to the fire.

"Dix, we're alone! For two whole days! Do you realize that this is the first time we've had the lodge to ourselves since we were married?"

He stood up and dusted his hands. "Cassie, all I've thought about for the past week is being alone with you." He grinned at her. "Come here, woman!"

She went into his arms and they kissed until Taylor tugged at her slacks demandingly.

They laughed and Dix lifted Taylor to include him. Taylor squealed with delight as the hug turned into a wild dance around the living room. Rags joined in, barking as he scrambled to stay out of their way.

Dix and Cassie stopped, still holding Taylor. "Well, we aren't entirely alone," he said.

Cassie squeezed his arm. "Later, darling. Later."

And later, when Taylor was asleep in his crib, Dix brought a quilt and laid it on the rug in front of the fire. Cassie turned off the lights and joined him on the floor. Slowly, carefully, they undressed each other, while their bare flesh gleamed red in the light of the fire. Dix put his arms around Cassie and she leaned against his warm body. She opened her eyes and looked over his shoulder.

"Oh, no."

Dix pulled away from her. "What's the matter?"

"It's Rags!" she said. "He's watching everything we do!"

Dix laughed and pulled her to him. "Oh, Cassie, he's just a damn dog."

"He is not! He's a damn *voyeur!*" She jumped up, naked, and led Rags down the hall to Taylor's room. She held the door open. "Go on, Rags," she whispered. "Now!"

With one reproachful look, he dragged himself into the room. Cassie closed the door and waited until she heard the thump as he dropped to his accustomed place by Taylor's crib, then she hurried back to the living room.

Dix was lying on the quilt, raised on one elbow.

"You look like a Roman emperor," she said softly, "waiting for a handmaiden to drop grapes into your mouth."

He grinned at her. "Well, how about it?"

She walked toward him, bending her knees with each step, thrusting her pelvis forward. "I've always wanted to undulate."

He reached up to her with one long arm. "And you do it so well. Come here to me."

She pulled back. "But the grapes, Caesar?"

"No grapes. Just you."

Cassie sank to her knees but he pulled her down on top of him. She lay along his body, feeling the heat of it, feeling him get hard beneath her. "Dix," she whispered, "oh, my darling."

Next to her ear, his breath took on a rasp and his hands moved down her back as if with a life of their own, to grasp her buttocks and push her against him. He entered her then, and she cried out in pleasure as he thrust himself deep into her, deeper and deeper.

"Dix!" she cried, and in one smooth motion he rolled with her until she was lying on her back on the comforter and he was on top of her, pounding into her, his eyes glinting in the flickering light from the fire, thrusting until she cried out in joy, "Dix!" At her cry he ground himself into her and she arched her body, lifting herself to receive him, to take him into her, as if to draw his very body into hers.

He cried out then, a deep wordless sound, and collapsed on her. She moved slightly, aware only of the throbbing of her body and the unbroken connection of his body and hers.

"Cassie," he said, voice breaking, and it was her turn to put her arms around him, to hold him close, to encompass him in her strength while he, spent, returned from the little death.

They dozed together until the fire burned down to embers and they were awakened by the chill in the room.

Together they showered and put on their nightclothes, saw Rags out and back in, and tucked Taylor's covers around him. Together they climbed into their double bed, pulled up the covers and turned off the light.

"Old married folks," Cassie whispered.

"Old married man," Dix corrected her, "with wife who undulates." He put his arms around her. "Old married folks. Yes."

And then, as old married folks will do when the night is cold on the farm and snow drifts down on the dark branches of the cedars and covers the dry spiky weeds, they made a quiet kind of love.

Chapter 5

On New Year's Day, Cassie Steele made her plans for 1957. During the holidays, Dix had barely mentioned a move to Oklahoma City, perhaps because he realized that after the autumn's hard work, she was more committed to the land than ever. Moreover, they both knew that preparing to run for Congress would mean that he would have to be away from home more and more as he crisscrossed the district meeting voters and building relationships with local Democrats. In the spring she and Henry Starr would sprig the pastures to Bermuda grass, and with normal rainfall and any luck at all, the place would be ready for cattle in the spring of 1958.

Two days after Dix left the farm the telephone rang.

"Is this the wise old country lawyer?" a woman's voice asked. "The one who sent me a Christmas note about strolling the lanes with her faithful dog Shep at her heel?"

"Fran! You idiot! For one thing, the dog's name is Rags, and—"

"Fran's the name, designing's the game, Cassie, and I must say that I have a rather large bone to pick with you. Except for that card, I haven't heard from you in months. Have you gone to seed up there in the boondocks?"

Cassie laughed. Fran, her only friend from Ballard and her best friend from Texas, had made a name for herself in Dallas as an interior designer who could create the proper settings for the new-rich country people who struck it big in oil and immigrated to mansions on Turtle Creek Drive and Preston Hollow.

"I haven't gone to seed, my dear girl. I'm working my tail off changing this dirt farm into a cattle ranch, and I'm a wife and mother, too, you know, and a practicing attorney."

Fran laughed. "Practicing law and getting even richer, if I know you."

"So far I've taken in about thirty-five dollars."

"My God, what kind of cases are you taking? Traffic tickets? Wait till I tell Steve Reilly about this!"

Cassie winced. Steve Reilly had been Cassie's boss in Dallas, then her lover, and finally her law partner. He was her mentor through every step of her rise from the position of legal secretary to that of a wealthy oil and gas attorney. "No! Don't tell Steve!"

"Well, I suppose—look, I'm coming to visit you, kid. Would two weeks from Monday be good? I'll need to leave early Friday to drive back to Dallas."

Cassie laughed. How like Fran it was to present her with a ready-made schedule and expect an immediate yes or no. She had to give her credit, though. A "no" would not faze her, and there would be no concealed resentment. Fran was what she was and she expected the same blunt honesty from her friends.

"Yes! Do come, Fran!" Until she said the words, Cassie did not realize how true they were. "I need you in my life."

On Monday afternoon, Frances Jordan rolled to a stop in the muddy road in front of the house. Before Cassie could cross the veranda, Fran was complaining to her or to herself or to anyone who happened to be in earshot.

"Look at my poor car! Why someone with Cassie Steele's money won't even gravel her damn road is beyond me. And the damn mud is red! All over my new—I swear to God, Oklahoma is so backwoods that it's—"

"Fran, Fran!" Half in laughter, half in apology, Cassie ran across the yard. "I'll have it washed, I swear! I won't let that nasty old red mud sully your beautiful—" She looked at the sleek blue automobile and realized what she was seeing. She whistled softly. "Your beautiful new Mercedes sports car."

Fran smiled smugly. "Like it?"

"Like it? I—" She shot a look at Fran. "Interior design must be paying big bucks these days."

Fran became terribly nonchalant. "Oh, I didn't buy it. It's a little gift from a friend."

Cassie was uncomfortably aware that Fran's friends were usually rich, middle-aged oil men who were still married to the wives who had worked side by side with them on the long climb from the West Texas oil fields to the wealthy suburbs of Dallas.

Fran looked away. "How do you like the color?"

"I like the color." Into one sentence Cassie tried to put her love for Fran, what their long friendship meant to her, and her full acceptance of Fran's decisions. "I like the color just fine!"

Fran looked at her carefully. "All right then," she said, and laughed. "All right!"

They hugged, laughing, until Fran said, "Where's that boy of yours? I want to see Taylor!"

"He was just waking up when I heard your car. Let's go in and—"

"Cassie, I have a jillion questions! How is Dix? *Where* is Dix? Has he started campaigning yet? And when is this one due?"

Cassie stopped on the veranda steps. "What do you mean, 'this one'?"

"Don't be dense, darling. This baby, of course. How far along are you?"

"Oh, for goodness' sake, Fran, I'm only a few weeks late. I haven't even seen the doctor yet!"

Fran put her arm around Cassie's waist and urged her up the steps. "You forget that I was around when you were first pregnant with Taylor. I recognize that sickening radiant glow, love. You're pregnant, all right."

Taylor went right to Fran Jordan. Cassie was delighted, but she could not resist some gentle teasing. "How do you do it? You're

like honey to the bears, Fran. You attract everything in pants."
She laughed. "Or in diapers, for that matter."

A shadow came into Fran's eyes, but it was gone as suddenly
as it had appeared. "Get 'em young, I always say. Get 'em young
and train 'em right. Now I want to hear all about Dix and the
farm and your old friend—I forget her name—the teacher."

"Naomi Bencher? I haven't heard from her lately. She's in Hawaii running a library for the Army, and she's very much involved
in the statehood movement. And Dix—"

As they talked, she realized, Fran was looking around the room,
measuring, comparing and, finally, rejecting. Cassie started to describe her plans for the farm, but Fran shook her head abruptly.

"It won't do, Cassie, it simply will not do," she said. "You know
Dix will win his seat in Congress and then you'll have all sorts of
people here: government people, the press, politicians, everybody
who *is* anybody in Oklahoma. And this place is a horror. Where
did you get this furniture, anyway?"

"Why, it was just here. I suppose most of the things are discards
from the Steeles' house in Ballard."

Fran turned slowly, surveying the room. "The thirties. Art Deco
was marvelous but never in the history of the world were chairs
and sofas so obese. Do you know what was here before they moved
in this stuff?"

"No, I have no idea—" Cassie hesitated and suddenly was five
years old again, clutching her grandmother's hand while she
pressed her face against the front window of the lodge. "Yes," she
said softly, "I remember it. Granny and I were outside on the
veranda, looking in." She saw the long rolls that were carpets
wrapped in canvas, and sofa shapes draped with sheets. "There
were tables with fancy carved legs, and bookcases and a big desk,
oh, and a secretary." She laughed. "I wouldn't have known the
name then, but it had leaded glass doors and a desk with pigeon
holes." She shook her head. "It's funny, Fran. I haven't thought
of those things for years."

Fran's eyes glittered with excitement. "Where are they now?"

"Heavens, I don't know. They could have been given away or burned—"

"Or stored, Cassie! Have you been through all the outbuildings, the barn and all?"

"Oh, sure, long ago. There's no furniture."

"The attic? Is there an attic?"

"Yes, but I've never been up there."

Fran moved fast. In a matter of minutes, she had plumped Taylor into his playpen, had summoned Henry to bring a ladder, and was sliding aside the large trap door in the ceiling of the hall. She sneezed as dust sifted down and then, disregarding her Neiman-Marcus suit, she clambered into the attic.

"What do you see?" Cassie called.

"You wouldn't believe—" There was a muffled sneeze and then an awed voice. "My God, what isn't Victorian is Eastlake."

"What's Eastlake?"

Fran's dirty, excited face appeared at the opening. "All solid hardwoods, machine-carved. It's about like stainless steel now, but in fifteen years it will be sterling silver, and fifteen years after that, fourteen-karat gold. I found the secretary. It's dirty, but in perfect shape. Cassie, the desk has a burled-cherry roll top!"

"Great. I guess."

"Well, you can guess all you want to, but I know. It's my business to know."

It also became Fran's business to redecorate the entire lodge. For four days she wandered through the house, jotting ideas and measurements in a leatherbound notebook. She gossiped with Cassie, catching up on old times in Ballard and Dallas, and she became Taylor's bosom buddy. Occasionally she even consulted Cassie about the plans for the house, but it seemed to Cassie that the questions were *pro forma* and were asked only because it was she who would eventually pay the bills.

Fran left on Friday with promises to return in a month or so, and five days later Cassie drove into San Bois to see Dr. Hill, a small round man who, as he said, had been doctoring in San Bois since heck was a pup.

"Well," he said, raising his bushy white eyebrows, "from what I hear, this baby's got a married mama and a legal papa, and a fine one at that."

Cassie blushed, remembering the first time she had seen Dr. Hill, when she had made no bones about the fact that she was not married and had refused to identify the father of her unborn child.

"You want to go with natural childbirth again, Cassie?"

"Yes, I do. That is, if Henry Starr will sharpen his ax."

They laughed together, remembering how Henry Starr had insisted on putting a sharp ax under the bed in the clinic's delivery room. One of his superstitions. "It'll cut the pain," he said.

After the examination, Dr. Hill said, "You look to be in good shape, Cassie, even if being thirty-two will make you a little long in the tooth for child-bearing."

"Thanks a lot!"

He laughed. "Now, Cassie, it isn't *that* old. Why, I could tell you stories—but I won't. I do want you to get yourself in top condition, though. Long walks, that's the best thing. Get yourself in the habit of taking long brisk walks."

"When is the baby due?"

He raised his eyebrows. "Thought you'd have figured that out by now. September, I figure."

September, Cassie thought. Then the baby must have been conceived at Christmas, when she undulated. She smiled.

"What are you smiling about, girl?"

"I'm happy, that's all," she said, but she was thinking that while she took those long walks she would practice her undulations.

Dr. Hill smiled, too. "And I'm happy for you, Cassie Steele. I'll see you next month."

Cassie had seen Dr. Hill again before Fran called and ordered her to get out of the house. She packed up clothes for herself and

Taylor, and went to spend two weeks with Dix while Fran Jordan moved her crew of workmen into the lodge.

Driving to Oklahoma City was like traveling to a different country. As they drove west from San Bois, the landscape changed from the wooded foothills of the Ozarks to more gentle country and to flatlands where winter wheat grew in individual fields as large as some of the farms in the hills of Eastern Oklahoma. As they came closer to Oklahoma City they saw acres of kaffir corn and silos to store feed for dairy herds. Fat Jerseys and Guernseys grazed the pastures, instead of the Hereford beef cattle they saw in Eastern Oklahoma.

Cassie's first sight of Oklahoma City was of a confusion of skyscrapers and steel derricks, as if the place had not figured out whether it was a city or an oil field. Dix drove past the state capitol, where there were pumping units on the grounds of the capitol building itself, units that reminded Cassie of the toy glass birds that swing down to sip water, change balance, sit back and then swing down to sip again.

Dix pulled to a stop. "This is the Skirvin Tower, honey, where I live. You'll be able to shop right here in the Tower at Ballict's or you can go to Rosenthal's, in the Biltmore Hotel."

"I heard of Balliet's, even in Dallas, but I had no idea it was in your apartment building!"

"Oh, there are other surprises here, too, for li'l ole country girls like you. Perle Mesta, 'the hostess with the mostes',' had an apartment in the Tower."

"Why would Perle Mesta—"

"Because her daddy built it, that's why. He built the Skirvin Hotel, across Broadway there, back in the thirties. Tonight we'll take Taylor and go to dinner at the Oklahoma City Golf and Country Club. We'll go early, but they're accustomed to having small children there. You'll like it here, honey, I swear."

Cassie suspected he was leading up to another try to get her to move to Oklahoma City, but perhaps she was wrong. Dix busied himself with the doorman, unloading their luggage from the trunk and making arrangements for it to be taken up to his place.

At last they had Taylor and themselves and all their possessions in Dix's apartment. It was pleasant, even luxurious, but it was small, and Taylor crawled from room to room, looking for Rags.

"A honeymoon for three," Cassie said.

"Three and a half," Dix said, patting her stomach. "At least, I assume you brought the baby with you."

"I never go anywhere without her."

"Her?"

Cassie smiled. "Or him. Taylor, how about you? Do you want a baby brother or a baby sister?"

"He would probably want a puppy." Dix took Cassie's hand. "How about you, darling. Would you settle for another dog?"

"Not at this stage of the game." She grimaced. "When the time comes, I may wish I had!"

Later that day, Dix introduced Taylor to Mrs. Lebiff, who lived on the same floor and had a miniature poodle named Mitzi. With her pink-varnished toenails, Mitzi was not the best substitute for Rags, but she kept Taylor happy.

During the next two weeks, Cassie met the men who would be working to get Dix elected to Congress in 1960. "I want to meet them while I still have a waist," Cassie said, but her first meetings with liberal Democrats left her somewhat disenchanted. They appeared to be committed to Dix Steele's cause, and to be hard workers, but only a few shared his zealous idealism.

"That's as it should be," Dix told her one night, over dinner at Delores. "The candidate must be the leader, at the head of the pack, but he needs the pack as much as it needs him, not only to get him elected but also to rein him in if he gets a wild hair up his—if he takes off on an inappropriate course."

Cassie smiled at a passing fancy. In the restaurant's setting of dark wood paneling and wrought-iron grilles, she could picture Dix, with his unruly black hair and his thin, high-bridged nose, as a Spanish grandee. She realized what he had said, however, and shook her head sadly. "You mean that a leader must compromise his beliefs?"

"No, dear, I mean politics is the art of the possible."

"Isn't that a rather cynical approach?"

Dix chuckled. "Not cynical, love, only practical."

Cassie discovered that she need not worry about Dix's making compromises. Only the most liberal Democrats fully supported Dix's involvement with the black movement in the South, but he persuaded those people that he could win, and ignored the others. Cassie herself was torn. She agreed with Dix, even though she knew that his stand would cost him votes, but she worried about his personal safety as Dr. Martin Luther King's nonviolent movement engendered increasingly violent reaction.

After two weeks of city life and city sounds, Cassie was ready to go home. As they turned off of Highway 12, however, and Dix slowed the car for the last half-mile of dirt road leading to the lodge, she became more and more worried about what she would find. She trusted Fran implicitly, but she had left the redecoration of the lodge in her hands, all of the work, all of the decisions. She might hate what Fran Jordan had done to her house.

Dix sensed her anxiety. "It will be okay, darling. It will be fine. You know Fran. You can trust her. And don't forget what she did with your little house in Dallas."

Cassie took a deep breath. He was right. Fran had done a beautiful job, working with very little money to turn the run-down, filthy place into a charming, comfortable house. But in effect Cassie had given her a blank check to work on the lodge. What would she have done? It was not the money that worried her, but something far more important. If she did not like what Fran had done, if she hated it, would it ruin their friendship? When she saw Fran's Mercedes and knew that in a few minutes she would have to tell her friend what she thought of the job, her heart sank.

Dix carried the sleeping Taylor up the veranda steps, but Cassie trailed behind, afraid to go inside.

Fran had seen them coming and held the door open for Dix to carry Taylor inside. She stopped Cassie at the door. "Wait," she said. "Let him get the baby into bed. I want to do the grand tour for both of you at once."

Dix came back with a smile curling the corners of his mouth. He winked at Cassie.

"Okay!" Fran said, throwing the door open. "Enter and behold!"

Cassie edged through the door, noticing that the floor was covered with rush carpeting that would trap dead leaves or snow or the red dust of the road. She looked through to the living room and stopped dead. "Fran," she breathed, "I can't—it's beautiful!"

Fran laughed with pleasure, but followed Cassie into the living room without saying a word.

Even on the gray February day, the room glowed with a light of its own. The walls were a warm eggshell white and the hand-hewn plank that served as a mantel over the fieldstone fireplace had been cleaned and rubbed with wax to a honey color. The tall cherry secretary gleamed at the far end of the room, and a walnut desk with a brass banker's lamp sat at the other end, catching and warming the pale daylight. There were other pieces of attic furniture, oak straight chairs with newly woven cane seats, massive Victorian bookshelves and a cherry quilt rack with an antique afghan ready for anyone who wanted to stretch out on the new couch for a nap. Interspersed among the antiques were new armchairs which were large but not obese, and covered with bright chintzes. A large Persian carpet covered the refinished wide plank floors. It was worn, like its twin in the dining room, but its colors glowed.

Cassie knew that the big dining room table had not come from any attic. It was a mahogany hunt table, set against the wall as a buffet table, although it could be moved into the center of the dining room for a sit-down dinner for twelve. The pictures on the walls were an intriguing mixture of old family photographs, a few good oils in heavy gilt frames and, in the hall, a topographical map of the quadrant that included the farm and San Bois Creek.

Cassie went back into the living room and turned all the way around, slowly, absorbing what she saw. Surely, she thought, surely only Fran Jordan would have the sense of style and the touch to take such an eclectic collection of furniture and pictures and make it look exactly right somehow for the home of a rising young Oklahoma politician and his pregnant lawyer-wife who lived with his small son in an Edwardian house set in the middle of what was becoming a working cattle ranch.

Cassie laughed out loud at the thought.

"What are you laughing at?" Fran said. "What's wrong?"

"Nothing's wrong. It's perfect! I just realized that it is exactly what Dix and I are, what the farm is: a little bit of everything, all thrown in together. It's eclectic, but when you think about it, so are we!"

Fran spent the night, as delighted to tell the story of the job as Cassie and Dix were to hear it: the fabric that ended up in Houston, the painter who showed up on the job so drunk that he fell off his ladder, but so drunk that the fall didn't hurt him.

The next morning Fran packed her sports car and left for Dallas. Cassie was sorry to see her go but delighted at having her family to herself. She was eager to walk the farm and see how the clover was doing, and to lean on the fence and discuss ranching matters with Henry. And she would settle into the house. She would dig out the magazines she liked and the books she and Dix were reading, and she would let Taylor scatter his toys around the place. Then their beautiful house would belong to them, and Cassie would be home at last.

Chapter 6

The summer of 1957 was a time of growth. The Bermuda grass in the pastures sent roots down deep into the soil and thrived during days of hot sun alternating with day-long drizzling rains. Like her land, Cassie relaxed and let the new life within her grow. She followed Dr. Hill's regimen of good diet and exercise. Often she took Taylor for walks, but fifteen-month-olds are not constructed to walk briskly along a path. He toddled here and there like a yellow chick, darting to pick up a leaf that caught his eye, to watch a roly-poly bug, or to poke a finger into an insect tunnel in the red clay. For serious exercise Cassie chose Rags for a walking companion. He quartered the land ahead of her, starting a rabbit in a fence row, sniffing after an unseen animal or chasing a squirrel up to an oak branch where it would lash an indignant tail and chatter complaints about the invasion of its territory.

Cassie and Rags walked to the high field, which once had been the site of a tenant shack with gray unpainted board walls and a rust-streaked tin roof: the house where Cassie had lived as a child, where her grandmother died and father was killed when she was thirteen. Cassie paused, looking at the pasture but seeing the un-painted winter-grayed shack and that last night, the hot airless night when Bo had pinned her to the floor, slavering as he told her what he was going to do to her, seeing her father take down his loaded shotgun, seeing the three of them scuffling, seeing Bo's dirty finger tighten on the trigger. She closed her eyes tight, as if she could close out the memory of what happened then, the vision of her father's face exploding. And then the fire, the flames, and she was running, screaming, through the black night. She shook her head, denying it, and forced herself to look not at the past but at the present and the Bermuda grass sending out green runners across what once was the packed earth of the dooryard.

Someday cattle would stand and chew their cud in the shadow of the big oak tree where Cassie had made her play-place, where she mothered her rag doll Francine, rocking her to sleep, cooking pretend mush for her in a cracked enamel pan. The grown-up Cassie, swollen with the growth of her real baby, could hear her child-self singing tunelessly one of the songs her grandmother had taught her:

> "And if that lookin'-glass don't shine,
> Papa's going to shoot that beau of thine."

Abruptly the grown-up Cassie laughed aloud. Her grandmother had taught her the song but she had not told her what that particular verse meant. There was an old hill-country belief that if a young girl lost her virginity, her face would no longer be reflected in a mirror.

Another morning, Cassie crossed the rickety wooden bridge over San Bois Creek and climbed the hill to the building that had been Turner School. The white paint had flaked away and the doors and windows were boarded up, but Cassie thought she could hear voices there, too: the laughter of children and Miss Naomi Bencher's firm voice: "You must learn, Cassie Taylor. You must get away from here."

One hot day, Cassie walked in the woods behind the lodge, down a gulch that would run with water in heavy rain but was dry and rocky in the summer sun. The gulch snaked past a steep bank on one side, where oak and cedar trees rose from thick undergrowth, a jungle of pokeberry plants. On the other side of the gulch was a limestone cliff forty feet high and pocked with small caves, some no more than two or three feet deep. Between the caves, spring water seeped down the gray rock in trickles of moisture that sustained airy ferns and clumps of bright green moss.

Rags ranged up the banks into the woods and along the base of the cliff where there was a wealth of smells to trace and holes to investigate. Cassie was aware of him, but she concentrated on keeping her footing on the loose rock. When he started barking, she looked back but she could not see him. At the same moment she realized that his bark was muffled and had a hollow echo.

"Rags?" she called, and she whistled for him, but the distant barking did not stop. She turned back, following the sound, and realized that it was coming from the cliff itself. "Rags!" she shouted. The barking stopped and Rags appeared, wagged his tail and disappeared as quickly as he had come. He had found a cave, she realized, a deeper one than most and she was afraid that he would trap himself. She stumbled across the rocky gulch, pushed into the clump of willows where she had last seen him, and found a cave with an opening large enough to admit a human being. She had not seen it when she walked past because the opening was concealed by the willows and by a thin fall of water from the ledge above them.

As curious as Rags, Cassie edged past the trickling water and into the cave. Rags stopped barking and came to her, wagging his tail and whining softly.

Watery light fell on the walls near the opening, but was lost in the darkness at the back of the cave. The walls were rough limestone glazed with the minerals that had dripped down them through the years. The sand floor was as damp as the walls. Cassie shivered. It was cool, almost chilly in the cave, but more than that, she had an eerie feeling that this was an ancient place, one which had been inhabited long before the white man came into the Indian Territory.

As her eyes became accustomed to the gloom, Cassie saw that a low rough table was set near one wall. She could make out the shapes of several things on the table, notably a candle stub protected from mice by an upside-down Mason jar, and an olive-drab match container. The threads of the container were rusted but the wooden matches within it were dry. She leaned over the table to strike one and light the candle.

As the flickering light rose, Cassie could see that the cave was seven or eight feet wide and about that deep, with a lime-encrusted ceiling just high enough to let her stand erect. On the wall just above the candle were strange tracings, carvings in the stone, of circles and squares with rounded corners and wavering lines running like snakes between the geometric figures in a pattern that was obviously intentional but had no meaning to her.

The cave had been used in prehistoric times, she thought. She had seen pictures of similar carvings in books. There was a theory, however, that the stone carvings in a cave near Heavener were not prehistoric but were runes cut into the stone by a group of Viking explorers who had wandered south and far inland from the Atlantic.

Neither Vikings nor prehistoric men, however, stored their matches in Army surplus containers, and on the table there were signs of more recent occupation: a rusted cast-iron skillet, a tin cup, a bedroll of blankets shredded by mice or other animals. There was a kerosene lantern, empty, and a small stack of mildewed magazines, pulpy paper with badly printed photographs of nude women.

"Bo," she said suddenly. Bo Taylor had been here. When she was a child, she knew that he had a hideout in the woods, but she never knew where it was. She was thirteen when she left the farm. Twenty years. She considered the rust and the decay. Was it appropriate to twenty years of disuse, or had he come back now and again? If he had, she thought, if he had come back, it must have been years ago, before he was sent to prison. The tightness in her shoulders eased, and for the first time she became aware of the sounds in the cave, of the slow steady drip of water from the ceiling and Rags's soft whine.

She looked down at the dog. He had stopped barking when she entered the cave. Why? And why was he standing, instead of lying at her feet the way he usually did when she paused on their walks? Standing, and whining, with his tail tucked between his hind legs, staring into the darkness at the back of the cave.

Cassie shivered as she had before, but it was not from the dank chill of the cave. It was because she, like Rags, felt that something was there, something indefinable but inherently evil. Suddenly she needed to be out in the fresh air, in the strong cleansing light of the sun. She blew out the candle and ran clumsily to the opening. With Rags at her heels she pushed her way through the trickle of water and the willows and burst out into the hot sunshine.

She hurried down the gulch, gaining distance, and for once Rags stayed right with her. When the gulch angled to the south, Cassie stopped and looked back. There was the clump of willows, and high on the cliff above the opening to the cave was a huge slab of limestone.

With the slab of rock as a marker, she could find the place again, easily. She shivered once more, there in the full sunshine. She could find it if she wanted, but she would not. She never wanted to see the cave again.

Dixon Steele was away during much of August of 1957, and Cassie missed him, but with her pregnancy in its eighth month and the summer's heat at its peak, she was happy to take life easy. She limited her walks to short strolls along the road. Nose to the ground Rags ranged ahead on trails only he could find, and Taylor toddled along with her, squatting to pick up an occasional treasure and to hold it up to Cassie for identification.

"Wot dis, Mama?" he would say, and, "Wot dis?"

"A rock, Taylor. A June bug. Ugh, a worm." As the question

count grew, Taylor's eyes would dance with delicious anticipation.

"Wot dis, Mama?"

Then Cassie would grab him, as he knew she would, and hold him close. "It's my Taylor! It's my darling boy!" She would kiss his thin little neck until he dissolved in giggles and pulled free to start the game all over again.

By Labor Day, the sun was too hot and Cassie was too big for even those slow walks. She wandered through the lodge searching for a cool haven, but not until the sun went down and a damp breeze blew up from the creek could she find surcease from the sweaty, clinging heat. Then, too hot to think and too exhausted to read, she would collapse into a chair in front of the television.

It was from the grainy black-and-white pictures that she gained a deeper understanding of Dix's commitment to the black movement in the South. Night after night she saw the faces of powerful Southern whites appear and their mouths spew out a message of hatred directed more at "Northern agitators" than at the Negroes themselves. Belying their words, however, were the pictures of Negroes in streets across the South, gathering together and then scattering before the onslaught of a ragtag army of policemen and dogs and farmers and loafers. In September, Governor Orval Faubus of Arkansas chose to lock the doors of the Little Rock public schools rather than to comply with a federal court order for desegregation. Governor Almond of Virginia was quick to follow his lead.

Dix came home that weekend, tired and dispirited. "Arkansas," he said. "Only a few hundred miles from here, Americans, Negro Americans, are being deprived of their constitutional rights. You'd think we would be marching, wouldn't you, Cassie? You'd think that we free Americans would rise up against tyranny, that we would take our pitchforks and our granddaddies' swords and march to the defense of our republic. But nobody's marching. There's no anger out there. There is only apathy."

"Perhaps people just don't understand, Dix. Except for war, few of the major public events or trends really touch our personal lives."

He slammed his fist on the arm of his chair. "But this does touch our lives when it shapes the lives of our brothers and our sisters, damn it! Why can't people understand that?"

Cassie shook her head helplessly. "I don't know, darling. I just don't know."

"Oh, hell, Cassie, I shouldn't try to take it out on you." He put his arms around her and forced a laugh. "Hey, I can still reach around you, but just barely!" He pushed her away gently, with his hands on her shoulders. "I'm home now, honey. For the duration."

"You mean till the baby comes? Dix, you don't have to be here. I can handle it."

"No way!" He hugged her to him. "You had our first baby all by yourself, but I'm going to be around for this one!"

Cassie put her cheek against his shoulder and only then allowed herself to go weak with relief. "Oh, Dix, I do love you."

His laugh rumbled in his chest. "You better love me, babe. It's a little late to back out now!"

Somehow the heat was less oppressive when Dix was at the farm, and somehow Cassie felt less gigantic. She was delighted but almost surprised on the morning when she realized that the slight backache she had felt all morning had developed a rhythm. She went to the front door, and leaning on the door jamb, looked down at Dix who was teaching Taylor to catch a beach ball. "Dix," she said quietly.

"Cassie! Is it—I—" His face turned red and then very white. "Come on, Taylor," he said, suppressing the tension in his voice, "I think Ruby Keeler has your lunch ready." He hurried Taylor around the house toward the back door and Cassie stepped out on the veranda to look down toward San Bois Creek. In what seemed to be a split second, Dix exploded through the front screen door, tossed her prepacked suitcase into the back seat of the car and ran back to her.

"Come on, now, darling. Take my arm. Let me—"

"Dix!" Cassie said. "Wait!" Her body shook from head to toe. Dix, frightened, put his arms around her but pulled back when he realized that she was shaking with laughter.

"Hey," he said indignantly, "what's so damn funny?"

"You!" she said, but the laughter broke off as abruptly as it had started. "Dix, help me to the car. Now!"

Cassie laughed no more, but her labor was mercifully short. At 2:14 P.M. she was delivered of a healthy seven-pound girl. Miss Martha Hendricks Steele was born.

Martha's first visitors at home were Amelia and James Steele. When Cassie placed her daughter in Amelia's arms, the woman smiled proudly, a proper grandmother, but tears ran down her face. Cassie was puzzled by what appeared to be an overreaction until sudden understanding struck her like a blow to the stomach. Julia. It was the memory of her own daughter that affected Amelia so strongly. She had held her own baby girl just so, and she had watched her grow into a lively, headstrong girl of seven years, and she had watched her die. Julia had died because of an accident that was James Steele's fault, a result of his cold stubbornness.

James himself bent to take little Martha from Amelia, but in a surge of protectiveness Cassie intervened and clutched her baby to her breast.

"She wants to nurse," she explained lamely, but when James Steele looked at her, she could see in his eyes that he knew. He knew.

Dix hugged his mother and did not see the exchange between Cassie and James.

"I would like to hold the baby," James said.

"Yes." Cassie turned to him but she did not surrender Martha.

"She looks nothing like Taylor," James said.

"She's only a week old."

His face was as hard as limestone. "She doesn't even look like a Steele."

Cassie's anger rose. "Well, she is one. Half a Steele, anyway. I'm her mother and Dix is her father."

James smiled. "Is he? Are you quite sure of that, Cassie?"

"You—you can't—"

"Hey," Dix interrupted. "It's my turn to hold Martha!"

Cassie gave the baby to Dix and crossed the room. She put her forehead against the cool glass of the window by the front door and tried to get hold of her emotions. How could he do it? How could anyone be so cruel? She had not let him hold the baby, but that surely was not enough to cause him to say such a thing, to imply that she had cuckolded his own son. She knew that he was a hard man, even a cruel one, but she felt that she would never, ever understand him. She turned slowly to face the room.

Amelia and Dix sat on the couch, their heads together as they smiled at each other over the baby. James watched them. He was old, Cassie saw, an old man standing alone. He was hard, yes, but it could be a remembered rigidity, a last battle for control but also against the end of life. His cruelty was the impotent cruelty of old men, reduced from life-shattering action to petty, hurtful jabs. Nothing that he could do now could hurt her or destroy her. She was the winner, in the end, by virtue of her age.

James turned, as if he felt her watching him, and she smiled. He looked at her steadily, but his eyes slid away and she knew that she had found at last the ultimate weapon with which to fight James Steele: the knowledge that he no longer could affect her life.

Chapter 7

The second Friday of October, 1957, was a beautiful Indian summer day. Cassie took her children for a walk by San Bois Creek. At six weeks of age, Martha went along just for the company but for a boy of eighteen months like Taylor, the walk was an education in itself.

Cassie sat on the bank of the creek, holding Martha, while Taylor selected a river-rounded stone, discarded it for another, then tossed that one away when he picked up another that evidently came closer to meeting his criteria for the ideal. Martha dozed off and Cassie spread a folded shawl to pad the sun-warmed gravel and, laying the baby next to her, leaned back and let the sun soak into her body. She kept an eye on Taylor, which was not difficult since he ran up to her every few minutes and stood over her to show off his newest acquisition. Like most small children he knew exactly when his mother was escaping into her own thoughts, and he was quick to make sure that her mind stayed where it belonged: on him.

"See dis, Mama," he said, thrusting at her the stone which was at least temporarily the ideal of pure rockness.

Taylor was not aware, however, of the duplicity of mothers who can heap fulsome praise on rock and on bringer-of-rock without losing one thread of a complex web of thoughts.

The boy himself was a thread in Cassie's web that warm, sunny morning. The sunshine was another, and Martha, and the good condition of the Bermuda pasture were others, and the stone that was poking her shoulder, and Dix. And Dix. Dix would come home that night from a week's trip through the western part of the congressional district, and during that week, the rule of celibacy Dr. Hill had imposed on them had expired.

Cassie admired Taylor's latest rock and adjusted Martha's hat to shield her tiny nose from the sun. Another thread, enmeshed with thoughts of Dix and her children, was for her law practice, but she had planned carefully and there were no cases, new or continued, to prick her conscience. She stretched in the warm sunshine and another thread wove its way into the tapestry of her thoughts: the idea of giving up the law entirely. She played with the idea as a child plays with a new and appealing toy, examining its surfaces, poking at it to see if the surface would readily rebound, handling it, pushing it away and bringing it close to see how it would fit with all of the sharp and knobby projections that made up her life.

She admired another stone for Taylor and then she admired her new idea, for herself.

She could be at home all the time, she thought, if she gave up the law. She could stay home with her children. Something within her that had been as tight as a clenched fist relaxed as if to display the precious jewel it had clutched, and only then did Cassie realize the pain associated with that clenched part of her. It had been difficult enough to leave Taylor for the hours she spent in the law library in Ballard, or in court. And there were the nights that she had to spend in a hotel room because the weather was too bad for her to drive back to the ranch or because she had to make an early appearance in court. She always called and talked to Taylor, she checked with Ruby Keeler and Henry Starr, but all the phone calls, in time, could not make up for not tucking her son into his bed, for not kissing him good night, or for failing to smooth down the cowlick where an unruly tuft of fair hair tried to stand alone. It had been bad enough when there was just Taylor, but now there was Martha, too, a tiny girl completely dependent on her mother for food and love and protection.

Cassie sat up, exclaimed over Taylor's latest find, and shifted her body to cast a shadow on Martha's sleeping face.

Money was not a problem. She and Dix had enough money to live comfortably and to entertain well if he should be elected to Congress. She might not achieve the rarified heights of that other Oklahoma girl, Perle Mesta, but the Steeles could certainly afford to give parties appropriate to a freshman congressman and his wife.

Most important of all, of course, was the thought that she could be at home for Dix. She could be a proper wife, free to campaign with and for him, to care for his children, to see to their investments so that he could devote his time to his career. If—*when* he won the Democratic primary and thereby the election to the House of Representatives, she could make a home for him in Washington, one to which he would be proud to bring his triumphs and to which he would know he could bring his failures.

What was the law, after all? A system society had imposed upon itself in an effort to keep the wolves of chaos away from the communal campfire of civilization. A system of rules to be codified and argued and rewritten until it appeared to the layman that two and two did indeed make seven. There were other lawyers, though, to do the arguing. There was a lawyer for everyone who needed one or, if the cases were interesting enough or the parties to the suit rich enough, there would be two or three lawyers or even ten or twelve. To Cassie, too, the law was fascinating, an intellectual exercise. Bereft of her practice, would she be bored? She realized that having the time to be bored might well be the greatest wealth of all.

When the car lights flashed in the road, Cassie pulled on a heavy sweater against the chill of the evening and ran out to meet Dix.

"Darling, you're finally home!"

Dixon Steele climbed out of his car wearily, but he grinned and hurried across the yard. "Cassie." He kissed her and then he held her at arm's length. "You know what day this is, woman?"

She laughed. "You couldn't possibly be referring to the fact that Dr. Hill's six weeks are up and we can—"

"Damn tootin', I am! Don't tell on me, Attorney Steele, but I broke the speed limit on Highway 12. Cassie, it seems like it's been forever since we—"

"Hush!" she said, shaking his arm. "Ruby Keeler's bringing Martha outside."

Dix gave her a quick hug and hurried to the veranda. "Ruby Keeler, where's my beautiful daughter?"

The girl giggled. "I got her right here, Mr. Steele—I mean, Dix, sir." Dix had insisted that she call him by his first name, but she was not comfortable with it. "Here's Taylor coming, too."

"Daddy!" Taylor threw himself at his father's legs and Dix caught him and lifted him high.

"Boy, look at you! You're taller than I am now!"

Taylor laughed with delight. "Mama! Lookie, Mama! I'm big!"

Cassie took him and held him close. "Then I'd better hug you before you're too big to hug."

Dix carefully took Martha from Ruby Keeler. "Oh, you beautiful baby," he whispered. "How did your old dad get himself such a daughter?"

They took the children inside and Dix lit the wood laid in the fieldstone fireplace and sat down with Taylor in his lap. Cassie made drinks and they sat companionably with their children while Ruby Keeler clattered pans in the kitchen.

"You look so tired, darling," Cassie said. "Was it a rough week?"

Dix stretched and rearranged Taylor on his lap. "Yeah. Rough but productive. I'm making progress with the large-scale farmers, I think. The wheat subsidy is the—" He hesitated. "Say, that reminds me. Cassie, do you know anything about a farmer from somewhere around here, a man named Jackson? Ward Jackson?"

"No." Cassie tickled Martha's tummy. "I don't think I've heard the name."

"I got the impression that he's a sharecropper. The ACLU left a call with my secretary and they say—"

"The American Civil Liberties Union? Why on earth are they interested in an Eastern Oklahoma sharecropper?"

He shook his head. "Damned if I know. I used to work with the ACLU, Cassie, and they've got a lot of great people, but the yahoo that called me didn't seem to know his ass from his elbow."

"Dix, Taylor will—"

"Oh, sorry. I keep forgetting that he's old enough to pick up words like—"

"Ass ehbow," Taylor said, smiling happily at his own prowess.

Dix laughed. "Thanks a lot, buddy. Now maybe I'll remember what a quick study you are." He turned back to Cassie. "Anyway, this guy wanted me to take on Jackson's case, just like that, when I have no idea of what it's about."

Cassie shook her head. "That's not like the ACLU. There must be some element of the case that—"

"Well, this guy who called did say that Jackson is a Negro."

Taylor wriggled out of Dix's arms. "Tay go see Wooby now, Daddy." He ran for the kitchen.

Dix sniffed. "Roast chicken, right? That boy's got a nose like a bird dog."

"Dix, that phone call—you don't suppose the ACLU will get themselves involved in a new kind of reverse segregation, do you?"

"What do you mean?"

"Well, Southerners act like they think that all Negroes should be segregated because of their skin color: Negroes are bad, that is, because they are black. But if the ACLU decides to back the Negro in any case where one is involved, won't that be a sort of segregation, too? Won't the ACLU be saying in effect that Negroes are right because they're black?"

Dix was very still for a minute. "I don't like that," he said thoughtfully. "I don't like that at all, Cassie. It's a view that leaves too much unsaid, too much history forgotten."

"Can history be held as a precedent in the law? It seems to me that each case—"

"It not only can, it must! The court has to consider social history. In a case involving a Negro, the traditional designation of him as a second-class citizen is a factor that can't possibly be ignored."

"But wouldn't it depend on case law? In this situation, for instance, this Ward Jackson case—"

Dix laughed. "This case about which we know nothing at all, right? I don't know what that guy had in mind, or if there was anything to it, and I didn't have time to get in touch with one of my pals at the ACLU and find out more. I just told him that I couldn't possibly work with or for the ACLU right now, what with the state senate and my private practice and campaigning, too. I flat don't have the time."

"Darling, about law practice—my law practice—" Cassie hesitated, figuring out how to tell him about her thoughts on the creek bank that morning. Ruby Keeler called from the dining room to tell them that dinner was on the table, and the moment was gone. Cassie was relieved, in a way, not to tell him, because their brief discussion of the ACLU case had shaken her fine resolutions of the morning and awakened in her feelings that she thought were dead and gone. Dix did not have the time to check into it further, but she had time. She had nothing but time.

From the care with which Dix touched her that night Cassie might have been made of spun sugar. She stood very still, in the center of their bedroom, while he removed each garment of her clothes, stroking her body gently as if to be sure that it was the body he remembered so well. By the time he pulled down her panties and cupped his big hands on her buttocks, Cassie was quivering, every cell of her skin alive and wanting his touch. Slowly Dix removed his own clothes and slowly, gently, he lifted her and placed her on the bed. He lowered himself upon her carefully and lay still, letting both of them feel his hardness against her.

"Dix," she whispered. "Now, darling, come to me."

He entered her slowly, carefully, and she felt herself swell around him, felt the throbbing in her body.

In his eyes she saw need change to urgency. "Cassie, I can't—"

She reached up to him and pulled him to her. "Now, darling! Now!" she cried and on one long deep thrust they exploded together into delight.

They relaxed together then, happy with even that brief, careful encounter, as refreshed as dry earth after a thundershower.

"It's been so long," Dix whispered. "I've needed you so damn much."

Cassie put her hand on his bare chest. "Darling, I didn't know how much I needed you. When I was so pregnant, so big—"

She felt as well as heard his deep laugh. "You were immense!" He slid his arm around her and pulled her close. "But I still wanted you. God, how I wanted you!"

Cassie felt a surge of happiness. "We have so much, darling. A son, and a beautiful daughter, and each other."

He kissed her gently. "And now we are together again, my dearest. Our two halves make a whole."

Cassie woke in the chilly dawn. A cold front had moved through Eastern Oklahoma during the night and Indian summer had disappeared in rain mixed with snow. She shaped her naked body against her husband's warm back. For once, she did not plan her day or her week. For once she was content to do no more than bask in the comfort of being with him for the brief respite before Martha woke and at the top of her lungs demanded nursing for one end and a dry diaper for the other.

Later in the morning, however, Cassie went into the living room where Dix had set a card table in front of the fire and was writing a brief. She interrupted him briefly to question him about the ACLU call and to offer to call his old friend there and find out more about the Ward Jackson case.

When Taylor went down for his nap, Cassie and Dix sat by the fire and she told him what she had learned from the ACLU. "This Ward Jackson is a Negro, as you thought, Dix, a sharecropper on a dirt farm about fifteen miles from here."

"In what direction?"

"East of here." She looked at her notes. "It sounds like the place is on the road past the old Indian cemetery. You may remember that there's a little crossroads store, and he said that Ward Jackson lives five or six miles southeast of that."

Dix leaned back. "I don't know much about that area."

"It's rough country back there: hills and little valleys that are just barely arable. Anyway, Jackson is about thirty and he took over working that land when his father died, about twelve or thirteen years ago."

"The dates are pretty vague, aren't they?"

"Jackson can't read or write, it seems, so he isn't good at exact dates. Guess who found out he even lived up there? The district truant officer. Jackson and his wife have four kids, the oldest about eight, and none of them has ever gone to school."

"For God's sake, why not? Surely even the hill people know they have to send their children to school."

"Jackson's boss won't let him." Cassie looked at her notes, even though she did not need to. "It's a peculiar set-up. I told you that Jackson took over the place when he was just a kid, when his father died. He doesn't have a tractor or a pickup, either. He works that land with a hand plow and a mule, Dix, in 1957!"

"No pickup truck? How does he get his supplies? Groceries, clothes for the kids, seed corn?"

"He rides his mule down to that crossroads store."

"Hell, Cassie, those places charge an arm and a leg for everything. If he bought his stuff in San Bois he'd save enough cash to pay for a damn pick-up!"

"He doesn't have any cash, darling. He gets credit at the store for his crops."

"And who owns the store?"

Cassie grimaced. "The same man who owns the farm. But Ward Jackson has never seen him. He only sees the owner's agent."

"God! To live like that—why doesn't he get out, Cassie? Get a job in town or—"

"The truant officer asked him that, too, and that's why he got in touch with the county social services, who checked it out with the ACLU. Jackson can't get another job, the landowner's agent tells him, until he pays off the debt."

Dix sat back and stretched. "You mean, what he owes to the crossroads store? That can't be much."

"Not that debt, Dix. It's one that his father owed the land-owner." Cassie watched him carefully. "The agent tells Ward Jackson that the owner will send him to prison if he tries to leave before he pays off the debt that Ward's father owed the landlord."

Dix raised his head and looked at Cassie. The disgust in his eyes was replaced, slowly, by an inward look as if he were examining bits of information in his mental files, sorting and reclassifying them to find an explanation. Then, suddenly, the inward look was gone, replaced by fury. He slammed his fist on the card table. "My God, Cassie, it sounds like a case of involuntary servitude!"

Cassie nodded. "That's what the ACLU thinks, too."

"I don't believe there's been a case of involuntary servitude since the First World War."

"He told me there has been one case, in California in 1947, but the ACLU is overloaded with segregation cases right now and he hasn't even had time to look it up, much less get together with the U.S. attorney's office." She hesitated. "That's why they want you, Dix."

"I can't, damn it. You know that. Much as I'd like to get in on this one, I just don't have the time."

Cassie took a deep breath. "I do, Dix. I have the time."

He shook his head. "Sure. You hardly have anything to do,

Cassie. Just run a farm and be a nursing mother and run after a toddler. To start with, you'd have to spend hours of research in the law library in Ballard, and Ruby Keeler can't miss school to—"

"With the holidays coming up I could work out days when she could be here with Taylor, and I could take Martha with me. And later, if this thing stretches out, Ruby Keeler says her sister Shirley Temple is fourteen now, a freshman in high school, but she needs to take the spring semester off and earn some money. I'm sure it would work."

He looked doubtful, but her excitement was contagious. "You know, it might, at that." He grinned at her. "If anyone on earth could make it work, Cassie, it has to be you. Say, don't forget my folks, hon'. Mother has Luella to help her, and I know she would love to have the kids at her house."

Cassie looked away. "That might not work out." She forced herself to look directly at him. "Dix, you haven't even asked me who the defendant is."

"Okay," he said, smiling, "so who plays Simon Legree to Ward Jackson's Uncle Tom?"

"You haven't read the book for a while, I guess. Simon Legree was the overseer, not the landowner. He was just the agent."

"So what? According to law, the owner is responsible for the actions of his duly appointed agent. So, who's the landowner in this case?"

Cassie looked at the fireplace and the warm flames of the burning oak logs. "Your father."

Chapter 8

Cassie's journey back to the battleground of the law was not without hazards. She had hoped, for instance, to be able to discuss the ramifications of the case with Dix, who was much more experienced in constitutional law than she.

"Look, honey," he said, "I can see why you need to pursue the Ward Jackson case, but I have to stay out of it. Whether my father is guilty or not is up to the jury, but I can not work against him. He is still my father."

The United States attorney was no problem at all. He was glad to appoint her a temporary member of his staff. In fact, since a case involving James Steele would be a political hot potato in Oklahoma, he was obviously relieved to dump the whole thing in her lap. The only help he could give her was one law clerk who would do some of the research she needed.

The best offer of assistance that came, unfortunately, was one she was compelled to refuse. The ACLU wanted to be in on the case but she asked them to stay away from it. The ACLU was far too entangled in the Southern struggle to be seen as neutral in a case that involved a Negro and slavery. Cassie was sure that the judge in the case would forbid the jurors' reading or watching news reports on the trial itself, but they would still be subjected to daily TV and newspaper reports on ACLU involvement with the black troubles in the South. In Oklahoma, Cassie had a fair chance of choosing a jury that was moderate in racial matters, but she was afraid that participation by the ACLU might push even a moderate jury member into voting his race rather than his conscience.

Her list of witnesses was brief: Ward Jackson, of course, and James Steele. She hesitated over calling James's agent, Cliff Boatwright, to the stand, but her hesitation solved her problem. James Steele listed Boatwright as a defense witness. Cassie was pleased because she would have more freedom in cross-examination than in direct.

Cassie began by visiting the Jackson family. She had worried about being able to talk comfortably with Jackson's wife, Biddy, but she had Martha with her, and no mother could resist a plump, happy five-month-old whose smile revealed two tiny pearly teeth. After the first moments of shyness, the Jackson children were as enthralled with Martha as their mother was. The late February sun was warm that morning and Cassie was given the seat of honor: the old rocking chair on the front porch. While Biddy and her children made friends with Martha, Cassie contended with the flood of memories the Jacksons' tenant shack brought forth. At noon all of them dug into the picnic lunch Cassie and Ruby Keeler had put together that morning: fried chicken and biscuits, apples and oranges, and a chocolate cake for dessert. When she saw the Jackson family eating and realized that the simple picnic was undoubtedly the best food they had ever eaten, Cassie was overcome by rage. It was James Steele's doing, just as it had been James Steele who had seen but had ignored the squalor in which Cassie's own family had lived. He was a businessman, after all. Profit was all that mattered.

Two days later James Steele called her. "This is a very foolish thing you are doing, Cassie."

"Oh, no, James. It is not foolish to try to rectify the wrong you have done Ward Jackson."

His voice was level. "Do you really think for one minute that you can win a court case from me?"

"From your attorney, you mean."

"I will represent myself."

"James, is that wise?" She took a deep breath. "Have you been to that farm? Have you seen the way the Jackson family lives? It is appalling."

"Cassie, you seem to have contracted some of Dix's fuzzy-minded idealism. You know damn well that a—a family of that sort would reduce the nicest place to a pigsty in no time at all."

"You mean, a Negro family."

"I didn't say that."

"You didn't have to, James. I know what you think."

"My opinions are my own business, young lady, not yours."

"They become everyone's business when you deprive a man of his constitutional rights."

James's voice rose to an angry roar. "I am not guilty of that charge and you know it! We'll go to that courtroom and I will take you apart, you hear? I will destroy you in open court!"

Cassie fought to stay calm. "We will see about that, James."

"I could ruin you now, you know. No one has yet made the connection between you and your brother, but I could make sure that it is publicized."

Cassie's heart sank, but she laughed with more bravado than confidence. "Are you so frightened? It's silly to think it would ruin me to have word get out that my half brother was in prison."

"He is no longer in prison, Cassie. He was paroled and broke parole to come back to this part of the country—to western Arkansas, in fact. The Fort Smith police have a warrant out for him."

"For breaking parole in California? That seems rather—"

"For murder."

Cassie flinched as if he had struck her. She wanted to hang up the phone, to walk away and forget it all. "For the murder of—"

"Of a child." James was all too eager to tell her about it. "A very nasty case, it seems. A little boy, four years old. There appears to be quite solid evidence that it was Bo Taylor who took the child from his yard, attacked him sexually and threw his strangled body into the ditch where it was found four days later."

Cassie's forehead broke out in sweat. She was afraid she was going to retch. Bo free? Bo hiding from the police? Where would he go? Where would he hide? "No," she whispered. "Oh, no."

"Why don't you just withdraw this ridiculous charge against me?"

She was shaking like a leaf, but she tried to think quickly. "No, James, I won't do it. And don't forget that if you put out that story to destroy my reputation, you will spoil Dix's chance of being elected to the House. Do you really want to do that?"

James laughed unpleasantly. "You don't know what I'll do, Cassie, do you? And you won't know until I've done it."

"That's enough! I don't have to listen to this!"

She slammed down the receiver. How foolish she had been to think that James Steele no longer could interfere with her life. He was old but he was strong and, damn it, he was right. She did not know what he would do. She could not even guess. But James Steele's schemes were real, they were concrete, and they would appear in time, perhaps as something she could fight in open court.

It was something else that made her shake with fear. It was something dark and hidden, something that lurked in the deep caves of her mind. Bo Taylor. She did not know what he would do, but she knew where he would go. Oh, yes, she knew.

United States v. *Steele* opened late in March of 1958, in a courtroom jammed with reporters and the curious. The case had received much publicity as the first involuntary servitude charge to come to trial in years. There had been few, in fact, since the turn of the century. Cassie sat at the prosecutor's table with her clerk, Ned Bosley, who was almost hidden by the stacked results of his work in the law library. James Steele sat alone at the defense table.

He looked cool, but Cassie knew that inwardly he was seething. He surely hated the publicity as much as the trial itself.

James was alone at the table but not, to Cassie's dismay, alone in the courtroom. It was all too evident that he and the judge were old friends. Were they members of the same country club, she wondered, or were they drinking buddies at bar association parties? Or perhaps they were just part of the old boys' network, a clan that excluded Cassie Taylor Steele on two counts out of two.

James Steele's opening statement was not so much an argument as a move to establish a fatherly relationship with the jury. "*I know what is right,*" he seemed to be saying. "You can trust me. I will take care of you."

Cassie's own opening was more aggressive, fueled by her rage that involuntary servitude, that slavery, could exist in the United States of America almost one hundred years after the ratification of the Thirteenth Amendment.

As the state's first witness, Cassie called Ward Jackson. He gave his oath and went to the witness stand slowly, as Cassie had suggested he do, giving the jury plenty of time to look him over. He wore what he always wore, what he owned: a faded flannel shirt and bib overalls patched by an inexpert seamstress. He was not a big man, and his shoulders were slumped, either from guiding a handplow pulled by a mule or by the burden of his father's debt to James Steele.

Slowly and carefully Cassie took Ward Jackson through a recital of his life history, bearing down on those facts that touched on the elements of involuntary servitude.

"Do you ever do any work away from the farm?"

"Yessum, like I tole you, Mist' Cliff, he gets me to split wood for them to sell at the store, oak mostly, and some hickory. People from Ballard call out there, Mist' Cliff say, and he haul it to town in his truck."

"And were you paid in cash for this extra work?"

"No'm. Mist' Cliff, he say he give me credit at the store, but he never said how much he payin' me."

"Now, Mr. Jackson, will you tell the jury what Mr. Cliff Boatwright, Mr. Steele's farm agent, said would happen if you ever tried to leave the farm?"

James Steele's heavy voice interrupted. "Objection. Hearsay."

"Your honor," Cassie said quickly, "I am trying to establish the witness's state of mind, directing to the *Hodges* v. *United States* definition cited in my brief, a definition upheld by the Supreme Court stating that slavery is the state of entire subjection of one person to the will of another."

"Objection overruled," the judge said. Cassie watched, but she could not tell whether or not he smiled at James Steele. "Mr. Jackson, you may answer the question."

The courtroom was cool, but Ward Jackson's forehead was dotted with beads of sweat. "Yessuh," he said, and stopped.

"I'll repeat the gist of the question," Cassie said hastily, to avoid Jackson's having to listen to the flat uninflexed reading that the court reporter would give it.

She asked, and he answered. "Mist' Cliff, he say my daddy done owe Mist' Steele that money an' if I go to leave, they goin' put the law on me. Put me in prison, he say, down to Macalester, ain't goin' ever let me go."

"How many times did Mr. Boatwright make this statement?"

"Lots of times, yessum. Lots. Right after my daddy passed over, when I wasn't but eighteen or so. Reckon he say it more after me and Biddy married an' had that first baby." There was sweat on his cheeks, too. "Hit scare me, Miz Cassie, hit scare me somethin' fierce. How Biddy goin' do with that baby, me in the jailhouse? She cain't get no work, no place to live, nothin'."

"Why didn't you tell someone about this, Ward? When you went to the store, couldn't you have talked to someone there, asked for help?"

"No, ma'am! Mist' Cliff, he say, 'You open your mouth about

this here, nigger, an' we ain't goin' wait no longer. We'll put the law on you right now.' "

"So you were convinced that you had to behave exactly as Mr. Boatwright, acting as Mr. Steele's agent, told you to behave. You were wholly subject to his will."

"Objection. Seeking conclusion."

"Sustained. Jury will disregard."

Cassie continued, not surprised at the objection. "But you told the truant officer, didn't you, when he came to the farm? You told him all about it."

Ward Jackson looked at James Steele and seemed to draw into himself. "Couldn't help tellin'. Never seen such a man for axin' questions. Axed me, axed Biddy, axed them babies. Axin', why ain't them chillun in the schoolhouse?"

"And what did you tell him, Ward?"

"Tole him same as Mist' Cliff tole me. Ain't no black school and they sure as hell cain't go to no white school. Then he say, ain't no such a thing as black schools, white schools anymore. Say Oklahoma schools is inner—inter—"

"Integrated?"

"Yessum, that's it. That's what he say. And he say schoolbus pick them chillun up at the bottom of my path, take 'em to school, bring 'em back after." His eyes lit up. "He say that school goin' give 'em a hot lunch and books and a pencil, I don't know what-all."

"And you said?"

The light left his eyes. "I say I gots to ax Mist' Cliff, can they go to school."

"Why would you have to do that, Ward?"

"Mist' Cliff, he always say, don't do nothin' lessen you ax me first. I gots to ax Mist' Cliff."

James Steele was an impressive figure when he rose to cross-examine. He nodded to the jury as if to reaffirm the friendliness of his opening argument, but he frowned at Ward Jackson as a father might frown at a beloved but wayward child.

"Now, Ward, you don't need to be nervous. I just want to ask you a few questions."

Ward looked down at his work-gnarled hands. "Yessuh."

"You know who I am, don't you?"

"Yessuh. Miz Cassie, she say you Mist' Steele, the man that owns the farm I works."

"Fine, Ward, fine. There are a few little points to clear up. First, you said that Mr. Cliff Boatwright told you not to talk to people about your arrangements with him?"

"Objection," Cassie interrupted. "As Mr. Boatwright was counsel's agent, the arrangements were in effect made with Mr. Steele, not Mr. Boatwright."

"Question withdrawn," James said quickly. "Ward, you testified that you were discouraged from talking to outsiders at all."

"Yessuh."

"Then how did you meet and court a young woman? How did you find a wife?"

Ward raised his eyes and laughed softly, looking more relaxed. "I see her at the store, Mist' Steele. See her a couple of times, and one day I foller her when she starts out home. We gets down the road a piece, where they cain't see us from the store, and we talks a spell."

James Steele chuckled. "So perhaps you weren't completely under Mr. Boatwright's control after all."

At the prosecutor's table, Cassie gripped her pencil hard. James was undoing the careful work she had put in to convince the jury that this case was within the definition of involuntary servitude, that is, that Ward Jackson was entirely subject to Boatwright's, therefore to James Steele's will.

James leaned forward as if he had made a sudden decision. "When it came to marrying your wife, that was a decision you made on your own, wasn't it? You made it of your own free will."

Ward looked down. "No suh. I axed Mist' Cliff was it all right for me to take me a wife. I always gots to ax Mist' Cliff."

James stepped back, scowling. "And what was Boatwright's reply?" he asked quickly, as if to cover the moment before the members of the jury realized what they had heard.

"Mist' Cliff, he say he gots to ax you."

"No further questions," James said.

Cassie sat very still, letting Ward's words resonate in the jury's minds and trying to contain her sense of triumph. She could hear her old boss Steve Reilly saying it again and again, drumming it into her head. "Never ask a witness a question without knowing how he'll answer it. Never!" James had been away from litigation for too long. He had become careless.

Cassie was ready to call James Steele as her next witness when the judge summoned counsel to the bench.

"James," he said quietly so that the jury could not hear, "I repeat my earlier advice. Don't represent yourself in a case of this magnitude. I beg you to get an attorney." He smiled at Cassie. "I'm sure the state will agree to a continuance to facilitate your instructing new counsel."

Cassie opened her mouth but James spoke before she could. "Thank you, Dudley." He looked at Cassie contemptuously. "I don't require other counsel."

The judge shrugged his shoulders. "It's your choice, James. I just hope you aren't making a big mistake." He chuckled. "Remember, they say that the attorney who represents himself in court has a fool for a lawyer."

James's face reddened, but he nodded politely and went back to the defense table.

"The state calls James Steele," Cassie said.

He took the oath, his hand on the bailiff's Bible, and sat down. Cassie laid her notes on the table but she did not begin her questioning. She stared at James Steele, overcome by almost thirty years of memories. She saw him looking down at her from his shiny

Buick, dangling a rat-gnawed doll as a gift for a ragged child, standing over her when he threatened to annul her marriage to his son Jimmy, sneering at her while he told her the latest news of her criminal half brother, accusing her of cuckolding her beloved husband, Dix. Thirty years he had spent taunting her with his power, reminding her that she was nothing but a sharecropper's daughter.

Thirty wasted years, because now they were equals facing each other on the common ground of the law.

"Counselor?" the judge said irritably, but Cassie was already in motion, moving forward to question her father-in-law, James Steele.

After the necessary formal questions, she went directly to the case at hand. "There are murky areas in your relationship with Mr. Ward Jackson, it seems."

James smiled at her and at the jury like an understanding father. "I will be happy to clear away the fog for you."

"Thank you." She could smile, too, she thought, and just as falsely, but personalities were no longer involved in her questioning of James Steele. She had fallen into the natural swing of direct examination, the give and take of two minds, one probing, the other resisting. She took a deep breath. "Mr. Steele, is your business arrangement with Mr. Jackson documented?"

"No, it is not. Nor was there a written lease between his father and me nor his grandfather and my father." He chuckled. "His forebears were also illiterate, you see."

"You find that amusing, Mr. Steele?" Before he could answer, she said, "But as an attorney, you are surely aware that an illiterate's mark is as binding as a signature. Did you apprise Mr. Jackson of that fact?"

"We had a verbal agreement, Counselor. Under the circumstances a written one would have been superfluous."

"The circumstances, yes. They were somewhat unusual, weren't they? For all the history of closeness between the two families, you never saw Ward Jackson but dealt with him only through your agent, Mr. Cliff Boatwright?"

"That is correct, but I can explain—"

"It will not be necessary. Mr. Boatwright, as your agent, acted under your instructions. Now, in the matter of the debt that forced Mr. Jackson to stay on the farm permanently—"

"That is not true. Ward knows I would never hold him responsible for his father's debt."

"Especially since we can assume that the debt was never put into documentary form either."

"Perhaps Ward is confused and considers staying on the farm a debt of honor."

"You heard his testimony, Mr. Steele. I do not believe that Ward Jackson suffers any confusion as to the nature of his father's debt, with the exception that it appears he has never been informed of the dollar amount owed. He was told only that he was responsible for paying it. In the matter of the availability of a school for his children, you lied to Ward Jackson, didn't you?"

"I have never laid eyes on the man! My agent was the one who—"

"You agree then that your agent lied to Jackson? But we have determined that your agent is, in effect, you. Therefore you—"

"I do not agree! I think Ward misunderstood—"

"Just as he misunderstood his responsibility for his father's debt, I suppose. And you told him not to talk to people about—"

"My agent! I mean, my agent told him no such thing!"

"Of course. Merely another misunderstanding on Ward Jackson's part. He thought that he owed his father's debt, that he could not leave the farm, ever, or send his children to school, that he could not discuss his problems with anyone and, above all, that he was required to ask your permission before he married."

"That's not true! He said he had to ask my agent—"

"And your agent had to ask you."

"He did not! Ward was lying!" He made an obvious effort to

calm himself. "This is an elaborate fiction created for some purpose I cannot begin to fathom."

"Created? For an illiterate man who has spent his life in a sharecropper's shack, Ward Jackson must have a truly amazing imagination. One would think that this sharecropper would have been capable of writing *Gone With the Wind,* if only he could read and write. What motive could a sharecropper have for creating what you call 'an elaborate fiction'?"

"Perhaps you can answer that, Counselor. You are more knowledgeable about sharecroppers than I."

Cassie froze. She had been walking back and forth, moving freely in the swing of question and answer, question and answer, but his low-voiced comment brought her up short. She had been willing to deal with the here and now, to leave their shared past buried, where it belonged, but James had changed the rules of the game with one small, vicious dig. Cassie could no longer be a dispassionate prosecutor relying only on the facts of the case.

She took one step toward him, stiffly, and then another. "Yes," she said softly, "I probably am more knowledgeable." With a quick movement she turned toward the jury. She paused for one moment to let them look at her, to give them time to see her black Yves Saint-Laurent suit, her impeccable silk shirt, her discreet but genuine gold jewelry and the sleek line of her long legs, down the sheer stockings to handmade Ferragliami pumps. "The witness," she said calmly, "is referring to the fact that I am a sharecropper's daughter. Like Mr. Ward Jackson, I spent my childhood in a tenant shack. Unlike Mr. Jackson, however, I was able to get an education and, more important, I was able to leave. I was not a slave, bound to the land."

"Objection!" James shouted.

"Sustained. Counsel, please confine yourself to questioning the witness. Your personal history is not an issue here."

Oh, yes, it is, Cassie said to herself. James Steele has made it an issue. She walked to her table and looked at her notes to regain her equilibrium. Suddenly she had a sense of being free, of taking off in unfettered flight. She approached the witness stand briskly, speaking as she walked.

"Mr. Steele, what is your annual gross profit on the land farmed by Ward Jackson and on extra work such as the wood-splitting that he performs for others?"

James cleared his throat. "I cannot tell you specifically. For accounting purposes, my farm leases are lumped together."

Cassie moved back a few steps to make sure that the jury could see his face. "It is difficult for me to believe, Mr. Steele, that a successful businessman does not know the profit figures on one of his productive assets."

James looked away. "Difficult to believe, perhaps, but true."

Cassie took a few steps one way and then the other. "Let's make a guess, shall we? Perhaps as two farmers approaching a problem together, we can find some numbers. Is your gross profit on that farm less than one hundred dollars per annum?"

"Certainly not." He smiled at the jury. "If I make that little, I am not a very successful businessman."

Some of the jury members chuckled, but Cassie ignored them. "From that specific farm do you make as much as twenty-five thousand dollars per annum?"

"My God, no!"

"We have made some progress, then. We've come from 'I don't know' to somewhere between one hundred dollars and twenty-five thousand dollars. Shall we try to narrow the gap?"

He glared at her. "I suppose I could take a stab at it. I'd say that in a good year, I might gross three thousand dollars on the place."

"Gross, sir? Or gross profit?"

"Gross profit," he said softly.

"Gross *profit*." Cassie turned to the jury as if to make sure that they heard it.

"Of course, out of that comes the—"

"I am not concerned with your net profit, Mr. Steele. Let's see. Under the usual tenancy agreement, you receive one third of the gross profit, right? Then that means that the two thirds Ward Jackson keeps comes to quite a sum. Jackson earns six thousand dollars a year in gross profit."

As one man the jury swiveled to stare at the ragged black man at the prosecutor's table. He looked as surprised as they did.

"Are my calculations correct, Mr. Steele?"

His fury was obvious. "I suppose so."

"Six thousand dollars. I wonder where Ward Jackson spent all that money. Not on rent, because you, of course, furnish his family with living quarters of a sort. Not on food. I've seen the Jacksons' larder: beans, cornmeal, a bit of fatback. He doesn't own a pickup truck, although he could have bought a dandy one with just half that much cash. Clothes? Well, we see him before us, don't we? I just wonder where all that money went."

"I'm sure I don't know," James said stiffly.

Cassie raised her eyebrows. "*Don't* you, Mr. Steele? Now, how was Jackson paid for outside work, wood-splitting and all? Oh, wait, I believe he testified that in lieu of cash he was given credit at the crossroads store where he buys his beans and cornmeal. And the man who owns the store is—"

"I own the store, and you know it!" He looked up at the bench angrily. "Your honor, I object to this entire line of questioning. How much I earn on my investments is not at issue."

The judge looked at Cassie. "Counselor?"

"I will confine my questions to one point which is clearly at issue, your honor, the matter of payment to Mr. Jackson for splitting wood. I remind the court that the matter of the defendant's receiving compensation for a servant's outside work was at issue also in United States *v*. Ingalls, as cited in my brief. In the present case, both Mr. Jackson and Mr. Steele have testified that payment was in the form of credit issued by the store owned by Mr. Steele." She turned to the jury and smiled. "We have not been shown a statement of the amount of credit, but in Mr. Steele's business, apparently, nothing is ever written down on paper and there is no proof that the store owner, Mr. Steele, did indeed credit Mr. Jackson's account for his labors."

"Wait a minute, now," Steele said. "That store is actually owned by J. and J. Steele, a corporation. It is a separate entity."

"I see." Cassie smiled like a Cheshire cat. "It would be quite interesting to follow that particular line to find out if indeed any amount credited to his account at the store was fair compensation for the work Ward Jackson did. It might be argued that James Steele the landowner in effect rented Mr. Jackson to J. and J. Steele, store owner, in a manner clearly commensurate with the conditions of involuntary servitude."

"Objection. Counsel is in an area of pure conjecture."

"Sustained."

"I withdraw my comment, your honor. I would like to ask just one final question, Mr. Steele, to help me as well as the jury understand the somewhat confusing financial aspect of your relationship with Ward Jackson. The total gross profit from that farm operation, according to your estimate, was around nine thousand dollars. If you took your third, Ward Jackson should have received some six thousand dollars. Obviously, he did not. That money did not go into his pocket nor, apparently, did it increase his so-called credit at the crossroads store. My question is this: Whose pocket did it go into? For God's sake, Mr. Steele, where is that six thousand dollars?"

Chapter 9

Cassie received no answer to her question about the missing $6000 and finally began to wonder if there were an answer. She rested the state's case.

James Steele called the witnesses for the defense, a parade of well-dressed men who made James sound like God's gift to Eastern Oklahoma. Cassie was relieved when he called a less respectable-looking witness, his farm agent. Cliff Boatwright, a small, wiry man, scuttled across the courtroom to take the witness stand. His eyes moved constantly, never quite settling on anyone or anything.

With sympathetic questions, James tried to establish Cliff Boatwright as a misunderstood man who was merely trying to do his job.

"Is it true, Mr. Boatwright, that you told Ward Jackson not to talk to people or that he had to ask your permission before making personal decisions?"

"Never said no such thing, Mr. Steele. He was lyin', he was."

"And in regard to the Jackson children attending school: did you tell Ward that there was no black school and that his children could not attend the white school?"

"Hell, no, excuse me. I never did."

"Did you tell him that he could not move away from the farm?"

"No, sir! You know how niggers is, can't get anything straight in their heads."

"Objection," Cassie said. "Will the court order the witness to refrain from racial slurs?"

"Sustained," the judge said sternly. "Mr. Boatwright, such words have no place in a court of law."

Cassie glanced at the jury. Would they understand that such words had no place in their minds, either?

James forged ahead. He elicited from Boatwright a description of Ward Jackson and his family that was as effective as any racial slur: a stereotypical picture of a shiftless man with a slovenly wife and four half-wild children wearing dirty rags. Cassie made a note on a yellow legal pad as she contrasted his picture of the family with hers: a hard-working poor man with a shy, eager wife and four well-loved children.

"Place is dirty as sin, Mr. Steele. I try to get them folks to clean it up, but I reckon they like livin' like pigs."

Cassie noticed one juror nodding and then another, as if what they were hearing confirmed their suspicions. She made another note.

When James finished with his witness, Cassie rose immediately so that Boatwright's picture of the family would not linger un-questioned in the jury's minds. "Mr. Boatwright, does the house on that farm have electricity?"

"No'm."

"Running water? Plumbing?"

"Hell—excuse me—no, ma'am!"

Cassie thought back to her visit to the Jacksons. "Is there a good spring on the place?"

"Fine spring, yessum, a dandy spring. Not exactly on the place, but—"

"How far is this spring from the house?"

Boatwright looked toward the defense table as if to get instruc-tions, but Cassie moved to interpose her body between him and James Steele. "How far, Mr. Boatwright?"

"Reckon it ain't more'n half a mile, if it's that."

Cassie moved in on him. "I clocked it on my odometer, Mr. Boatwright. The Jackson family has to carry water over a mile." She saw that the women jurors, at least, reacted to that. Perhaps they were wondering how clean a house they would keep if they had to carry water more than a mile, one bucket at a time.

"They got a mule, ain't they?" Boatwright said. "Reckon they can haul water with that there mule."

Cassie switched direction. "How much money does Mr. Ward Jackson clear each year?"

"Don't know that. Depends if he's careful with his money."

"What money? What money is that, Mr. Boatwright?"

"Well, what he earns, croppin' on the shares."

"Are payments on his father's debt deducted from that amount?"

"I don't know nothin' about that."

"We can't seem to discover, Mr. Boatwright, exactly how much he does earn. Does he ever have any money, any cash to put in his pocket?" From the corner of her eye she saw James Steele move his head slightly, indicating that Boatwright should not answer the question. "Your honor! Defense counsel is coaching the witness!"

The judge turned to look at James, who smiled pleasantly.

"I'm sure you're mistaken, Counselor," the judge said. "Please continue with your cross-examination."

"But I saw—"

"I said, please continue. Eileen, will you read back that last question?"

The court reporter read, " 'Does he ever have any money, any cash to put in his pocket?' "

Cliff Boatwright smiled at Cassie, looking as smug as his employer. "I don't know."

Cassie wanted to grab his thin shoulders and shake the truth out of him, but she clenched her fists at her sides. "In previous testimony, Mr. Boatwright, you told the court that you had never told Ward Jackson not to talk to people."

"Yessum. It's the truth, too."

"Is it, Mr. Boatwright? Mr. Jackson has given us a different impression. You further testified that you did not tell him that there was no school for his children. I remind you that you are under oath. Do you still maintain that your statements are true?"

"Yessum."

Cassie noticed patches where his shirt was darkened by sweat. She let him wait for a few minutes while she went to the table and looked at her notes. "Let me get this straight," she said finally. She held up her left hand and ticked the points off on her fingers. "You say, under oath, that you did not tell Ward Jackson that there was no school. You did not tell him not to talk to people, you did not make him ask for your permission to make personal decisions, and to your knowledge no money was deducted from his earnings to pay his father's debt. Is that correct?"

"Yessum, I reckon that's about it."

Cassie glared at him. "This court does not ask you to 'reckon,' Mr. Boatwright. It asks you to tell the truth. I'll repeat my question. Is that correct?"

"Yes!"

"Ward Jackson testified that you did tell him those things and that you repeated them frequently. Do you maintain that in each case Jackson misunderstood or lied—in other words, that a poverty-ridden illiterate Negro created a masterpiece of a story from nothing but his own imagination?"

"Yessum, he was just makin' it all up, just lyin'."

Boatwright was sweating heavily and his eyes darted from Cassie to the jury, to the audience, to James Steele, and back to Cassie.

"Only one more question, Mr. Boatwright."

The man relaxed visibly and Cassie moved close to him.

"You testified that you never told Ward Jackson that he could not leave the farm. Is that the truth?"

Boatwright let out a relieved sigh. "It sure is true! Why would I go and tell him a thing like that when he can go any ole place he wants to go? It's a free country, ain't it?"

Cassie paused for a minute, hoping that the jury would see the

man as she did. "Is it a free country, Mr. Boatwright? Is it, for
everyone? Did you not, in fact, serve Mr. James Steele by making
very sure that it was not a free country for Ward Jackson? Where
is the money Ward Jackson earned and was never paid, Mr. Boatwright? Tell me that. Where is that money?"

The defense rested its case and court was recessed until nine o'clock
the next morning. Cassie packed her briefcase, going over the
testimony in her mind. Everyone had left by the time she went out
of the courthouse, everyone except the press. Four reporters surrounded her. She fought off their questions with replies of "No
comment," but they followed her down the granite steps asking
new questions or rephrasing the old ones. Three elderly men in
bib overalls were sitting on a sun-warmed bench by the sidewalk.
Cassie glanced at them, amused that the local sit-and-spit club was
in session despite the shouting reporters.

For one instant, the level of noise fell and Cassie heard one of
the old men speak to the others in a nasal Oklahoma twang: "Yeah,
she ain't nothin' but a nigger-lover."

Cassie flinched as if she had been struck by a cast stone.

"No comment," she yelled at the reporters. "I mean it! For God's
sake, leave me alone!" They paused and she hurried to get into
her car and speed away.

Ruby Keeler, still on spring vacation, was in the hotel suite with
Martha. "How'd it go, Cassie? Does it look good for Ward?"

"Yes. No. Oh, I don't know, Ruby Keeler." Cassie leaned down
to kiss Martha, and the touch of her soft baby cheek warmed her
even as it made her aware that she felt dirty from that day of lies,
too soiled to touch her innocent daughter. "Let me get a shower,
and then I'll tell you all about it."

Cassie undressed hurriedly and stepped into the shower. She
turned the water on full so that it pounded on her bare skin. There
was something besides the lies to wash away: the old man's comment made her feel as dirty as if he had spat tobacco juice on her

rather than an epithet. When she felt cleansed she adjusted the handles and let the water flow over her while she relaxed from the tense give-and-take of the courtroom.

Ruby Keeler wanted to know how it had gone, but Cassie could ask herself the same question and still be unable to answer it. She ran the testimony through her mind, testing for weak points, searching for strengths she could emphasize in her closing argument. James Steele had slipped several times, but so had she. It appeared that the case would come down, in the end, to the question of whether the jury believed Cliff Boatwright or Ward Jackson. And, of course, how much skin color would influence the final decision. The bath soap escaped her slippery hand and she felt that it could be an omen for the attack she had mounted in court. She felt that she almost had hold of the case, almost but not quite, and that it could slip away from her at any second. She was appalled at her own inadequacy.

"Oh, God," she moaned. "I need help! I should have gone with the ACLU after all." She stepped out of the shower and toweled herself dry, rubbing so hard that the blood rushed to her skin. Suddenly she stopped, holding the towel. "But I didn't. I didn't call on the ACLU and that's that. I have to handle this alone."

Cassie did not answer Ruby Keeler's questions that evening. "Wait," she said, "wait until it's all over." As always, she enjoyed playing with Martha and nursing her and tucking her into bed. She called Dix in Oklahoma City, and although they meticulously avoided mentioning the case, she was sustained by his voice and his love for her. She was restless, then, and left Ruby Keeler in charge while she went for a long walk through the quiet streets. By the time she returned to the hotel she knew what she would say in her final argument. For better or for worse, she knew what she had to tell the jury.

The defense argued first. James Steele might not have set foot in a courtroom for years, but he had not forgotten how to charm a jury. He was an impressive figure with his hulking look of power and his well-cut, expensive suit. He strolled back and forth in front of the jury box, meeting the eyes of each member in turn, letting them see the imposing outward man while he described the equally impressive man within. After a jocular remark about being too modest to blow his own horn, he switched to the third person to describe "his client" and his background: a history of charitable works, of participation in banks and other institutions all over the state, of political activities and, in short, of his commitment through the years to the growth and prosperity of the state of Oklahoma.

With a smile for each member of the jury, he summed up his argument. "Why would this man—why would I stoop to so base an act as that of which I am accused? The simple answer, my friends, is that I did not." He moved closer to the box and spoke to the jury confidentially, involving each of them in his dilemma. "All of you are good men, or good women, and true. You have hired people to work for you, an assistant, a yardman or a maid, a clerk, a salesperson. Many times it has worked out well and you have been pleased. Other times, unfortunately, it has not. Your employee has stolen from you, perhaps, or lied to you, or lied *about* you. He has told others, 'the boss said this or the boss said that,' when the boss never once made such a statement."

He stepped back from the jury box and frowned, and his heavy eyebrows almost met at the bridge of his nose. "Such an employee should and will be removed from his job." He moved forward then, and smiled warmly, like a storyteller bringing his tale to a happy ending. "Remember, my friends, what St. Paul said in his second letter to the Thessalonians: 'If any would not work, neither should he eat. For we hear that there are some which walk among you disorderly, working not at all, but are busybodies.' "

Steele looked across at Cassie as if to make sure that the jury saw the connection, nodded to the jury and returned to his place at the defense table.

Cassie stood up before the judge could call on her. She marched briskly to the bailiff's table, purposely clicking her high heels on the hardwood floor, creating a bustle in the courtroom. "Bailiff," she said, "may I borrow your Bible?"

Every eye in the room watched her march back to the prosecutor's table. The jury was no longer under James's spell. They were dying to find out why she needed a Bible in such a big hurry. She held it high as she confidently thumbed the pages, letting the jury see that she knew her way along the paths of righteousness.

James Steele had planned ahead and had plenty of time to tell a clerk to find a suitable scripture. He had that advantage, but she had one, too. She was a sharecropper's daughter, as he was so fond of reminding her, and she had had a grandmother who loved to read as much as the granddaughter loved to listen. Since their choice of reading material was between the old newspapers tacked over the gaping cracks in the walls of the tenant shack and Granny's well-thumbed Bible, Cassie had learned about Bonnie and Clyde and the New Deal, but she had learned more about the Bible.

She almost panicked when she could not find the passage she remembered, but she did not let it show. Maybe it was not in Psalms, after all, or even in the Old Testament. She spotted it, and with hidden relief she laid the open Bible on her table and turned to face the jury.

All twelve were staring at the Bible as if it were a ticking bomb. She hid her pleasure and addressed them in a grave voice.

"Ladies and gentlemen of the jury." She moved slightly to block their view of the Bible and their eyes went automatically to her face. "When I left this courtroom last evening, I felt good. Not good about myself or my presentation of this case, but about our American legal system. This courtroom yesterday was a fine example of all that we hold to be true and good. Here, in this courtroom, was the judge, the umpire, as it were, who maintains fair play. Here was the defendant, free to fight the charges made against him. Here was I, representing the United States of America, not just to attack the defendant and not to win, but simply to protect our fellow American from mistreatment. And you were here, you the jury, who will make the final decision as to what is right and what is wrong. Yesterday, this courtroom *was* America at work, defending our Constitution, making certain that every American's rights are upheld and that every American has a fair chance to be a happy, independent citizen of our country."

She walked slowly toward the jury box as she spoke. Everyone in the jury glanced at the ticking Bible, but she would regain their attention with her next few sentences. "Yesterday I left the courtroom feeling good, and I walked down the front steps of this building, the federal courthouse, and an old man made a remark about me."

Cassie had their attention now, and she said it slowly and emphatically. "The man said, 'She ain't nothin' but a nigger-lover.' "

There were gasps in the room and then a subdued mutter. The judge tapped his gavel quietly and the mutter sank into a tense silence. Cassie was aware of the sounds and then the silence, but she was watching the jury's reaction. Some members appeared to be shocked, a few were as embarrassed as if they had used the phrase themselves sometimes without stopping to consider its implications, and one man would not look at Cassie at all.

"He was right," she said in a ringing voice. "I *am* a nigger-lover!" Cassie heard the nervous titters behind her, but she looked at the jury and suddenly she knew: I have them, by God! I have them!

She stepped back and smiled at the jury. A few people smiled back, tentatively.

"I am a nigger-lover," she said quietly, "and a spic-lover and a Hebe-lover and, for my sins, I am even a redneck-lover." Relieved laughter ran through the courtroom, but Cassie spoke over it. "Because I am an American-lover. I love Americans and I love America, a place where we can bring our whole country into one courtroom and use the might of a great nation and the good sense of our citizens to protect an American, one of us, from harm, whether he is white or Negro or Christian or Jew. Whether he wears ragged overalls like Ward Jackson or—" She sketched a gesture toward James Steele. "Or a three-hundred-dollar Oxxford suit.

"The court will instruct you as to the legal definition of involuntary servitude, or slavery, and then you twelve people will decide for yourselves and for the rest of us whether this man, Ward Jackson, has suffered slavery. Let me, for just one minute, refresh your memories as to the condition of slavery, because it is difficult for free Americans to imagine being enslaved. A slave's very existence, as we heard yesterday, is at the pleasure of his master. He is not given money for his work, so he cannot buy the conveniences, the washing machine, for instance, that most of us enjoy. For that matter, he does not even have running water. Every drop of water a slave uses is carried by bucket for over a mile. In a day of two- and even three-car families, he has a mule. He can't buy clothes for his wife or even decent, nutritious food for his children. Worse than his physical deprivation, however, is the fact that he has no control over his own life. His master forbids him to chat with people he meets, to leave his place of employment. For God's sake, his master prevents his sending his children to school! He cannot even marry without getting his master's permission. A slave is deprived of physical comfort, he cannot exercise free will and, worst of all, he has no hope."

Cassie walked toward the prosecutor's table, shaking her head, and then turned and started walking back to the jury box. "We are a pretty easy-going bunch, we Americans, within the rules of our society. We work and we go fishing and we go to baseball games. If our neighbor prefers football, that's okay with us. It's a big country, we say, it's up to you, we say." She laughed. "We say, 'Everyone to his own taste, said the old lady as she kissed the cow.' "

She placed both hands on the railing of the jury box. "But some things we can't be easy-going about. We cannot stand idly by while one man subjects another to his will, while he uses an American citizen as if he were a beast in the field. We cannot permit one man to get rich by denying another man his rights as an American, as a human being and a child of God." She looked at the members of the jury, one by one, and then she said, "This is a red-letter day, ladies and gentlemen of the jury, because this is the day that you can make a statement of your faith in our country to all America. This is the day you can tell the world." Her voice rose to a shout. "We will not accept slavery!"

Cassie went quickly to her table and leaned on her knuckles, one hand on either side of the Bible, until she knew that every member of the jury was looking not at her but at the Bible. She picked it up, open to the passage she had found. She looked across at James Steele and read it in a loud firm voice, " 'The Lord is known by the judgement which he executeth: the wicked is snared in the work of his own hands.' "

Cassie turned to the jury then and said, "There is more." Her voice sank until the jury had to strain to hear her. " 'For the needy shall not always be forgotten: the expectation of the poor shall not perish forever.' "

It took the jury two hours and forty-eight minutes to find James Steele guilty of holding Ward Jackson in the condition of involuntary servitude.

Chapter 10

The trial was done and the jubilation finished. The courtroom emptied until only three people were left: Cassie Steele, Ward Jackson and James Steele.

James looked up from the papers he was putting into his briefcase. "Cassie, I would like to speak with you for a moment. In private."

"Ward," Cassie said, "will you wait for me in the hall?"

"Yessum, Miz Cassie, I sure will."

They faced each other, James and Cassie, as they had faced each other in open court, but now there were no judge and no jury.

"I hope you are happy," James said with open distaste. "You have made me an object of scorn."

Cassie heard his arrogant anger but what she saw was a tired old man with hunched shoulders. He was still stern, and heaven knew he was hateful, but she could feel his pain and she felt the sorrow she might have felt for an old lion in a zoo, a toothless weak creature that had once been king of the jungle. "I am sorry it came to this, James."

He raised his chin and his eyes flashed with anger. "I don't need pity from the likes of you!"

The likes of me, Cassie thought. A sharecropper's daughter? Poor white trash? A nigger-lover? Suddenly she was as angry as he. "You brought it on yourself! I'm a damned good lawyer, but I couldn't have gotten you convicted if you were innocent!"

James would not look at her. "I will sell that farm to your Negro, if he wants it, at a reasonable price. I will finance it myself, on very easy terms."

Cassie laughed. "So now you are sorry for what you did to the man—'an humble and a contrite heart'? You're a damned good lawyer, too, James, and you certainly do understand the effect remorse has at a sentencing hearing and the importance of staving off a civil suit."

He looked at her then. "I am sure you will not believe that I knew absolutely nothing about Boatwright's arrangements with Jackson, and that this is my genuine attempt to make amends to the man."

"But you should have known. If it was your business to take in the money, then it was your business to know how it was made. You put your intent into writing and I'll turn it over to Ward Jackson's lawyer as soon as I find him one. He can negotiate with you."

James set his jaw. "You understand, Cassie, that I will never forgive you for the humiliation you have visited on me. You could have come to me privately and accomplished the same result."

"I doubt that!"

"Nor will you ever forgive me my sins, I see." He looked at her for a minute. "It's a pity, in some ways. We are cut from the same cloth."

"I also doubt that, James."

"We are. I think I recognized it the day you first came into my office, looking for a job, and I knew I was making a mistake in hiring you. We both know what we want, Cassie Taylor, and by God, we go after it. You think about it. You'll see what I mean."

Cassie did think about it, although she did not want to. The man was dead wrong. They had nothing in common. Nevertheless, his words nibbled at the edge of her mind all the time she and Ward went to the hotel, packed up Martha and Ruby Keeler and Martha's gear and started the drive east.

"Ward," she said, "Mr. Steele has made an offer you will want to discuss with your attorney."

"With you, Miz Cassie?"

"No, Ward, I can't represent you since I acted as prosecutor in this case. A young lawyer named Tom Blankenship has just opened an office in San Bois. I think you'll like him. Now, Mr. Steele is offering to sell you the farm, if you want it, and to finance the sale with easy terms. That would mean low interest and low payments."

Ward was dumbfounded. He opened his mouth, closed it again and finally said, "Me? Own that farm?"

Cassie laughed. "Somehow I get the impression that you would like that."

"Yes, ma'am, Miz Cassie. You say I could—oh, just you wait till I tells my Biddy! She gone be so proud!"

"What's more, Ward, after you sue Mr. Steele, you'll be able to get a good little house built, with running water and electricity."

He turned in the car seat to look at her. "I done did that, Miz Cassie. I went to court on him oncet already."

"Now you'll file a civil suit, Ward. The lawyer in San Bois can handle it all for you. This conviction means that you're sure to win a civil suit for damages."

"Miz Cassie, how me and Biddy ever gone thank you?"

Cassie slowed for the turn off Highway 12 toward the country store. "Learn to read. And get Biddy to learn to read, too. When you go into San Bois to see your lawyer, go to the school. They have an adult literacy program. That means they teach grownups to read.

"Yes, ma'am. I do that. And I sees that Biddy do, too. What else you want us to do?"

"Just one more thing, Ward. It was our system, the American system, that saved you from Mr. Steele, so pay it back by bringing up your children to be good people and good citizens."

"They good kids, Miz Cassie. I sees to that." He hesitated. "Mr. Steele, he sells me the farm and all, like he say, they gone put him in the jailhouse?"

After her fine talk about America, Cassie was torn, but she told him the truth. "No, he won't go to prison. For one thing, he has the money to appeal the case right up to the Supreme Court, but even before that, his generosity to you and his standing in Oklahoma will get him off with a stiff fine. No, Ward, the James Steeles of this world don't go to jail. I never said the system was perfect."

The publicity engendered by *United States* v. *Steele* brought Cassie new clients; in fact, more clients than a lawyer who was also a wife and mother could handle. There were days when she felt that her true home was her aging Cadillac convertible as she sped back and forth on the road between the ranch and the county courthouse in Ballard. Her reputation as a poor man's lawyer cut down the size of her fees, but it gave her great personal satisfaction.

Her arrangements for her children, however, provided no satisfaction at all. Shirley Temple Vance had done fairly well as a short-term baby sitter for Taylor while Cassie argued the case against James Steele, but as a mother's-helper she was no use at all.

Shirley Temple was fourteen but in some ways she seemed to be older than that, and more knowledgeable. She was a small thin girl with red hair in a mass of tight permanent-waved curls. With her pointed chin and pale yellow eyes that never quite seemed to meet Cassie's, she had a foxy look. She had a deep and abiding love of makeup, and unfortunately her favorite lipstick that spring was fluorescent purple. She wore so much black mascara that Cassie was afraid that her upper eyelashes would become glued to the lower ones. Still, there was something about the scrawny little thing with the wildly inappropriate makeup that touched Cassie. The child was trying too hard, perhaps, but at least she was trying. Moreover, Shirley Temple liked the children and Taylor adored her from the start.

With some misgivings, Cassie hired her to help out with the children. It soon became clear that Shirley Temple was too slovenly to do the job. For Cassie to work all day at her practice and come home to a filthy house and sour-smelling children and the mounds of washing that Shirley Temple had "not quite got around to" was depressing. Dix complained, too, that there had to be someone better. Cassie argued that the child was only fourteen and would learn, but she had her doubts. Even scaling down her law practice in order to be at home more was not a solution. She felt guilty: she was neither a good mother nor a good lawyer. Then, one evening in early April, Henry Starr came into the living room to talk and although it was not at all what Cassie had searched for, a solution appeared, a way for Cassie to be a mother and accomplish something.

"Saw old Tom Butler at the feedstore today and heard some news. Seems like they got them a right bad dry spell down to east Texas. A real drought."

"I'm sorry to hear that. Isn't it too early in the year to tell for sure, though?"

"Nope. And last year bein' so dry, they ain't got no grass."

As a rancher who did not yet own a single steer, Cassie could still sympathize with those who had cattle but no grass to feed them. "That's bad, Henry. Really bad."

"One man's poison's another man's meat."

"What's that supposed to mean?"

"Tom Butler had him a phone call. Long distance. There's this fellow looking for somebody up here that'll graze his cattle through the summer and on into the fall."

Cassie laid down her pencil. "He wants to rent pasture?"

"Yep. Seems like most folks round about San Bois, they got all the stock they can handle."

"Except us."

"Yep."

"I was going to buy cattle later this spring."

"I know that." He wheezed a laugh. "Was thinkin' as how it might be better for you to practice on somebody else's stock."

"Henry! That's—" Cassie stopped and looked at him hard. "You don't think I can do it, do you?"

"Never said nothin' like that, Cassie. Just don't want you gettin' in over your head. Ranchin's hard work, mighty hard."

"I can work!"

"I never said you couldn't."

Cassie picked up the pencil and tapped a slow beat on her desk. "It might not be a bad idea, at that. You don't think the Texan would be hesitant about making a deal with someone new to ranching?"

Henry grinned. "Tom said he told that fellow all about you. Said you're about the hardest worker in these parts, and the most up-and-comin' when it comes to ranchin'."

Cassie laughed with pleasure. "How much a head will he pay, Henry, and how many cattle does he have?"

He told her and she grabbed a clean piece of paper and made some quick calculations. "Could you and I handle that many head?"

"What you goin' to do about them little kids? Shirley Temple ain't doin' much of a job."

"I know. I'll just have to do the best I can till spring, when Ruby Keeler graduates. If I'm on the place all the time, I can try to work with Shirley Temple."

Henry shrugged, divorcing himself from the problem. "Maybe you can, maybe you can't. Depends."

Cassie turned to a new page of her pad and scribbled figures. She wished she could discuss it with Dix, but the state senate was in session, and anyway, she was certain that he would support whatever decision she made. "Henry, let's do it! I know it will be a lot of extra work, so I'll tell you what I'll do. I'll pay you your regular salary, and we'll split the profits." She jumped up from her chair and thrust her hand out to him. "Do we have a deal, partner?"

Henry Starr stood up slowly and wiped his hand on the leg of his overalls. He shook Cassie's hand, tentatively at first and then more firmly. "Yep, partner, I reckon we got ourselves a deal."

For the next three weeks Cassie and Henry worked "from cain't see to cain't see." Their main job was building fence, replacing rotted posts and rusty barbed wire all over the farm. In the high pastures where they would keep the bulls, they had to strengthen the existing fence, sinking longer posts and hanging extra strands of wire. For the places that defied the posthole digger on the tractor, Henry bought dynamite and with a few well-placed charges blew holes into the solid rock. The explosive made Cassie so nervous that she made Henry store the leftover dynamite in a padlocked shed a good two hundred yards from the house.

The hard work trimmed Cassie down to pure muscle. In the full-length mirror she could see that her stomach was almost as flat as it had been before she became pregnant. Her thick blond hair was short, in what the Bon Ton Salon in San Bois called a pixie cut, a convenient style for a woman who had no time to fool with curlers. The sun had bleached pale streaks into her hair and had tanned her skin to a warm toast color. With her height and her high cheekbones she could have been one of those strong Scandinavian women who had worked alongside their husbands to open up the Midwestern prairies. She laughed at herself in the mirror. There was no question about it, she was a farm woman. Even though she ignored it, however, Cassie still had the air of elegance that her friend and teacher Naomi Bencher had spotted in a rawboned adolescent. It would be easy to imagine her picture in *Vogue,* perhaps modeling a Balenciaga chemise.

In spite of the hours of work she put in, Cassie saved time to be with her children. In May of 1958, Taylor was over two and was into everything. His vocabulary increased at an astounding rate. Like most children his age, he was fighting for his right to be independent, but between tantrums he was a loving little boy. Martha was eight months old, a smiling dumpling who was happy

anywhere and everywhere as long as her diaper was dry. She loved
to sit in the playpen on the veranda hugging her soft doll and
waving at every bird that flew by.

On the day when the Texas cattle were delivered, Cassie made
sure that Shirley Temple kept Taylor and Martha on the veranda,
where they could watch but be protected from the trucks and the
nervous cattle. At first Cassie stayed with them while Henry helped
the drivers unload the cattle in a cloud of red dust, but then she
had to be part of it and she joined the men in the dusty road,
flapping her arms and yelling, "Soo, cow! Soo!"

"That's what you say to pigs, ma'am," one of the Texans said,
"and anyways, that there's a bull. If it was me, I'd kind of stay
out of his way."

Finally the bulls were safely locked into the high pasture and
the cows and their calves were grazing the lush grass of the bottomlands. The men sat down on the veranda to drink the cold
beer Cassie passed around. The head driver wiped the red dust
from his sweaty forehead. "Boss wants you to move them calves
away from their mamas in a week or so. Most of them's already
seven or eight weeks old."

"That ought to be a good time for it," Henry said. "We got us
a full moon coming in ten days. Always ought to wean on the
third day before the full moon."

The driver turned to him. "That a fact?"

"Yep. Leastways, it's what they say around here."

The driver nodded slowly. "Seems like my grandpappy used to
say that, too. He come from Arkansas himself."

Cassie shaded her eyes and looked down toward the cattle in
the pastures by the creek. "But I thought they should be weaned
at six weeks."

The head driver grinned at her. "You sound like one of them
Texas Aggie boys, ma'am. They done read every book there is,
but they ain't never laid eyes on no cow. Them calves is pulled
down, what with the drought and the haulin'. Boss reckons they
need a little extra time with their mamas."

"Oh, of course." Cassie sat down quickly and confined herself to making notes about the vaccinations the cattle had already received and the dates when they had been dipped to prevent ticks and sprayed for flies.

Dix came home almost every weekend, usually too exhausted from the week of campaigning to do much more than lie around the house and chat with Cassie. One warm evening at the end of May, they sat on the veranda. Cassie had nursed Martha, but she was reluctant to put her down and kept rocking her long after she was asleep. The cows were restless in their new pastures, lowing occasionally in harsh rising moans which the bulls answered in grumbling bellows.

"Sounds like they're lonesome for each other," Dix said drowsily. "When will you put the bulls in with the cows, Cassie?"

"Oh, not until late summer." It was nice to know more about cattle than at least one person in the world. "When they're on good grass like this, the cows will come into estrus, into season, every forty days. Their gestation period is like humans, nine months; and you don't want your cow throwing a calf in the fall when the pasture is poor, because it will drag her right down. So you turn the bulls in with the cows along in August, and then you'll have calves in the spring when the grass is good."

Henry came around the corner of the house and eased himself down on the front steps. "Evenin', Cassie, Dix. Hot work today."

"Want a glass of lemonade, Henry?" Cassie said.

"Sure thing, if you got it there handy." He took the glass from her and took a long drink. "Dix? You got a shotgun on the place?"

"As a matter of fact, I do. It's broken down, in a box in the office closet. Why?"

"Reckon you better get her out and load her up. We lost us a calf last night, and from the looks of the carcass, it was coyotes."

"I don't know," Cassie said. "To keep a loaded gun in the house, with Taylor around—"

"Can't afford to lose them calves, Cassie."

Dix patted her knee. "We'll keep it behind the door in the office.

Taylor never goes in there. And I'll show you how to make sure the safety is on."

"Well, all right," she said reluctantly.

They listened to the cattle for a few minutes. Cassie shifted Martha in her lap. "Do you think the stock is getting used to the place, Henry?"

"Yep, they'll settle down soon enough. Let them get their bellies full of that good grass and clover and they ain't never goin' to want to go home to Texas. They won't want to leave this place."

They sat in a companionable silence, listening to the lowing of the cattle and the clattering buzz of insects in the summer night. "Who would?" Dix said comfortably. "Who would ever want to leave?"

At times during the next month, Cassie looked back on that evening on the veranda and thought that it was the last time she had sat down for two hours straight and maybe the last time she had sat down at all. There was always something to be done for the cattle, and usually it was something that should have been done at least two days earlier. They had to be wormed and dusted for ticks; and even the tiniest cut had to be smeared with salve, or within twenty-four hours flies would have laid their eggs in the wound and the maggots would turn it into a nasty running sore. The Texas cattle were white-faced Herefords, not registered stock but of good bloodlines. They were bred for meat production, in-dividual beef factories producing steaks and roasts and hamburger and, as a by-product, organic fertilizer for Cassie's pastures.

The cattle were not pets, but Cassie did name one cow, the one with the irritating habit of leaning against a barbed-wire fence and staring off into space. It was hard on the fence and on the cow's hide, and on Cassie herself, who had to smear a new cut almost every day. She named the cow Ella Mae, because the creature had precisely the same dreamy look that her father's cousin Ella Mae Hodge had worn when she listened to "Stella Dallas" on the radio back in Whitman. It was expensive to have the veterinarian come and she soon learned to treat simple ailments from her book on the diseases of cattle. Once she asked Henry Starr to treat a cow with some exotic symptoms that were not listed in her book.

"Oh, that's holler tail," he said, and treated it with a mixture of salt and vinegar crammed into a slit in the cow's tail and tied up with a piece of woolen yarn. Cassie was almost afraid to go to the pasture the next day, but the cow healed and thrived. After that, however, she relied on her book and the veterinarian.

With Cassie at home most of the time, Shirley Temple worked harder. Cassie was happy to encourage her, and she took every opportunity to teach the girl not only the fundamentals of child care but also to open her eyes to new ideas. The overdone makeup lightened, then disappeared, and Shirley Temple showed more interest in the world as well as in her work.

In July, Dix asked Cassie to accompany him on a trip to the southern part of the district. "The folks down there don't believe I have a wife, honey, or think that I won't bring you because you have two heads or something."

Cassie could not decide if the trip sounded more appealing because she would have three days with Dix or because she would have three days away from the cattle, but she was eager to go. Martha had recently weaned herself to the bottle, and nursing was no longer a problem. Henry hired Bubba Vance to help him, and Cassie would leave the children with Shirley Temple, whom she was beginning to trust. Henry reassured her that he would make sure everyone toed the mark.

Dix was getting tired of campaigning but Cassie took to it like a duck to water. When Dix spoke, she was so proud of him that she wanted to wave her own private flag. He took the high road in politics, talking not just about the individual voter's needs but about his responsibility to the state, and to the nation. After his speech she delivered her carefully memorized three sentences. It was when they left the platform that she had fun. It was her job to chat with the wives while Dix talked to the husbands, but as the word got around that she was a farmer and rancher, too, she had to field questions about cattle salves and soil conservation plans. They could tell that she knew what it was to be poor, to live as a sharecropper. But she also knew how to plow a straight furrow and to cast clover seed and to drill in Bermuda sprigs. She knew how to work, and she understood how hard they had to work to provide a living for their families.

When the political evenings were over, Dix and Cassie had time for each other. In three different hotel rooms on three different nights, they talked and talked, starved for conversation not interrupted by children or telephone calls or the minor crises of ranch life. And then, of course, they made love, delicious love enhanced with the slightly disreputable spice of love in a hotel room instead of their own marital bed.

As they drove home, Dix reached across and put his hand on her arm. "Cassie, will you go with me again?"

"Oh, yes!" she said. "But do you want me along for the love-making or the politics?"

He laughed explosively. "Both! It's a real luxury, at the end of the evening, not to have to round up some floozy—"

"Dix! If I ever hear of you—"

"Don't worry, honey. You're all the woman I'll ever need." He glanced at her and then looked back at the road. "It's politics, too, Cassie. My campaign manager said it this morning: 'She's your secret weapon.' He said that your beauty doesn't even put off the women, not when you're talking with them and their husbands about something as important as making a farm pay."

"Well! Be careful, sirrah, or you will turn my pretty head!"

He laughed. "Come on, now, you could feel their reaction to you, their approval."

"Well, yes, I suppose I could. I guess I'm homefolks, in a way."

"Yes, love, you are. And I'm the city slicker with a fancy Yale law degree and an apartment in Oklahoma City."

"Dix, they love you!"

"No, honey, they admire me. They love you. You bridge the gap. That's why I need you in my campaign. That, and the fact that I get so damn lonesome for you when we're apart."

"Dix. Oh, Dix." Cassie rose in the seat to kiss his cheek. After a few minutes, though, another thought came to her. "Can we bring the children with us sometimes?"

"Sure. I'd like that, and I think the voters would, too. But not every time, okay? Not when we have to stay in some sleazy motel."

"Oh, no. I wouldn't want them to be in—"

"I mean I want the sleazy motel rooms to be our thing, honey, just for us."

Cassie giggled. "My God, you're right! The sleazier the better! Do you think we're some kind of perverts?"

"Nah," he said, "not perverts. Just homefolks, that's all. Home-folks who like to get away from home now and again."

"Well, that's a relief, I think."

Shirley Temple Vance proved to be a quick learner. By August, she had made herself indispensable. She came to Cassie in the pasture one morning, carrying Martha and with Taylor trailing behind her. "Cassie, can I talk to you?"

Cassie shoved Ella Mae away and turned to face her. Why, she thought, Shirley Temple has grown this summer, and I never even noticed. "Of course you can, dear."

Shirley Temple looked down at her worn sneakers. "School's goin' to start right soon. I was wonderin' could I stay on with you all while I go to school? I won't take no pay, just room and board, and I'll help with the kids and all. I need a chance, see, that's all. Just a chance to get ahead."

Cassie felt a surge of tenderness toward the child. Shirley Temple was only fifteen, but it seemed that she was already setting goals for herself. "Of course you can!" she said. "But I will insist on paying you, just as I did Ruby Keeler."

"Thank you, Cassie. Oh, I thank you!" The girl smiled, that rare neat smile of hers that always reminded Cassie of a fox.

Cassie drew back slightly but then she smiled too, and gave Shirley Temple a big hug. "We will love having you!" she said, and she hoped that she was right.

During the next few years, Cassie looked back to that brief vacation as an eddy in the rushing waters of a stream in spring flood. The river of time carried them past Martha's first birthday in September and her second in 1959, to Taylor's fourth birthday the next March and to the threshold of the Democratic primary in April of 1960.

Cassie tried to cling to the little islands in the flooding stream: Martha's first tentative steps, Taylor's learning to use the potty, and one delightful week she spent with Fran in Dallas, seeing old friends and stocking up on clothes at Neiman-Marcus. Certain events stood out: the successful completion of her first contract with the East Texas rancher and of another the next year, and the campaign tours she made with Dix, when they kept a secret watch for sleazy motels.

The political meeting in San Bois, however, did not give Cassie and Dix even a glimpse of a sleazy motel. It was held at the Baptist church. As a hometown boy with a hometown wife, Dix drew a big crowd. Cassie spotted Ward and Biddy Jackson and their children, all wearing new clothes, the postmistress, Tom Butler from the feedstore, and even Dr. Hill.

After the rally Dix and she stood outside the door to shake hands. Ward Jackson nodded shyly to Dix and turned to Cassie. "I'm learnin' to read, Miz Cassie," he said, "and Biddy, she's learnin' too."

"I'm glad to hear that!" Cassie shook his hand. "How did you folks get to town tonight?"

"I got me a pickup! Mr. Tom Blankenship, he helped me to get it and he learned me to drive."

Biddy Jackson smiled shyly at Cassie. "We thanks you, Miz Cassie, we surely does, and we prays for you every night."

"Thank you, Mrs. Jackson. Thank you very much."

The postmistress shook Cassie's hand, and Dr. Hill greeted her, and then Deputy Sheriff Beasley stood before her, grinning unpleasantly. "Reckon you know, Cassie, the Arkansas police still got a warrant out on your fine brother Bo, got him charged with murder and child molestation."

Suddenly Cassie felt tired, very tired. "I know."

"Then I reckon you know he's headed this way. Somebody spotted him in Haskell County last week."

Beasley, chuckling, moved on and Cassie greeted the next person in line and the next, but her mind was spinning. Where was Bo going? Where else? The farm. But what would he do if he came to the farm? And what would she do?

John Kennedy's victory over Hubert Humphrey in the Wisconsin primary on April 5, 1960, appeared to both Dix and Cassie a good omen. They had become more and more interested as Kennedy bowled over the other Democratic candidates: Stuart Symington, Lyndon Johnson and Adlai Stevenson. "He's young, like you, Dix," Cassie said, "and, like you, a war veteran and a liberal."

"And, like me, he has a beautiful wife. I like the man's ideas, and what's more, I think he can beat Nixon."

On the night of the primary election, Cassie and Dix were together in the Skirvin Tower, watching the returns come in on television. Dix had gone across to the Skirvin Hotel to greet his supporters earlier, and although it was becoming clear that he had won an easy victory, he did not want to go back until his opponents had a chance to deliver their messages in concession speeches. "I'll have my time," he told his campaign manager. "Let them have the limelight for a while."

Cassie admired his generosity, but when each man in turn asked his followers to give Dixon Steele their wholehearted support, she saw that even with Dix something more than generosity was involved. She still had a lot to learn about politics.

They went across to the hotel together, and together experienced the applause of the wildly enthusiastic crowd. Together they went through the room, shaking hands, hugging and being hugged, and together they stood at the podium. Then Cassie stepped back and Dix gave a brief talk, thanking his opponents one by one for their good sportsmanship, thanking his supporters for their unflagging enthusiasm and the hard hours they had worked. The supporters cheered themselves as loudly as they had cheered Dix until he patted his hands on the air to quiet them.

"I would like to thank one more person, not the last on my list, but the first. I want to thank the kingpin—or perhaps I should say queenpin of my supporters, of my family, of my life. Folks, please help me show my gratitude to Cassandra Taylor Steele, my wife."

The crowd went berserk as Dix pulled Cassie to the podium. She stood with his arm around her, and although she knew that the cheers were mostly for him, for the victor, she looked out at the smiling, shouting faces, saw the wildly beating hands and thrived on the heady sound of applause.

Chapter 11

Cassie was delighted with the results of the primary and very proud of Dix, but she could not avoid seeing the problems his victory added to their already complicated life. Winning the primary meant an automatic election to Congress, so the first thing they would have to do was to find somewhere to live in Washington. What would happen to the ranch? Henry could not handle the cattle alone, and Bubba Vance was not a reliable assistant. She would have to talk to Henry and try to figure out a solution.

The day after the primary, she and Dix went straight back to the ranch. For two days they just loafed, resting from the arduous campaign. They played with the children and took long walks, just the two of them, talking about what had gone before and what was to come. The spring growth enhanced their talk and their sense of new beginnings. In the woods redbud trees bloomed, the pink flowers bright among the dark cedars and the rough trunks of the oaks. Every gully was filled with dogwood, its flat leaves like small green lily pads floating in the air and delicate white flowers lighting the shadowed gullies. As it was and had been every year, spring in Eastern Oklahoma was a delight to the eye and a heartening reminder to the soul that a fresh start was always possible.

Dix had to go back to the city on the third day, and Cassie set herself to making plans. She had long talks with Henry Starr, and she broached to Ruby Keeler the idea of moving to Washington with the family. For every item that Cassie checked off her list, however, she added two others. Moving was always a chore, she knew, but when it involved not only people but also making arrangements for a working ranch and a herd of cattle, it became a major exercise in logistics.

As an added problem, small things had begun to disappear from the house and toolshed: half of a ham, the bolt cutters, a butcher knife, a chicken Ruby Keeler had boiled for salad, a hammer. The losses were not big, but they were irritating. They were also inexplicable. A suspicion swam to the surface of Cassie's mind but she immediately forced it down to the depths of thought, beneath consideration. Ruby Keeler was with them for the summer, replacing Shirley Temple, and Cassie knew that she was as honest as the day was long and although Bubba Vance was not overly bright, Cassie was sure that he was not a thief. She refused to confront that other possibility. Instead she reduced the small losses to one more item on her list of things to be handled eventually.

With all that she had to do, Cassie reached the point of being too tired even to sleep. One Wednesday night in May, she dozed fitfully in the hot night, rousing now and again to sink back into an uneasy rest.

Later, much later, she came fully awake. She craned her neck to see the lighted figures on her bedside clock. Three-twenty. She had an uneasy feeling of having been awakened by something outside of her own mind, by something other than the churning of her thoughts.

Taylor, she thought. She sighed and sat up on the side of her bed to pull on her cotton robe. Or Martha. She got up and tiptoed barefooted down the hall, but in the dim glow of the nightlight near the door, she saw that Taylor was sound asleep, lying on his side with his teddy bear in an iron grip. Across the hall Martha was sleeping on her stomach with her rump sticking up in the air.

Cassie smiled in the darkness. Martha was changing from a

baby into a little girl. She would be three in September, and already her vocabulary far surpassed Taylor's at that age. She touched Martha's curls lightly, but looked up at the sound of a muffled clatter down the hall. Someone was in the kitchen. That must have been the sound that had awakened her, not the children. Ruby Keeler, she thought, waking in the night to the perpetual hunger of the young, going to the kitchen for a glass of milk and a few cookies. Cassie smiled. At thirty-five, she was not that young, but milk and cookies sounded good to her, too. She tiptoed out of the children's room, pulling the door closed behind her, and went down the long back hall to the kitchen.

At the door of the kitchen she stopped short. In the light from the hall behind her, she could see that the refrigerator door was open and that someone was leaning over and reaching into it, but the hair was shaggy and too dark to be Ruby Keeler's hair, and the shoulders in the dirty blue workshirt were wider than a girl's.

She must have made a sound, a gasp of disbelief, of protest against what she already knew to be true, because the shaggy head jerked and the person straightened and turned around.

He turned around and looked at her and then slowly, slowly, he began to smile. Small, even teeth flashed white against the tanned, weathered skin and the blackness of a week's growth of beard.

He had come in the night, as she had known that he would. He was there, as she had always known that he would be, sometime, someday.

It was her brother. It was Bo Taylor.

Cassie stood in the doorway, her hand on the doorknob, and as surely as if it were written in fire in the night sky, she knew that all of her life, that all that had been done to her and all that she had done to others had brought her there to that frozen moment in time when she and her half brother would face each other across a room. Man and woman, brother and sister, sharing their father's blood, the evil and the good, the weakness and the strength, they were spawn of the same father and of the same red dirt of Oklahoma. Bo Taylor had made his way through the dark paths, killing not for survival but for the pleasure of giving pain, and Cassie had fought for her husband, her children and her land, and for the right to be herself. And through their two lives, this moment had been waiting to be born, this moment in which they would confront each other. Half sister, half brother, each in some way a part of the other.

Seventeen years. It had been seventeen years since she last saw him in a park in Ballard. It was the night she gave him the money to go to California. Bo had changed very little. In the ragged blue workshirt and khaki pants, his body was thicker and more powerful, but his shaggy black hair still fell over his low forehead and his black eyes were still as cold as a snake's.

He was the first to move, sliding across the floor to switch on the overhead light. As if to isolate her family from infection, Cassie pulled the kitchen door closed behind her.

"Well, Cassie." He smiled, showing his small white teeth. His left dog tooth was missing.

"Bo." Cassie's mind began to function again. "You were the one. You stole the food and the tools."

He grinned. "Never did. They was rightfully mine. You're my sister, ain't you? I'm family."

"Not my family. None of mine. That's all over now. You've been living in that cave, haven't you?"

He shrugged.

"Well, you've got to get out, you hear me? I don't want you hanging around here."

"No," he said softly. "That there cave is my place. I ain't fixin' to leave it."

Cassie pulled the cord of her bathrobe tight and straightened her shoulders. "You've got it all wrong. I own that cave. I own this land, all of it. How long have you been there?"

He shrugged again. "Two weeks. Maybe three. Don't have no calendar."

"That's long enough! You've got to—Bo, are the police looking for you?"

"Reckon so." He scowled at her. "They ain't goin' to find me, though, lessen somebody takes a notion to phone over there to Arkansas and turn me in."

Cassie remembered suddenly what James Steele had told her before the trial, the story she had pushed from her mind in her preoccupation with *United States* v. *Steele*. She should have taken warning from Deputy Beasley, too. A little boy's body, a naked body, had been found in a ditch at Fort Smith. She forced herself to walk, not looking at the wall phone, to the sink and draw a glass of water.

"It wouldn't be me that called them, Bo. Like you said, you're family." She turned and leaned against the drainboard, holding her glass, and made herself smile at him. "I remember one time when the deputy came looking for you. Deputy Skeet Beasley, remember him? Somebody had frightened a little girl down in San Bois. Granny made me lie for you, Bo, made me say that you were home the night it happened. Do you remember that, Bo? I lied to the police for you."

"Give me a glass of that water."

A little of the tension went out of Cassie's spine. She turned around to take down a clean glass and fill it from the tap. "You can stay on in the cave, Bo. You'll be safe there. Or better still, I'll try to get hold of some money and help you get clear out of the country." She turned around with the glass. "To Mexico, maybe, or—" She stopped because he had wrapped his fist in the cord of the telephone receiver and, as she watched, he jerked it out of the phone and held it up to show her the dangling wires. "Bo! What are you—"

He turned toward her and she did not need to ask. It was all there in those cold black eyes.

"Bo, I swear, I wouldn't have—I never would have—"

"You liar. You always was a liar. Tellin' the old woman on me, tellin' Paw."

"I didn't, I swear it!"

"You was the one sent me out to California, too, and then you told them police out there about me." He moved toward her slowly, like a cat, like one of the housecats that were dropped in the woods to go back to their natural state, back to the wild. "You was the one got me sent to prison."

"No!" Cassie backed along the counter, still holding the glass of water. "That's not the way it was at all! Bo, that's crazy!"

He tensed and went into a half-crouch. "Crazy." He moved toward her again, like a cat creeping up to pounce on a bird.

"I don't mean you," Cassie said tearfully. "All I meant was that I didn't tell anyone—I wouldn't tell—"

His hand snaked out and grabbed her wrist, and the glass flew through the air and sprayed water in his face. He wiped the water away with his free hand and then slapped her across the face, backhanded.

"Don't hurt me!" she cried. "Please don't hurt me!"

He twisted her wrist until she fell into a heap at his feet. He laughed then, a laugh as low-pitched and dangerous as a snarl. He dropped her wrist and she rubbed it with her other hand.

"Crazy. That's what they said out there. Them doctors and all, they called it by four-bit words, but that's what they was sayin'. But I was too smart for them fellows. I told them what it was they wanted to hear. Told them I didn't want nothin' to do with no little kids. Told them I only wanted to come on back here and get me a job on a farm. Crazy, sure, crazy like a fox, that's Bo Taylor!"

"Go away, Bo," Cassie sobbed. "Just go away. I swear I won't tell. I swear it on the Bible. Please. Just go away."

"Sure, Cassie, sure. You swear it on the Good Book. Just like all them Bible-thumpers that come to see me in prison. I told them what they wanted to hear, too. Yessir, I'm saved. Yessir, I'm goin' to change my ways, yessir. Hell, all they wanted was to get shut of me, get me out of that nice clean state of theirs. Bastards. Every last one of them. Bastards."

Cassie tried to push herself up from the floor. "Bo, I've got some money in the house. I'll get it for—"

"You stay put!" He kicked her hard on her left thigh.

"Oh, God!" She fought back the tears. "Bo, please don't—please, won't you just go away?"

He grinned down at her. "Not till I get what I come for."

Cassie wiped her eyes with the back of her hand and looked up at him, at his loose mouth and glittering eyes, and then she saw that an erection was straining against the fly of his khaki pants. Her flesh crawled. In spite of her fear that he would kick her again, she crossed her arms over her breasts and whispered, "No. Please."

He laughed harshly. "Hell, Cassie, what do I want with you? I like young ones, you ought to know that by now. I don't want no old broody hen like you. I want that other one."

Cassie closed her eyes. Oh, God, she thought, not Ruby Keeler. Please don't let him get Ruby Keeler.

He kicked her again and she cried out and pushed herself back into the corner.

"Look at me when I talk to you, girl! I want that young one, that little one I seen around the place."

Cassie could not figure out what he was talking about. "Martha? Little Martha? But she's just a baby."

"Hell, no! The boy. That there little boy with all the yellow hair. He's the one I want. Go on now, you go get him for me."

She would not allow herself to understand him. She tried to speak, to tell him that there was no meaning in what he had said, no meaning at all, but she could not put words into any order that made sense. "I can't—there's no—you wouldn't—"

"You hear me, girl? I said, go get him!"

"No!" she cried. "Take me, Bo! Take me instead! I'll do whatever you want. Anything! Just don't—"

"Shit, I ain't goin' to fuck no old gal like you. I want me a little one to—"

"No!" She jumped up and grabbed his arm. "Bo, you can't—"

He hit her again, not a slap but a full-armed punch in the face, and the pain exploded in her head like dynamite. She clapped her hands to her face and blood ran out between her fingers. "My nose," she cried. "You broke my nose!"

"That ain't all I'm going to break if you don't—hell!" He hit her backhanded and knocked her against the counter. "Get out of my way! I'll go get him myself."

"No! Oh, please!"

He turned to her suddenly and through swelling eyes she saw that he was smiling. "Yeah," he said softly. His eyes glittered. "Yeah, that's it. You come on now, Cassie, come along with me. It'll make it even better if you're watchin'." He grabbed her arm and pulled her toward the door to the hall.

"Wait, Bo, wait! You're hurting my arm! I'll—I'll take you to him."

He dropped her wrist and stepped back. "Well, goddamn. Miss highfalutin' Cassie herself. When it comes down to it, you're just a bitch like all the rest of them, ain't you?" He raised his voice to a falsetto. "Anything you want, Bo, just any old thing. Just don't hurt me no more, and I'll give you anything you want, even my own kid." He shoved her toward the door. "Okay, bitch, go on now. But don't you try to pull no tricks on me, you hear?"

"No tricks, Bo. No tricks."

She stumbled down the long back hall and past Ruby Keeler's door, praying that the girl would not wake up. At the next door she hesitated.

"This his room? Get on with it!" Bo shoved her and she fell against the door and pushed it halfway open.

"I'll get the light," she whispered, and before Bo could stop her, she reached around behind the partly opened door. It was not the light switch that she was feeling for behind the office door, but the cold metal of a gun barrel.

In one swift movement she spun around and slipped the safety catch off of the shotgun. "Get back, Bo," she said tightly. "Get back or I'll shoot!"

"You goddamn fuckin'—"

"Get back, I said. And get your hands up or I swear to God I'll kill you!"

"I'm goin', I'm goin'." He raised his hands above his head and backed down the hall toward the lighted kitchen.

Cassie moved after him, watching him through swollen eyes. He hesitated in the doorway and she raised the gun and pointed it directly at his face. "Into the kitchen! Go on, back up against the refrigerator!" She followed him into the kitchen and closed the door with her heel.

Sweat matted Bo's thick hair and ran down his face. "Listen, Cassie, I was just funnin' you. I never had no mind to hurt that little—"

"Shut up!" Watching him carefully, Cassie wiped her left hand across her upper lip. The blood from her nose had subsided to a trickle. Bo moved his foot and she gripped the shotgun with both hands and raised it.

"Cassie, girl, let me tell you—"

"You aren't going to tell me anything, Bo Taylor. You are not going to say one word. Do you understand that?"

"Yeah, sure, but—" Cassie waved the gun and he clamped his lips shut and nodded angrily.

"You have one chance, Bo, and that's all. We're going to walk down that road until you're off of my land. I'm going to follow you and I'm going to keep this shotgun aimed right at your back, you hear? There's a full moon tonight, so I can see you, I can see every move you make. You're going to walk down the middle of that road, Bo Taylor, and if you stray one inch to the left or the right, I'll shoot you dead in the road. Do you have that straight?"

His small black eyes were shining with hate. "Sure, I got it. Sure. And then you'll set the law on me, sure as hell."

"I sure as hell will. And there's another phone in the office, one you didn't find."

"You'd turn on your own brother that way?"

"My brother!" Cassie spat the words at him. "You're no brother of mine!"

"We got the self-same blood, Cassie Taylor, and you know it. My paw was your—"

"No! she cried. "Papa might have been weak, but he never was evil!"

"Can't bring yourself to be my sister, can you? You and that old bitch Granny always was just alike, so goddamn uppity you thought your shit smelled like roses." He started to lower his hands.

"Get your hands up, Bo! I'll shoot, I swear it!"

"And get blood all over them pretty little hands of yours? Naw, I've got you pegged now, Cassie. Hell, you ain't got enough gumption to shoot nothin'!"

He moved like lightning. He jerked the red-checked oilcloth from the kitchen table and threw it at her face while he grabbed at the barrel of the shotgun. Cassie fought to keep her grip on the gun and she pulled the trigger and the oilcloth fell away from her eyes and where Bo's face had been there was only blood and flesh flying outward like a great red flower opening in yellow sunlight, exploding as once her father's face had exploded before her eyes.

Time stopped and everything hung in the air, suspended in the sound of the explosion and then Bo crumpled and collapsed onto the floor as if losing his face had tired him, had so exhausted him that he had to lie down and take a long, long nap. And Cassie went down, too, down on her knees, and tried to open her hands and throw the shotgun away from her, but her fingers had cramped into position, were fixed on the gun, on the trigger, forever, and never would she be able to put the gun away from her, never in her life.

"What have I done?" she whispered. "Oh, God in heaven, what have I done? Dix—" The name stopped her. Dix. Honest and ethical and idealistic. How could he ever accept what she had done? How could he ever forgive her for killing? How could she forgive herself?

A cry sounded from somewhere far away, "Mama!," and there was the thud of running feet in the hall and another cry, "Miz Cassie!"

"Stop!" Cassie screamed. "Don't open that door!" She made the association between the running feet and the cries from the other part of the house. "Ruby Keeler, don't come in here! Take Taylor in Martha's room and stay there with them. Don't leave their room, you hear? Get them quieted down, but don't any of you come out of that room!"

There was a pause and then the retreating sound of running feet and a distant wail and a voice calling, "Martha, baby, it's okay, I'm comin'. Ruby Keeler's comin' for you!"

Cassie closed her eyes and took a deep breath. The spring on the screen door squeaked and she opened her eyes and looked up, directly into Henry Starr's pale brown eyes. He looked down at the thing on the floor, at the shotgun in her hands, and then back at her. He nodded once.

"Your brother?" he said softly.

"Yes."

"Reckoned it was. You hurt bad, Cassie?"

"I don't think so."

"Give me the shotgun now."

Her fingers could release it to Henry. He pushed the safety catch and carefully laid the gun on the drainboard. Cassie tried to get up, could not, and had to wait until Henry helped her to her feet.

"I'd better call now," she said. She looked at the kitchen phone and the receiver lying on the floor. "He didn't know about the office phone. I can call the sheriff from there."

Henry pushed a kitchen chair toward her. "Sit down a minute first, Cassie."

He watched her sink onto the chair and then he took up the oilcloth from the floor and draped it over Bo's body.

"I better call," she said again.

"No rush. He ain't goin' no place." They looked down at the red-and-white-checked heap on the floor. "Reckon maybe we ought to think some about this here before we do anything. Let me get a look at your face."

He soaked a dishtowel in cold water and dabbed at her face as gently as a mother cleaning a new baby. "That hurt?"

Cassie shook her head.

"Nose ain't broke, then. He give you a good wallop, though. Reckon you'll have you a black eye, maybe two."

He rinsed the dishtowel in cold water, wrung it out and folded it neatly. "Hold this on your eyes, Cassie."

It was easier when her eyes were covered and she did not have to look at the oilcloth. She heard Henry pull a chair close to her and heard the seat squeak as he sat down.

"Thing is, Cassie," he said, "you get that deputy in here and all hell's goin' to break loose. Bein' as how you're a Steele and Dix's goin' into Congress and all, and this here Bo bein' your brother, there's goin' to be a big fuss, reporters and I don't know what-all." He hesitated. "And a trial, too, I reckon."

"I killed him," she said flatly.

"I know that, Cassie. And from the looks of you, you was defendin' yourself, but that don't mean there won't be no reporters swarming like bees to a queen."

In the same dead voice, Cassie said, "He wanted Taylor." She lowered the dishtowel and for a long moment she and Henry Starr looked into each other's eyes, sharing the knowledge of what could have happened, of what would have happened.

Henry's voice was as flat as hers. "Reckon we ain't goin' to call nobody. Reckon we're goin' to bury him out there in the woods, same as you'd bury any dead varmint."

"Yes," Cassie said softly. "Of course."

"Reckon we ain't goin' to tell nobody about it, nobody in the whole world."

"What about Ruby Keeler? She knows something happened in here tonight."

"Ruby Keeler, she'll know what her grandpa tells her to know.

Varmint got in the kitchen, one of them stray housecats gone wild, and you come and got me and I shot the thing."

Cassie tried to smile at him, but it hurt her face too much. "Henry Starr, you are a good man."

He did not smile either. "And you're a good woman, Cassie Steele. Don't you never forget that."

I am not so sure of that, I'm not sure of that at all, Cassie thought, but she did not say it aloud.

Cassie and Henry worked fast. By the time the sun was edging up from the mountains to the east, they had wrapped the body in the oilcloth and then in an Army surplus tarpaulin and had loaded it onto the trailer hitched to the tractor. Between them they got the kitchen cleaned up and Henry took the bloody rags out and added them to the bundle on the trailer while Cassie tiptoed into her room to pull on jeans and a shirt. She went back to the kitchen to make sure they had not overlooked anything. There was a tentative knock at the door from the hall.

"Ruby Keeler? Come on in." Cassie turned away from the door to hide to her face.

"Miz Cassie, the little ones are settled down and back to sleep."

"I know. I listened at their door. Thank you, Ruby Keeler."

"What was all that—" For the first time she saw Cassie's face. "Mercy, are you all right?"

Cassie tried to smile. "What a night! I heard something out back and I went out there and sure enough, it was one of those wild housecats. I fell down, and it got past me and into the kitchen, but I got your grandfather and—well, he'll tell you about it later, Ruby Keeler. We want to haul the thing off and bury it in the woods so the children won't see it and be upset. You stay with them, okay?"

"Yessum," the girl said obediently, but her dark eyes were sharp with interest.

Henry was going to have his work cut out for him with this

one, Cassie thought, but then she remembered that Ruby Keeler was a hill-country girl like Cassie herself, and very likely an old hand at keeping family secrets. "It's all right, Ruby Keeler. Everything is all right now."

"Yessum. I'll stay with the young ones like you said."

Henry drove the tractor while Cassie stood behind him, bracing herself with one hand on his shoulder and with the other, carefully balancing the brown package that he had brought from the shed in the pasture.

The tractor left the pasture and pulled up a hill and down to the old riverbed where in that wet summer a foot-wide stream of water cascaded over the rocks. Cassie was watching for the landmark, but even so, she almost missed it. At the last minute she spotted the slab of limestone poised on the face of the cliff.

"Here, Henry. Stop here."

"I don't see no cave."

"It's there behind those willows. Let me check it first."

Cassie had to look closely to find the entrance. The thin screen of water was heavy from the rains, and the willows were larger than she had remembered and were thick with leaves.

She slipped past the falling water and pulled the flashlight from the hip pocket of her jeans. Its disk of light moved through the cave. It touched the lantern hung from a spike driven into the wall, hesitated on the strange carvings in the stone, slid across the low table stacked with Bo's belongings: a butcher knife and the missing bolt cutters and a few mildewed magazines. It stopped on a pile of bones near the wall. The disk wavered, but Cassie held it on the bones. A calf. She would have to count the calves in the weaning pasture.

The light moved on, touched something pale blue, passed it and went back, drawn to it as if the color were a magnet. Not wanting to, hating to, Cassie crossed the sandy floor of the cave and picked it up. A little boy's shirt, about a size four. There was a brown stain on the shoulder. Dirt? No. Blood. Dried blood. She laid the flashlight down and folded the shirt carefully, sadly, like a mother folding away her child's outgrown clothes, and laid it down on the table, in the decent darkness. She took up the flashlight and stumbled across the cave and outside to the safety of the early morning light.

"What's the matter, Cassie?" Henry took a step toward her. "You sick?"

"No. Oh, God, yes. I'm sick." She told him what she had found and his weathered face hardened.

"For God's sake, Cassie, let's do it and be done with it. Let's get this varmint in the ground where he ought to be."

They half-carried, half-dragged the bundled tarpaulin into the cave. Cassie would have taken it farther in, would have laid it on the low table, but Henry would not do it.

"Lived in the dirt, let him be dead in the dirt."

Cassie drove the tractor down the riverbed and around a bend while Henry scrabbled up the hill with the brown package. He set his dynamite charges under the slab of limestone and let the wire reel out while he climbed back down. They went up the hill across from the cave, Henry paying out the wire behind them.

When they were behind the crest of the hill, Henry connected the wire to the electric terminals and lifted the plunger handle. "You want to do it, Cassie, or you want me to?"

"You, Henry. Wait, though. Shouldn't we say something first? A prayer or something?"

He scowled at her. "Say God's Word over an animal like him? It ain't fitting."

"He was only half an animal, Henry. He was half a man, too. And he was my half brother."

"Half of this and half of that, it don't make up to much, does it?"

Cassie looked down at the green willows and the sheet of fresh water that concealed the entrance to the cave. "Maybe that was what was wrong with him, Henry. Maybe that was what was always wrong."

She knelt down on the matted brown oak leaves and Henry reluctantly took off his hat.

" 'Our Father , Who art in heaven, hallowed be Thy name. Thy kingdom come. Thy will be done on earth, as it is in heaven. Give us this day our daily bread. And forgive us our trespasses—' "

After she had said the words for Bo she hesitated and then said them again, for herself.

" '—forgive us our trespasses, as we forgive those who trespass against us. And lead us not into temptation, but deliver us from evil: For Thine is the kingdom, the power, and the glory, for ever. Amen.' "

She stood up then and looked down at the cave for the last time. "Please, Lord. Please make him whole."

Cassie lay down in the leaves and Henry put his hat back on his head and crouched down beside her and rammed the plunger down into the box.

A giant invisible hand pushed at Cassie and then the thump of the explosion hit the hill and echoed up and down the rocky gulch. She raised her head and watched the limestone slab hover and fall, sliding down with slow dignity to crash into the dry rocks of the riverbed. It teetered for a moment and then slumped back against the cliff, hiding the green willows, hiding the falling water, hiding the entrance to the cave.

As the dust settled, a trickle of water found its way over the top of the slab and traced a dark line of moisture down to the bottom of the dry stone. Another trickle pushed through and then another until the water ran down in a thin sparkling sheet, darkening the limestone and washing the slab that covered Bo Taylor's grave.

Part Two

For my days are consumed away like smoke . . .

My days are gone like a shadow,

and I am withered like grass.

—*Psalm 102, The Book of Common Prayer*

Chapter 12

 On a warm June evening Dix and Cassie sat in the living room at the ranch. They could have been an old married couple settled with each other and with their own ways, the husband studying his papers, the wife knitting. The scene, however, was less placid than it appeared. Dixon Steele's papers were position assessments typed by a member of his congressional campaign staff and Cassie's knitting, a practice square, was a wad of yarn interspersed with holes caused by dropped stitches.

She worked the yarn off her finger, where it left a painful red ring in the flesh, and murmured a frustrated expletive.

Dix pushed up the glasses he had begun to use for eyestrain and looked over at her. "What did you say, dear?"

"Just what you thought I said."

He laughed. "It spoils the effect, Cassie, when the happy housewife mutters four-letter words over her knitting."

Somehow her right forefinger had become part of the stitch on the needle. She extricated it with another curse. "I'll never learn to knit, darn it. Ruby Keeler is a good teacher, but I just can't get my fingers to do what my mind tells them to."

"Maybe it's one of those things you have to learn as a child," Dix said, comforting her. "I'm surprised that your grandmother didn't teach you."

Cassie's mind went back to the tenant shack and its empty

rooms, to their empty life. "We never had much to *do* with," she said.

Dix put down his papers. "You know, you've been talking about your childhood a lot lately. Is something bothering you?"

"No!" she said. "Nothing at all!"

He looked at her as if he were waiting to hear more. "I just wondered."

Cassie dropped the yarn and needles in her lap. The knitting was meant to occupy her mind, to keep her from thinking about that night in May, but it had failed in that as surely as it had failed to produce a usable piece of knitted fabric.

She wanted to tell Dix about Bo's death. She wanted terribly to share her burden, but she could not. With his idealistic moral views, he would probably feel compelled to do something about it, perhaps even to report it to the authorities. No. He would never throw her to the wolves. It was worse than that. He would have to live with the secret that he was married to a murderess.

There. That's it, she thought. That's the word. Whether she was justified in defending her son and herself was, in the end, a moot point. She killed Bo Taylor. She murdered him. She shot him down like a mad dog.

Murderess.

During the weeks that followed, the word rode on her shoulder like a great black raven.

It was a hectic time. Besides helping Henry Starr with the cattle, Cassie had to prepare the farm and the house for the two years' absence ensured by Dix's winning the congressional primary in a solidly Democratic district. Obvious winner or not, Dix spent almost as much time on the campaign road as he had before the April primary.

"I want to meet as many people as I can," he said, "and I want them to know that when they need me, I'll be there and I'll be accessible."

Cassie missed him, but she began to believe that it was better for him to be away from the ranch, and from her, for a while. When he was at home, there were misunderstandings, little things that became big ones, spats that exploded into full-fledged arguments.

"Oh, Dix, I'm just too tired tonight."

Dix rolled away, to his own side of the bed. "You're always too tired. You aren't pregnant, are you?"

"No!" She laughed with relief rather than amusement. "I am most definitely not pregnant."

"What the hell is wrong, then? You never want to make love."

There in the moonlit bedroom Cassie hesitated, hearing San Bois Creek chuckle over its rocky bed, listening to the lonely night call of a whippoorwill on the ridge. "I don't know. I'm just tired, I guess. Getting ready to move to Washington, trying to plan for—" Her voice faded away.

On his side of the bed, Dix was very still. "It's my fault then?" he said finally. "Because I went and got myself elected to Congress? I thought you were all in favor of it."

"I was—oh, Dix, I am! It's just that—it's me, Dix. I'm the problem, not you."

"Then why won't you talk about it? Goddamn it, Cassie, a husband deserves better than this!"

Cassie raised herself on her elbow and glared at him. " 'A husband deserves'? I don't remember promising 'to obey' in our wedding ceremony."

"Damn it, you know what I mean."

"No, I don't! Why don't you tell me, Dix, tell me just exactly what you do mean."

"That I deserve to be a part of your life and—oh, hell, why talk about it? Nothing's going to change." He rolled over and presented her with a cold, unyielding back.

"Maybe you're right. Maybe it will never change." Cassie rolled away from him, too, away from any opportunity to ease the tension between them.

They lay there silently, two rigid figures in a double bed, backs

turned to each other and their love for one another: two backs
that silently shouted the words that the man and woman were
afraid even to whisper.

Cassie met Fran Jordan in Tulsa by boarding the Washington flight
and taking the first-class seat Fran had reserved next to her own.
As the plane lifted from the runway, Cassie's heart lifted, too. For
the week that she and Fran spent househunting in Washington,
there would be no tense conversations with Dix, no arguments,
and above all no demands made on a body that seemed to have
become sealed off from all emotion on one dreadful night in May.
Dix would be away from the farm also. He planned to take Taylor
and Martha to Ballard to visit their grandparents. Cassie had seen
Amelia a few times, on neutral ground, but she had not laid eyes
on James Steele since the day she humiliated him in open court.
He made it clear that she was no longer welcome in his home.

"I've been doing my homework," Fran said happily. She pulled
a sheaf of papers from a black leather briefcase. "I've talked to
congressmen and senators and politicians and, more important,
I've talked to their wives, so I have a pretty good picture of the
pecking order in Washington."

"But won't it all change if the Democrats get in? If Kennedy
beats Nixon?"

Fran laughed. "Here is Saint Fran's first letter to the Oklahomans, love. Washington, the real Washington, is a bureaucracy,
and bureaucrats are much more interested in safeguarding the
status quo than in who happens to be President at the moment.
A department chief cares a lot more about his pension than about
changes in the top levels of the administration. That is, except for
the fact that bureaucrats have a vested interest in having a Democratic Congress. Liberals mean big government and big government means more government jobs. The more Indians there are
in the ranks, the more importance for the chiefs, as well as more
pay, and therefore bigger pensions."

"I'm sure that's not what John Kennedy has in mind!"

"I'm trying to tell you, Cassie, that it doesn't matter what he or any other candidate has in mind. Look, suppose a real penny pincher is elected President. Out comes Executive Order Number Whatever: 'Governmental expenses will be cut to the bone or else.' So the department chief goes out right away and hires himself a high-powered Assistant Director for Budget Compliance, and *he* hires five GS-Fifteens and ten GS-Twelves and an absolute bevy of GS-Fives—all of this just to find out what the bone actually is."

"I feel sort of dizzy."

"You and everyone else in Washington, love. You and everyone else." The stewardess delivered champagne cocktails and Fran got down to business. "Georgetown, Cassie. The word is Georgetown."

"Where in God's name is Georgetown?"

Fran sighed and flagged down the stewardess for another cocktail. "Miss, I'm going to need another of these, maybe even several. And keep them coming to my poor ignorant friend, too." She turned back to Cassie. "Georgetown has always been a good address, but it's catching on now with the younger, more with-it members of Congress. Since *they* took a house on N Street—"

" 'They'?"

"The Kennedys, who else? All aside from the fact that he might be President, Jack and Jackie have style!"

"You know them, Fran?"

She looked slightly embarrassed. "Well, no, but I met them once, at a party. Anyway, Georgetown is the place for you and Dix: a small house, good for entertaining but not ostentatious enough to offend senior congressmen and their wives, and just different enough to make people think twice before they assume that Oklahoma people still spit tobacco juice and do their trading in wampum."

Cassie laughed and relaxed as she had not done since that night in May. "Fran, I'm so glad you'll be with me for the househunting.

You're a breath of fresh air, and I need some fresh air in my life right now."

"I wondered." Fran was watching her closely, her eyes bright with curiosity. "You really aren't yourself, love. Is there a problem? Surely not with you and Dix?"

"No! Well, yes, in a—Fran, I don't want to talk about it." The brief surge of pleasure was gone. "I can't talk about it."

Fran looked away quickly. "All right. Let's talk houses. Now, how much are you willing to spend and how much space do you need?"

Cassie was relieved to concentrate on mundane matters such as bedrooms and bathrooms. "Oh, and we'll need a bedroom for Shirley Temple."

"Now, wait just a—" Fran laughed abruptly. "Oh, I guess you mean Shirley Temple Vance, Ruby Keeler's little sister."

"Not so little, now. Ruby Keeler is starting college in Tahlequah this fall, and Shirley Temple is going to take her place in our family."

"If I remember Shirley Temple right, that won't be all she takes. She looks like she's no better than she should be."

"Come on, Fran! She's just a child. Sixteen years old!"

"And you know as well as I how little that means in the backwoods. I'd watch that one, Cassie. I'd keep a good eye on her."

Fran's energy never flagged as they looked at house after house, but Cassie became more and more confused. Was the house on O Street the one that needed a new kitchen? Or was it the one that had the beautiful master bedroom? Finally they settled on a place on R Street, a solid red-brick with a graceful stairway and the requisite number of bedrooms and bathrooms. In their room at the Four Seasons, Cassie read the contracts while Fran planned their strategy. "Don't bother reading the lease, Cassie. You'll want to buy that house, not rent it."

"Oh, no, we won't. I've done some research, too. Most first-time representatives just lease a place for two years, possibly with an option to renew the lease."

"But you'll make money on this house, Cassie, especially at this price. A really messy divorce is a buyer's dream. That's why you want to buy rather than rent."

"What makes you so sure we'd make money on it?"

"You're a lawyer, love, and good at it, but I'm good at my profession too, and part of my job is recognizing trends. As a matter of fact, I've been nosing around, and I'm thinking about buying a small house myself, as an investment."

Cassie peered at her. "With what? A 'gift from a friend,' like the Mercedes?"

Fran's face froze. "I didn't know my love life offended you."

"Oh, no! I didn't mean to—"

"I know what you meant! It will probably make you feel better to know that I intend to buy the house with money I've earned from my business."

"Of course!" Cassie said quickly.

Fran gave her a half-smile. "All right, all right, Cassie," she said. "I don't know why I'm so touchy about it. After all, I did accept the car, and the trip to—"

"Don't tell me, Fran! I don't want to know!"

Fran was calm, but there was an edge to her voice. "There seem to be quite a few things lately that you don't want to know or don't want to tell. What's going on?"

Cassie looked at her watch. "The real estate agent will be waiting for us." She took up her handbag and hurried to the door.

Fran stopped her. "Don't you need to call Dix and get his approval on the price of the house?"

She had already made that decision. After all that had passed between them, it was the least she could do for him. "No, Fran, I don't. I'm going to pay for it." She did not quite look at Fran. "Like you. I'm going to buy it with the money I've earned myself."

Fran started to speak, but shrugged, picked up her own purse and followed Cassie out of the room.

Cassie thought that the week in Washington had done her a lot of good, but as she drove home from the airport in Tulsa, her depression returned, as heavy on her mind as before. Was she always going to find returning to the ranch threatening? Would she never again see it as a refuge, a place where she could recharge her batteries, the one place on earth where she could relax and be an Oklahoma girl?

Dix was at the ranch, waiting for her with their children. At four, Taylor was a thin wiry boy whose blond hair was almost platinum from a summer of Oklahoma sunshine. Martha, almost three, was as pale as porcelain with huge blue eyes and blond hair that hung in ringlets in the damp heat. Ruby Keeler had gone to Tahlequah to preregister at Northeastern State College. Taking her place at the ranch was Shirley Temple Vance, who hovered in the shadow near the front door, watching Cassie.

Cassie hugged and kissed the children, and when Dix put his arms around her she consciously relaxed and tried to find the old sense of security. It was not there. She pulled away and chattered to him and the children about the house and Washington and all of the things she and Fran Jordan had seen and done.

When the children were settled in their beds, Cassie and Dix sat on the veranda in the eerie light of the full moon. Dix was calm and cheerful, but in spite of herself, Cassie was jumpy. Her journey, she felt, had not yet come to an end. She kept the conversation to a mundane track, describing the house in Georgetown in more detail and explaining the rationale for buying rather than renting it.

"I think Senator Kennedy lives in Georgetown," Dix said.

"Why, yes, I believe Fran did mention it."

He laughed. "You know, these similarities keep cropping up, don't they?"

"What are you talking about?"

"About John Kennedy's career and mine," he said, leaning back in the wicker rocking chair. "We're both young, right? And we have rich fathers. We have good war records and we got our starts in state politics."

Cassie chuckled. "If I didn't know better, I'd think you were saying that you could be running for President someday, too."

Dix was silent for a minute. "Why not?" he said softly. "Why not?"

"But, Dix, be realistic about it! You aren't John Kennedy, you're—"

The telephone rang and Dix went inside to answer, but Cassie could hear his half of the conversation through the open window. The caller was Cully Meecham, Dix's campaign manager, a man she could not abide. Cully was a small wiry man with the undernourished appearance common to poor boys who had grown up in the Dust Bowl. She couldn't understand how Dix could bear to be with him. Dix was tall and lanky and beautifully dressed. Cully, who appeared to buy his suits by mail-order from Monkey Ward, as the country people called Montgomery Ward, capered along behind Dix like a cur following its master. He came close to Fran's description of what Easterners thought of Oklahomans. He did not spit tobacco juice, but he was a bigot to the core and he was in his glory when he was making deals involving favors and duebills. The wampum he traded in was political influence. Perhaps Dix tolerated Cully because, as the man himself bragged, he would do anything to win, anything at all.

"What do you mean, it's coming unstuck? Cully, I promised to push for the dam, didn't I? What the hell does he want now? . . . We can't do that. No, I mean it! I've already made a commitment to the boys in Oklahoma City. . . . Well, I suppose I could—Cully, we're spreading it too thin. Look, the election's in the bag. You know it, I know it, and for Christ's sake, all your good old boys know it. Why do I have to deal with this sort of . . . oh, sure, I'm aware that there will be another election in two years, but . . . okay, okay. Do what you have to do, but keep me filled in."

The screen door slammed and Dix dropped into the rocker so heavily that the wicker screeched in protest.

"What was that all about?" Cassie said.

"I don't want to talk about it."

Cassie's anger flared. "Deals. The great white knight is making political deals, but he doesn't want to talk about it." She stood up and looked down at Dix. "What's the matter? Are you afraid that old word will raise its ugly head if we discuss this? What is that word, anyway? Oh, yes. Sell-out."

Dix jumped to his feet and loomed over her. "I don't need your sarcasm, Cassie! My God, you're an adult. You know how these things are done, not just in politics, but in business, too. In fact, you wanted it, didn't you? You wanted to be a wheeler-dealer."

Cassie swallowed hard. "People change, don't they? Maybe you've changed, too. You've always been so ethical, Dix, so fine. It was one reason I married you."

Dix turned away from her. "Maybe it was the only reason."

"What do you mean?"

"Well, it sure wasn't for sex, was it?"

Later that evening Cassie and Dix got ready for bed. They were extremely polite, like two strangers forced by circumstances to share a room for the night.

"Shall I turn off the light now, Cassie?"

"Yes, please, if you're sure you're ready."

They lay down, each to one side of the bed, establishing a demilitarized zone between their bodies.

"Oh, hell," Dix muttered and suddenly he rolled over and invaded her territory, clasping her body to his. "Oh, God, Cassie! I love you so much!"

Chains fell from Cassie's arms and she wrapped her body around his. "Dix," she cried. "Darling!"

He entered her in one thrust and her body enfolded his as she gave herself to him freely, with ecstasy. Then Bo violated her thoughts, the knowledge of what he had done to that little boy in Arkansas, of what he would have done to Taylor, and she felt the very tissues of her body shrivel. She released her grip on Dix's back. She did not pull away but all she could do was lie there, inert, while he drove into her again and again, while Bo's face exploded, reformed, and exploded again and again and again.

Dix gripped her to him for one last thrust but when he released her, her limp body sank back on the bed. His breath came in great gasps for air until he subsided and was as limp as she.

"Cassie," he whispered. "Cassie, darling, what's wrong?"

"Nothing," she said, wishing it were true. "Nothing at all."

Dix raised himself on an elbow and switched on the bedside lamp. "Why won't you tell me?"

Cassie closed her eyes against the sudden glare. "Nothing is wrong, I swear."

"I don't believe you."

She began to cry softly. "I just—I just can't talk about it."

"You mean, you *won't* talk about it."

She opened her eyes then and saw his angry closed face. She shook her head helplessly.

With a muttered curse, Dix switched off the lamp and lay down with his back to her. Cassie rolled over, too, but her eyes were wide open, staring into the darkness.

Long after Dix's breathing had fallen into a steady, even rhythm she lay awake, clutching her pillow to her damp face.

Chapter 13

 In early September, Cassie and Dix flew to Washington to arrange for the move and to see what Fran Jordan had done with the house. While Dix paid the cab driver, Cassie unlocked the front door and threw it open.

"Welcome to our house, darling!"

"Your house," he said harshly. "You paid for it, didn't you?"

"Dix, I explained my reasoning on the—"

"Never mind. Let's have a look at it." He went ahead of her into the front hall. The fresh white paint set off the aged wooden floors, clean and waxed, and the rich muted colors of an antique Persian rug. Dix turned to Cassie and for once gave her a free, open smile. "I like your house already, Cassie. I think it will be a good place to live."

Cassie sighed in relief. "Wait till you see the parlor, darling, and the library!"

"And the bedrooms?" His voice faltered but he smiled. "I hope Fran didn't forget to fix up a bedroom for you and me."

They toured the house together. Cassie was delighted with the results of Fran's hard work. The furnishings were as eclectic as those on the farm, but the decor of the downstairs rooms, those which would be used for entertaining, was formal, even elegant. On the second story, the bedrooms were casual but comfortable, as were the big playroom for the children and the small sitting room off the master bedroom.

As they went through the house, Cassie felt excitement building within her, and hope. Surely in this new house, this new place, she could put Bo's death behind her. She could shuck off the guilt and live her life as she wanted to live it, loving and being loved.

The master bedroom was at the back of the house and its large windows looked out on Georgetown's big old shade trees and on the small backyard which Fran's landscape designer had divided between a formal garden for entertaining and a compact play area for the children. The bedroom itself connected with a dressing room that had closets large enough to hold twice as many garments as they owned. Everything was done, everything complete, right down to fresh towels hanging on the rods in the bathroom. Dix was looking at the bedroom furnishings: the antique four-poster bed, the matching walnut chests with wooden handles carved into fruit shapes, the thick Oriental rug with a cream-colored background and a pattern of blue as rich as the blue of imperial porcelains.

Dix whistled. "Cassie, this must have cost you a fortune!"

Cassie's latest balance sheet appeared in her mind. She had made astute investments, primarily in Dallas real estate, and even buying the Georgetown house and its furnishings had barely dented her new worth. "Dix, I *have* a fortune."

Dix went to the window and looked out at the trees. "I'm not happy about your spending it on a house for us."

"What difference does it make whether the money came from your account or mine? We share children, and a bed—" She hesitated. "We share a life, darling. Why can't we share money, too?"

Dix turned from the window and looked at her directly. "Do we share a life? Lately I've begun to wonder."

For all his height, for all his self-confidence, at that moment Dix looked as vulnerable as his four-year-old son. Cassie ran to put her arms around him and to bury her face in his chest. "We do, darling! Don't you know that you are the most important person in my life? Without you, I'm nothing, I'm nobody!"

Dix clutched her to him and it was as if Taylor were holding onto her in the night, as if only she in all the world could stave off the terrors of the night. "Cassie," he said softly, and kissed her, tenderly at first and then with increasing urgency. Cassie kissed him, too, feeling the core of ice within her melt away. She needed him, she knew, more than she had ever been willing to confess even to herself. He pushed her away, smiling, and crossed the room to lock the bedroom door. He came back to her then and put his arm around her to guide her to the bed.

Fumbling, they undressed and pulled down the bedspread. The sheets were as blue as the pattern in the rug and as smooth and cool as only fine Egyptian cotton could be.

They were together, then, alone in the world, alone in their love. The fumbling was over and their movements were practiced and sure, as together they released the pent-up hungers of the summer. Afterward they lay back on the silky sheets.

"Why do we let things push us away from each other?" Dix said. "Why do we do this to ourselves?"

Cassie turned her face away. It was not Dix's fault, it was hers and he knew it as well as she. But he would not assign to her the blame for their estrangement. Not Dix, the moral man, the gentleman.

With a surge of admiration and appreciation, of love, she turned back to him and apologized in the only words she could afford to use. "I love you, darling, with all my heart and soul."

He put his arms around her. "That's all I want, that's all."

Slowly, comfortably they explored each other's bodies as if they had come home again after a long sojourn in other countries. For once Cassie could consign her guilt for Bo's death to the past and live only in the present.

She was with Dix again, physically and mentally, and nothing else mattered a hill of beans.

Their short stay in Washington was like a second honeymoon, but Cassie and Dix were back in Oklahoma when the exciting news about New Orleans came. For the first time, a Southern city was going to obey the law and desegregate its public schools. Dix was delighted. He knew that the admission of four little black girls, first-graders, to previously all-white schools was little more than a gesture, but the importance of the gesture far exceeded the number of people who would be directly involved. Cassie had more a sense of relief than of triumph. Nobody, she thought, not even the most militant white, could object to the presence of a little girl.

Both Cassie and Dix, as it happened, were misled by hope. On the television news that night they saw the little girls approaching school: spotless children, their hair meticulously braided, their appearance so sparkling that their mothers might have washed their daughters along with their dresses, dipped them in starch and ironed them to perfection. Then suddenly the screen was crowded. There were police everywhere and young white men waved their fists and shouted unheard below the newscaster's commentary.

"Plenty of police," Dix said as if he were doing a technical critique of the exercise. "I'm glad to see that. And it looks like a good plan for moving the children right into their building. Look at those police barricades, Cassie."

Instead, Cassie looked beyond the barricades and what she saw made her gasp in horror. The most active protesters were not young men, rowdies and layabouts. They were women, young mothers with faces contorted by hatred, American mothers screeching with anger and screaming invective at the little black girls who held hands and walked steadfastly toward the education that they as Americans deserved. The little girls slowed, their eyes white with fear, but they kept walking forward.

"Look at the police," Dix said. "They've doubled their line there by that group of toughs. They'll need to—"

"Look at the faces, Dix! Look at the women's faces!"

"My God," he said softly. "Oh, my God."

Cassie rubbed the tears from her eyes. "How long will it take, Dix? For God's sake, how long?"

He came across the room to sit down on the couch and take

her hand in his. "I don't know, darling, No one knows. But you see why I have to keep working at it, don't you?"

Cassie closed her eyes but the vision lingered: the angry faces, the silently screaming mouths. "Oh, God, yes."

On the rare occasions that fall when Dix was at the farm, he was usually on the telephone, talking to Oklahoma Democrats, to the heads of the national party, and often to Martin Luther King and his aides. Cassie sympathized with his efforts more than she ever before had, but the hours he was closeted with the telephone left her feeling deserted and lonely. She sometimes felt that she was no longer involved in planning their life as a family. She loved Dix, though, and she trusted him implicitly. While he made his plans she concentrated on their children.

At three Martha was a delight. She was as wiry as Taylor, but her disposition was less volatile. As she cooked dinner for her dolls on the toy stove she had received for her birthday, Cassie could see her resemblance to Granny, with her calm, well-paced progress through life. Martha was endlessly curious and was inclined to sum up her findings in statements that were sometimes based on a spectacularly skewed vision of the world.

"Mama, you know why there are trees?"

"Why, darling? You tell me why there are trees."

"So the leaves don't fall down till they're the right color."

Dix called her pronouncements "The Gospel According to Martha," and shook his head in disbelief: "How the hell do you get an eighty-year-old brain into a three-year-old body?"

Through the fall days Dix appeared to be more interested in the presidential campaign than in his own. "I just wish," he said one night in October, "that John Kennedy would make it clear that he intends to push for immediate desegregation."

"I thought he made his view pretty clear at the Democratic Convention," Cassie said.

"He needs to do it again and to be more specific." He laughed.

"But who am I to talk? I've had to soft-pedal my own position, so why shouldn't he? Winning elections means making some compromises."

Cassie's throat tightened. "That sounds like something Cully Meecham would say."

"So? Cully is one of the savviest politicians in this state."

"Too savvy, if you ask me. And too damn ready to compromise. Just be careful that he doesn't decide to shift his support to some other candidate, Dix. You'd be nailed to the wall before you caught sight of his hammer."

Dix stood up abruptly. "You must think I'm a fool! Cully is loyal to a fault, and I'm damn lucky to have him for a campaign manager. I've wished I could find a man like him ever since I first got interested in politics."

Cassie laughed uncomfortably. "Remember the old saying: Be careful what you wish for, because you just might get it."

The evening ended, as most evenings had begun to do, with Cassie creaming her face at the bedroom dresser while the clatter of voices floated in from the living room where Dix watched the late show on television. Cassie wiped off the cream and looked at herself in the mirror. Why was he so touchy? And why was she so ready to criticize? She turned away from her reflection, not wanting to look too deeply into her own eyes because she was afraid of what she would see there.

To no one's surprise, Dixon Steele walked away with the congressional election. His Republican opponent conceded shortly after the polls closed, with a rueful comment that he might as well have conceded back in April when Dixon Steele won the Democratic primary. He promised to return and fight the good fight another time, but he gave the impression that he and his party knew that it would be like spitting into the wind.

Dix made his victory speech early, too, and celebrated with his supporters. When he could gracefully leave, he and Cassie drove home to the farm. As they drove through the crisp November night their full attention was on the reports broadcast over the car radio. The outcome of the presidential election was a cliff-hanger. Even when they had reached the farm and turned on the television, the lead was swinging back and forth between Kennedy and Nixon like an apple on a string. No network was ready to issue the usual flat statement "awarding" the election to a candidate on the basis of mystical, possibly mythical, factors which were never explained because, apparently, no one who watched network television was capable of understanding a concept which had to be defined in words of more than two syllables.

A cold front blew into Eastern Oklahoma during the night, and Cassie and Dix woke to a gray rainy day. They turned on the radio, however, and the day grew brighter by the minute. John Fitzgerald Kennedy was the President-Elect of the United States. It did not matter that his margin of victory was only 100,000 votes and that there were allegations of voting chicanery in Illinois and Texas. Nothing mattered but the fact that John Kennedy had won.

Dix was elated. "Remember what he said, Cassie? We'll have 'a new generation of leadership—new men to cope with new problems and new opportunities.' "

"And you'll be part of it," Cassie said. "You'll be one of those new men!"

When Dix came down to earth he immediately began to make plans. "I want to get to Washington and get involved in the transition process. It will make a difference when committee assignments are parceled out. I don't have enough pull to get Ways and Means, but I don't want to be buried in some housekeeping committee, like the District of Columbia, that never gets any publicity or any real power."

In what seemed to be a matter of days, the Steele family was transported to Washington. Cassie was happy with what now seemed to be the last major decision she herself had made for the family. The house was perfect for them, as was Angelina, who greeted them at the door. Cassie had hired her to cook and clean and to help with the children when Shirley Temple was in class. She was a jolly woman, almost as wide as she was tall, with a broad brown face and a warm smile.

Taylor went through the house like a whirlwind, exploring every nook and cranny, but Martha took her time, walking sedately from room to room. When her leisurely tour was completed, she nodded once, briskly. "Mama, my babies will like living here."

Shirley Temple Vance trailed along behind Martha and Cassie. She seemed to be somewhat in awe of the place, but she was not too overwhelmed to mutter rebelliously when she discovered that she would be sharing a bathroom with the children.

The girl's complaints irritated Cassie. She knew the Vance family's shack had no bathroom at all, only a weathered outhouse badly in need of shoring up. Once again she wished Ruby Keeler had wanted to come to Washington instead of sending her younger sister. The girl was somehow unsettling. She was pretty enough, with her pert nose and thick red hair, but her amber eyes never quite met Cassie's. Cassie consoled herself with the thought that Shirley Temple would learn soon enough that she was in the big time now and that her childish country ways were a disadvantage in the city. Ruefully, Cassie thought that she herself might be in for a cultural shock, too.

"Cassie?"

The whiney note in the girl's voice irritated Cassie, but she forced herself to smile. "Yes, Shirley Temple?"

"Bein' as how you're goin' to be around home today, would it be okay for me to take a walk and look around some?"

"It certainly would!" Cassie was delighted that the girl was taking an interest in her surroundings. "Let me give you a city map."

As they settled into the house on R Street, Dix took over more and more of their long-range planning. At first Cassie was delighted with the time it saved her, but as her participation in major decisions ebbed, it seemed, a tide of minutiae flooded her mind.

One of the first items on her agenda was to get Shirley Temple enrolled in school, so she brought up the matter a few nights later when she and Dix were sitting in the library with flames crackling in the fireplace. "There's a high school a half mile from here," she said, "so tomorrow I'll go over and—"

"She doesn't want to go to that school, Cassie, and I'm inclined to think that she shouldn't."

"She came to you about it? What's wrong with the place?"

Dix got up and went over to the bookshelves. Looking at the books, his back to her, he said, "It's the level of education, Cassie, that's the problem."

"The level of education! For a girl who reads nothing but movie magazines? A country girl who went to the consolidated high school in San Bois, Oklahoma? What on God's green earth are you talking about?"

He turned to face her. "Look, we've taken on the responsibility for her, haven't we? We're committed to see that she gets an education. I think she should be in private school."

"Dix, why on earth would we send her to private school when we'll be sending our own children to public school?"

"Now, honey, that's a decision we won't need to make for months yet. Taylor won't start kindergarten until next September."

Cassie stood up, too. She had just remembered an offhand comment made by a new neighbor, but surely it was not a factor Dix would even consider. "I thought we decided on public school years ago," she said tensely.

Dix flushed. "I've been asking around and apparently almost no one in government puts his kids in the Washington public school system because—"

"Because the other students are Negro?"

"Of course not! I told you it's the level of education. People like us put their children in private schools, not public."

"What do you mean, 'people like us'?" she said sharply. "A freshman congressman and a sharecropper's daughter?"

"Listen, I'm young, I'm able and I'm ambitious. People say this job is just a stepping stone for me."

"People? What people? Cully Meecham?"

His face went red with anger. "Hell, yes, Cully! But he's not the only one! I'm going a long way, Cassie, and you'd better get used to the idea!"

Cassie was startled by his vehemence as well as by the strength of his ambition. "Dix. Darling. Let's talk about this calmly. Do you really think you can rise to—"

"That's enough!" His voice dropped and tightened with fury. "I didn't ask for your opinion and I'm not asking for it now. My political career is my business, not yours!"

"But you haven't even mentioned this before!"

"When would we have had time? All you ever want to talk about is new towels for the master bathroom or the children or what Angelina's making for dinner."

Cassie flinched. "That's not fair. I've wanted to discuss politics with you, but—"

"But you haven't. It's all been on my shoulders. Well, I've got broad shoulders, Cassie. I've set my course and if it means living a certain way or sending our children to certain schools, that's what I will do."

She was shaking with anger, but she tried to speak calmly. "This isn't you talking. Surely it isn't!"

He scowled at her. "It's me, all right. There's no point to any further discussion."

"Then you'd better get yourself on that District of Columbia committee after all, and get to work on raising the level of education! Taylor is going to go to public school or—"

Dix pulled a book from the shelf and slammed it down on the coffee table. "Or what? You want your kids to get a poor education, is that it? And how are you going to explain it to them when they discover that they can't go to the college they want because they don't have a good educational background? Tell me that, Cassie. Just tell me that!"

"No." She sat down and forced herself to speak in a level voice. "You tell me, Dix. You tell me how you are going to explain it to your Negro friends and to Martin Luther King, not to mention your own conscience. What will you say? 'Oh, yes, I'll sit at the lunch counter with you and I'll ride the bus with you and I'll go to the polls and vote with you. I'll even use the same men's room as you, but I won't send my children to school with your children.' You tell me, Dix, tell me how you're going to explain that and how you're going to convince them that you aren't just using them to build your political image."

Obviously shaken, Dix picked up the book and restored it to its place on the shelf. "Cassie. You're doing it again, aren't you? You're trying to make things sound straightforward when they aren't simple at all and they sure as hell are not easy."

"Nothing is easy," Cassie said. "Nothing is ever easy, is it?" She softened her voice. "But maybe you're right. Maybe I am making too much of it. Still, the next time Shirley Temple wants to discuss schools, send her to me, will you?"

"As long as she goes to a private school."

"All right, all right! When it comes to Taylor, though, we'll have to talk about that."

They went upstairs to bed, but they did not make love. Cassie was exhausted and she suspected that Dix was, too. Tired as she was, however, she was tense, caught up in the injustices of life. She hoped, how she hoped that the new President would provide the leadership they all needed in order to deal with old problems, and with new ones, too.

It was high time for some new beginnings.

Chapter 14

 With her family organized in the house on R Street, Cassie had a chance to investigate the city. She discovered that there were three Washingtons in the District of Columbia rather than one.

The floating, temporary Washington was made up of tourists. The Steele family moved to Georgetown after the summer season, but even on gray November days, clumps of tourists plodded through the cold rain from one sight to another. Invariably an awed group of tourists stood at the Lincoln Memorial and stared up at the statue of the Great Emancipator.

Less temporary than the tourists were the elected, the wave of office holders who swept into Washington every two years, or four, or six. They stayed as long as they could maintain equilibrium on the shifting sands of politics, only to be washed away by the arrival of a new wave. Each of the elected trailed a queue of appointees, from the highest aide down to the one-session college intern. It was a fast-moving, high-stepping crowd surrounded by lobbyists who darted into the fray to argue and persuade, a circle of political wheeler-dealers.

Then there was the third Washington, the foundation of permanent residents. Like every other city, Washington had its service core, plumbers and policemen and pediatricians, but they were outnumbered by the permanent government workers who kept the wheels of state turning, if only at the speed of God's mills. There was a nonbureaucratic substructure, too, the socially adroit who gave a certain continuity to the changeable political scene. A congressman comes and goes, after all, but a witty hostess with a first-class chef can last a lifetime. Another sort of continuity was provided by the elder statesmen who pontificated on park benches or in book-lined rooms. They were, in fact, repositories of the unwritten history of Washington. They knew where the bodies were buried and precisely who had dug the graves. Their female counterparts had come to Washington as wives or, in a few instances, as politicians, but had stayed on when the party was over.

Cassie discovered that Fran Jordan's friend Blair Fuller was from another group entirely. She had been married, briefly, to a young Georgia congressman, Fran had reported, and was in her early thirties. She was small, with thick black hair brushed back from a high forehead. Her eyelashes were thick and black, and her eyes were that nameless color that changes from amber to purple, depending on the color of a scarf or a sweater. On the day Cassie first met Blair Fuller for lunch at a Washington restaurant, Blair's eyes were as emerald a green as the silk of her Empire-waisted dress.

Her first words to Cassie were, "I think I hate you."

Startled, Cassie dropped onto a chair across the table. "Why? What on earth have I done?"

"It's not what you've done, it's what you are. My God, woman, you were born to wear clothes! Just look at you! It's a Chanel, of course."

"Well, yes." Cassie blushed. She knew she looked good in her suit of rough white tweed trimmed with navy braid, but Blair's comment embarrassed her. Even in her confusion, she was fascinated by Blair's faint, appealing Southern accent, but she would learn eventually that she could judge Blair's conversational partner sight unseen by the variation in that accent. She sounded more Southern when she talked to males, and when she talked to Southern males, her consonants melted like butter on a warm day.

"How tall are you, Cassie? Five ten?"

"Oh, no. Only five eight."

"*Only* five eight. Do you have the slightest idea what hell it is to try to dress well when you're only five feet and one inch tall?"

"But you look great!"

"I look good," Blair said. "I'm well-groomed and I'm well-dressed, but I do not look 'great.' That's a word reserved for show-stoppers like you."

"Blair, stop it! You're making me blush!"

"Okay, okay." She flagged down the waiter and ordered gimlets. When he left, she smiled. "So, how are you finding Washington?"

"To tell the truth, I'm still looking for it." She started to explain her theory of the three separate Washingtons, but Blair buried her face in her hands and groaned.

"Smart, too! I can't bear it. I simply cannot bear it." She raised her face to heaven in mock supplication. "O Lord, why have you visited this plague upon me? What have I done to deserve her?"

"Oh, you idiot!" Cassie dissolved in laughter. "Fran should have warned me. You are too much!"

"No, Cassie, *you* are too much. I'm too little."

Cassie laughed. "Can a little person and a giant ever find happiness together?" She stopped laughing then. "I meant it when I said Washington confused me. I need a friend." She heard the note of pleading in her voice and stopped before she said too much.

Blair had heard it, too. "We will be friends, Cassie. I need a friend, a real friend, too. Now tell me, what's wrong?"

"Nothing is *wrong*, exactly. I just feel sort of at sea."

"I'm not surprised! You've been tossed into the Washington pool without even a pair of water wings."

Cassie hesitated. "I really need to know about schools and shops and, most important, how to be a good congressional wife."

"Well, I can help you while you're treading water. I've lived here all my life."

"A native Washingtonian?" Cassie laughed. "Somehow I've

never considered the idea of people being born and growing up here."

"My father was born here, too, and his father and his father. There are other families like ours, who were here in Georgetown when they were building the White House. People say we've been here so long we lived in caves." Her eyes sparkled. "They call us the 'cave-dwellers.' "

"So you really know Washington."

"Do I ever! Now, when it comes to being a congressional wife, there are just three simple rules: Keep your freezer full, your eyes open and your mouth shut."

Cassie laughed. "A full freezer, that means I'll need to do a lot of entertaining, right? Be 'the Hostess with the Mostes',' like Perle Mesta."

"Hush!" Blair scanned the room as if she were looking for KGB agents. "Don't say that name in public, don't even think it! Jacqueline Kennedy can not abide the woman! I doubt if she'll ever let her set foot in the White House."

"Why? What did Mrs. Mesta do?"

"Mrs. Mesta doesn't have to *do.* Mrs. Mesta *is,* and that in itself is enough to offend Jackie Kennedy. But you must entertain, yes. I suspect that you're already a tremendous help to your Dix. A good-looking wife is a great political asset."

Cassie remembered the campaign in Oklahoma, leaning on a gate, chewing a straw and having long discussions of livestock and crops and the land. "I guess I did help him, Blair, back in Oklahoma, but that was easy. I liked being a big frog in a little puddle. It was comfortable."

Blair laughed. "That won't last, that little-puddle satisfaction. Cassie, power is the name of the game in Washington, and power is infectious. Believe me, the more you see of power, the more you'll want it."

"Listen, I'll be happy just to be a good wife and mother. I have no political ambitions."

"How about Dix?"

Cassie remembered their conversation about private schools. "I'm not sure," she said defensively.

"Well, if he doesn't have political ambitions now, believe me, he will. When he hangs around the House and sees what can be done when you have the power. Remember, power corrupts."

"And absolute power corrupts absolutely. But not Dix, Blair. You don't know Dixon Steele."

"He's human, isn't he? Anyway, by corruption I didn't mean something that changes a good guy into a venal crook. I mean the desire for power, the wanting to have a bigger piece of the pie."

Instantly Cully Meecham's face appeared in Cassie's mind, and she remembered bits and pieces of overheard telephone calls. A desire for power. "But don't some men avoid it, Blair? Surely not everyone who is elected to office is power-mad."

"No, there are a few who—but think about it, Cassie. The man—or woman—who campaigns on a platform of cutting government spending and after the election is the first one in line for a congressional fact-finding mission to Hawaii. *His* mission, of course, is not corrupt or wasteful, because he knows how important it is to see Hawaii with his own eyes rather than relying on biased reports."

Cassie nodded thoughtfully. "I see what you mean. I'll have to be careful, and to ask Dix to be careful, too."

"I wouldn't hold my breath."

Cassie thought of that conversation frequently during the short December days, but there never seemed to be a time when she could tell Dix about it. In fact, there never was time for them to talk about anything. Dix was busy maneuvering for committee appointments and organizing a staff. Even when they went to the farm for Christmas, Dix had to spend most of his time on the telephone and the rest closeted with Cully Meecham or other Oklahoma politicians. He went back to Washington the day after

Christmas, but Cassie lingered at the farm until it was time for Shirley Temple's school to open.

The Democratic sweep of the congressional election meant that there were more applications for good committee assignments than there were seats. It was easy to put off a first-term congressman from Oklahoma, especially one who was entangled in the thorny jungle of desegregation. Washington was in the first flush, however, of its love affair with John and Jacqueline Kennedy, admiring their youth and style and rejoicing with them at the November birth of their son John-John. Jack Kennedy had barely managed to win over the American electorate, but he took Washington by storm. The strength of the liberals in the party was reinforced by their liberal President. Desegregation was a hot potato but it was one the party was forced to grasp. Dixon Steele became an exemplar of the policies the Democrats were bound to uphold.

Cully Meecham almost lived in the house in Georgetown. He and Dix spent hours in the library, talking and talking and talking. Dix, in the end, got the committee appointments he wanted. What he and Cully traded for them, what deals were made, Cassie did not know. She was not at all sure she wanted to know.

Shirley Temple was enrolled in private school and by December underwent a sea change from country girl to young sophisticate. The twanging country music she liked was replaced by Chubby Checkers and Connie Francis. She changed from full-skirted cotton dresses to sweaters and skirts and wore a hairdo inspired by Jackie Kennedy. She even worked on her accent, and Cassie had to control her amusement when Shirley Temple's speech changed direction, sometimes in midsentence, and her words came out not through her nose but from between locked jaws.

Cassie was not surprised when the girl said she wanted a raise in the allowance she received in addition to bed and board. Cassie agreed that Washington was more expensive than San Bois and gave Shirley Temple a generous increase. What was more, the girl said, she wanted them to use just one first name for her. Cassie thought "Shirley Vance" would do nicely, but Shirley Temple had a teenager's unerring ear for the characteristics of the pack.

"I want y'all—I want you to call me 'Temple' now. Temple Vance."

Dix noticed the changes in the girl but, like most men, he saw the whole rather than the parts. "Shirley—I mean, *Temple* is growing up, isn't she? How old is she now, anyway?"

"She's seventeen, Dix."

"Seventeen. Well."

Later, much later, it occurred to Cassie that Dix sounded disappointed, but by then she did not have time to examine the thought. It was mid-January, and the presidential inauguration of John Fitzgerald Kennedy was at hand.

The inauguration ceremony was held on Friday, January 20, 1961. The official party stood on a platform, exposed to the wind, while the audience huddled on the Mall, glad to have other bodies nearby to provide some shelter against the damp 20-degree weather. Later that night political Washington ignored the cold, however, to turn out for the five inaugural balls.

When Cassie descended the stairs of the house on R Street, even Shirley Temple caught her breath. Cassie wore blue, a cool-blue silk dress that matched her eyes. It was deceptively simple in cut, clinging to her slender body and emphasizing her excellent figure. After some thought, she had decided against a bouffant hairdo, suspecting that most of the women at the ball would be copying Jacqueline Kennedy's hairstyle. Instead, Cassie wore her hair down, parted on the left side and falling to her shoulders in a cascade of honey blond.

Dix went to her and kissed her hand with knightly gallantry. He moved close to her to whisper, "You are a knockout, darling. Half saint, half sinner. You'll have every woman in Washington insane with envy."

"Except for Mrs. Kennedy."

He laughed. "Except for Mrs. Kennedy. But someday, maybe—"

She pushed him away so that she could admire his finery. His height and slim build were set off by his dress suit of white tie and tails, and his dark eyes were warm and, for once, were interested only in her. Suddenly she was overwhelmed by love for her husband. Careless of her dress she put her arms around him. "Dix. Oh, I do love you!"

Their tickets were not for the ball at the Mayflower, the first ball, where former President and Mrs. Truman would be. Not even Cully Meecham could manage that. They were at the second ball, however, and happened to be directly in front of the door when President and Mrs. Kennedy made their entrance. Cassie caught her breath in excitement. It was a grand moment, with the President so tall and young and energetic and with his wife a beautiful young woman in a stunning white chiffon sheath. Her diamonds glittered and glinted in the lights of the ballroom, and in her billowing floor-length white silk cape, she seemed to appear in a whirl of white smoke.

The two of them passed through the center of the room, the President shaking hands and laughing, his wife smiling shyly and greeting friends in a soft, breathy voice. To Cassie's surprise, the President stopped when he came to her.

Dix stepped forward. "Sir, I am Dixon Steele, the freshman congressman from Oklahoma. May I present my wife, Cassandra Steele?"

"Cassandra?" the President said.

"Cassie," she said nervously, "Cassie Steele."

The President introduced both of them to Jacqueline Kennedy. She looks so tired, Cassie thought, so very tired. Mrs. Kennedy spoke to Dix, and the President turned to Cassie.

His eyes scanned her body in a way that made her draw back. Television did not do justice to his magnetism, both personal and professional. He was attractive and very masculine and, people said, the most powerful man in the world.

"Cassie," he said as if to imprint the name in his memory. "Cassie Steele."

Jacqueline Kennedy took her husband's arm and they moved on, greeting people, shaking hands, as the crowd wheeled around them as if those two beautiful young people were the axis about which the world revolved.

"What a gorgeous woman!" Dix said, and then he put his arm around her and whispered. "But not half as beautiful as you, darling."

Cassie relaxed against his shoulder, feeling beautiful and beloved. "Thank you, Congressman Steele," she said. "Thank you very much indeed!"

"Inaugural ball" was a misnomer, because no one danced. Instead, the guests milled around, seeing and being seen, clumping to tell jokes or make minor political deals and then wandering away to repeat the jokes or extend the deals. As the liquor flowed, the decibel level increased, and Cassie was delighted when it was after two and time for them to leave.

They tiptoed into the house and upstairs, but when they went into their bedroom, instead of getting ready for bed they stood together and exchanged the first deep kiss they had shared in a long time.

"My darling," Dix whispered. "I was so proud of you tonight."

Without speaking, they helped each other undress, slowly and carefully at first until they were frantic, half-drunk with excitement and love and with their need for each other. In bed Dix entered her immediately and she was as ready as he. Their desire detonated in one burst and they fell back on the bed gasping for breath.

"It's been so long, Cassie. So damn long. God, that was good!"

"Yes," she whispered. "Yes, but not—"

"Not what?"

"It was more desperation than love."

"Oh, you want love, do you? You want all the trimmings?"

Suddenly he pulled away from her and walked naked to the window. He threw open the curtains, and the lights of the city made moving patterns on his bare skin and on the walls and ceiling of the bedroom. "Look at me, Washington!" he said. "Look at me, world! Watch me make love to my wife!"

"Idiot!" she cried, but he was already back in bed with her. His right hand moved over her body, touching the places only he knew.

"So you want all the trimmings. That trimming? This one? And how about this one?"

"Darling," she breathed. "Dix, I—"

"Don't talk. Just feel."

She surrendered herself to his touch, silently, until the throbbing of her heart took over her body and became as loud as thunder. "Now, darling! I can't stand any more!"

Even then he held back, sliding himself against her damp, waiting tissues, touching and retreating, entering and withdrawing until she was frantic with desire.

"Oh, please!" she cried. "Please!"

With one sure thrust he entered her and they rose and fell in time with the throbbing of her heart, rising and falling together, one creature created from two until he cried out and lifted her, grasped her body to his, triumphed and then fell back with her onto the bed.

They lay there then, affirmed, one to the other, exhausted and intertwined.

Gradually sense replaced sensuality and they talked freely and openly, as they had not done for months. They talked about Washington's influence on their lives and they talked about the need for them to pull together, for the children's sake and for their own.

Long after Dix had dozed off, Cassie lay awake and stared at the play of lights on the ceiling above her. She had not thought of Bo that night, nor of his death. Their lovemaking had been as it was before, in the old days, the good old days: sensuous and amusing, explosive and comforting.

She loved Dix. She had loved him from that long-ago day when they sat on the bank of San Bois Creek and skimmed flat stones on the water. Only now, however, only as a woman of thirty-five, could she realize the full potential of that love. He was a fine man, a good and wise man.

On that night of John F. Kennedy's inauguration, Cassie Steele came home at last from her journey through dark and perilous waters.

Chapter 15

Congressman and Mrs. Steele settled into a comfortable Washington life but Cassie was vaguely uneasy. She and Dix were close that night in January, so close, but they had made love only twice since then and each time it was brief, almost perfunctory. There was a gulf between them that seemed impossible to bridge.

Cully Meecham came to dinner the first night in March. It was a warm night and Cassie had opened the French doors to the back garden. The sounds of spring played in counterpoint with the muted rumble of the city's traffic: the soft buzz of night insects, the assertive clicking of a cicada near the screen doors and somewhere in the night the repeated cry of a barred owl.

"Don't you agree, Cassie?"

She looked up, startled, at the sound of Dix's voice. "I'm sorry. I must have been wool-gathering."

"Cully thinks I should go home for a week or so and touch base with the party leaders and my constituency."

Go home, she thought. The farm. Of course! That's what they needed: a touch of home. A vacation from the Washington hothouse.

"Oh, yes, Dix. Yes! I'll go, too, and we'll take the children. Temple can't miss a week of school but she can stay with Angelina."

"There y'are, Dix." Cully laughed. "I always say there ain't nothin' as good for a man as a willin' woman."

Cassie flushed. "May I give you more coffee, Cully?" she said.

"Sure thing, Cassie, and then maybe you'll excuse me and Dix. We got to talk a little politics and you won't want to bother your pretty little head with all that."

Through clenched teeth, she said, "Of course. Would you like to have your coffee in the library? I'll ask Angelina to bring a tray."

"Thanks, darling," Dix said, smiling as if he had not heard his wife insulted and then summarily dismissed.

Cassie took her own coffee into the living room. Dix probably had not even noticed. A willing woman, indeed! And the man's automatic assumption that a political discussion would be over her "pretty little head." She drew back her fist, but stopped. She did not really want to hit the sofa pillow. She wanted to hit Cully Meecham.

To Cassie's disgust, Cully Meecham was waiting for them when they pulled to a stop in front of the farmhouse. She was delighted to take the children and escape to the outdoors. While Dix and Cully put their heads together to work out the week's schedule, Cassie and the children walked the farm with Henry Starr.

Thanks to Henry and his dim but hard-working son-in-law Bubba Vance, the farm was in apple-pie order. Martha walked next to Cassie as sedately as Cassie walked with Henry, but Taylor darted this way and that, investigating everything in sight.

Cassie duly admired the tautness of the barbed-wire fences and the appearance of the freshly painted barn, but her mind behaved like Taylor, leaping from the incredible cobalt blue of the sky to the sound of cicadas in the woods, to the flash of a robin's breast in the sunshine, to the smooth feel of the red clay she picked up from the road, crumbled and let trickle between her fingers.

"Your garden looks good this year, Henry."

"Yep. Planted on the new moon and it shows, don't it? Aim to sell some of the produce in town and take the rest over to my daughter. She'll put it up in Mason jars, enough for them and me both. I wouldn't give you nothin' for them store-bought canned vegetables. Ain't got no taste at all."

Cassie pictured Bubba Vance's slovenly wife working at her wood cookstove, hauling water from the well to sterilize fruit jars. It occurred to her that it might just be a mild food-poisoning bacteria that gave home-canned food the zest Henry liked. "That's hot work, Henry, canning with a woodstove. Why don't you have Bubba bring her over here and let her use my electric stove for the canning? It will be easier on her, too, with the running water."

Henry stopped and looked at her. "Well, that's mighty neighborly of you, Cassie. I reckon she'd like that right well. Workin' in your kitchen there will be kind of like a vacation for her."

The children went with Henry to see the new kittens in the barn, and Cassie strolled down to San Bois Creek alone. She turned to look toward the hills where a limestone cliff served as her brother's tombstone. She could not see it from the creek but she knew it was there. It would always be there. It had been almost a year since the night she shot Bo Taylor but her guilt still existed, like a poison encapsulated in her soul.

Firmly she turned her back on the hills and walked on till she came to the shade of an oak tree, a place where she and Dix had once made love. The rich smells of the countryside surrounded her and the soft chuckle of the rippling creek encompassed her as the land worked its old magic, reminding her of who she had been, who she was and who she would be. Unfortunately, it also brought up the old memories of that hot night when she heard noises in the kitchen.

Spring had burst upon Washington by the time they returned to the house on R Street. Almost before Cassie was aware of it, Taylor had his fifth birthday and it was April and she was thirty-six and was taking Temple and the children to see the cloud of cherry blossoms around the Tidal Basin.

In the spring of 1961, the Cherry Blossom Festival was over-shadowed by the dark events in Cuba: the CIA-designed fiasco at the Bay of Pigs. Washington thrived on rumors and they reached a new high in the weeks after the aborted invasion of Cuba by American-supported Free Cuba forces. Would the promised air support have helped? Why were the CIA codes in such a shambles? Why did President Eisenhower approve the plan? Why did President Kennedy agree to it?

"The whole sorry mess seems to be another CIA foul-up," Dix said angrily. "I half suspect that it was bungled just to embarrass Jack Kennedy."

"Oh, no!" Cassie said. "Surely not even the CIA would spend so many lives just to make a point."

"Maybe not, but it sure as hell shows a lack of judgement on their part."

"Perhaps on *his* part, too." Cassie was startled to find herself thinking the unthinkable, saying the unsayable. "President Kennedy could have stopped it, couldn't he, if he thought it was a bad plan?"

"Of course, but his advisors recommended that he do it, and—"

"And a President has to do what his advisors tell him to do?" She tried to stop herself, but she had to say it. "How about you, Dix? Suppose your advisors—suppose Cully recommended some course of action. Would you follow through on it even if you thought it was wrong?"

"I'd want to hear both sides first, and take it all into account in making a decision, but I'm not the President, Cassie. My decisions don't affect millions of people."

"Your decisions affect thousands of Oklahomans, though. Don't they count?"

He glared at her. "This is not a court of law, Counselor. My God, Cassie, a man has to do what he thinks is right, and Jack Kennedy thought he was right. What more can you ask of him?"

"I'm sorry. I thought that maybe you could do something to—"

"Never mind," he said curtly.

They went up to bed shortly after the argument, but Dix did not reach out to her that night.

Cassie lay awake for hours thinking. "What he thinks is right" was the phrase Dix used. How could a man know? A President, a representative, or for that matter, a woman? She turned restlessly in bed, unsatisfied with her thoughts.

She tried to give Dix her unqualified love and trust, but he apparently was coming to believe that his own personal compass needle pointed directly toward what was right and to deny the possibility of other, alternative rights.

On one of the few nights that Dix was neither in the house nor at a committee meeting, the two of them sat in the library, a picture of a handsome young congressman and his wife enjoying a quiet evening at home. Dix, at the desk, read through a mountain of paperwork reports that seemed to grow rather than shrink, while Cassie curled up on the couch with a book open on her lap.

She did not see the words, however. Instead, she saw the scene that had occupied her mind constantly since the trip home to the farm. Again and again it played itself through like an endless filmstrip that ran ceaselessly, day and night.

She could stand it no more. "Dix?" she said suddenly. "Can we talk for a while?"

He stacked his papers, frowning. "I'm bushed tonight. Can't it wait for tomorrow?"

"No," she said. "I have to tell you something." Her voice was firm, but when he sat back in his chair and looked at her, the words would not come. "Dix, I—" she said, and stopped. He was so far away from her, sitting at his desk like a judge hearing evidence.

"Well?"

"Dix, I—could you come over here? Please?"

Something in her voice evidently reached across the gulf that separated them. He looked surprised, but without a word he crossed the room to sit down on the couch beside her, not touching, but close by.

Cassie tried to find a way into the story. "Do you remember when you had to go to Oklahoma City for a special session of the state senate? Just a few weeks after the Democratic primary?"

"Last May? You want to talk about last May? For God's sake, Cassie! I've got a heavy day tomorrow and I need to get some sleep."

"No!" She turned toward him. "Please, darling, please hear me out! Last May. I was in bed, at the farm, when I heard something—" She looked down at her hands twisting a handkerchief in her lap. "Or someone—in the kitchen. It was Bo."

"Bo Taylor? Your brother? I thought he was in San Quentin."

"He was in our kitchen." Cassie began to tell him about that night. She was calm when she told him about the warrant from Arkansas, but as she told more and more, her voice became high and breathless. At some point, she realized that Dix was holding her hand tightly, and then later, that he was holding her close and she was half-crying, half-talking into his shirt front.

"I killed him, Dix. I shot him dead."

Did he pull away from her? Did the grip of his arms weaken slightly? She kept her head against his shoulder, afraid to look up at his face, afraid to see what was in his eyes.

"My God," he said softly. "Oh, my God."

"Henry helped me—clean up," she said, pushing ahead because now that she had told so much, she had to tell it all. "He helped me take Bo—take the body away." She took a deep breath. "Dix, if it is impossible for you to—if you can't stand to be with me because of what I've done, tell me now, will you? Please tell me now. I can't take any more wondering if—"

"Wondering? Wondering if *I* can stand it? For God's sake, Cassie!" He pushed her away and she had to look at his eyes. There was no disapproval there. She saw only concern.

He took her two hands in his and looked straight at her. "You had no choice, my dear, no choice at all. You have no more to feel guilty about that than a mother tiger protecting her young. You did what you had to do, and I thank God you had the strength. Don't blame yourself."

"Oh, Dix. Darling. If you knew what a relief it is to tell you, finally."

"That's what I don't understand. It's been almost a year, Cassie. Why haven't you told me before?"

"Dix, I wanted to, oh, God, I wanted to." She hesitated. "But you've had so much on your mind that I hated to add to it."

"God, Cassie, is this what's been between us this year? Is this what made you withdraw from me?"

She looked down. "I suppose it is. The guilt has—"

"The guilt you've hugged to you, right?" He stood up abruptly and crossed the room to the desk. "That you couldn't tell me about."

"I was afraid you would feel that you had to tell—the police, I guess."

"You guessed." He turned to look at her and she caught her breath at the sadness in his eyes. "You guessed, but you had so little confidence in me that you were afraid to be honest with me. You did not trust me."

"No, Dix. No! It's just that you are so certain about things, so sure of what's right and what's wrong."

"Oh, God!" He sank into an armchair. "Have I become such a demagogue, Cassie?" Roughly he rubbed his hand across his eyes. "I have let you down."

She hurried across the library to kneel by his chair. "That's not so. If I had only told you about it from the first—"

He put his arms around her. "If you had told me—I don't know, dear, whether I could have helped you or not. I only know that I love you more than life itself."

Cassie felt herself relaxing into a freedom she had not known since that night in May. "Dix. Darling. That is all the help I need.

Just to know that *you* know and that you still love me, that's enough."

In bed that night each held the other, but it was not in passion. They held each other for the reassurance, like two children clinging together against the terrors of a dark impenetrable wood.

Cassie stumbled through her duties the next day, her mind far from the minutiae of everyday life. The House sat until late, and by the time Dix came home the children were sound asleep and Temple was in her room, ostensibly doing her homework.

Dix sat down in the library to sip a Scotch and water. "Cassie, I've been thinking all day about what you told me last night."

Cassie's heart fell. "I know that what I did was wrong, Dix, dreadfully wrong."

He shook his head impatiently. "That's not what I was thinking about. I can't see that right or wrong has much to do with it, Cassie. You did what had to be done. But the fact that you didn't tell me about it, I think that was wrong."

"But if I had told you—"

"I know, I know. You did not trust me." He set his glass on the desk and scowled at her. "And by not trusting me, you failed me."

She bowed her head. "I suppose I did."

"But I have failed you, too."

"Oh, no, darling, I—" She realized what he had said. "What do you mean?"

His pain seemed almost physical. "I've failed you, my wife, but I've failed my constituents, too, and my country."

"That isn't so, Dix. You work harder than most—"

He laughed bitterly. "Sure I do. I do my homework, don't I? I read the reports and I study the issues and when I am ready to cast my vote, I discover that it was pointless even to show up because the issue has been decided long before the bill comes to committee or even to the floor of the House. A deal has been cut, a deal based on politics or an exchange of favors. I might as well have stayed home."

Cassie sat up. "Come on, now, Dix. The same sort of thing happened in the state senate back in Oklahoma."

"Perhaps it did, but not on this scale. Look, last week we were asked to provide a supplemental appropriation to cover a shortfall in the Government Printing Office. I nosed around and discovered a three-year-old report from the Government Accounting Office. The shortfall at the GPO almost exactly matches the figure the GAO considers waste."

"That's appalling! Can't anyone do anything?"

" 'Anyone,' in this case, is a House committee. The committee received this report three years ago and it has yet to take any action. Which means that the GPO has received a supplemental appropriation each year and the waste has stayed the same or has even grown in proportion to the new budget figure."

Cassie looked at him across the room. "Dix, why haven't you told me about this before?"

"For the same reason you didn't tell me about Bo. I didn't want you to know something that might make you think less of me."

"But it's not the same thing, not at all!"

He picked up his glass and sipped his drink. "Of course not. But the end result has been the same. Our secrecy has driven a wedge between us."

"Yes," Cassie said. "Yes."

"So, no more secrets?"

"Of course!" She jumped up from the couch and he stood up to take her in his arms. "No more secrets, darling."

Cassie thought of that period as the springtime of their love for each other. They walked hand in hand through the narrow streets of Georgetown and they giggled together like children let out of school. There was constant political discussion and even more discussion of Dix's own role in the House. Gradually her mental picture of the night of Bo's death faded and was set aside, not to be forgotten, never to be forgotten, but to take its place in a parade of memories.

The idyll ended, however, on the night Dix came home late from a meeting. His face was tense and worried.

"Dix! What's wrong?"

He flopped down in an armchair in the library. "I've been with black leaders all evening. There's trouble ahead, Cassie. Big trouble. CORE, the Congress of Racial Equality, sent out a busload of people today, seven blacks and six whites who call themselves 'Freedom Riders.' They're headed for the Deep South with the idea of challenging segregation in every bus terminal—in restaurants and waiting rooms and restrooms."

Cassie sank onto a chair, remembering the fighting she had seen on TV when time and time again Southern whites reacted violently to black confrontation. "Oh, Dix, why? If they would only wait—the President has said that he's committed to racial equality!"

"He's committed all right, but he has been in office since January and the blacks have seen no clear-cut action." He stretched, easing his back. "The people I saw tonight think that Kennedy is too involved in foreign policy to do anything at home. They're tired of it, Cassie. Tired of hearing, 'Wait, this is not a good time. Wait till later.' If it comes to a showdown, though, they're sure that the President and the attorney general will back them, so they're taking matters into their own hands."

"There will be fighting," Cassie said softly.

"I know. And some of them may die."

Cassie monitored the reports of the first minor clashes. In South Carolina, three Freedom Riders were beaten and two arrested. The trip through Georgia was peaceful and in the Atlanta bus terminal, protected by Georgia State Troopers, the Riders split into two groups for the ride on to Birmingham. Then, near Anniston, Alabama, the Ku Klux Klan ambushed one bus, fire-bombing it and beating twelve passengers. In Anniston itself, the other bus was attacked by young toughs who dragged the Riders into the aisle of the bus and punched them until the police came. In Birmingham, a mob armed with lead pipes dragged the Riders into the terminal and beat them so badly that three had to be sent to the hospital. Police Commissioner "Bull" Connor provided no protection at all.

Dix came home with the good news that Robert Kennedy was trying to get in touch with the governor of Alabama to negotiate a peace. When nothing happened, the attorney general asked the blacks for a cooling-off period, but a CORE member said that American blacks had been cooling off for a hundred years.

The Freedom Riders' bus pulled into Montgomery, Alabama, where a mob of several thousand was waiting, with no police in evidence. A melee followed, with Southern whites beating everyone, Riders and bystanders alike. In the end President Kennedy's personal envoy lay on the sidewalk in a pool of his own blood.

Bobby Kennedy sent riot-trained federal marshals to the airbase outside Montgomery, where they were assembled by the attorney general's own representative, Byron White.

Martin Luther King, Jr., flew to Montgomery and called for a rally at the First Baptist Church. The church was attacked but was defended by federal marshals, the Alabama Highway Patrol and the National Guard. At last, it was over.

"Thank God no one was killed," Cassie said.

"But many were badly injured," Dix said. "Who knows, maybe it was worth it. Martin King says that Jim Crow has been eliminated from public transportation."

Cassie shook her head sadly. "Can anything be worth the kind of violence we have seen this week?"

Dix was at the House early those mornings, and stayed late, which meant that Cassie had more time to be with her children. They spent hours exploring Georgetown, from Towpath Row to the Old Stone House. At five, Taylor was blessed with sturdy legs and boundless energy, but Martha would not be four until September and her stamina was limited. If they planned a long walk through the gardens of Dumbarton Oaks, Cassie took the stroller along. She ambled and Martha rode amiably among the flowers while Taylor darted here and there in hot pursuit of the imaginary foe of the week: bears or monsters or tigers. By the end of June, summer had set in, as hot and humid as a Turkish bath, and Cassie lounged in the minute back garden of the house on R Street while the children played in their wading pool. Temple Vance, *née* Shirley Temple, sometimes joined them to lie on a beach towel and perfect her already impeccable tan.

Although she had been thirty-six for only a few months, it seemed to Cassie that her life was crashing toward forty. It was depressing to look at Temple, at all that smooth young skin with its peach-glow tan. Temple did not have crowsfeet or an incipient wrinkle between her eyebrows. Temple at seventeen was a fresh new woman, unmarked by life, unscarred.

At least Temple liked to read, Cassie thought, consoling herself. The girl was not just a beauty goddess. To Cassie's way of thinking, reading was a good in itself, even if the book was a paperback with a lurid illustration on the cover. Moreover, she had to give Temple credit: What seventeen-year-old girl would be more interested in economics than in high romance on the Scottish moors?

The two of them talked, sometimes, while the children splashed and laughed, and Cassie learned that Temple had other interests besides romance.

One sultry afternoon Cassie asked her, "Do you miss the farm and your family terribly?"

"The farm?" Temple's eyes were so blank that for an instant Cassie thought the girl had forgotten the question. "Hell, no. Why would I miss that old place and all them people?" She laughed and rolled onto her back, tugging at a bathing suit that had shrunk. Or perhaps Temple had grown, Cassie thought, making a mental note to take Temple shopping for a swimsuit in a larger breast size.

"*Those* people are your parents, Temple, and your brothers and the farm is your home. And ladies do not say 'hell' in conversation."

Temple laughed. "Guess I ain't cut out to be a lady anyways. I'm trying to work on my grammar, though. Can't get you a government job lessen you got pretty good grammar."

"I'll be glad to help you with that, dear. Is a government job what you want most?"

"No'm, not really. It's just a way I can stay here when you folks go back home, that's all." She paused and her eyes appeared to glaze over as she concentrated on her inner self. "I want—I want a house like this here, and a big car, and clothes like you got." She turned toward Cassie. "Reckon you think it's silly, coming from somebody like me, but I'll tell you, I want it all."

A shiver of recognition ran down Cassie's spine. Was this the Vance sister who was what she herself had been at seventeen? Ruby Keeler was honest and true, a hard worker, but she was not driven to succeed. She was a girl who recognized her limitations, something Cassie never did and never wanted to do. Like Temple, Cassie had wanted it all and she had driven herself to get it. "Then you're already planning to work your way through college, Temple?"

"College? In a pig's eye. That's too much work."

The tremor in Cassie's spine subsided. She appraised the girl. With her amber eyes and her mane of tousled red hair, she had the wary look of a young animal, a fawn, pausing in the border of a wood to survey the dangerous plains ahead. She looked at Temple again and saw her full rich lips and her pointed chin. Not a nervous fawn, she thought. More likely a young tigress lurking in the concealing shadows until her prey appeared. "Then how do you expect to get what you want, to get it all?"

Temple looked at her in surprise. "With a man, of course. I want to go to the big parties and know important people and all that. So I got to get through high school and get a job and the right clothes and then I'll get me a man."

A man. Cassie felt a twinge of guilt. She was proud of what she had done in the past, but the past was past; and now, in the spring of 1961, her real life was uncomfortably similar to Temple's imagined one. She was dependent on a man. Was she so different from Temple Vance after all?

She was relieved at the need to jump up from her chair and settle a small battle as to whether it was Martha's turn to hold the hose or Taylor's. She ended by being thoroughly sprayed herself and wrestling in the wading pool, laughing, with both children. She looked up once to see Temple watching, just watching, but Cassie turned away, unaccountably chilly on a hot day in June.

Chapter 16

 Taylor Steele clung to his mother's hand as they approached his new school and his first day of kindergarten. It was September of 1961 and the morning was already heavy with damp heat.

Cassie was prepared to deal with cold feet, shyness, even copious tears, but she was not ready to deal with her own sense of loss.

There were six other little boys dressed in the school's hot-weather uniform of soft white shirt, blue and white seersucker shorts, white knee socks and snowy white tennis shoes. The six little girls wore the same outfits with seersucker jumpers substituted for shorts. Taylor took one look at the other children, released Cassie's hand and without a backward look switched allegiance from his mother to his schoolmates.

A plump smiling teacher with a yellow pencil stuck in her bun herded the girls and boys into a line of sorts.

The other mothers, like Cassie, looked bereft and strangely empty-handed, except for one short brunette whose little girl was wrapped inextricably in her mother's full skirts. The mother's expression was confused, a mix of concern, embarrassment and a glimmer of pride, as if to say, "She needs me! Mine still needs her mother!"

The other mothers and Cassie, their children officially delivered to the educational process, lingered as if they thought their offspring might need one last cheery smile of encouragement or, perhaps, in the hope that a child might reconsider and make a last-minute break to run to the woman who had provided for all of his or her needs for the past five years.

But there were no jail breaks and the scraggly line marched into the school. At the last instant the clinging girl flung off her wrappings and ran to catch up with the smiling teacher.

The mothers shuffled their feet and said, "Imagine! Three hours of freedom!" and "I know he'll just love it!" and "I'm free again!" but the shuffles did not become steps, and although they slowly dispersed, they seemed to be on rubber bands attached to the school door, half-expecting to be tugged backward but loath to move away and let the bands snap.

Cassie walked home slowly, wondering if she had been right to agree to Dix's choice of schools for Taylor. She suspected that she would feel as lonely outside the door of any school, but this particular one stuck in her Oklahoma craw. The only dark face in the line belonged to a little boy who, she happened to know, was the eldest son of the eldest son of an incredibly wealthy king of an oil-rich Arab country. Besides the cost of uniforms and accouterments for hot and cold weather, moreover, the tuition the school charged dictated that the students' parents would be wealthy. The admissions board made sure that they would be of a proper class. She knew that she herself would never have passed the board.

Dix refused to discuss the matter. "You can't use your children to make political points," he said. He did not explain, however, why it was all right to use them to enhance one's Washington image.

That autumn of 1961, the White House was the center of interest for the entire country. Jacqueline Kennedy's face was on the cover of every magazine but *Popular Mechanics* and the articles within reported on every aspect of the First Family's life. Although many of the articles were no more than wildly speculative fiction wrapped around a tiny kernel of fact, it appeared that the American public could not get enough of them.

Washington was no different. Khrushchev's drubbing of "the

new boy," in Vienna, was overlooked, and the August shock of
the sudden appearance of the Berlin Wall was almost ignored in
the capital's love affair with its new President and his glamorous
lady. There was excitement in the very air as Washington women
shopped for pillbox hats and designer dresses and, following the
First Lady's lead, planned intimate little dinners in place of the
vast noisy cocktail parties of previous administrations. It was a
style of entertaining which suited Cassie perfectly and that fall she
began to have a small reputation for her dinners. There was always
an element of surprise at the Steeles' dinners, an unusual guest or
an item not to be found on other Washington menus, such as
black-eyed peas, which Helen Corbitt of Neiman-Marcus called
"Texas caviar."

Dix invariably complimented Cassie on her parties, but she was
not satisfied. She was a lawyer, not a cook, even though she did
not practice her profession, but her decision to be a good congressional wife seemed to require no more than a deep understanding
of after-dinner mints. She and Dix discussed what was happening
in the House, but that was his career, not hers. She felt that she
was limited to the role of the happy little housewife who should
be content with having an opinion on menus and recipes but never
on the state of the union. She began to feel that she was being
reduced to Cully Meecham's "pretty little head."

The most coveted invitation in Washington that fall was for
dinner at the White House, but freshmen congressmen from Oklahoma did not appear on lists with such august names as Leonard
Bernstein and André Malraux.

In September, too, black Americans' enthusiasm for John Kennedy was rekindled when James Meredith applied to be the first
Negro ever to attend the University of Mississippi. This time there
was no hesitation and there were no delays. From the start, the
Kennedys backed Meredith's attempts to be registered. Through
rioting, through gas and shotgun attacks, through the arrests of
two hundred rioters (only twenty-five of whom were University

of Mississippi students), through the shooting deaths of a French correspondent and a bystander, the Kennedys kept up the pressure until James Meredith was duly registered as a political science major at Ol' Miss.

The Steeles went home for Thanksgiving, home to the farm for a week. The weather was dreadful the day they arrived in Oklahoma, hazy with damp cold, the fields yellowed, and against the darkening sky the bare trees stretched out branches like bony claws. It was spitting snow when they stopped in front of the house, but they had called ahead so Henry Starr had the furnace on and a roaring hickory fire in the fireplace. The house was filled with the sweet smell of hickory smoke and the rich spices of the stew Henry had thawed and set to simmer on the kitchen stove.

Taylor and Martha were exhausted by the long flight and were half asleep as they sat at the dining table and ate stew with their parents. Afterward they were happy to go to their warm beds.

Dix poured a tot of twelve-year-old bourbon for himself and one for Cassie. She sat back in her chair, sipping at bourbon as powerful as brandy and warming her feet on an ottoman near the fire. It had been months since she felt so relaxed, so comfortable in her skin. She set down her glass and stretched like an enormous cat, flexing every muscle from her head to her toes.

Dix chuckled. "You look like the cat that swallowed the canary."

Cassie laughed too, startled that he had picked up the same image. "That's how I feel, darling: cat-warm, cat-happy, cat-content. Meeow!"

"The kids are sound asleep. Let's go for a walk."

Cassie shuddered but she realized that with a warm house to come back to, and a warm bed, it might be pleasant.

Cassie laughed at Dix as he put on an old jacket and sweater and mismatched mittens: warm clothes that had been jammed into the back of the closet. "If only the House could see you now, Dix! You look more like a scarecrow than a congressman!"

"And is this the beautifully dressed Mrs. Dixon Steele? I think I'll take a snapshot and pass it around at your next dinner party."

"Not if you value your life!"

The snow had passed on to the east and a dark bank of clouds hung over the Ozarks. There were layers of mist downhill from the house, where cold air was warmed by the waters of San Bois Creek. The sky was clear by the house, however, the air was crisp, and above them a thousand stars glittered in a blue velvet sky.

Dix's voice was hushed. "It is beautiful."

Cassie was awed too. "We forget sometimes."

"Yes."

She turned and looked up at Dix. "We have to remember, darling. We must!"

They stumbled, crossing the pasture to the road. The darkness confused their senses and made them step over rocks that did not exist and tense their muscles for ruts that were not there.

Cassie almost fell.

"Here, love," he said. "Let me give you a hand."

She looked down at his mismatched mittens and laughed. "The red one or the blue one?"

Then, suddenly, his arms were around her and he was kissing her roughly, forcing her head back.

"Let's—let's go inside," she said weakly.

Like a good countryman, Dix built up the fire and checked the front and back doors while Cassie went in to cover the children. When they met in the living room, however, the countryman had disappeared. He turned off the lights and left the room lit only by the leaping red flames in the fireplace.

"Take off your clothes," he said abruptly.

"Here? But—"

"Here."

Watching him closely, watching his hard glittering eyes shining red in the firelight, Cassie pulled off her threadbare plaid jacket and torn sweater, but this time neither of them laughed at her outfit. Slowly she pulled her cashmere turtleneck over her head and let it drop to the floor unheeded while she stepped out of her wool socks and fur-lined moccasins and let her slacks slide down to her ankles. She hesitated then, wearing only a lacy beige brassiere and beige panties, and looked at Dix. He nodded once, firmly. She reached back to unhook her bra and dropped it, then she tucked her hands into the sides of her panties and pushed them down, slowly, until she could step out of them, one foot and then the other. She stood up with the red firelight playing over her body. Chin high, full breasts lifted, long slender legs stretched, she stood there tall and unashamed either of her body or of her nakedness. She looked again at Dix.

His eyes explored her body from her blond hair to her eyes to her lips to her breasts and her body and her long legs. He made an abrupt gesture of command and Cassie sank to the floor, to the thick Persian rug littered with her discarded clothes.

Dix looked down at her lying at his feet in the firelight and then, deliberately, he pulled off his old jacket and his wool shirt, kicked off his shoes and undid his fly and let his trousers fall, the change in the pockets jingling. Slowly, he pushed down his shorts, stepped out of them and stood above her. With his tousled black hair and his eyes gleaming red in the firelight, he looked like a savage standing over her, tall and strong and hugely erect.

Then he too dropped to the floor and bracing himself so that no other part of their bodies touched, he drove himself into her waiting, ready body. That one thrust into her released in each of them the passion that had built during those long minutes of stripping from themselves not only their clothes but also their civilization. Like wild animals coming together they released years, centuries, eons of lust in one mighty heave of coupling, his body driving down to impale her, and hers driving up from beneath to capture his.

They cried out then, as one, in a cry that might have come from deep in the silent woods, from a hidden cave in the hills, a lair where panthers coupled and screamed at the moment of release. They sank, sealed together as if by a stake driven through their two bodies. Dix was heavy upon Cassie, his lust fulfilled, his animal appetites satiated.

"Dix," Cassie moaned. "Dix, darling."

He grunted.

She cradled his head against her sweat-damp shoulder. "What would I do without you, my love? How could I live, without you?"

Dix rolled off of her and lay back on the floor.

He raised himself on an elbow and switched on a table lamp. "I want to look at you."

She smiled up at him, loving him. His face was shadowed but he moved and she could see his eyes. He looked at her not with love, not even with satisfaction, but as if he were appraising the body of a strange female and ranking it on some private scale.

Cassie caught her breath and felt behind her for her sweater, for a jacket, for anything that would cover her nakedness. Her fingers touched her cashmere pullover but lost the strength to grasp it in her sudden understanding of the need she felt to hide herself.

She was ashamed. For the first time in all of her years with Dixon Steele, her nakedness before him shamed her.

Had she changed so much? Perhaps she had become the proper little homemaker after all. Or did his look of appraisal impose the shame upon her?

"The light," she said. "Turn off the light."

"Why? We have to find our clothes."

In the light she gathered her things, in the light she led the way to their bedroom, but she had lost all sense of happiness. She was too much aware of his cool, measuring eyes on her back. She blinked, trying to hold back the tears. She had lost something, something important, but she did not know what it was.

In the early morning, before first light, Cassie was awakened by a cramp in her arm. She worked it out from under Dix's shoulder and for comfort, both of body and mind, she fitted herself against his back spoon-fashion. In his sleep he moved away from her and she rolled onto her back. The wild excitement of their lovemaking the night before looked very different in the dawn light.

It was then that she knew what she had lost. She was thirty-six years old, she had been married twice and she had borne two children. For God's sake, she had even killed a man! She wanted to laugh, but she could not. Instead she rolled away from her sleeping husband and used the edge of the blanket to stifle a sob because she realized that no matter how much she and Dix loved each other, no matter how good a life they shared, in the end he was a man and she was no more than his woman. She wept because she realized that at some moment during that night of abandon, Cassie Steele had lost her innocence.

Dix left in the crisp morning sunlight to meet with party leaders in Oklahoma City. Cassie watched him drive away, then on an impulse got Taylor and Martha into their jackets and wool caps and took them for a walk down the road.

Watching her children darting from road to ditch and back, and hearing their laughter, lifted her spirits a little. She might be a lost woman, but from the children's joy and curiosity about their world, she was at least a good mother.

The mailbox at the end of the road was stuffed with the usual junk mail from feed companies and farm equipment dealers, but there was one legal-sized envelope addressed to her. The return address was that of James Steele's law offices in Ballard. Cassie's hands shook. He has learned about Bo's death, she thought. Somehow he has found me out. She ripped open the envelope and skimmed the single page it contained. With great relief she saw that Bo's name was not even mentioned.

As you will understand, after our last confrontation it is difficult for me to write to you, especially when it is to ask a favor. It has come to my attention, however, that the breach between us has affected a third party whose innocence is obvious. I refer to my wife Amelia, whose loneliness for her grandchildren is overwhelming.

I proffer no apologies nor do I ask apologies of you. I ask only that Amelia may no longer be made to suffer by the estrangement between you and me.

I propose to drive Amelia to the farm on Sunday. I will wait in the car, and I will seek no contact with you or your children.

If this plan is acceptable, please call my secretary.

Cassie crumpled the letter in her fist. Let James come to the farm? After the way he had treated her through the years? After the way he had spoken to her when the Ward Jackson case ended? Never!

"What's this, Mama?" Taylor held up a stick with a cocoon attached to it. Cassie squatted down to explain cocoons to him and to Martha, who came running to see what her brother had found. Cassie stood up and listened, smiling, as the two children made elaborate plans to take the cocoon back to Washington and see what emerged. She touched Martha's hair and then Taylor's. They were so dear to her, so dear.

The children ran ahead to search for more cocoons but Cassie smoothed the crumpled letter and read again the part about Amelia's loneliness. James was right, damn it. Amelia should not have to pay the cost of their battles.

Her decision made, it was with a lighter step that she followed the children back to the house. She called Amelia right away and invited her to spend Sunday at the farm.

Amelia and the children were so glad to see each other that Cassie felt terribly guilty for having kept them apart. She glanced out the front window once, to see James sitting alone in his black Cadillac. She did not feel *that* guilty.

When she had finished setting the table and checked the chili one last time, however, she found herself walking straight through the living room and out the front door.

He got out of the car and took off his broad-brimmed black hat. "Cassie."

"James."

He *was* old, she saw, and he looked as tired as death. He had lost weight, too, and his once-bulky shoulders were thin and slumped under the cloth of his expensive suit. "Dixon is away?"

"Yes."

"I was hoping I could talk to you privately. Driving down here this morning, I realized that Amelia is not the only one who is suffering under the present arrangement. I, too, am lonely for my grandchildren." He took a deep breath. "I would like to end our estrangement."

"You were the one who caused it, James."

"No, Cassie Taylor, you caused it with your unfounded charges against me. You never proved that I was responsible for the actions of my farm agent."

"I proved it well enough to convince the jury."

"Juries," he said in disgust. "They'll believe anything if you tug at their heartstrings, and you damn near played 'Dixie' on that jury's heartstrings."

"James, I do believe you've made a joke."

He flushed. "This is not a joking matter."

Cassie smiled. "But it is the way to resolve the differences between us? I think we are past settling things amicably."

James seemed to gather himself. "As you know, I was fined heavily in the Jackson case. I paid that fine and I fired Cliff Boatwright and I helped Ward Jackson build a decent house for himself and his family. I have also made sure that his children are in school and are well-treated there." He stood a little straighter. "I have since joined and taken an active part in the NAACP, and I have made substantial donations to that organization and to Martin

Luther King's group, the Southern Christian Leadership Conference."

"All tax deductible, of course."

A flash of anger crossed his face, but he spoke calmly. "There are three reasons for these actions. First, whatever my responsibility in it, what was done to that young Negro and his family was reprehensible, and I wanted not only to make amends for it but also to ensure that a similar situation never develops."

Cassie started to speak, but James Steele waved her to silence.

"Second, I have come to realize that my son Dixon is right. Racial equality must be recognized and practiced, throughout the United States. Third—" He hesitated, turning his hat in his hands. "The third reason, Cassie, is that I want to bring to an end the acrimony between the two of us. For my actions against you, I sincerely ask your forgiveness. But if for no other reason, it should end, it *must* end, because by my own stupidity I have deprived my dear wife and myself of being with our grandchildren."

Cassie thought of the other things he had done to her through the years: the therapeutic abortion, the attempts to use Bo's situation for blackmail, the constant slights and insults. She wanted to laugh, but she knew that James's change of heart had cost him far more than money.

"She needs them to love," he said, "and I need them, too, very much. I need to see them grow and develop." He paused. "The older I grow, the more I need them and need to see in them the proof that when I go I will not just fade into nothingness. I need them to remember me and to know that I once existed."

Cassie looked away. She cleared her throat. "And what are our differences compared with eternity? Is that what you're saying?"

"Yes, I believe it is."

Cassie pulled her sweater close. "Ours is 'a tale told by an idiot,' isn't it, James?"

" 'Full of sound and fury,' " he said.

" 'Signifying nothing.' " She turned to face him. "We have

known each other since 1930, James. For over thirty years. I don't think that we'll ever be able to forget the pain we have inflicted on each other. Can we ever set it aside? Can we seal off the past?"

"I hope so, Cassie, with every fiber of my being. I hope so."

"I hope so, too, James. I'm willing to try."

They stood in the road and looked at each other, wary but willing. He cleared his throat. "Would it be possible for me to see the children?"

When Dix came home that night Cassie told Dix about it.

He frowned. "My father's getting soft in his old age, and for that matter, so are you."

"Do you think so?"

He looked at her speculatively. "Yes, I think you are." Suddenly he smiled at her with that wide-open grin she loved so much. "Cassie, what you did for my parents was very generous. I'm proud of you." He stood up and reached out to her. "Come on, babe. Let's go to bed."

Her knees went weak. He was no more than a man but perhaps, after all, she was no more than a woman. Was that so bad?

Chapter 17

If Cassie had known how pleased Dix would be by her reconciliation with his father, she would have made an effort toward it long before.

"I know what it must have cost you, Cassie, and I appreciate it."

Cassie did not tell him that it had not cost her all that much. Her battles with James had gone on for so long that he no longer had the power to touch her deeply.

Early in December, Dix had to make a flying trip to Oklahoma, but Cassie stayed home and worked on her Christmas preparations. She was in the sitting room addressing cards the morning that Blair Fuller called.

"What's this I hear about you being all alone while that scoundrel Dix is off gallivanting?"

"Blair, he is not gallivanting, he has political business in Oklahoma." She heard the defensiveness in her own voice and laughed to hide it. "And for heaven's sake, don't talk about it. You know Washington—they'll have us divorced before the week is out! While I've got you, why don't we go out to dinner tonight?"

"Sorry, but I promised my parents I'd go home for dinner and— Cassie, why don't you come with me?"

"I couldn't impose myself on your mother like that, Blair."

"Nonsense! They complain that I never bring any of my friends home. I'll call Mother, and I'll pick you up at six. Don't dress, it's just a family dinner and we'll probably eat in the den. I'm wearing a sweater and skirt."

A sweater and skirt, Cassie thought as she hung up. In old-money language that was sure to mean an imported tweed skirt, a cashmere twin set and real pearls. She dressed accordingly in a deceptively simple wool shirtwaist dress with a narrow leather belt. For jewelry she wore only a thin gold chain.

"You never told me you had a Mercedes sedan!" Cassie said as she closed herself into the car.

"You never asked, did you?" Blair fumbled with the gear shift and the car shot away from the curb.

Cassie realized that her friend was edgy and unusually nervous. "What's wrong, Blair?"

"Oh, damn, it's the parents bit, that's all."

Cassie's heart sank. "Oh. You think they won't approve of me as your friend."

Fortunately Blair had just stopped for a red light, because she turned toward Cassie, open-mouthed. "Not approve of *you?* Not like *you?* You've got it all turned around! I'm afraid you won't like *them!* My mother and father are—well—odd. The family thinks they're sort of dotty. You know, gaga."

Cassie was confused. "I thought—I don't know what I thought."

Blair, her fears revealed, had her mind on her driving again. "They're rather ancient. They married late and I'm the younger of two children. Their families were surprised, I hear. The truth is, Cassie, that no one expected either of them to marry. Each of them was assigned a position early in life, Dad to be the son who looked after his antique aunts, and Mother, the daughter who stayed home and comforted her parents in their old age. You know how families are."

Cassie thought back to her own family, in its ramshackle tenant house: her grandmother, holding the family together by hook and by crook, her drunken father, beaten down by the Depression, and the wild half brother she herself had shot dead on a May night.

"No," she said softly, "I don't know very much about families."

Blair drove into a circular driveway and Cassie caught her breath. The house was very large, one of the old Georgetown mansions, a Federal brick presenting its clean fine lines and tall windows to the gardens and the circular drive. She could imagine its owners: Blair's father would be tall and thin, with a narrow aristocratic nose, down which he would look at the interloper; and Blair's mother, whose family probably came on the Mayflower, would be tall and regal, cool to a sharecropper's daughter from Oklahoma. Blair stopped the car with a spew of gravel, and by the time they were out of the car, the front door was open wide.

The maid who greeted them had a pug nose and a fresh Irish face. She wore a neat gray uniform and a starched white cap.

"Hi, Kathleen. In the den, as usual?"

"Yes, Miss Blair. They'd like you to come right through."

Cassie had stopped dead in the hall. It was larger than their library on R Street and was hung with portraits of long-gone Fullers. One painting she recognized as a Copley and she was almost sure that another one was by John Singer Sargent. Through the doors to the left she could see a softly lit room furnished with brocaded chairs and fine examples of Chippendale tables and chests. To the right was a formal dining room with a beautiful Sheraton table that would surely seat twenty in perfect comfort.

"Come on, Cassie," Blair said, and led the way straight down the hall. Cassie saw some of the workings of the house then: a butler's pantry with glass-doored shelves holding a wealth of crystal and china, a huge kitchen where a plump white-uniformed cook stirred something in a restaurant-sized pot, and across the hall a small room which must have been the servants' living room, with a large television and a half-knit sweater on a side table.

They passed through the door at the end of the hall and Cassie paused in surprise. They were in a large semicircular room with windows all around its curve. It had probably been a solarium in some distant past, but now long tables stretched across half the room, tables cluttered with what appeared to be new and half-done projects involving the use of masses of reeds and grasses and scraggly branches. The other half of the room was equally cluttered with rattan tables and settees and floor lamps and five or six large rattan armchairs pulled up around a roaring fire in a stone fireplace set into the wall of the house itself.

"Mother and Dad, may I introduce my friend Cassie Steele. Cassie, my parents."

Two faces emerged from the welter of things in the rattan half of the room, not the long aristocratic faces Cassie had expected, but faces that were round and windburned and jolly. When the Fullers rose to their feet, she saw that their bodies were as round and jolly as their faces.

"Cassie!" Mrs. Fuller said, "Blair has spoken of you so often! Do come and sit by me and tell me all about your delightful children!"

The woman was dressed for a family evening in a wool knit dress that had probably given up its struggle to maintain a shape in about 1943. She wore serviceable lisle stockings and stout well-polished oxfords.

Mr. Fuller hugged his daughter and beamed at Cassie. His wool pants bagged from long acquaintance with his knees, and his Harris tweed jacket was comfortably shapeless. He wore a blue oxford shirt with a badly frayed collar, and his striped necktie bore reminders of many meals.

He bustled around them until both Blair and Cassie were comfortably seated and served with glasses of a superb dry sherry.

Almost immediately the maid Kathleen began setting a table Cassie had not noticed before, a rattan-framed table with a glass top that would seat six at most.

Mrs. Fuller began an apology. "When it's just family, we dine—"

"Exceptionally early!" Mr. Fuller said triumphantly.

With that, a conversation began that was confusing at first but became, to Cassie, pure delight. Mr. and Mrs. Fuller were warm and friendly and in their way as provincial in their "cave-dweller" society as the people of San Bois, Oklahoma, were in their dirt-farmer society. What's more, the Fullers obviously adored each other, but adored even more finishing each other's sentences.

Mrs. Fuller leaned close to Cassie. "When Blair proposed that she buy a house of her own, we said—"

"Go ahead!" said Mr. Fuller, beaming at his daughter. "The fledgling must leave the nest, we said, it must fly on its—"

"Own wings!" Mrs. Fuller smiled and took Cassie's hand. "But we want to hear about you, my dear. Blair tells us that you are not only a wife and mother, but an attorney as well. Do tell us all about your—"

"Latest case!"

"The truth is," Cassie said tentatively, expecting the conversational ball to be snatched from her at any instant, "the truth is that I haven't practiced law for several years. The last major case I argued was as prosecutor in a criminal case of involuntary servitude."

Blair inserted a comment. "She convicted her own father-in-law."

"Well!" Mr. Fuller said. "I do hope it hasn't led to—"

"Ill feelings!" Mrs. Fuller said.

"It did, yes, but we are reconciled now. In fact, my husband's parents are coming to Washington for Christmas." On a sudden impulse she added, "I would like very much for you to come and meet them."

Kathleen served dinner and they sat down to a simple and delicious meal of beef stew with homemade bread.

Mrs. Fuller replied to Cassie's compliment on the stew. "It *is* good, isn't it? We do have trouble getting it, though. Our cook, Rosie, is Irish and if we don't insist, she *will* use—"

"Mutton! Tell me, Cassie, does this 'involuntary servitude' business mean that your father-in-law owned—"

"Slaves?" Mrs. Fuller asked tremulously.

"Heavens, no! It was slavery only in the narrowest legal definition of the term."

The Fullers seemed to relax. "I didn't know. I thought perhaps in Oklahoma, one still kept slaves. Of course, our grandfathers were slaveowners, but that was—"

"Hundreds of years ago!" Mr. Fuller gave Cassie one of his warmest smiles. "We know so little of the far west. We do know that Oklahoma is near all those—"

"Mountains! Bobby, dear, it's quite close to—"

"Idaho! Of course, Margaret. And it has thousands of—"

"Indians!" Mrs. Fuller looked concerned. "Tell me, Cassie, are they pacified now or do they still take—"

"Scalps?"

Cassie laughed in delight. "Oh, they're pacified, Mrs. Fuller. In fact one of the tribes, the Osage, is quite wealthy from oil production on tribal lands. And for years the Cherokees have published a bilingual newspaper in English and Cherokee."

"My dear!" Mr. Fuller said. "Surely the Indians could not—"

"Read and write?" Cassie was embarrassed that she had finished his sentence for him. Apparently the habit was contagious. "The Cherokees did. A chief named Sequoyah devised a Cherokee alphabet years ago."

"Fancy! But to go back to your husband's father. Is he a farmer?"

"No, not really. He owns farmland, but he leases it out. He's an attorney too, and he's—" Cassie paused, wishing one of the Fullers would finish the sentence for her. How could she describe what James Steele really did? "I suppose you could say that he is one of the people who run the state of Oklahoma. He makes things happen."

"And Mrs. Steele, does she help him?"

Cassie thought of the wispy Amelia and the sherry bottles hidden in her hatboxes. "No. She doesn't go out much."

"She should," Mrs. Fuller said. "It's such—"

"Fun!" Mr. Fuller said. "We do everything together, Margaret and I. We do volunteer work and we visit the sick and we play with our two grandchildren and we sit on boards and we—"

"Bank boards," Blair interjected, as if she could see that Cassie, deluged with words, was visualizing Mr. and Mrs. Fuller sitting happily side by side on long planks.

"And corporate boards," Mrs. Fuller said, "and the Smithsonian and the National Gallery and—"

"But we always save time," her father said sternly, "for what we like most of all, for—"

"Bird-watching!"

"Bird-watching," Cassie said, dazed.

"Yes. And the high point of our year is coming up. Perhaps you and your husband and his parents as well might join us for the—"

"Christmas Count!" Mrs. Fuller bounced with excitement. "The tidal flats are simply magnificent for shore birds. We wear Wellington boots and dress warmly and carry along a Thermos of hot—"

"Buttered rum!"

She looked irritated. "I was going to say 'coffee.' "

"Then let's have some! Kathleen," he called, "coffee!"

Cassie was touched by the Fullers and completely confused.

Blair drove the Mercedes out of the circular driveway. "I told you they were nuts."

"If they're nuts, I wish everyone were! They are so kind and friendly and so much in love with each other—"

"In love?" Blair was obviously startled. "Do you know," she said slowly, "I think you're right."

When he returned to Washington, Dix was amused by Cassie's report on the Fullers, but his thoughts seemed to be far away.

"Is something wrong, Dix?"

"No. At least, I don't think so. I was fielding a lot of questions while I was in Oklahoma, though, questions about the number of military advisors in Southeast Asia."

"People in Oklahoma were worrying about Asia?"

"They are worrying about the President, Cassie, about his judgement. I explained that we need to show the flag in Southeast Asia, to prove to the Russians that we won't just cave in every time some Communist-backed invasion takes place."

"But in Asia? I thought the Asia thing was just a matter of civil war, the northerners trying to depose the ruler in the south of Vietnam."

"I thought that, too, Cassie, until the congressional briefing last week. The North Vietnam forces are definitely backed by the Communist Chinese, so the President has to send more military advisors to help the leader stay in power, a fellow named Ngo Dinh Diem."

"How many American advisors are there?"

"They aren't all advisors. There are some Green Berets and some infantry, too."

"How many Americans, Dix?"

"I don't have all the figures in my head, but I remember that the military command in Saigon has been increased from two thousand men to sixteen thousand."

"My God! Why haven't we known?"

"Not all that much has been said in the newspapers and on TV. Southeast Asia is a long way from Washington."

"But, Dix, if that rate of growth keeps up, there could eventually be over a hundred thousand American soldiers in Vietnam."

He shook his head. "That is simply inconceivable."

"I don't know, Dix. With all of the troubles we have here, the racial problems, the poor, sometimes I wonder. Is the President doing all this to impress the Russians with our strength as a nation, or is he following the advice Shakespeare's king gave to his son: 'and busy giddy minds with foreign quarrels'?"

"You know better than that, Cassie," he said.

She capitulated. "I suppose I do," she said, but she still wondered.

James and Amelia Steele arrived on December twentieth to stay for a week. Cassie was proud to show them the house with all its Christmas decorations in place and to settle them into the guest room she had created by putting a grousing Temple in with Martha for a week.

At first everyone worked terribly hard at getting on well, but the children's assumption that their parents and grandparents existed only to glorify the lives of Taylor and Martha Steele soon destroyed the stiff formality of the visit.

The next evening Blair Fuller and her parents came to dinner. Blair was obviously delighted to find that Amelia was as fey as her own mother. James Steele and Robert Fuller hit it off immediately, with James tracing the complexities of his oil and gas deals, and Bobby Fuller listening carefully but watching James as he might watch an exotic bird of bizarre habits: a bird he would never see *in situ* even on the most successful of all Christmas Counts. Amelia, whose sentences usually had no beginnings and no endings, was in her glory with someone to finish them for her. "Yes," Cassie heard her say several times, "yes, that's just exactly what I meant, Margaret."

Congress was not in session that week, but Dix made a point of taking Cassie and his parents on a private tour of the House and Senate and then, as Congressman Steele, to a bang-up lunch at Sans Souci, where everyone who was anyone knew everyone else—that is, everyone who was anyone.

Taylor and Martha, Cassie thought, were the real winners in the reunion. She loved the sight of James, his back straight and his voice pitched for a courtroom, solemnly reading a storybook to the small boy perched on his knee. And she watched with delight as Amelia played dolls with Martha, whispering and laughing with her until it appeared that she was a four-year-old, too.

*   *   *

On New Year's Eve, James and Amelia had returned to Oklahoma, Temple was at a party at a schoolfriend's and the children were sound asleep. Cassie and Dix sat together on a couch before the library fireplace, sipping champagne. The elder Steeles' presence in the house had allowed Cassie to distance herself from her marriage and that night, oddly enough, she was more relaxed with Dix, and more trusting.

"What a hectic year 1961 has been," Cassie said.

"Yes. I hope that next year will be—"

"Calmer." They laughed. "I'm sorry," Cassie said. "You can finish your own sentences, darling. But when we're as old as Bobby and Margaret Fuller, we may need—" She paused deliberately.

"Help!" He hugged her to his side. "I only hope we'll still be as much in love as they are."

"You noticed it too?"

"Cassie, how could anyone help but see it? Just imagine us at that age, still billing and cooing, too, I'll bet."

"Dix! We don't bill and coo *now!*"

"There's never enough time now, but there will be then."

She put her head on his shoulder. "Plenty of time, darling. We have all the time in the world."

At the beginning, it seemed that 1962 was indeed shaping up to be a quieter year. Dix was settled into the House, and although he would have to campaign for re-election later in the spring, he had no strong opposition. Taylor loved his school and Martha was enjoying her days at home. Temple was happier, too, that winter, and less sulky. She would be eighteen in a few months and her new maturity suited her.

One night in late January, Dix said, "I was at Taylor's school today."

"Why on earth were you—"

"I wanted to check on something and I'm glad I did."

Cassie was startled. "Something about Taylor?"

"Oh, no. In fact, I talked to his teacher for a few minutes before I saw the admissions woman and she said he's doing quite well."

"But Taylor is already in school. Why see the admissions clerk now?"

"For Martha. Wait, now, let me tell you. I heard that there was a long waiting list for admission to the school."

"Taylor had no problem."

"That was because a boy's father was fired by the SEC and went back to California at the last minute. Since the other kids on the list were signed up for schools, they could take Taylor. It won't be that easy for Martha. That's why she has to start preschool at the semester break. The kids who are in their preschool are automatically accepted for kindergarten."

"But she's so happy at home, and so little! Dix, what kind of hold does this school have on us?"

He frowned. "I have explained it before, Cassie. This school feeds a good prep school and it, in turn, feeds the Ivy League. Our kids need to go to the right schools, to get the best educations."

"At four years old? That's ridiculous!"

"Ridiculous? What makes you an expert? You weren't on that track. You didn't have the advantages our children have."

Cassie felt as if he had slapped her. "Thank you so much for reminding me that I grew up poor. I don't understand about the 'right' schools because I didn't go to college, is that it? Let me tell you, Dix, that I learned one hell of a lot on my own, and I think my children are bright enough to do the same thing!"

"*Our* children. To deprive them of the right schools, of the best available education, would be criminal."

"My God, is the time coming when a child will have to be born in the 'right' hospital so he can get into the 'right' preschool and the 'right' college? And are any of these 'right' schools integrated, Dix? Tell me, do black children get to go to the 'right' schools?"

"Now, look here," he said defensively. "I'm sure any of these schools would welcome blacks if they could just—"

"If the blacks could just afford it, right? But if they can't go to the best schools, the ones that lead to the best professions, then how are they ever going to be able to afford it?"

"That's a hell of a thing to say to me! You know how much I've supported integration!"

Cassie knew she had gone too far. "I know, darling, I know. All I'm asking is this: Shouldn't supporting integration be a whole-life commitment rather than just an intellectual or a political exercise?"

When Cassie saw Martha's immediate delight at having nine four-year-olds to play with and her instant love for the pretty young blonde who taught the Monday–Wednesday–Friday preschool class, she thought the entire argument had been irrelevant. Dix had said that you couldn't use your children to make political points and he was probably right. All that mattered in the end was Martha's happiness.

As she walked home, however, she was still uneasy about the decision. Was Dix telling her that a fine education would buy happiness for their children? How could she be sure that he was right? But then, how could she be sure that she was right, either?

Chapter 18

Another, more immediate problem came up in February, a problem with Temple. One of her schoolfriends, a girl named Betty Leland, invited Temple to go home to Baltimore with her for the four-day semester break. Temple wanted desperately to go and Cassie gave her permission after she had called Betty Leland's mother and made sure that the invitation was legitimate and had parental approval. Mrs. Leland's soft Baltimore accent convinced her that she could approve of Temple's first opportunity to visit a friend's home.

According to Temple, the visit to Baltimore was a huge success, but her gushing reports made Cassie uneasy. Her mind, trained for the law, found discrepancies involving who had gone where with whom, and when. She did not want to give Temple the third degree, but during the next few days she asked a few seemingly innocuous questions and the answers did not quite match.

Temple had been home for a week and was still glowing with pleasure over her trip the afternoon Cassie picked up the telephone in the library to call her hairdresser. Before she could dial, she heard a young man's voice.

"—know my mother. She's so out of it that she wouldn't have noticed an elephant walking into the kitchen. Don't worry, she didn't suspect anything at all. Now, how about tonight?"

"I think I can make it. I'll tell her I'm going to the library. On the corner, like before?"

"Sure thing, baby." He kept talking, endearments with anatomical allusions that made Cassie blush. She eased the phone onto its base and sat down across the room.

The slut, she thought, the little slut! Tricking me into letting her go to Baltimore and now using my house as a base for—she stopped herself. She did not know that anything had happened. She only suspected. She needed to find out what was suspicion and what was truth. Perhaps she and Dix should—no! It was not his responsibility, but hers. In fact, for some reason she could not explain even to herself, she thought it would be better if Dix knew nothing about it.

Dix had a late meeting that night, and the children were asleep when Temple came to the door of the library, wearing a coat and carrying a notebook.

"Cassie, I need to go to the public library. There's this paper I have to write and—"

"No. Come and sit down, Temple. There, by the light." The girl's grammar had improved, she thought, if not her morals.

"But if I don't go to the library, I won't—"

"Shall I walk to the corner with you, so I can meet him?"

Temple's mouth dropped open. "How did you know?" Her eyes narrowed. "You been spying on me, that's it, listening to my phone calls."

"Only one call, Temple, and that was by accident. Now, I want you to tell me the truth about the trip to Baltimore."

Temple tried to put the best face on it, but it was clear to Cassie that the thing had been a put-up job from the first. Betty Leland's older brother was a freshman at Georgetown University in Washington. He and his roommate went to Baltimore for the semester break, too, and the roommate squired Betty so that Temple and the brother could be together. There was just enough sophomoric stupidity in the story to give it the ring of truth.

"Temple, you have deceived me and I'm not sure yet exactly what I will do about that. To begin with, I think the time has come for me to talk to you about something." Cassie stopped to gather her thoughts and an amused awareness in Temple's eyes told her that a lecture would be a waste of breath. "You know about it, don't you, Temple? You know all about sex."

Temple laughed and with the laugh went her newly acquired good grammar and lockjaw accent. "Know about it? Hell, I seen it since I weren't knee-high to a grasshopper! Ole Bubba, my daddy, he'd take after Mama and the two of 'em would go at it right there on the floor, gruntin' like pigs. Root, hog, or die! Hell, yes, Cassie. I know about all there is to know!"

Cassie looked at her for a moment. "And you've done it, haven't you?"

"Sure as hell have! Started when I was 'bout thirteen, I reckon. Big ole boy at school. Wasn't very clean, but he knowed what his pecker was for!"

Cassie closed her eyes and put her head back on her chair. Oh, God, she thought. Eastern Oklahoma. Sharecroppers. There but for the grace of God— "What about Ruby Keeler?" she said suddenly.

"That Ruby Keeler," Temple said scornfully. "I don't think she's ever gone near enough to *touch* a boy, much less to—you know." Her Washington persona was returning, bringing with it a new confidence. "Well, now you know it all, Cassie, so I'll just go down to the corner and—"

"No. Did you sleep with this boy in Baltimore?"

Temple laughed. "Well, we didn't do much sleeping, but I know what you mean, and yes, I did."

"Did you use birth control?"

"That's not really any of your business, is it?" Temple said, but one look from Cassie convinced her that it was indeed Cassie's business. "He did, sometimes."

Cassie sighed. "And you feel no remorse, obviously. You have no regrets."

"Hell, no, why should I? And what's it to you, anyway?"

"Tomorrow I will take you to my gynecologist for an examination and blood tests."

"I don't need any—"

"Oh, yes, you do, if you want to be in my house, with my children. I could ask you to promise not to do it again, but I don't trust you, Temple, I don't trust you any farther than I can throw you, so I will ask the doctor to fit you with a birth control device. Now, here are the rules. You may go out on dates on Friday and Saturday nights if you are home by midnight, and I want to meet any boy before you go out with him. You will not, repeat, *not* entertain a boy in this house when my husband and I are out. And you will appear at my doctor's office at six-month intervals for pelvic examinations and blood tests. Is that understood?"

Temple's mouth sagged into a sulk. "What if I don't want to do all that? What if I won't?"

"That's easy. I will send you home to Oklahoma."

The girl went pale. "You wouldn't do that!"

"The hell I wouldn't. What's more, Temple, I want you to understand that I will be your judge and your jury and there will be no appealing my decision to my husband. You will have to watch your step carefully, because I will be watching you every minute."

"That's not fair!"

"*Life* is not fair, Temple." Cassie's tone softened. "I am not sending you to Oklahoma on the next plane, though, because I would like to help you make something of yourself. I can't forbid you to have sex, but please don't do it! Your whole life is spread out before you, Temple. Don't throw it away."

Tears rose in Temple's eyes. "I'll think about it, Cassie. I really will."

"Good. You can go now. Are you going to the corner?"

"Reckon he's gone by now. Reckon I'll just go to bed." Her shoulders were rounded in dejection, but Cassie made no move to stop her and offer her comfort.

*   *   *

One April morning, Cassie met Blair Fuller for a stroll among the cherry blossoms around the Tidal Basin. They sauntered through the crowds of tourists who oohed and ahhed over the beautiful trees Japan had sent before World War II. In spite of, or perhaps because of the crowds, the two of them achieved a special closeness that morning. Cassie noticed that Blair was particularly quiet.

"Is something wrong?" she asked.

Blair sighed. "I just can't figure out what to do with my life. Did you ever feel that you were just waiting for something to happen?"

Cassie glanced up at a cloud of pink blossoms. Oh, God, she thought, do I ever! "A sense of reacting rather than acting?"

Blair stopped and looked up at her. "That's it! In fact, I sometimes think that's all I've ever done, all my life. I've been on a conveyor belt: go to school, go to college, get married, have two-point-three children, be a proper wife and mother and a good hostess—except that when I was divorced I fell off the belt. I don't have the husband or the two-point-three children. And I feel like a failure. You know my mother and father. Do you think failure is in my genes?"

"Your parents aren't failures! They are two of the happiest people I know."

"But they dropped off the conveyor belt, didn't they? My mother never entertained. Sometimes I thought that she hardly noticed me. My aunts ran my life. If they'd left it to Mother and Dad, I'd probably have become an old maid ornithologist."

"How about your brother?"

"Oh, he followed the straight and narrow: Groton, Harvard, Harvard Law, Washington law firm, married a Vassar girl, two children, has a place on Foxhall Road. If it hadn't been for my divorce—"

"There, but for the grace of God, go you!"

Blair laughed uncomfortably. "I never thought about it that way, exactly."

Cassie wondered just how close their friendship was. Did she have the right to meddle in Blair's life? Her mind flew back to Dallas and she remembered how Fran Jordan pushed her to search for something with a future rather than settle for the mediocre. "Blair," she said suddenly, "what is it you want to do? And why don't you do what *you* want? Why don't you take control of your life?"

"I'm not even sure what I want. And my aunts would be—they still talk about The Divorce with capital letters."

"To hell with your aunts, Blair. We're talking about your life, not theirs! Why should you measure yourself by their standards instead of your own?"

"My standards?" Blair quickened her pace. "My standards are what I have been taught."

"And never questioned?"

Blair stopped and the stream of tourists divided to go around her. Cassie stopped, too, and waited.

"And never questioned," Blair said softly. "Never."

"But you did get a divorce when you found out that your husband was unfaithful."

"That had to be done! That was urgent!"

"And what you do with your life is not urgent?"

Blair's eyes flashed purple. "Damn you, Cassie, you and your lawyer's questions! Do I have to probe into everything?"

"When it is as important as making major choices about your life, yes. You'd better do a lot of probing."

Blair glared at her, then turned and walked on, her heels clicking on the sidewalk. "I've thought about going into social work, or nursing—anything that would let me help people. But what if I make the wrong choice?"

"You probably will, but where's the judge that will give you a ten-year sentence for making a poor choice? Everyone makes a few false starts. If I told you how many mistakes I've made—"

"Don't give me that! Look at you: a lawyer, a mother, a wife—

you have it all!" Blair looked up at her with a worried frown. "I hope I didn't say something wrong."

"No. Oh, no! Let's go have lunch, shall we?"

Blair glanced at her watch. "I don't have time. This is the afternoon I volunteer at the National Gallery. Listen, I'm sorry I cried on your shoulder. I'll get hold of my life somehow."

"Of course you will," Cassie said brightly, "and after all, Blair, what are friends for?"

After she dropped Blair off, however, she did not go straight home. Instead she drove to Rock Creek Park and sat in the car to examine the thought that had come to her at the Tidal Basin. Sometimes, she thought, you have to get outside of yourself. You have to put a frame around your life, hang it on the wall and step back from it in order to see it clearly.

Dixon Steele had married a strong, independent woman, but that woman had disappeared during the last year. What was left? *Who* was left? Dix seemed to be happy with her, but was she the woman she wanted to be?

She drove home and immediately became involved in Martha's life and, when he came home from school, in Taylor's. Only once during the afternoon did she think of her fears and then it was to deride them. She had been thrown off balance, she thought, by her talk with her friend. Blair's uncertainty about her life had spawned uncertainty in her own mind. She laughed to herself. Would such a thing ever happen to "Dear Abby"? Of course not. But Cassie was far less experienced at giving advice to the lovelorn.

Dixon Steele walked away with the Oklahoma Democratic primary and, with a weak Republican opponent, was guaranteed two more years in the United States House of Representatives. He and Cassie were in Oklahoma to hear the results and join in the victory celebration. More party leaders were present than had been at Dix's previous primary victory. At first Cassie wondered if James Steele had recruited them, but later, as she heard wisps of con-

versation and read between the lines of their fulsome congratu-
lations, she realized that it was not James but the size of Dix's
plurality that had brought them out. Dix's support had increased
dramatically, districtwide, and in the long run, politics was about
one thing and one thing only: votes.

She had no chance to discuss the victory with Dix. Their hotel
suite was always full of politicians, and on the flight back to
Washington, Cully Meecham sat next to Dix and engaged him in
a conversation Cassie could not hear from her seat across the aisle.
She paged through a magazine which had Jacqueline Kennedy's
picture on the cover. She wondered if Mrs. Kennedy felt as essential
as she did, standing on the platform next to the candidate, and as
useless as she when the ballots were counted and the candidate
was elected.

Back in Washington their lives fell into the old routine: the children
busy with school, Dix busy with the House and Cassie at loose
ends. She considered taking up volunteer work but she never
seemed to get around to it. Instead she read a great deal, both
books and newspapers. If nothing else, she could be an intelligent
sounding-board for Dix's ideas.

But Dix was rarely home. There were late votes and meetings
and his increasing involvement with the integration movement in
the South.

Summer dwindled away to fall and in September Martha was
enrolled in kindergarten at the same school where Taylor was a
first-grader. Temple, at eighteen, began her senior year in high
school, and the house was left to Cassie, Angelina and the biweekly
cleaning woman.

Cassie tried to get in touch with Blair Fuller, to have lunch or
do anything that would get her out of the house on R Street, but
Blair never was at home.

Dix was increasingly busy, and by early October, Cassie was
afraid that the strain was beginning to affect his health. He slept

so restlessly that she was awakened frequently by his tossing and turning. By the middle of October, he looked haggard, with dark circles under his eyes.

On Friday, the nineteenth of October, he came home from the Hill at noon.

"Dix!" Cassie cried. "How nice! Let me have Angelina fix some lunch for you."

He shook his head, taking an airline envelope from his coat pocket. "No time. Look, Cassie, I want you to take the children and Temple to Oklahoma for a while."

Cassie was shocked. "Dix! Is something wrong with your parents?"

"No, I can't talk about it, but I want you out of Washington."

Cassie stared at him. "Russia. It's Russia, isn't it? What on earth is going on?"

"I said I can't tell you!" he said angrily. "For once, will you just do what I say without arguing about it? Hurry now, and pack. I've got you on a late afternoon flight."

"No." Cassie went into the library and sat down. "I'm not budging until I know what this is about."

Dix glared at her but she summoned all of her strength to wait him out. He tapped the white envelope against his knee as if the soft, regular beat would help him measure his thoughts.

"All right," he said finally. "I can see that you won't go unless— Cassie, what I'm going to tell you is a state secret and is not to be revealed, not to anyone."

"Yes, Dix. I understand."

"The Russians have set up missile bases in Cuba that will be operable in a matter of days, if not hours." He took a deep breath. "On Monday, the President is going to announce a blockade of Cuba and to warn Khrushchev that any missile launched from Cuba will be considered a Soviet act of war against the United States."

Cassie sank back in her chair as if to withdraw from the situation. "And after that—" She stopped and swallowed. "After that, the Russians might attack us with atomic bombs."

He looked at her steadily. "Or before that. Now you see why you must take the children to Oklahoma."

"I see." She nodded slowly. "I can't, Dix. I can't leave you here alone."

Dix stood up abruptly. "Cassie, don't you understand what I'm saying? Washington would be their first—"

"Target. Yes. Will you come with us, Dix?"

"It's my duty to be here."

"Your duty! What possible effect can you have on the situation? A congressman from Oklahoma?"

He gripped the envelope until it crumpled. "Thanks for the vote of confidence, but whatever you think of my effectiveness, my duty is here."

Cassie stood up. "And so is mine. My duty is to be with you."

"What about the children?"

"The children." She was sick with fear for the children. "I could send them out with Temple, I suppose, but would they be safe there? If the atmosphere becomes radioactive, can you guarantee that they would be safe in Oklahoma?"

"No one can guarantee anything, not one damn thing."

"And what if Russia decided to hit the Oklahoma oil fields? Dix, we can't send the children away. They would be frightened."

Dix looked defeated. "At our wedding I promised to take care of you. And now—"

"You have!" She hurried across the room to put her arms around him. "And you will again. This will pass, Dix, I swear it! All this will pass!"

"Oh, God, I hope so." He tried to smile. "Cassandra. All of your predictions come true, don't they?" He hugged her and said, "I have to get back to the House. We're supposed to keep a pretense of normality."

For once Cassie did not consult Dix about her plans. She told

Angelina she could take the weekend off, and she took out a list of the guests she had invited to a dinner party on Saturday. We don't have to be all *that* normal, she thought. Before she could start her calls, the telephone rang.

"Cassie, dear, I'm frightfully sorry to cancel at the last minute, but Brad's mother is ill and he's packing the car now so that we can go to her."

"What a pity. Where is his mother?"

"Actually, she's in Kentucky. In the hills."

Another phone call.

"I do hate to cancel, but we're flying out to Wyoming this afternoon. My father—"

It appeared that Dix's secret was no secret at all.

The phone rang again. "An emergency call from Nancy's college—Jim and I must regret your dinner party—oh, it's Antioch, in Ohio."

When the children came home that day, Cassie saw them in a new light, as if they wore an aura of the past. Martha brought four pages of artwork to explain. One was a house with two windows and a sketchy square that Martha said was "of course" the TV. After lunch she condescended to take a nap even though, as she carefully reminded Cassie, she was now five whole years old. Taylor, as always, dumped his backpack in the hall, but for once Cassie picked it up instead of withholding an after-school snack until he had picked it up himself.

At six-and-a-half, Taylor was weedy, but as sturdy as a young tree. He was teeming with news of the first grade, of who hit whom and what the teacher said and of what was going on in the classroom zoo, which consisted of a snake, a turtle, a guinea pig and Taylor's personal favorite, a large black rabbit. Again Cassie felt that the scene was bathed in the yellow light of premature nostalgia: in this house, in October of 1962, a boy ate a snack and told his mother about a bunny named Robert.

Sunday was interminable, as was Monday, until 7 P.M. when

President Kennedy spoke to the American people on television and threw down the gauntlet for the Soviet Union.

During the next few days, Dix was at the House or in committee almost continuously, but he took every opportunity to call Cassie and, in veiled language, give her the latest inside news from the White House.

By Wednesday, the Russians still had not acted upon the ultimatum. Taylor reported that six members of his class were absent with flu. Cassie wondered what kind of flu required a period of recuperation in the Kentucky hills or Ohio or Wyoming.

On Thursday, Adlai Stevenson confronted Valerian Zorin of the USSR in the United Nations Security Council and showed the Council, and the Americans who were watching television, aerial photographs of missile installations in Cuba.

It was Saturday, October 28, when the waiting finally ended. Dix came home to tell Cassie that the Russians had agreed to remove their missiles from Cuba.

That night Dix came to Cassie. He seemed to be as defenseless that once as Cassie herself. They made love less in passion than mutual comfort and in relief that they were still there to make love, that their children were safe, and that the lights of Washington still glittered in the autumn haze.

Chapter 19

Blair Fuller called Cassie early in November. "This is your friend the graduate student."

"What? Where!"

"At Georgetown University, right here in Washington."

"I've tried to get hold of you for weeks."

"It's your own fault, Cassie. Remember the day of the cherry blossoms? Well, I went up to a place we have in Maine and spent the summer. I thought a lot, and I read a lot, and then I thought some more. After that, I had some long talks with my old professors at Vassar. My grade-point average wasn't too bad, considering the fact that all I thought about was boys, and they thought I could make it in grad school. Then I spent a week trailing Mother and Dad around those godforsaken tidal flats, and I came to a decision. And here I am, an overaged grad student in political science."

"Blair, I can't tell you how pleased I am! Do you like it?"

"Cassie, I love it. All those little cells in my brain are jumping up and down and saying, 'Hey, why did you let us sleep so long?' And there's more. It may just be me and colleges, but I find that I'm thinking about boys again. Well, a boy."

"A fellow student!"

"No, actually, a professor."

After a good talk, they agreed to get together for lunch, even though it might have to be delayed until the Christmas holidays, when Blair would have a break from reading and writing.

Cassie hung up the phone and looked around the library, vaguely dissatisfied with it, or with herself. Perhaps she should go back to the law, or on to something else. She could discuss it with Dix, but instinctively she knew that he would not like the idea at all.

Spending time with Dix, however, for discussion or any other reason, was rare that winter. He was seldom at home and when he was, he was closeted in the library reading through stack after stack of reports. He could not take the time for the family to have Thanksgiving in Oklahoma, but in early December he received an urgent call from Cully Meecham and had to fly to Oklahoma.

To Cassie's surprise, Temple asked if she could go there, too, to see her parents. Cassie had been aware of changes in Temple since their talk the previous winter and Cassie's imposition of rules. The girl appeared to be more mature and to have better control of her time. Her grades had improved, too. She must have changed more than Cassie had expected if she wanted to see the parents she had so scorned. Dix seemed to have no objection, so Cassie agreed to Temple's plan.

Four days later, Dix and Temple were back in Washington. Cassie met them in the front hall. "Temple, you look like the cat that swallowed the canary," she said after greeting Dix. "You must have had fun in Oklahoma."

"Yessum, I sure did."

"How are your parents? And your brothers?"

"Okay, I guess." She took her bag and went up to her room.

Dix was somewhat distant.

"Was it a good trip, darling?" Cassie asked.

"Yes, good enough. I'll tell you about it later. Right now the first thing I want is a good shower." He carried his suitcase up the stairs.

Cassie stood in the hall alone. There was a time, she thought, when after four days away, the first thing Dix would want was his wife: a good woman rather than a good shower. She shrugged and went to tell Angelina when to serve dinner.

Later, when the children were in bed and the house was quiet, Cassie and Dix sat before the fire in the library. Cassie savored the moment. A warm fire, curtains pulled against the dank cold of a winter night, her dear husband safely home from his journey: she sighed in pleasure.

"Cassie." Dix's harsh, businesslike voice shattered the silence. "I have been asked to run for the United States Senate."

"Dix! What an honor! We'll have to think about it, of course, and consider the time we would have to spend campaigning and away from the children. When do they want an answer?"

"I have already accepted."

Cassie felt as though he had struck her. "Without—without even asking my opinion?"

He did not quite look at her. "They wanted an answer right away."

"But if you'd told them that we—that you needed—if you had insisted on a few days to—"

"I told you, they wanted an answer and I gave them one. I accepted. Aren't you even excited?"

"Yes, of course, but it's so—"

"It's so terrible that I didn't discuss it with you before I accepted? 'Please, Mommy, can I run for the Senate next year?' "

"Now, wait! I didn't say you had to have my permission. That's not what I meant, and you know it!"

"You think Jack Kennedy did that when they asked him to run for President? Do you think he put his thumb in his mouth and whined, 'Please, Jackie, oh, please, can I be President of the United States?' "

"That's not fair, Dix! You're not Jack Kennedy and I'm not Jackie Kennedy! You and I have always made our plans together. We've always talked about things and worked out—"

"Maybe I'm tired of talking everything to death, did you ever think about that? Tired of endless discussions about where to live and which school to pick for the children. I don't want to talk about the Senate now, or ever. I'm dead tired and I'm going to hit the sack. Good night."

Without a good-night kiss, without another word, he was gone.

Cassie sat alone, stunned. Who was this man? Where was her beloved husband? Had he always been this, underneath, or had she created him by accepting his domination? She could find no answers. Finally she banked the fire, turned off the lights and went upstairs, too. The door to the sitting room was closed. She changed into her nightgown and got into bed, into the empty bed.

The Christmas holidays came, and with them came James and Amelia Steele. Cassie was glad to have them in the house because in their presence Dix was more forthcoming. The division in their marriage was papered over temporarily and although Cassie felt the flimsy fabric could rip at any moment, it was a relief to have even a semblance of a happy marriage.

The elder Steeles, however, were not entirely taken in by the show. Amelia escaped her adoring grandchildren for long enough to seek Cassie out in the kitchen. "—Dixon looks so tired—I do hope it's not the flu or—"

Cassie hastened to tell her that Dix was just worn out from a heavy workload. Even as she reassured Amelia, though, she wished that it were as simple as that.

She noticed that Dix avoided private father-son talks as assiduously as he avoided conversations with Cassie herself. She did not think James was aware of it, but one morning he cornered her in the library, away from the rest of the family.

"What is bothering Dixon?" he asked.

Cassie was caught off guard. "I don't know," she said, but she found herself telling James the little that she did know. "He's been, well, distant since he came back from his last trip to Oklahoma. Do you suppose he's worried about running for the Senate?"

"That shouldn't concern him, not this early. After all, the primary won't be held until April of 1964. Not that he'll have a great

deal to worry about then. He has strong support in all factions of
the party and I've told him that by the time he begins to campaign
actively I'll have quite a large war chest for him, all the financial
backing he needs and more."

Cassie rubbed her cheek. "Could it be this trip to the South,
then? He's planning to go next month."

James scowled. "I have done my best to talk him out of that.
Oklahoma is integrated, but there is still enough opposition that
his blatant support of Martin Luther King will hurt him at the
polls." His eyes narrowed. "It isn't something between the two of
you, by any chance?"

"No!"

"I just asked, that's all. I'm concerned about the boy."

The boy, Cassie thought, when James had left the library. The
boy. Perhaps that in itself was the problem. Dix was forty-one,
but he was acting like a child. A sudden insight made her stop in
the middle of the room. He was behaving like their child, like
Taylor, who had a way of withdrawing when he was in trouble.
She had laughed inwardly about Taylor's habit because his very
withdrawal was a dead giveaway that something was up. It was
sure to be followed by a note from his teacher or an impassioned
accusation by Martha.

With Dix, however, she had no clue to the problem. When
Christmas was over, she thought, when the elder Steeles had gone
back to Oklahoma, she would ask him about it point-blank. Surely
if they talked about it, they could work it out.

Both the older and younger Steeles were invited to a formal
dinner party at the Fullers' house. Bobby Fuller wore a dinner
jacket with the greenish tint of age and Margaret a silk jersey dress
with a faulty zipper anchored with a diaper pin. James, in his well-
cut dinner jacket and Amelia in a diaphanous gown from Neiman's
made their host and hostess look positively shabby. There was
nothing shabby about the dinner, however, with a main course of
squab served on museum-quality china and eaten with silverware

so heavy that Cassie wondered if wispy Amelia would be able to lift her fork. Kathleen, with two rosy-faced girls to help her, served the table as punctiliously as a butler in an English country manor.

Blair was there, of course, as were her brother and his wife. They set Cassie's teeth on edge. Kenneth Fuller was a pompous and self-important product of what he himself called "the right schools." He apparently had some position in the State Department, but he was less interested in his work than in himself. Unfortunately his wife, Muffy, was seated on Cassie's left. She took the lockjaw accent to a new high—or low—as she enhanced her self-esteem by attempting to destroy that of everyone at the table, including her husband's parents.

"Such poppets! I sometimes think they've entered their second childhood, but then it may be that they never escaped their first. You're from Oklahoma, you say? Oh, yes. One of those rough, uncultured states. I do think one always keeps the nature of one's native land, don't you? But I'm sure your parents sent you east to college. You didn't go to college. A finishing school, perhaps. No? But how very—how very *unique* of you."

Cassie was delighted to turn to the guest on her right. Joe Howe, Blair's young professor, was tall and thin and rather shy, with piercing blue eyes and a sandy beard. They had a pleasant talk about history, his field of interest, and Cassie was interested to learn that he had strong antiestablishment leanings.

"The United States should be brought before the World Court," he said emphatically. "Kennedy's interference in Vietnam is criminal."

"But Jack Kennedy is a liberal Democrat," Cassie protested. "Look at the stand he has taken on civil rights."

"You mean, the stand Robert Kennedy has taken. He is his brother's conscience. But even he is too rich to be a pure liberal. In the best of all possible worlds, he and other rich people would voluntarily share their wealth with the poor."

Cassie looked at the head of the table, where Bobby Fuller was excitedly telling Amelia about the Christmas Count. At the foot of the table, Margaret Fuller was happily finishing sentences for James Steele, who looked somewhat disgruntled.

"I suspect that if you suggested that to Blair's parents," Cassie said, "they might just do it."

"How about your father-in-law? Would he—"

"Heavens, no! In fact, if you so much as suggested it, he would probably have you hauled off and shot as a communist."

Joe Howe turned to look directly at Cassie. "And how about you?"

It was a question that brought her up short. "I don't know," she said slowly. "I feel that I am my brother's keeper, but I have worked hard all my life to earn my money."

"Then you feel no social responsibility? You do not feel compelled to help the poor?"

"Damn it, Joe!" Embarrassed, Cassie looked around but no one had noticed her agitation. "I *was* the poor," she said more quietly. "My father was a sharecropper. Do you know what that means?"

"I've read *The Grapes of Wrath*, of course, and the Agee–Evans book, *Let Us Now Praise Famous Men*."

"Reading about it isn't being there, Joe. You haven't known absolute poverty. My grandmother used to say, 'Pride ain't worth a hill of beans.' It took me a long time to understand that the phrase had a double meaning. You could *eat* beans. What kind of family do you come from?"

He looked down at his plate. "My father is an investment banker. And, yes, I have had plenty of advantages: country clubs, private schools. Yale. I suppose you think that makes me a limousine liberal."

"Are you going to become an investment banker, too?"

"God, no! I'm going into the Peace Corps in the spring."

"Good for you! Do that, Joe, live with poverty on a day-to-day basis, learn what it means to be hungry, day in and day out. Then come back and we'll talk about poverty again."

"I will," he said, "and I'll hold you to that."

"One thing, Joe." Cassie turned her wineglass in her fingers. "If you run across a child who has a spark, an eagerness to learn, perhaps, or the drive to climb out of that pit, encourage him—or her, will you? Help him."

Joe's blue eyes were steady. "I will, Cassie Steele, I promise you that. I will."

Blair called Cassie early the next morning. "Well?"

"Well, what?"

"What did you think of him?"

"Of Kenneth, your brother?"

"Cassie, stop that! You know who I mean. Joe. Joe Howe."

"I know, I know. Blair, I liked him immensely. For a communist, he's—"

"He is not a communist! He just has ideals, and a highly developed sense of responsibility for his fellow man."

"I was teasing, dear. Blair, I admire him, partly because he is obviously willing to learn. And I think it's great that he's going into the Peace Corps."

There was a long pause. "You mean, *we* are going into the Peace Corps, Cassie. We are going to be married and go as a couple."

"Blair! That's—that's—" Cassie could not decide whether it was wonderful or terrible. She pictured the two of them dwelling in a mud hut, teaching children, patching up minor wounds, working with the natives, digging drainage ditches. Working together. A wave of envy swept over her. "That is great, Blair! Wonderful news! Have you told your family?"

"Just Mother and Dad. I don't think Kenneth and Muffy are going to approve, nor, for that matter, will the aunts. But Dad said I'm a grown woman and should just let them all go—"

"Hang!"

Blair laughed. "Right! So we're going to slip away, just the two of us and Mother and Dad, and have a simple wedding ceremony."

Cassie could imagine it, Blair and Joe upright and serious, with Bobby and Margaret giggling like children involved in an elaborate plot to fool the grownups.

"What about Joe's parents?"

"I've met them, and if you can believe it they're even stuffier than Kenneth and Muffy. Joe says we'll tell them afterward and they can get their stewing out of the way during the two years we're gone."

"Two years. I'm going to miss you terribly, Blair."

"I'll miss you, too."

"Oh, no, you won't! You'll be as dotty as any other bride!"

"Cassie, it's early to ask this since we won't be going till late spring, but speaking of dotty, will you visit my parents sometimes?"

"Frequently! And the three of us can sit and cry huge crocodile tears over your being away."

Blair giggled. "Just don't forget that Joe and I will be *with* the crocodile."

Amelia and James left two days later and the house was quiet again. Too quiet, in Cassie's opinion. Dix seemed to have withdrawn even from the children, and they moped around the house like abandoned puppies.

On New Year's Eve, Cassie and Dix went to a few parties but Cassie conjured up a headache and they went home early. By custom rather than desire, Dix opened champagne and they sipped at it while they made desultory conversation.

After thirty minutes, Cassie could take no more. "Dix, for God's sake, we have to talk! What's bothering you? Is it this trip to the South? Or the senatorial race? What is the problem, anyway? Dix, please don't shut me out of your life."

"What makes you so sure I have a problem?"

Cassie kept her voice calm. "It isn't just me, darling. Your father asked me about it. Even your mother was worried."

Dix put down his glass and stood up. "That's great," he said, looking down at the fire. "That's just great! All of you sitting around gossiping about 'poor Dix.' That's a big help."

Cassie jumped on the word. "Do you need help, Dix? You know that if there's anything I can do, anything at all. It's the Southern trip, isn't it? I know it's important to you."

He turned to her and scowled. "Hell, yes, it's important! More important than you can imagine."

Cassie's spirits rose. Finally, she had broached the wall between them. "Can you tell me about it?"

He hesitated. "I guess I'll have to, just to get you off my back. You must not let any word of this get out, not so much as a hint. It could ruin everything." Grudgingly, he pulled an armchair close to hers, but his face was open to her for once, and as eager as Taylor's when he reported on the latest exploits of Robert Rabbit.

"You know about the troubles the Freedom Riders had in Birmingham last year, of course."

"Yes, the race riots—"

"Not race riots, Cassie. The only rioting was done by white hoodlums. They beat those nonviolent protesters within an inch of their lives; in fact, they put three of them in the hospital. And why were they allowed to do it? Why didn't the police interfere? The police knew what was happening, and they ignored it. They allowed Americans to be beaten in the streets simply because they opposed the illegal Jim Crow laws."

"I remember," Cassie said softly. "I remember."

"And do you remember why the police did nothing to protect the victims? It was because their chief, Police Commissioner T. Eugene Connor—because Bull Connor sat in his office two blocks away and did nothing. He said afterward, it was because the police were shorthanded. After all, he said, it was Mother's Day."

"But what has that to do with you?"

"I'm coming to that. Martin Luther King has called Birmingham, Alabama, the most segregated city in the United States, and he intends to attack segregation at its very root." He leaned closer to Cassie. "This spring, in April, King is going to mount a major protest there: sermons, sit-ins, marches, the works."

"And you will—"

"And I will be there to help. Cassie, the two men I admire most in the world have asked for my help. Reverend Martin Luther King and Attorney General Robert Kennedy have asked me to serve as liaison between the protesters and the federal government. I will stand witness to the events, and at the same time I will be the main channel of communication between the two of them. Bobby Kennedy doesn't want any major confrontations."

Cassie took a deep breath. "You'll be in danger, Dix."

"Kennedy has promised me all the protection I need."

"In political danger, too. It will come just at the time of the Oklahoma primary, won't it?"

Dix waved his hand, dismissing her comment. "I can't let politics interfere, Cassie, not when I know that I am doing the right thing."

Cassie's spirits lifted. It was the old Dix talking now. Her Dix. "But why do you need to go South now?"

"I'll consult with Martin King and bring his plans back to Bobby Kennedy so that they can coordinate their strategies."

"Will you have protection on this trip, too?"

"I won't need it, Cassie. I'll go not as a congressman but as a private person. I'll even wear a plaid shirt and jeans so I can fade into the red-neck background."

"It scares me, Dix."

"I have to go. King and Kennedy can't be seen together and it's hardly the sort of thing that can be handled on the phone."

"Does it have to be you?"

"Yes." He looked at her for a moment and then away. "I must go, Cassie."

Something else was there, behind his words, but she did not question him about it. She was not at all sure that she wanted to know. "Yes," she said. "I can see that you must."

Cassie could not go to sleep that night. Instead, she lay thinking about what Dix had told her and trying to understand. Dix heard his call as clearly as Saint Peter had heard his when he left his boat to become a fisher of men. She could understand that, and she could admire it. It was the undisclosed motive for the distance between them since he returned from Oklahoma that frightened her, even more than the journey itself.

Dix was planning his trip but he still had a congressional district to represent. He flew to Oklahoma January 7, for one night, to attend the ribbon-cutting ceremony at the new dam the Army Engineers had built in his district.

Wanting to spend what time she could with Blair before she and Joe Howe were married and left Washington, Cassie made a date with her to see a movie and have a drink afterward.

With its 1962 Academy Award spurring sales, *West Side Story* had a line two blocks long. After one look at the patrons drooping in the cold rain, Cassie and Blair decided to forego the movie and settle for a glass of white wine at a lounge near Blair's apartment.

"It's probably just as well," Blair said. "I really need to get home and work on a paper."

Although she had told Temple not to expect her before ten-thirty or eleven, Cassie left Blair's and was at home by nine. She hung her raincoat in the closet and stood in the hall for a minute trying to decide whether to watch television in the library or read in her own bed. She chose reading and was in the upstairs hall when she heard a noise in Temple's room. She tapped lightly on the girl's bedroom door. "Temple? Are you all right?"

Temple answered in a muffled voice. "Just a minute."

It was more than a minute. It was several minutes before she opened the door just enough to slide into the hall and pull the door shut behind her. She rubbed her eyes, but the gesture did not conceal a glint of excitement.

"You got home early, Cassie. How was the movie?"

Cassie started to explain about the long line at the movie but stopped abruptly when she became aware that a faint odor clung to Temple like the scent of cheap perfume.

It was the smell of sex.

"Temple," Cassie said quietly, "open the door."

"Why do you—no!" Temple's eyes flashed, amber as a caution light. "I don't have to. This is my room!"

"And this is my house. Open the door or I will do it myself."

Slowly, reluctantly, Temple opened the door. Near the bed, near the rumpled bed with its tossed sheets, a bare-chested young man was pulling on his jeans.

Cassie fought to keep her voice level. "Temple, who is this—this person?"

Temple pulled her robe tight around her body. "It's Larry Denby, from school."

The boy was dressed and was looking desperately at Cassie, who blocked his path to freedom. "Temple," Cassie said, "you stay right here. And you—" She gestured to the boy. "You come with me."

She preceded him down the stairs, crossed the hall and opened the door. He started to pass her, but she waved him to a stop. "You must never come to this house, you hear? I don't want to see your face, ever again."

"Yes, ma'am, I hear," he said and then he was past her and disappearing into the rain.

Cassie locked the door and went straight to the library to make a telephone call. She went upstairs, then, and checked on Taylor and Martha. Both of them were sleeping soundly. The innocence, she thought, the lovely unsullied innocence of childhood. She walked down the hall to Temple's room. The girl was at the window, looking out at the night.

"Pack your things," Cassie said. "You are flying to Oklahoma at nine-thirty tomorrow morning."

Temple whirled around. "You can't do this!"

"I can, and I have. I've made the reservation and your ticket will be held for you at the airline counter."

"But who'll meet me? How will I get to the farm?"

"As they say down there, Temple, that's your look-out."

"You wouldn't send me off like—"

"I would, and you know it. You've known it all along, haven't you? You knew it tonight when you brought that boy here, into my house."

"But we didn't do anything! I heard you come in and we—"

"You stopped so that I wouldn't catch you in flagrante delicto? Would that have made any difference? I warned you, Temple, and there's no getting out of it. Whether you and that boy had sex is immaterial."

Temple flounced across to her dresser and made a brave show of fluffing her tousled hair. "What's so damn bad about sex? Listen, I'm a big girl now, almost nineteen, and I've got a right to do what I want with my body!"

"Not in my house, you don't."

Temple spun around. Her eyes were hard and narrow. "*You* have sex in this house, you and Dix. Don't think I haven't heard you at night. You really go at it, you two. But you're married and that makes you Miz Butter-won't-melt-in-your-mouth, doesn't it, no matter how much you yell when Dix puts it to you. So I'm not married. What does that make me, a whore?"

Judy O'Grady and the colonel's lady, Cassie thought, and smiled slightly.

Temple's lips thinned and twisted into a snarl. "You think it's funny, do you? You think it's all real funny that it's okay when Dix puts it to you but it's sin when Larry puts it to me. But then Dix is a good man, he's a congressman, ain't he?" She smiled suddenly, a thin evil smile. "He's good in other ways, too, though. He's good in bed, ain't he?" She laughed harshly. "But why do I have to ask you that, Cassie? Maybe I know how he is in bed. Maybe I been to bed with him myself."

Cassie became aware of a pulse throbbing in her throat. "You're lying!" she said flatly.

Temple grinned. "Why would I lie when telling the truth is more fun, a hell of a lot more fun? Maybe you ain't so high and mighty as you think. Not when you know that your man Dix puts it to me, too!"

Cassie did not move, did not change her expression, but she felt that all of the blood had drained from her, from her head, from her heart. She looked at Temple, whose face was changing from evil to fear.

"Pack your things," Cassie said. She left Temple's room and went to her own room, to *their* room, the one that had belonged, in some other life, to a happy couple named Cassie and Dixon Steele, a couple who trusted each other and loved each other and made one person of two.

She closed the door carefully and looked down at their bed, stared at it as if she had some rare form of visual aphasia and no longer could remember what things were or what purpose they served.

Finally she lay down on the object, the bed, in her clothes.

Later, much later, the first gray light of morning crept across the figure of a woman, fully dressed, lying gray-faced and rigid, staring up at the ceiling above her.

Chapter 20

 When Dix came home from Oklahoma the next night, he looked tired, but Cassie herself was exhausted, drained by her emotions and her lack of sleep.

In the library, he thumbed through the mail. "Have you already put the children to bed?" he said casually. "Or is Temple giving them their bath?"

Cassie bent down to poke at the fire. "I sent Temple home."

"Home?" he said, but she did not turn around. "You mean home to Oklahoma? Why on earth did you—" He stopped.

Cassie did not look at him. "I caught her with a boy in her room."

"Oh, God. That little—" He looked at her blankly and then turned away. "There are some calls I have to make."

"Not yet. Dix, is there anything you want to tell me?"

"No. There's nothing, nothing at all. These calls are important. I have to get hold of—"

"Dix." Her voice was leaden. "Don't make me ask you, don't make me beg for the truth. Please don't do that. If what Temple told me is true, I have to know it. I have to hear it from you."

"Damn it, how am I supposed to know what she told you!"

For an instant Cassie felt life flowing back into her exhausted body. She wanted terribly to believe that Temple had just wanted to hurt her, that it was a brazen lie. "Oh, Dix! If that's the truth, then—"

He scowled at her. "God, Cassie, you know I love you! Don't you trust me anymore?"

Cassie reached out to touch him but her hand stopped in midair, as of its own volition. There was an odd ring to his voice, like the clang of a cracked bell.

They stood there for a moment, looking at each other, with hope on Cassie's face and defiance on Dix's. Suddenly he sank down in an armchair and covered his eyes with his hand. "No," he said. "It isn't fair. I have no right to ask you to trust me." He pushed himself up from the chair slowly, like an old, old man and walked to the window to stand with his back to her. "I did not sleep with her, Cassie, but I came close. It was when we took that trip to Oklahoma."

Cassie shuddered. "At the farm? Not in our room. Please God, not in our bed."

"At a motel near the airport. You remember that our flight to Washington was delayed? We went to a—"

"I don't want to hear it."

"But I want to tell you, Cassie. I want to—"

"You want to clear your conscience?" Suddenly Cassie was enraged. "You want to tell me all about it, don't you, so you can quit worrying about it. You seem to have trouble remembering this, but I am your wife. I'm not your priest. I can't help you do penance. I can't tell you to say two Hail Marys and go and sin no more!"

Dix turned to face her. "You asked me to tell you and now you stop me. What do you want of me?"

Cassie's breath caught in a sob that wracked her body. "I want— I want it not to have happened. Oh, God, I want you to have kept the promises you made at our wedding, the vows to be faithful."

"But nothing *did* happen! Can't you get that through your head? And I really am sorry, Cassie, deeply sorry."

" 'Sorry' doesn't quite cut it, does it? 'Sorry' is what you say when you bump into a stranger on the sidewalk."

"What would cut it, Cassie? If I promise you that I'll never be tempted again?" He looked down at the floor. "If I tell you that the knowledge of what I almost did has been tearing me to pieces?"

It was then that the past few weeks became clear to Cassie. When Dix was so withdrawn, so far away, he was not trying to stay away from her. He was trying to distance himself from himself. "I see," she said slowly. "I understand it now."

Dix's face lightened with relief. "You understand how a thing like this can happen, then? You understand that when a man is away from home and the girl is obviously experienced and is so goddamn willing—"

"No! That is exactly what I don't understand! You say you love me, but the first time you have a chance—"

"Not the first time I've had a chance, Cassie. Not by a long shot. And not the first time I've turned it down. Why are you so angry, anyway? I told you, nothing happened."

"You did tell me that, didn't you? And you expect me to believe you like a good little wife, a spineless clinging woman who will forgive her man anything and everything as long as he tosses her a scrap of love now and then?"

Dix sat down and looked up at her. "You are overreacting, you know."

She looked down at him coolly. "I don't think so. You ask too much of me, Dix. Too much."

"Cassie, I—"

"Make your calls, Dix, make those damned important phone calls. I am tired. I am going to bed."

"Are you going to be able to forgive me?"

"I'll have to think about it, but not tonight."

During the days that followed, Cassie and Dix maintained a polite relationship, but no more than that. Dix threw himself into his plans for the trip south.

Cassie considered searching for a new mother's-helper as a replacement for Temple. No, she thought, no! She could raise her children herself.

Far more important than finding a mother's-helper was finding a way that she and Dix could salvage the wreck of their marriage. When the children were tucked in bed that night, Cassie sat in the library and tried to think it through. Dix was a good man, who had fallen from grace. A phrase sneaked into her mind: "A man has his needs." She had heard that again and again, from the time her father's whiney voice had tried to justify his actions. But Dix was married. He had a wife who was only too willing to meet his needs!

She got up, restless, and went to the window. It was snowing lightly that night, white flakes floating down through the cone of light from the streetlight on the corner. She shivered with cold, but the chill was within herself, as she faced the truth. Their relationship had changed with their move to Washington. There were times when their lovemaking had been great, but there were more times when she had felt no desire, had felt dull and disinterested. Something had gone out of her when they moved to Washington.

Abruptly she turned away from the window. Something had not gone out of her, not really. Rather it had come into her on one hot May night in Oklahoma. Theirs had been a marriage of trust, of complete honesty, and she had brought into it a dark secret that she had not shared with her husband. In trying to protect him, or more likely, to protect herself, she had created a chasm in their marriage. She had not told him that she was a murderess. She wanted him to trust her, but she had not trusted him enough to confess her crime.

His sins were, in the end, her sins, and her sins were his. As they had so often shared joy, they would have to share sorrow in order to rebuild their trust, and their marriage.

She heard the front door and hurried to sit down on the couch and open a magazine. "Dix?"

He came into the library. "Cassie, I'm sorry I'm so late. I would have called but I couldn't get away."

The sound of his tired voice, the haggard look of his long face touched her, hurt her, and at the same time lifted her above her misery.

"Shall I fix you some dinner?" she said.

"No, I ate with Cully." He rubbed his forehead. "He's still trying to talk me out of going South. God, can't the man see beyond the voting booth?"

"He doesn't have your high standards, Dix."

He looked at her quickly, obviously surprised by the sympathy in her voice.

"He doesn't have your ideals, either." She smiled. " 'He loved chivalrye, trouthe and honour, fredom and curteisye.' "

"Chaucer?"

"Yes. 'He was a verray parfait gentil knight.' "

"Hardly 'parfait,' " he said sadly.

"Who is? Dix, I've been thinking—"

"So have I." He let his body sag into a chair. Sitting there with his hands flat on his thighs and his face haggard, he reminded Cassie of the statue of Abraham Lincoln in the Memorial.

"We need to talk," she said softly.

"About Temple?"

"No. I believe you, Dix. It's something else."

He straightened his back. "Now? Can't it wait till I come back?"

"What do you mean?" Cassie sat forward on the couch. "When do you plan to leave?"

"Tomorrow. Wednesday."

"Oh, no! Why didn't you tell me?"

"I haven't told anyone when we're leaving, not even Cully. We want to get away early in the morning so that we can get into Selma at night. On the last leg of the trip, Cokie will drive and I'll sit in the back seat."

"Cokie?"

"Cokie Palmer, the black man who will take me to Martin King."

A chill ran down Cassie's spine. "Don't go, Dix! Stay here with me! Let someone else go."

"I promised, Cassie. I gave my word."

Cassie sank back in her chair, defeated. "I know. I know you did. Have you packed?"

"I won't need much. One suit. A plaid shirt and khakis."

She got to her feet. "I'll help you pack."

When his small case was closed Dix went in to pull down the spread on the single bed.

Cassie went to the door. "No, Dix. Sleep in here, with me."

He looked up. "Are you sure?"

"I'm sure."

They made love that night, tentatively at first and then with more confidence, in affirmation of the love that had almost been destroyed by their reliance upon it. As if to protect each other from personal doubts and public fears, they clung to each other in the darkness.

Dix called Cassie Wednesday night, as he had promised to do each night that he was gone. "We're in Georgia," he said. "Had some trouble with the car but we're going to drive through and should make Selma by dawn. I won't call you again till tomorrow night, Cassie, but I wanted you to know that everything's all right."

"Do be careful, Dix. And remember that I love you."

"I love you, too, darling. Got to go now." The phone went dead.

Cassie waited for Dix's call that night, but she dozed off on the couch and did not wake until one o'clock in the morning. Dix's late arrival, she thought, probably meant that his meetings were running late. He would call Friday morning, she knew, or at least by Friday night.

After a busy day with the children, Cassie waited for a call from

Dix. At midnight, in desperation, she called Cully Meecham at his hotel.

"No, Cassie, you didn't wake me up. I just now came in."

"Cully, did you know that Dix left Wednesday morning?"

"Yeah, I found out yesterday. I kept telling him, Dix, you're flirting with trouble. This little ole trip could cost you a hell of a lot of votes."

Cassie told him about the call from Georgia and Dix's promise to call her each night. "I'm not even sure he got to Selma, and I don't know who I can call to find out. I thought he might have told you—"

"What the hell, Cassie, he's probably stuck in some backcountry gas station with more car trouble. I wouldn't worry your pretty head about it."

"Forget my pretty head, Cully. I'm worried sick, and I have to *know!* Is there anyone you can contact?"

"Okay, okay. Look, let me make a couple of calls. I'll call you back."

"Hurry, Cully! Please hurry!"

He called back at 2:15 A.M. "Ain't been able to find out much. Like me, they figure it's probably car trouble. He's out in the boondocks someplace, waiting for a part."

Cassie's hands were shaking. "He's not with Reverend King?"

"No. Hasn't shown up yet. They're checking from that end, too."

"The police, Cully. We've got to get the police."

"Now, whoa up there, Cassie. Tell you what, you go to bed and get you some sleep. Let me handle this and call you in the morning."

"Call me tonight! If you find out anything at all, call me!"

"Sure thing, honey. Now, you just let me handle it."

How well Cully Meecham handled it was evident in the banner headline on the front page of the Saturday morning paper:

CONGRESSMAN MISSING. Cassie crumpled the newspaper. Trust Cully to go for the publicity, she thought. Anything for votes. She called his hotel.

"Haven't found out anything yet, Cassie, but then if he's at some gas station—"

"What gas station wouldn't have a phone or a car to take him to a phone? Damn it, Cully, if you don't call the police, I will!"

"The police down in Selma, Cassie? You think they're going to knock themselves out looking for a white friend of Martin Luther King's? You just relax and let me take care of this."

"I saw how you took care of it, Cully. I saw the headlines. Listen to me, Dix is my husband and from now on I'm going to be the one who handles it, hear? I'm going to call the FBI."

"They won't do anything about—"

"The hell they won't! You just wait and see."

Cassie took a few moments to calm herself and then dialed the Department of Justice. By using a rational voice and by absolutely refusing to be put off, she finally found herself talking to the man who was chief assistant to an assistant of Robert Kennedy.

"I saw the story in the paper, Mrs. Steele, and I do understand your concern, but this may well be no more than a simple breakdown in communications."

"Or it might be something else entirely," she said as calmly as she could. "Are you aware that Congressman Steele went to Alabama at the personal request of the attorney general? Perhaps Mr. Robert Kennedy should be consulted in this matter."

"Well, yes, I am aware that—but the attorney general is a very busy man and—just what is it you want us to do, Mrs. Steele?"

Cassie's patience was wearing thin. "I want you to call in the FBI. Sir."

"On what grounds?"

She spoke clearly and slowly. "On the grounds that I suspect that Congressman Steele has been taken by some white group, perhaps the Klan, and kidnapping is a crime which the FBI is clearly empowered to investigate."

"Yes, well, this might have to be bucked up to—I mean, I will check into this and call you back right away."

Cassie made a few quick phone calls, but she need not have hurried. "Right away," in government parlance, apparently meant three hours. When the phone finally rang, she jumped to answer it.

"Mrs. Steele?"

"Yes." She recognized the voice instantly. "Is this—are you the attorney general?"

"Yes, I am. It took some time for your message to reach me, but I want to assure you personally that agents from the Montgomery FBI office are on their way to Selma right now."

Cassie's shoulders relaxed for the first time that day. Someone had taken charge. Someone who could get things done. "Thank you, sir. I sincerely thank you."

"There is no need for that, Mrs. Steele. I just hope that we can put your fears to rest. It may be no more than crossed wires, you know. I do want you to know that either I or my staff will be in touch with you as soon as there is anything to report."

"I'm leaving here in half an hour. I have a flight to Montgomery and a room reserved at the Southern Hotel there."

"Do you think it is wise for you to go?"

"I have to," Cassie said. "I must go."

"I can see that. When you arrive, will you call the local FBI office and give them your room and telephone number?"

"Yes, I will. And thank you—thank you again."

"You will hear from us."

One of her quick calls, earlier, had been to Blair Fuller. On the way to the airport, she said, "Now, don't you worry about the children, love. I will take good care of them."

"I hated to ask you."

"Don't give it a thought. As you said one time, what are friends for?"

Cassie checked into the Southern Hotel and from her room called the FBI. Nothing to report. Nothing. She gave them her number and then, out of the need to be doing something, anything, she drew a bath, leaving the bathroom door open so that she would be able to hear the phone. It did not ring. She went to bed and, finally, drifted into a fitful sleep.

It was still dark outside when the telephone rang but Cassie woke instantly. "Yes? Yes, who is it?"

"Miz Steele, I only got a minute, y'hear?"

Although the voice was little more than a whisper, she recognized the soft liquid accent of a Southern black man. "Yes," she said. "Yes!"

"They taken him on the highway, 'fore he got to Selma. Three white men. They put him in a blue car. Listen close, now. They taken him on the state road towards Catherine, 'bout five mile out, I reckon. You got that?"

"Yes. Tell me, is he all right? Is he—"

She was speaking into a dead phone. She hung up and looked at her watch. Four-forty-five A.M. Did the FBI man its phones at night?

A sleepy voice answered. "Federal Bureau of Investigation."

"This is Cassie Steele, Mrs. Dixon Steele. I know where he is!"

"What? Wait, let me get this down." The voice was now alert and eager. "How did you find out? And where is he?"

"Someone—a black man—called me just now and said they took him before he even got to Selma, kidnapped him on the highway. I want to go with you to get him. I *have* to go!"

"That wouldn't be a good idea, not a good idea at all. Where is he, Mrs. Steele?"

Cassie hesitated, then said firmly, "I'll tell you in the car, when we're on the way."

There was a pause. "I'll have to call to the agent-in-charge. You wait right there and I'll call you back."

"Hurry! For God's sake, hurry!"

Cassie dressed quickly in woolen slacks, a turtleneck and a heavy sweater. She was tying her walking shoes when the phone rang again.

"This is Tom Pearson, Mrs. Steele, agent-in-charge. We'll pick you up at the hotel in fifteen minutes. Now, don't get your hopes too high. It could be just a crank call."

"I'll be waiting for you in front of the hotel!"

In the first of the two FBI cars, Cassie told the driver to head for Selma. Agent Pearson, sitting next to her, sighed. "Look, I promise that we aren't going to stop and throw you out on the roadside. Tell us everything the caller said."

By the time she finished her brief report, one of the agents in the back seat had unrolled a topographic map. He folded it into a more manageable rectangle and passed it up to Agent Pearson. Cassie realized that the four men in the car had become very quiet.

"What's wrong? Is there a town there, or a village?"

Pearson cleared his throat. "It's where the highway department is putting in an earthen dam to protect the road from runoff."

"Yeah," the driver said. "Road gets flooded out almost every year. Any kind of a storm will do it, even a good all-night rain."

The two cars slowed as they drove through Selma. After all of the publicity Cassie was surprised to see that it was only a small town and, moreover, one that could have been in Eastern Oklahoma.

The cars did not resume speed when they left the town on the road toward Catherine. It was as if the urgency had gone out of their mission. She wanted to tell the driver to go faster, but she began to realize that for some reason she was as reluctant as they to reach the end of their journey.

Five miles out of Selma, the two cars pulled to the side of the road and stopped. Pearson got out and Cassie would have followed, but he said, "Wait, let us check it out first."

The agents strung themselves out along the road, staying on the blacktop as they peered down on each side at the red clay ditches choked with winter-killed weeds. Fifty yards up the road, an agent raised his arm and gave a shrill whistle. The other men hurried to him. There was talk, but Cassie could not hear what was said. There was gesturing, and pointing, but she could see nothing. Two men ran back to the second car and took armloads of long steel rods to the men up the road. They trailed out, single file, following a path of their own making.

Cassie could wait no more. She jumped out of the car and ran up the road.

"Stay back!" someone yelled. "Don't mess up those footprints!"

She looked down and saw there was a path of sorts, the one the FBI men were avoiding. There were footprints in the clay, prints that could have been made in terra cotta. Evidently they were made after a rain and had been baked by a day of winter sunshine.

The agents stopped in an area where a now-abandoned bulldozer had scraped the red earth into the beginnings of a dam. Agent Pearson gestured and they formed themselves into a line. They faced west and stayed in rank, no more than two feet apart.

Cassie watched as they jammed their steel rods down to break the sun-dried surface and then pushed them into the moist soil beneath the surface. Probing, she thought, probing for—she wrapped her arms around her chest, holding herself together with physical strength.

One of the agents stopped abruptly and raised his hand. His two neighbors moved close, broke the surface, and probed carefully in the red earth. They nodded, but no one spoke. Two men came forward with shovels which Cassie had not noticed before, and at a gesture from Agent Pearson, the others moved between the shovelers and the road, screening their actions from Cassie's view. She saw only their bent backs and, after a few minutes, a glint of steel as a shovel was cast aside.

Agent Pearson moved across to see what Cassie could not, and then walked heavily out to the road, to her.

"You've found him," she said.

"Yes, ma'am, we have."

"And he's—"

"I'm sorry," he said gently.

"He's dead."

Pearson looked down at the clay on his shoes. "Yes."

"I want to see him."

"Ma'am, why don't you wait until we get him—"

"Now," she said tautly. "I must see him now."

Pearson looked at her for a moment. "Yes, ma'am."

He took her arm and helped her through the weedy ditch. With polite formality, he guided her along the path the FBI agents had made, carefully avoiding the footprints of those others, of those men who had brought Dix to this place.

The screen of agents opened and she saw him.

He was lying on the raw red earth. His hands were tied behind him with a rope so tight that his shoulders were pulled back, almost dislocated, and his plaid shirt was stretched taut across his chest. There was a dark stain on his shirt, over his heart, a brown stain tinged with a darker red than the clay beneath him. His face was badly bruised and across his forehead there was a long narrow wound that was almost as black as his tousled hair.

His dark eyes were open, staring at her.

Cassie dropped to her knees. "Dix," she whispered. "Oh, my poor darling." She sagged over him but she lifted her chin and forced her head up, forced herself to see him clear, his battered face and his long, still body.

It was an instant of utter silence, as if the world itself had stopped. Agent Pearson put his hand on her shoulder but she shrugged it off. She had to be alone with Dix, alone to share with him that one last moment of absolute peace.

She leaned forward and took his face in her hands. "Dix," she said once more. His cheeks were ice cold in the winter sunshine.

"Dear God, take him home. Take him now," she said, and with her fingers she closed his eyes.

Part Three

Save me, and deliver me from the hand of
strangers . . .
That our sons may grow up as the young plants,
and that our daughters may be as the polished
corners of the temple.

—Psalm 144, The Book of Common Prayer

Chapter 21

Cassandra Steele's moment of peace ended in FBI bustle as the agents insisted on returning her to Montgomery while they handled the crime scene and local police and the transportation of Dixon Steele's body. Cassie did not object. She had said her farewell to Dix in releasing his spirit to God and his body to the FBI. Moreover, the FBI's arrangements had nothing to do with reality. She knew it was only a bad dream because it could not be true. In reality she was not there, not standing on the red clay of Alabama, and Dix was not dead. How could Dix be dead, after all, when she was alive? It was a nightmare, only that, and eventually she would awaken from it.

The FBI men spoke softly to her as they retraced their earlier trip: back to Selma, back to the highway, back to the Southern Hotel in Montgomery. Cassie sat where they suggested and said what was expected while she waited for it all to be over, to wake from the dream.

At the hotel, however, a hungover reporter from the Montgomery paper was lying in wait and his drawled but insistent questions cracked the shell Cassie had created to enclose herself and the dream.

"Mrs. Steele, does the FBI believe the assassination was the work of one man or of a group?"

Assassination? Cassie put up a hand as if to ward off the word. Why would he ask such a question? But the squinty reporter with the rasping drawl had already managed to shake the foundation of her belief. There was a possibility, however remote, that she was not asleep but awake, that the incredible had become credible.

"Mrs. Steele can't answer your questions now!" It was Agent Pearson who spoke. "We'll have a full statement for you later this morning." He took Cassie's arm and guided her into the hotel lobby. "I'm afraid he's just the first, Mrs. Steele. I would suggest that we fly you back to Washington right away."

"I suppose—is there a flight this morning?"

"The attorney general's office is sending an Air Force plane, ma'am. It will be here by the time I drive you to the base. Will you need time to pack?"

"Dix?" she said. "What about Dix?"

"Later," he said. "When the local police have finished their— will you make arrangements in Washington for someone to meet his—his plane, or shall I?"

"I will. Yes, I'll take care of that."

"Good. It will be good for you to have something to organize, to keep you occupied." He looked at her closely. "Are you all right, Mrs. Steele?"

"All right?" What a strange thing to say, she thought. What an odd question to ask. "Yes. I'm all right."

More reporters were waiting when she came down from her room, and there were more questions. Agent Pearson told them to wait for the FBI statement, and since Cassie herself did not have to speak to them she did not realize that the lobby of the Southern Hotel was only the beginning.

The kidnapping and murder of Dixon Steele, a member of the United States House of Representatives, shocked the American public to the core. Every newspaper, every television reported his death and followed up with virtually minute-by-minute updates on the progress of the search for his killers. Between updates, editorial comment repeatedly tackled the questions that so shocked all Americans. "What has become of our country? What is to become of us when free speech is silenced by death, when political questions are decided by assassination? Are we to become a banana republic where the slate of the ruling party is automatically voted into office and the opposition is automatically voted dead?"

Flying north in an Air Force transport plane, however, Cassie Steele was less concerned with constitutional questions than with personal ones. How do you tell your children? Over and over again she asked herself that question. How do you tell a six-year-old boy and a five-year-old girl that their father will never again come home? She blocked from her mind the larger question that she knew she would have to face sometime, somewhere along the line, because at that moment, at that point she could not even allow herself to comprehend the enormity of it: how could she herself live, how could she continue to exist in a world without Dix?

The plane landed at Andrews Air Force Base, where Cully Meecham was waiting to meet it. For once Cassie was glad to see him. "Cully," she said. "Thank you for coming."

He jerked his chin in embarrassment and took her arm to guide her to the waiting car. When they went past the guards at the gate, Cassie realized how kind the attorney general had been to arrange for her to land at an Air Force base, because a mob of reporters blocked the street. Respect for her husband and for her loss might have restrained them somewhat, but still they all but crawled into the car with her. There were shouted questions and cameras jammed against the windows and curses as they were pushed aside by other reporters.

"For God's sake!" Cully yelled. "Driver, get us out of here!"

"Thank you, Cully," Cassie said when they were in the stream of traffic flowing into Washington. "Thank you so much."

"Oh, Cassie, Cassie." Cully's voice had no trace of his usual Oklahoma twang. "What the hell are we going to do, Cassie? He was such a good man, such a *good* man."

"I know," she whispered. "I know."

Cully struck his knee with his clenched fist. "He could have gone the distance, damn it! He could have had it all!"

"You don't mean the—"

"Yes, goddamn it, I mean the presidency! Cassie, I told him, I said, 'Don't go down there, Dix. Don't mess with that race stuff. It's not your responsibility.' I told him, but did he listen to old Cully? Hell, no! He had to go down there and get killed for it!"

"Yes," Cassie said softly. "He had to go." She turned and looked at Cully. In spite of his ranting, his eyes were full of tears. She saw him then, saw him clearly and saw what Dix had meant to him. Cully was a small man, in body and spirit. He was a man who needed someone to look up to, a leader, and he found that man in Dixon Steele. Cully found his leader and, to keep him heroic, was happy to serve as spaniel to the king, to guard Dixon Steele against his foes, to ease his way and to handle the dirty little jobs that could tarnish the sterling silver of a hero.

With an unaccustomed surge of warmth toward the man, Cassie asked herself what he was to do now, with his hero gone. He would be asking himself the same thing, she realized, the same question she had not yet been able to face: "How can I live without Dixon Steele?"

The car turned onto R Street and Cassie saw that the reporters had already found the house. Men and women, cameras and TV cables, were scattered over the front sidewalk and even on the narrow brick steps. Cully ran interference for her, forcing a path through the mob, and Cassie hurried behind him without answering the screamed questions or looking, as requested, at the television cameras. In a few minutes she and Cully were in the front hall and the door was safely closed and locked behind them.

"Mama!" Taylor ran down the stairs and into her arms.

Cassie clutched his thin body to hers, holding onto him as if he were a life buoy in a surging sea. Martha flew down the hall to be included in the hug. Cassie held both of the children, delaying the inevitable moment when she would have to find the words to tell them about their father.

She realized that Blair Fuller was standing in the hall and she freed one arm and held it out to her friend. Blair moved in to hold Cassie, clinging to her like another child, sobbing.

"This is all turned around," Blair said shakily. "You're supposed to be crying and I'm supposed to be comforting you."

"I am crying," Cassie said.

Blair pushed back to look up at her face. "I don't see any tears."

"No," Cassie said. "I know."

"Cassie," Blair whispered urgently. "I told the children about—about their father. I hope it's all right."

Cassie felt a heavy burden drop from her shoulders. "All right?" she said. "Blair, thank you! You can't imagine how I've dreaded—"

"Yes, I can. My imagination is there even if it's as invisible as your tears."

"I'd like a few minutes alone with the children, Blair."

"Of course. I'll give your Mr. Meecham a drink in the library."

Cassie took the children upstairs to the master bedroom which, she realized, would henceforth be her room. Only hers. For an instant she looked ahead, toward the changes waiting for her, but she closed her mind to the future. She could face only one thing at a time. Only one.

"Taylor. Martha." She sat down on the bed with a child on each side of her and put an arm around each of them. "Blair told you about—about your daddy."

"When the men killed him, did it hurt?" Martha said. "Did he cry?"

Cassie closed her eyes. She had to be honest with them, because in a child's mind an unanswered question could become a festering wound. "I think it hurt, yes. I don't know if he cried."

Within her arm Taylor's body was stiff. "I don't know why they did it. I don't know why they had to go and do that to my daddy."

"They were bad men, Taylor. Terrible men. You see, good men like your father think and make decisions to do good things, but bad men don't think. They just do it, whatever it is, they do it without asking themselves whether it's right or wrong."

Martha pulled at Cassie's sleeve. "Mama, Blair said—Mama, what's heaven?"

Cassie bit her lip. "Heaven? Heaven is—well, it's being with God."

"Is Daddy with God? In heaven?"

Cassie hesitated. Honesty was essential but she had no proof one way or the other. Perhaps in the absence of evidence, proof lay in believing what you wanted to believe. "Yes," she said firmly. "Yes, darling, Daddy is in heaven."

To her surprise and relief Taylor's rigid little body eased itself into the curve of her arm. "With God?" he said. "Mama, is it like Blair said? Is Daddy with God where there's not any bad people and snow and he's happy all day every day?"

Cassie hugged him close. "Yes, dear. That is exactly the way it is."

"Does he miss us?"

"Yes, love, I'm sure that he misses us, just as we miss him. But we're still a family, aren't we? We have to remember that we're still a family."

"Mama?" It was Martha's turn to ask.

"Yes, Martha?"

"Is Daddy going to come home soon? From heaven?"

Cassie braced herself. She had to hold up until it was over, until she answered every question honestly. "No, Martha. Daddy won't be coming home."

Martha looked up at her in alarm. "Not ever?"

Cassie put her cheek against Martha's. "I'm afraid not."

Taylor buried his face in her shoulder, but she could feel the sobs that racked his body. "Taylor, Taylor, it will be all right, you hear? I promise you, it will be all right."

Taylor's tears set off Martha and tears ran down her face. Cassie held them close, longing to join in their crying but unable to break out of her steel cocoon of grief. Their sobs became no more than hiccoughs.

Martha moved restlessly in her grip. "Mama, can I play with my Barbie dolls now?"

"Of course you can. How about you, Taylor?"

"I'm hungry."

"It won't be long till dinner, but ask Angelina to give you a snack, dear."

"Me, too!"

"Yes, Martha. You, too."

"And my Barbies!"

"And your Barbies."

The children ran out of the room and Cassie stood up slowly, stretching her tired muscles. She glanced at the window and then at the door to the sitting room, but the place was full of memories, memories that attacked her like Furies. She could not face them, not yet. She looked at herself in the mirror but she did not even notice that her blue eyes were set in bruised circles of exhaustion and loss. She pushed at her hair distractedly and left the room.

She heard the voices in the front hall, but she had to go down the stairs to see the speakers. With Blair were Amelia and James Steele. They paused, their coats half on, and looked up at her. James looked old, so old, and Amelia was so pale that it seemed impossible that she had survived the flight from Oklahoma.

"Cassie," she said weakly. "Oh, Cassie, what are we to—"

Cassie hurried to take her into her arms. The two women stood and held each other without speaking, seeking surcease in sharing their pain.

"Cassie. My dear." James's hand was heavy on her shoulder and she knew that she was supporting him rather than him supporting her. She turned to put one arm around him and saw Temple Vance carry two suitcases into the house and slam the door in the reporters' faces.

Amelia must have felt Cassie stiffen. "... brought dear Temple—wanted to be with the children ... hope it's all right that we ..."

"Yes," Cassie said, looking at Temple. "It's all right, Amelia."

"Cassie?" Temple's amber eyes looked straight at her and she could see the pain in them. "I want to—I'm sorry, Cassie. So sorry for—for everything."

"Yes," Cassie said. "I know. I can see that you are."

Temple's eyes filled with tears. "Taylor and Martha . . . do they know?"

"Yes. Blair—" Cassie looked at Blair in the library doorway. "Blair, thank you for telling them."

"I thought I could spare you that one duty, Cassie, and Mother and Dad thought it was the right thing to do."

"They were right, and so were you."

"I'm sure." Cassie took James and Amelia into the library where Cully poured sherry for Amelia and a stiff slug of bourbon for James.

James sat down in Dix's armchair. "Can you—will you tell us about it, Cassie, all about it?"

Cassie told them everything, from Attorney General Kennedy's call right down to the color of the clay in Alabama. She kept secret only the one last moment which was essential to her, that last moment she shared with Dix. Amelia cried softly throughout her recital and James clutched a white handkerchief in his hand. Blair and Cully listened, too, without comment. Cassie was dry-eyed. There would be a time, she thought, she hoped, when she too could weep, but she could not afford to, not yet.

When she had finished they sat in silence, a silence which seemed to Cassie to accuse her: "You, the defendant took this man into your life and carelessly allowed him to be killed." Amelia was obviously far too distraught to lay blame. Did the accusation come from Cully Meecham, who had lost his white knight and his ride to the heights of national politics? It was more likely that the indictment came from James Steele, an expert at assigning guilt.

James, however, only cleared his throat. "I think we should go to the hotel now, Amelia, and have some dinner and go to bed."

"Where are you staying, James?" Cassie said. "The Four Seasons? Maybe Cully can—"

Cully's face brightened at the prospect of a chore to do, a service to be performed. "Sure," he said. "I have a car and driver waiting, Mr. Steele. I'll be happy to drop you at your hotel."

They were gone, finally, and Blair Fuller made light drinks for Cassie and herself, added a log to the fire and sat down on the couch. "I've made a list of the phone calls, Cassie, and there are telegrams to read and decisions you'll need to make about—about the services and—"

"Not now, Blair. Please."

"Of course. Dix's—his secretary is coming out to the house tomorrow. She can work in the upstairs sitting room, out of your way, to field phone calls and reporters and the like."

"Blair, bless you, you've thought of everything."

"Hey, I've had help from my parents and even from my brother, who knows all there is to know about protocol. And Joe Howe spent the day here helping out." She smiled. "He's good with children, Cassie. Wonderful with children. Some day when—oh, and Angelina is fixing a casserole for you and for me, too, if you'd like me to stay."

"Yes, oh, yes! Please do stay. I don't want to be—"

"I'll sleep here, too, if you like, dear," Blair said quickly so that Cassie would not have to say the word "alone." "Otherwise I'll come back tomorrow to deal with the people who drop in."

Cassie flinched at the thought of a parade of people walking through the house expressing their regrets but not expressing their certainty that she was to blame for Dix's death. It did not matter, though, because she knew. Even if it were never put into so many words, she knew. Men forty-one years old, members of the House of Representatives, did not just die. They did not just go down South and get themselves murdered. A woman who was widowed at thirty-seven was suspect. Such a woman had obviously done something wrong, had made a bad decision, had worn the blue dress rather than the yellow, turned right at the corner instead of left. Cassie's stomach churned with guilt. Surely she had done something that contributed to Dix's death but she might never know what it was that she did. All that she could be sure of was the fact that she had failed him. She had failed everyone. She had not kept him alive.

Cassie and Blair ate their casserole at a low table in front of the fireplace. Blair was almost too sympathetic. She was ready to listen while Cassie talked out her pain, but to Cassie she seemed to have become an enormous ear. She wanted Cassie to talk, but Cassie could not. She would have to pick her words carefully to hide her failure as a wife. She would have to be too careful. It would be like following faint trails through dark swampland and Cassie was tired, far too tired to begin such a perilous journey.

After Cassie had supervised her children's baths and their getting into their pajamas and nightgown, she hugged each child in turn, clinging to each for a moment too long in an effort to draw on their resources, on their youth.

Martha's little body began to shake. "I want my daddy to come home," she sobbed. "I want my daddy."

Taylor stood alone. Cassie could see how hard he was trying to be strong but his eyes filled, too. She reached out to him and wordlessly he went into her arms. Cassie closed her eyes in pain. They needed her. They needed so much of her, and she had so little to give.

The next few days at the house on R Street dissolved into a confusion of people coming and going, of faces appearing and disappearing without rhyme or reason. Cassie moved through the days as if through a dream, one from which she might never wake. People came to her for decisions but she could no longer make even a simple decision and the people went away, either to make their own decisions or to leave the original question unanswered and dangling in midair like the string of a helium-filled balloon.

Attorney General Robert Kennedy and his wife came to the house on the second day after Cassie's return. Ethel Kennedy was warm and loving, and her tear-filled eyes showed that she shared

Cassie's loss, but Cassie found herself comforting Bobby Kennedy.

His voice was low and miserable. "If I hadn't asked him to—"

"He was honored," Cassie said. "It meant a great deal to him. It meant everything."

Kennedy ducked his head. "Everything."

"He was—" Cassie hesitated. "My husband believed so strongly in peaceful integration of the—"

"I know." The attorney general took her hands in his. "If there is anything I can do, anything at all, will you call on me?"

The intensity in his voice underscored his words.

"Yes," Cassie said. "Yes, I will."

"Later," Ethel Kennedy said, "later, when you've had time to— to heal, you must bring your children to Hickory Hill."

"Yes," Cassie said, but although she knew that Mrs. Kennedy meant well, she could not believe that healing would ever come.

Dix's brother, Jimmy, came and set up camp near the drink tray in the library, his pouting, overweight wife, Maggie, at his side. Cassie's old teacher Naomi Bencher flew in from Hawaii, a staunch military figure in the uniform of a major of the Women's Army Corps. Fran Jordan came from Dallas with Cassie's old friends: Steve Reilly and his wife Dorothea, and Myrtle Frawley. They put their arms around Cassie and cried, and were there when a stir in the front hall announced the arrival of the most august of comforters, the President of the United States.

President Kennedy came alone except for his Secret Service men, and like most official mourners, he had little to say. "Your great loss—sorely missed on the Hill—a death with meaning—an indictment of racial prejudice—"

Meaning, Cassie thought later. What meaning? And who was indicted, the ignorant men who killed Dixon Steele or the country that fostered such hatred among its people? The concept was too complicated to be analyzed by a mind which could no longer make an independent decision even as to which dress to wear or which chair to sit upon.

On the third Tuesday in January, 1963, a day that was windy and bitterly cold, United States Representative Dixon Steele was transported across the Potomac and was buried with the full military honors his World War II military service had earned. Cassie kept her children close during the graveside service, kneeling, finally, to put an arm around each of them. Awkwardly she got to her feet when a young Marine approached her with a thick triangle of bunting, the flag from Dix's casket, but she made no move to take it. In a flurry of whispers someone took the children's hands and someone else encouraged her to accept the flag. She took it then, and clutched it tightly to her chest, but it only served to make her more aware of the void where her heart had once lived and loved and pumped the fluid of life through her body. Her chest felt hollow because her love, her reason for living, was in the gray metallic casket at her feet, the casket that would soon be covered with soil. Her love was in that cold box, her very life.

A soldier raised his bugle and the sweet sad notes of "Taps" rose to the gray sky. The last note hung in the air, and Cassie began to shake, almost imperceptibly to begin with and then in large uncontrollable motions that racked her body. Someone, James, gripped her elbow with surprising strength.

"The car," he said gruffly. "Let me get you to the car."

He guided her across the winter-killed grass and helped her into the black limousine. From the window Cassie watched the scene as she had watched the grainy newsreels of the forties, seeing the people but not connected with them, not even with her own children. She watched until the meaning of what she saw swept over her.

"Oh, no!" she cried and bent suddenly to wrap herself around her pain. For the first time since Dixon Steele's death, Cassie wept.

Chapter 22

 By the first of February, the last visitor had left and the household on R Street was reduced to Cassie, her children, Temple, and, during daytime hours, Angelina. At first Cassie tried to return to her former schedule, busying herself through the day with shopping and lunches and chores, waiting to have her dinner until after the children had gone to bed, but that made the days too long. She had built her schedule around Dix's for so long that her own days had no shape or form. What she had thought to be a busy and productive life was hollow at the core.

The evenings were even worse. She had dined with Dix in the past or, when he had a meeting or was out of town, she had asked Angelina for a tray and read while she ate, or watched television, enjoying the self-indulgence, but she could dine on a tray every night now and find no pleasure in it.

A drink before dinner was not a treat when she had to share it with the televised image of Walter Cronkite rather than with Dix, and to dine was merely to eat, to absorb into her body enough calories for maintenance.

She went up to her own room earlier and earlier each night, leaving the vacancies of the library for the dubious comfort of her bed. Once she was in bed, however, once she had turned off the light and pulled her blankets to her chin, she would be fully awake, her mind churning with wishes and doubts and concerns. Sometimes she could relax and doze, until her hand reached out in the darkness and found no warm shoulder, no tousled hair, found nothing but a smooth cold sheet. She would wake from her doze then and confront the enormity of real life. Dix was not merely out of town and sleeping in a hotel in New York or Oklahoma City. Dix was not sleeping at all. Dix was dead, and his body was moldering in a cold grave in Arlington Cemetery. Dix would not come to her bed, would never again come to her bed. What she would get was what she had. Nothing.

Sometimes that knowledge freed her to weep, to release the pain in tears, and she would not wake until the gray light of dawn revealed her tossed bed sheets and her tear-soaked pillow. Other nights, most nights, she could not bear confronting the facts. She would turn on her bed lamp and read the night away. She could force her eyes to move from sentence to sentence but she could not force her mind to comprehend those sentences. The light of the lamp would hold the dawn at bay, though, until she could rise from her bed and busy herself with the minutiae of another pointless day.

Cassie tried to spend more time with her children, but perhaps she tried too hard. She discovered that she had no place in worlds crowded with schoolfriends and Barbie dolls and Saturday morning cartoons. She could sense their rejection of her, of their long-faced nervous mother.

Cassie saw Blair frequently at first but as the days rolled by, Blair was more and more involved in her plans for marriage and the Peace Corps. Even as she recognized that and tried to share Blair's joy, she found herself resenting her friend's happy commitment to a future that held only lonely misery for Cassie.

James Steele called her late in February. "We miss you and the children, Cassie. Will you visit us for a few weeks?"

"The children would have to miss school."

"Would it hurt them so much? They're bright kids, they could catch up. Amelia needs—" He stopped abruptly, but he had made his point.

Cassie thought briefly of her children's unhappiness, and then of her own lonely dinners and interminable restless nights. "Yes," she said slowly. "Perhaps we need something, too, perhaps a change of scene."

The prospect of leaving Washington even for only a short time provided Cassie with the impetus for a shorter journey that she had not yet been strong enough to make. Alone, she drove to Arlington Cemetery. She walked through rank on rank of headstones until she found the neat stone marker engraved with a few words:

DIXON LANDIS STEELE
1921—1963

A simple cross was centered beneath the dates of his brief life.

Cassie knelt on the cold ground and whispered the Lord's Prayer and then she rose to her feet and stood, head bowed, as if waiting for a message. After a few moments she raised her face to the sky and smiled, because she knew that Dixon Steele had freed himself from the mortal flesh in the grave at her feet. He had risen, the true Dix. His spirit had risen to become a part of the glory that was God.

She looked down at the grave again, though, and her smile faded away. She had loved the mortal flesh, too. She had loved his body as well as his spirit. Her eyes filled with tears and she turned away, both comforted and made more miserable, and stumbled across the mist-damp grass toward her car.

A young woman stood near the path, a woman who might have been Cassie herself staring down at a grave that was so new that the raw earth had not yet been covered with sod.

As Cassie walked by, the woman turned and raised her hand in a quickly aborted gesture.

Cassie stopped. "Can I help you?"

Tears welled up in the woman's eyes. "No. I'm sorry. My husband—"

"Oh, my dear." Cassie gestured toward the grave she had just left. "Mine, too. My husband, too."

"I'm sorry. Was it the war? Or was it—disease?"

Cassie looked at her blankly. The war? Then she realized that the woman meant South Vietnam. She had never thought of it as a war. Disease? Perhaps Dix had died of a disease, but it was not one he had carried within his body. It was a disease of the times, the cancer of racial hatred. "Disease," she said aloud. "Yes."

The woman ducked her head but not before Cassie had seen the desolation in her eyes. "My husband—he was killed in the war. He was what the government laughably calls 'a military advisor.' We—I have three children under ten, and now they have no father."

"I am—I'm sorry." Cassie had enough grief to suffer without sharing a stranger's, but she knew that she had to stand and listen because the woman had to say the words.

"We—I have two sons," the woman said. "Will they grow up and have the same thing happen to them? How can we just ignore this—this obscenity in South Vietnam? Do we have to sit back while they send our children to war, too, all of our children?"

Cassie took a deep breath. "I don't know," she said. "I just don't know."

The young woman reached out to touch Cassie's sleeve. "Of course you don't," she said more calmly. "You can't know. I'm sorry. I shouldn't have—but it's such a—a waste!"

Cassie nodded slowly. "A waste. Yes."

James met them at the airport. Taylor and Martha sat in the back seat and chattered about the farm animals they saw grazing in the pastures along the highway. Cassie and James, however, were silent, each involved in his own thoughts as they passed through the neutral colors of the winter landscape, the pale wheat stubble in the fields, the gray barren branches of the trees and the mist-dulled evergreens.

The town of Ballard had changed since Cassie's days there, first as a young legal secretary and later as Jimmy Steele's wife. The new buildings downtown dwarfed the six-story bank building where James Steele's law offices had been located, and Ballard in general had a look of prosperity that was not there before.

James steered the car into the circular driveway in front of his house and Cassie's first sight of the wide front porch and the solid stone of the big house triggered a flood of memories. She remembered the rainy day when she and Jimmy, newly married, had driven his Cadillac convertible up this drive. She remembered the day she had left this house and fled to Dallas, never to return as Jimmy's wife. Most of all she remembered Dix: the wounded Army captain coming home from war, supporting himself on a stout cane. She remembered the night when she sat in the living room with the Steeles, with all the Steeles, and realized that in choosing Jimmy she had married the wrong brother.

James stopped and the front door of the house opened instantly to reveal Amelia and, behind her, the maid Luella. The children ran to clasp Amelia around the waist. Amelia cried with happiness but Luella's smile was like a white banner of welcome across her dark face.

"I got our yard man Jessie comin' to get them valises, Mist' Steele," she called. "Don't you go strainin' your back, you hear?"

James nodded and took Cassie's elbow to guide her up the front steps. "I'm glad you came."

"I'm glad, too," she said softly, watching her children greet their grandmother. "It was the right thing to do."

Later that night, however, Cassie was less certain. The children and Temple were settled into the guest room, and Amelia put

Cassie in the bedroom she had shared with Jimmy Steele. She was nervous about it until she became aware of the vast difference between going to bed in the room she shared with Jimmy twenty years ago, when she was a bride, and that Georgetown room she shared with Dixon Steele until the last few weeks.

Unlike Georgetown and Washington, Ballard was quiet at night. There were no sirens, no honking cars, no unexplained shouts in the street. Ballard was a town where they rolled up the sidewalks at nine o'clock and everyone in town went home to bed. For the first time since Dix's death she was able to relax. She sank gratefully into a deep and dreamless sleep.

When she awoke, however, she knew that coming to Ballard had solved nothing. Dix was still dead, and she was still alive. She felt more restless than ever.

Amelia and James asked to have the children to themselves for the day, to show them around Ballard and to introduce a few of Amelia's friends' grandchildren as playmates. Cassie was relieved to have the day to herself. James had arranged for a car for her to use, and in it she drove around Ballard alone, revisiting the town she had known when she first came there, seventeen years old and without even a high-school diploma. She drove past the seedy rooming house where she had first lived, and down to the river to the juke joint named The Riverside, where Jimmy had taken her to eat fried fish and drink Pearl beer and dance. It had burned to the ground, and from the look of the rain-washed soot on the few jagged timbers that still stood next to a parking lot long since reclaimed by weeds, it must have happened long ago. She drove along the streets she had walked that summer of 1942, when she escaped from her hot boardinghouse room to the streets of Ballard and walked alone through the night, looking into the lives of the families along her way, lives as open to her view as the windows of their houses. She drove into the gates of the country club, around the parking lot and out again, remembering the night she had crouched in the weeds to watch a Packard convertible sail by, filled with laughing young people in fashionable clothes.

She left the country club to explore the road beyond, driving past farmhouses that had once been gray wood with defunct washing machines on their porches but were now freshly painted and prosperous-looking. In the forties, the children she had seen were still products of the Depression, thin and sickly, and now they wore warm clothes and had round, rosy cheeks.

Cassie's own children were at the Steeles' house when she returned. They rhapsodized about the town and its ice cream store and its schools and playgrounds and "neat vacant lots" for digging and hiding. Each of them apparently had made a best friend already, and their faces glowed with excitement. Cassie realized that they had not looked that happy since Dix's death.

After dinner, when Temple had put the children to bed, Amelia and James invited Cassie to stay on in Ballard with the children, to live with them.

"—so good for the children—a small town is so much better—"

"I don't know, Amelia," Cassie said. "My place is—" Her sentence, like Amelia's, went unfinished. What was her place? Was there, in fact, any place for her in a world without Dix? "I don't know," she said again.

As much as the children enjoyed Ballard, during the next few days Cassie realized that Ballard was not the place for her. Living in Amelia's house meant that she had no recourse even to the time-killers of life: meal-planning and shopping and cleaning. Ballard might offer a lot to children, but for adults it could provide very little. The public library appeared to stock virtually the same books it had offered in the forties, and the shops, she was sure, displayed the same clothes. If the days were empty, the evenings were worse. Amelia and James went to bed early, shortly after the children's bedtime, and Cassie was left to her own skimpy resources, to reread a mystery novel or rework a jigsaw puzzle. Ballard moved to a different drummer, a slower beat than Washington.

James bought bicycles for the children, something forbidden to them in Georgetown's heavy traffic, and they rode for hours every day, coming in with rosy cheeks and voracious appetites. The two of them obviously thrived on the quiet of the big house and the safety of small-town streets.

They had been in Ballard a week when James asked Cassie to come to his study after dinner.

"I was going to read to the children."

"—can do that if they—" Amelia smiled at Martha. "If it's all right with—"

"Let Gammy read!" Martha said instantly. It suited Taylor, too, especially when his grandmother promised to read *Green Eggs and Ham*.

Cassie sat down, as directed, in James's study and recalled with sad amusement Dix's description of his terror at command appearances in his father's study. Cassie was not apprehensive, however, and was not even very curious.

"You are probably wondering why I want to talk to you privately."

Cassie nodded politely.

"First, Jimmy called last night and asked me to apologize for his staying such a short time when he and his wife went to Washington for Dix's funeral."

Cassie was startled. She had forgotten about Jimmy.

"His wife, Margaret—or 'Maggie,' as she prefers to be called—was unwell."

"I'm sorry."

"I'm sorry, too," James said flatly. "Amelia and I see very little of them, you know. Maggie is a very self-centered young woman who seems to need to be the center of attention on every occasion."

"Even at Dix's funeral?"

"Even at Dix's funeral." He scowled. "But I didn't ask you in here to discuss Maggie's egotism. The governor of Oklahoma called me this afternoon and asked that I approach you in his name."

"Yes?" Cassie said, and waited to hear one more expression of regret that Dix was gone, and of outrage at the method of his passing.

"The governor wants to appoint you to finish Dixon's term of office in the House."

His words jerked Cassie's mind into the present. "What did you say?"

"As you know, Dixon's term as a United States Representative does not end until January of 1965, almost two years from now. As I'm sure you also know, filling the position of an elected official who dies in office is the responsibility of the governor. He can call an election, which is expensive and in this particular political climate, somewhat risky, or he can appoint someone to fill the position. This has been a subject for discussion in the party, and the consensus appears to be that the appointment of a politician might jeopardize the election of a Democrat to the U.S. Senate in 1965."

"But why me, James? Why me?"

"To appoint a widow to fulfill her late husband's term is nonpolitical, you see, a gracious gesture. In this specific case, moreover, this—this racist assassination will garner a great deal of publicity, whether the state wants it or not. Appointing you to fill Dixon's term would guarantee that such publicity would be appropriate to the governor's moderate stance on the issue of antisegregation."

"But I know nothing of politics, James. I'm only a mother."

"And an attorney and a highly successful oil-and-gas investor, and a rancher. Don't sell yourself short, Cassie. You are a person of substance."

"I've only thought of myself as Dix's wife—" Cassie stopped abruptly. There was a time, she remembered, when she too had considered herself successful in broad fields, but that was before they went to Washington, before she became a simple helpmeet, a homebody wife whose success or failure was measured in terms of her husband's career. A spark of life kindled, somewhere deep within her, and grew into a small warming fire, the first sign that she had not, after all, died with Dix. She moved uneasily in her chair, feeling oddly disloyal.

"No," she said. "No, James. I couldn't possibly accept it."

"Why not? It wouldn't hurt, you know, just to think about it.

You might also consider your children." He lowered his heavy brows. "If it's the thought of your future that's stopping you, Cassie, remember that Taylor and Martha have a future, too. They deserve more than a mother who is steeped in self-pity."

Cassie glared at him. "I am not—"

"I'm sorry, my dear. That was a tactless remark. I'm afraid that just now none of us is thinking as clearly as he should. Please, don't reject the governor's proposition out of hand. Give it some serious thought."

She shrugged. "Oh, all right. I'll think about it. But I warn you, I know what my final decision will be."

At breakfast the next morning Cassie kissed Taylor and Martha and turned to James. "I'd like to drive down to the farm for the day."

Taylor and Martha begged to go with her, but James raised his voice to drown their clamor. "No. Your mother needs some time alone. Moreover, your grandmother and I plan to take you to lunch and the new Disney movie."

"Mama," Taylor asked nervously, "will you be back by bedtime?"

"Yes, dear. I promise. In fact, I'll probably be back in time to have dinner with you and hear all about your day with Grandma and Grandpa."

As she drove down Highway 12, however, Cassie regretted leaving the children behind. Taylor's chatter would have filled the silent car and answering Martha's questions would have prevented this drive from recalling painful memories of the times she had driven the same road with Dixon Steele. Not even her promise to James to think about the governor's offer could do that.

She saw a silo she remembered, one that was built toward the end of the war. She saw it with Dix when he was home on convalescent leave, when she took him to the farm for a picnic. It was a hot day in early June of 1945. Not long after VE Day. The two of them went swimming in San Bois Creek and Dix kissed her for the first time. He kissed her and then pushed her away because she was his brother's wife. She remembered the idyllic weekend they spent at the farm later, years later, when her divorce from Jimmy Steele was final and she was responsible only to herself. She remembered Dix coming to the farm to see the son he did not know he had sired. Most of all she remembered the good times after they were married, when Dix was in the Oklahoma State Senate and she was building a country law practice. She remembered that time more clearly than the others: the time when they were happy together, happy in their marriage, and in love. So much in love.

She drove James Steele's car from the blacktop of Highway 12 onto the red dirt of the road to the ranch. On an impulse she stopped the car and on foot climbed the hill to the place where she had lived as a child. The tenant house was gone, as were the privy and Granny's chicken house. The dooryard had long since been plowed and harrowed and seeded to pasture. The only evidence that remained to show that it was once a place where people had lived and had died was a clutter of rusty objects at the base of a post oak tree, the place where Cassie used to play at cooking for her dolls and feeding them, and singing them to sleep.

She could almost hear it in the cutting wind of February: a little girl's thin, tuneless song.

"And if that mockin'bird don't sing,
Papa's gonna buy you a di'mond ring."

Only memories remained of the tenant shack and of her grandmother. Everyone was gone. Her half brother Bo had killed their father and, years later, she herself had killed Bo. But Granny had died of natural causes, if poverty and hard, backbreaking work could be considered natural. Cassie's eyes filled with tears and she turned and stumbled down the hill to James's car. Besides her children, she had loved, truly loved, only two people in her life, Granny and Dix, and they were gone now. Everyone was gone, and she was alone.

She drove slowly along the dirt road, past the woods, and stopped at the picket fence around the old hunting lodge, her house.

She had expected the place to be cold and cheerless, but smoke curled from the fieldstone chimney and dissipated against the gray sky.

The front door opened and Henry Starr came out to see the car, a grizzled man in bib overalls. Cassie was surprised to see how much white was in his hair. Henry's getting old, she thought, and I have never noticed it. She let herself out of the car and hurried across the frost-killed grass to the veranda.

"Henry," she said, stopping at the bottom step.

He came down the steps to put his arms around her tentatively. "Cassie, I was mighty sorry to hear. He was a fine man, a real fine man."

Cassie nodded wordlessly, returning his hug.

"Come in, now," he said. "The house is warm." He shepherded her up the steps and through the door. "Mr. Steele, he called down here, said you was on your way. I just now made us a pot of coffee."

Cassie went to the fireplace to warm her hands. "I'd love a cup, Henry."

He came back with a tray balanced precariously in his big work-roughened hands, gave her a cup of coffee and took one for himself.

"Let's sit down and get warm," she said. Henry nodded and perched on the edge of a chair as he had always done before. Cassie herself sat on the couch and stretched out her legs to let the heat from the fire warm her flannel slacks.

"You comin' back here now, Cassie?"

"Why, I—what do you mean?"

"Ain't that much to hold you in Washington now, I reckon. Thought maybe you was plannin' to get back to ranchin'."

"I haven't made any plans."

"Reckon not." His eyes were sad. "Reckon you ain't, not yet. It's a good life down here, though. You remember."

Yes, Cassie thought, but that was the problem. She remembered. She left Henry to drink his coffee and walked through the house. Every room was full of Dix, laughing, swinging Taylor up to his shoulders, tickling Martha, hugging Cassie, sharing a story with Henry. On that gray winter morning the house resounded with his absence, like an empty wooden box struck by a thrown rock.

She went into the bedroom and saw their bed, the one where they first slept together and, on awakening, heard birds singing and saw sunlight glittering on the ripples of San Bois Creek. It was the bed where they made their babies. The bed they shared in happiness and anger, in joy and disappointment. Their bed. Dix and Cassie's bed.

"No," she whispered, "no." The farm, it appeared, was not the place for her. She could not stay there, not with the memory of Dix lying in wait behind every door. But neither could she stay in Ballard, at James and Amelia's house, nor could she measure out the days in Washington with shopping and idle chatter. Time-killers, after all, were not painkillers.

That afternoon she and Henry discussed farm matters, but her mind was not on the business of ranching. Instead she found herself thinking more and more about the business of government.

Chapter 23

Cassie drove back to Ballard that afternoon, and after dinner she asked James to meet her in his study.

"I might do it," she said. "I might just be able to handle it."

James straightened in his chair and took a cigar from the humidor on his desk. He looked younger, suddenly, and his eyes were sharp and alive. "Of course you can do it. You won't just be on your own, of course. I'll do anything I can to help, and there's Cully. I'm sure he'll agree to stay on as your chief aide."

"Cully," she said thoughtfully. "Yes, there's Cully."

"I'll call the governor, then, and tell him that you will accept the appointment."

Cassie pressed the tips of her fingers together. "No, James. I haven't yet decided for sure. I want to think about it some more. But one way or the other, I think I should be the one to make the call to the governor."

James looked surprised, but he nodded. "Of course. Whatever you say." He shuffled through the papers on his desk, avoiding looking at her. "There's something else, Cassie. About the children—"

Fear knifed Cassie's heart. "They're all right, aren't they? Did something happen while I was gone today?"

"No, no, they are fine. They couldn't be better. That, in fact, is what I want to discuss with you." He took a deep breath. "Amelia and I would like very much to keep your children here for a few months; say, to the end of this school year."

"James! I can't just—"

"Please, hear me out. We would enroll them in school, of course, and see that they attended Sunday school as well. You've seen them these last few days, Cassie. You've seen how good life is here, for children. And if you decide to accept the governor's appointment, I might point out that you will be extremely busy in your new post and that meetings and the like will keep you on the Hill many evenings. Wouldn't it be better for Taylor and Martha to be here, where they are busy and happy, than in Georgetown where they would have to spend evening after evening with only Temple for company?"

"What about Temple? Would you—"

"Yes, we want her, too. She can go to high school here." He looked at Cassie shrewdly. "I rather think that a touch of small-town life might be good for Temple as well."

Cassie had to agree with that.

"I'm sure you would find it easy to visit the children frequently. The large Oklahoma oil companies maintain fleets of jets, you know, and schedule flights for their high-level employees. They would be only too happy to let a member of Congress hitchhike, as it were."

"As it were. Yes. And in return they would expect me to—"

"Cassie, if you are to take national office, you must rid yourself of naïveté. They will expect no more than a smile and, perhaps, a friendly attitude. Prices have risen, you know. An elected official can no longer be bought for a few free plane rides."

No, Cassie thought, no. If she were to try to fill Dix's shoes, she had to be like Caesar's wife, above suspicion. She could afford to buy her own tickets on commercial flights. "Let me think about it, James. And let me find out what my children have to say."

He nodded approvingly. "Of course. The decision is yours, Cassie."

"And theirs."

"And theirs, yes."

Yes, she thought, her children had to be involved in the decision. But the question of how hard she was able to work at her job in Congress involved other children as well. She thought back to her conversation with the young widow at Arlington. Could they, could Cassie, simply sit back and let the government send young men to die in South Vietnam? Could she watch while it happened to her children, to all of the children?

No, Cassie thought. No.

As she helped Temple get the children ready for bed, Cassie analyzed the situation, thinking it through. As she had learned to do in the law, she separated the subject into component parts, letting each issue stand alone. Accepting or rejecting the governor's offer, for instance, had to be considered alone, not in conjunction with a decision on where the children would live.

It was not as easy to separate questions involving human beings, she discovered, as it was to split those based on abstract legal theories. If she left the children with Amelia and James and went back to Washington, she would be alone in the house on R Street. There would be no sounds of life, no laughter and no tears, only the sound of the mantel clock ticking away the minutes and the hours and the days. But if she accepted the governor's proposal, and took the children back to Washington with her, James was right: She would have practically no time with them. But could she abandon them to the Steeles, even for four months? If she could do that and accept the appointment, she could continue Dix's work. Somehow she felt that he would be with her, sharing the job.

While she helped Taylor and Martha into their pajamas, she brought up the idea of their staying with their grandparents.

"In Ballard?" Taylor said. "You mean, us stay here in Ballard? And go to school here and everything! Wait till I tell Bobby Owen! Me and him's going to build us a fort!"

"And work on your grammar, too, I hope. Martha, what do you think of the idea?"

"Gammy and Gampaw took us where Susy lives, and she has *four* Barbies and a Barbie house! She said I could play with them, too. Mama, if we stay here, can we get me another Barbie?"

"I think we can swing that, honey."

"Maybe *two* Barbies?"

"Hey, don't push your luck!"

When she had kissed the children good night, she started to go back downstairs, but Luella stopped her in the hall. "Miz Cassie? You got a minute we can talk?"

"Of course. What is it?"

"Miz Cassie, me and Jessie and the rest wants you to know how bad we feels about Mr. Dix's passing."

Cassie closed her eyes for an instant and then looked directly at Luella. "Thank you. I appreciate that."

"There's more. Mr. Dix, he was on our side. He wanted us to get equality and all that."

"I know. He felt very strongly about integration."

Tears filled Luella's dark eyes. "But with him gone, who's gonna help us now? That's what's worryin' us, Miz Cassie. Who's gonna help us now?"

"Oh, Luella!" Cassie put her arms around Luella and she cried too. If Luella, living in Oklahoma which was a moderate state, felt the loss so greatly, what would other blacks feel, in the deep South, everywhere? Were they missing Dix as much as she? Were they, too, wondering, Who will help us now?"

Cassie released Luella, stepped back and dried her eyes. "I will, for one," she said definitely. "I will help you. I can't do all that much as a private citizen, but—" She hesitated for only a moment because suddenly the decision was clear-cut. "The governor has asked me to take my husband's place in the House of Representatives and I will do it. I promise you that, Luella. I will help you."

Luella straightened her back. "Yessum. Yessum, I believe you. And I thank you. We all thank you."

Cassie tried to smile. "I haven't done anything yet, you know. You'd better wait till we see what I can accomplish."

Luella hurried off to finish turning down the beds, and Cassie went down the stairs slowly, one step at a time, considering the ramifications of the promise she had made.

James and Amelia were in the living room.

"James," Cassie said firmly, "I have decided to accept the appointment. And Amelia, I will leave the children with you until the end of the school year."

James stood up, letting his newspaper slip to the floor. "Cassie, dear, I am delighted. I'm certain that you'll do a fine job of filling out Dix's term."

". . . to have the children with . . ." Amelia clasped both of Cassie's hands in hers. ". . . such a delight to . . ."

During their phone conversation, Cassie felt that the governor was trying to tell her something between the lines. There was an implication that she was to consider her role as a representative as a stopgap, a position more honorific than real. She was not certain he meant that, however, and she realized that she was an unknown quantity to the governor, just as he was to her. She would have to talk with him again in order to clarify their positions.

Cassie went back into the living room where James and Amelia were waiting. "I have talked with the governor," she said, "and I have agreed to go to Oklahoma City on Monday. I will be sworn in, then, to fill Dix's term of office." She cleared her throat and tried to put into her voice the self-confidence she could not feel. "I will become a congresswoman, a delegate from Oklahoma to the United States House of Representatives."

Cassie was surprised when Cully Meecham met her plane at Dulles Airport. "How did you know which flight to meet?"

He grinned like a fox. "Oh, I find these things out. You can depend on old Cully." He looked at her directly for an instant, but his eyes slid off to the side. Cully was not a man for direct looks, no matter how sincere he was. "I mean that, Cassie. Things are going to be tough for you, going into the House and all, and it's going to get worse. I'll be there for you, you hear? You just say the word."

Cassie was touched by his profession of support, but while he loaded her bags into his car she distanced herself from his concern. She knew that it was going to be difficult, terribly difficult to take on Dix's job, to try to fill his shoes as a U.S. Representative. Perhaps Cully knew, as she did, that it would be even more difficult, since it would require her to function as a woman, and at the same time to set aside her all-consuming sense of loss. She would need help, but she was not at all sure that she wanted it to come from Cully Meecham. There was something about Cully that reminded her of a forest creature, an animal that avoided clearings flooded with sunlight. The woods where Cully walked could be dark and even dangerous.

At the house on R Street, Cully carried Cassie's luggage upstairs and then paused in the front hall. "I reckon you'd as soon have a little time to yourself now, Cassie."

It suited Cassie for him to go, but once he was gone she found herself wishing that he had stayed.

The house was cold and empty. There was no Temple to amble through the room grumbling about school or Cassie's house rules. There was no Angelina singing in the kitchen. There were no children running down the stairs to greet her. There was no Dix.

The sound of a rattle at the back door drew Cassie into the kitchen. Angelina was there, having let herself in with her own key. "Mizteel! I no expec' you till night! I come to turn up the heat, fix you a little something to eat." Suddenly her broad face crumpled. "Oh, Mizteel, ees bad, so bad."

Cassie ran to put her arms around Angelina and for a few

moments they stood together, holding each other, mourning together as women have done since the world began. Cassie pulled
away first, wiping her eyes, straightening her shoulders.

"Angelina, I have to get hold of myself."

The woman shrugged. "I never understan' these Anglo peoples.
Why not to cry? Why not to show way you feel?"

"Because—" Cassie hesitated. "I don't know. Because that's the
way it is. Or the way I am."

When she had finished the light supper Angelina had prepared,
Cassie stared blankly at the leaping flames in the fireplace, wishing,
wanting. After a while she picked up the telephone and dialed the
number she had now memorized. "Mr. Pearson?"

The FBI agent-in-charge in Montgomery recognized her voice.
"No news, Mrs. Steele. Or I guess I should say, Congresswoman."

"No. Please don't. I was just—hoping—"

"Listen, you keep hoping, hear? We'll catch them, I swear it.
But remember that it's going to take time, time for someone to
remember something he saw, or heard. Time, even, for one of them
to get drunk and let something slip. We'll get them in the long
run, I promise you that."

"You don't mind my calling you to ask—"

"Hell, no! Sorry, I mean, please do call me. Then I can tell my
bosses honestly that there's congressional pressure on this one.
Believe me, I don't want this to get filed away any more than you
do. You keep on calling, hear, and you keep on hoping. We'll get
them."

Cassie replaced the receiver carefully, as if a sudden crash of
noise might destroy the delicate thread of Agent Pearson's investigation. Hope, he said. Hope. What was there to hope for? Even
if the FBI caught the killers, it would not bring Dixon Steele back
to her.

After a miserable sleepless night, Cassie took a shower and had
just finished dressing when Angelina knocked on the bedroom
door. "There thees lady, Mizteel, she say she your friend."

"It's all right," Cassie said. "I'll go downstairs and see."

Halfway down the stairs she saw who it was, and she ran the rest of the way. "Fran!"

"Oh, Cassie, my dear!" Fran hugged her. "When I was here for the funeral, I couldn't—" She pushed Cassie to arm's length. "Honestly! Just look at you!"

Cassie was more interested in looking at Fran. Rarely had anyone looked so good to her. She realized suddenly that she and Fran had been friends since 1942. Twenty-one years. She looked at Fran, who was surveying Cassie just as carefully, and for the first time since that morning in Alabama, there was some lightness in her heart. She even giggled. "So? What's to see?"

"You're a frump, Cassie Steele. You've let yourself become an absolute frump!"

Cassie looked down at herself: a dun-colored jersey dress with one gold chain for jewelry, midheight heels on sensible brown pumps. "What's wrong with me? I look like what I am."

Fran's eyes snapped with anger. "What you are? Or what you'll settle for being?"

"Oh, come on, Fran." Cassie turned away sadly. "I'm a middle-aged widow." As always, the word caught in her throat, but she forced herself to go on. "I'm the mother of two children, and I'm in Washington only to fill out Dix's term of office. I have no illusions."

Fran grabbed her arm. "You stop right there, Cassie Steele! As usual, you have it all backwards. Look, you are a United States Representative from Oklahoma, right? There are four hundred and eighteen men in the House and only seventeen women, but you are one of those women. That gives you power, kid, it gives you leverage. Not to mention considerable fame. Are you even aware that your name is known all over the country?"

Cassie shook her head. "You mean, Dix's name is known. I'm only his widow."

Fran closed her eyes. "Dix, yes. God rest his soul." She opened her eyes, then, and peered at Cassie. "Nevertheless, you are a congresswoman, with the power to do great good—or nothing at all. Second, you're a mother. Third, you're a widow, yes, but you aren't a frump! Cassie, you idiot, you are thirty-seven years old, at the prime of your life! I absolutely refuse to let you sink into middle age in a welter of self-pity! You hear me, girl?"

Cassie raised her chin and grinned as if a burden had been lifted from her shoulders. "I hear you, girl. I hear you just fine!"

Fran hugged her, hard. "Then for God's sake, fix me a Scotch and ask me about my horrendous flight from Dallas."

"Scotch at ten o'clock in the morning?"

"Scotch instantly, if you want to live to enjoy your power!"

Fran rushed Cassie from store to store selecting a new wardrobe for her, what Fran called congressional clothes. "Don't forget, Cassie. Dress not for what you are but for what you want to become."

"Then we'd better look at Levis and Oshkosh overalls, because when Dix's term is finished I'm going to go back to Oklahoma to be a farmer."

Fran looked at her and started to speak, but stopped. "We'll see," she said finally. "We'll just have to see about that."

As they moved from store to store Cassie was surprised by the number of people on the street who hesitated then turned to watch her pass. An old lady scurried up to take her hand. "My dear," the woman said, "oh, my dear," and disappeared into the crowd. Most clerks recognized her instantly, and those who did not, looked up when she handed them her charge card, startled by her name.

A young clerk, a pretty blonde, said "Mrs. Steele? Mrs. Dixon Steele?" Her eyes filled with tears. "Oh, Mrs. Steele, I'm so sorry."

Cassie was embarrassed, but Fran stood by, watching the episode with a thoughtful expression. "Cassie," she said as they left the store, "is Cully Meecham still around?"

"Oh, yes. He's been so much help. And surprisingly sensitive."

"I've always sort of liked old Cully."

Fran had to fly back to Dallas before the day that Cassie entered the House of Representatives, but Cassie dressed to suit Fran's commands: a well-cut gray wool suit ("No, Cassie, not black, this is business, not a funeral."), a pale pink silk blouse and black pumps with heels of just the right height, what Fran had called, "Somewhere south of floozy but north of frump." Blair Fuller and Cully Meecham were in the gallery to provide moral support. The majority leader met her and offered his arm as he escorted her down to the well of the House. As they walked in, conversations stopped on both sides of the aisle and people rose to their feet in tribute, not to her but to Dixon Steele, who had been one of their own. Speaker McCormack took her hand and held it for a moment of silent sympathy before he swore her in. She was escorted, then, to the seat that had been Dixon Steele's, and as the normal chatter of the House rose around her, she sat with her hands folded, feeling very much like a new kid on her first day in school.

She felt very much the same way at the first meetings of the committees to which she had been assigned. The testimony of witnesses went on and on as they relied on sheer numbers of words to obfuscate the meaning of what they were saying. The members of the committees seemed to be no more concise. Cassie thought that some of them asked and parried questions for an hour at a time to set up an opportunity to deliver one short, pithy sentence that might make the six o'clock network news.

Cassie herself said little in committee and nothing in the House. Like most freshman congressmen, she had been advised to keep her ears open and her mouth shut, and moreover she needed to learn the jargon and study the issues. There were times, however, when she wondered if her presence served even the minimum requirement of filling Dix's place with a warm body.

One aspect of being a congresswoman surprised her. In Ballard or Dallas, a widow was a drug on the dinner party market. For a widow, for Dixon Steele's widow, who was a member of Congress, there were more invitations than she could accept. At first she refused invitations but later in the spring, at Cully's urging, she began to go to a few large parties which she could leave early without becoming entangled.

Cully, as usual, was her escort in late March for a party at the Venezuelan Embassy, where attendance was virtually compulsory for a U.S. Representative from an oil-producing state. As always, Cully introduced her to a few people and then tactfully faded into the crowd. Cassie circulated, chatting with people she knew, alert for clues as to OPEC's next move. She knew she looked good, in a pale blue ankle-length dress she and Fran had selected. If she had not been certain, she would have been reassured by the Venezuelan undersecretary. His attentions were almost embarrassing, as was his fascination with her long blond hair and, from the way his eyes made frequent little journeys in that direction, with her bosom. Her distaste for his invasive looks was sweetened by the OPEC tidbits he was revealing. She listened, and smiled, until he realized that he was saying too much and stopped abruptly. He dabbed at his forehead with a red silk handkerchief and looked around the room in desperation.

"Señor Cameron!" he called out. "Señora Steele, may I introduce Señor Cameron? Señor, this lady is the new representative from your fine state of Oklahoma."

A rasping baritone answered from behind Cassie. "I know that, Ricardo, but I have not had the privilege of meeting the lady."

The Venezuelan made a hasty escape into the crowd, but Cassie hardly noticed. The owner of the baritone voice appeared and captured her entire attention.

The man was huge, she thought, at least six foot four, with broad, heavy shoulders, big competent-looking hands, and a wide open face with ice-blue eyes set slightly far apart and fringed with sandy eyelashes that matched his eyebrows and his thick curly mass of blond hair. His left cheek was marked by an old scar and she was sure that his nose had been broken at least once. He looked about forty. He was not bad looking, in his craggy way, but he wore a suit that was simply appalling, polyester double-knit in a beige color that had no resemblance to any color existing in nature.

"Mackenzie Cameron, ma'am," he said in that deep-timbred voice. "We haven't met, Congresswoman, but I know you are Mrs. Dixon Steele."

"Cassandra Steele," she said, hearing the tightness in her voice. "Cassie Steele. You aren't in my district, then."

"Cassie Steele." His smile was an open, friendly grin. "Now, that sounds more like Oklahoma. Folks call me 'Mack.' You're from Lapland, aren't you?"

"Yes." Cassie smiled too. Only another Oklahoman would know the area called Lapland, "where Arkansas laps over into Oklahoma."

"I'm from Sooner country, myself," he said. "My daddy was a dirt farmer up Guthrie way."

The Sooners were the settlers who jumped the gun on the day of the great Oklahoma Land Rush. They went into the Territory the night before the Rush and claimed the best parts for themselves. This man was definitely not a dirt farmer like his father, however. She knew of his oil company, an independent with the reputation of making more money than the U.S. Mint. "You're Cameron Oil, of course."

"Yes, ma'am. I've been pretty lucky, comin' and goin'."

Cassie looked at him carefully. There was an amused intelligence in the man's eyes that did not match the country-boy diction. "I think you're pulling my leg, Mr. Cameron."

He answered her just as formally. "I cannot say that I would not enjoy doing that, Congresswoman Steele."

Cassie drew back and the amusement left his eyes. He immediately stepped to one side as if to give her room to move, to escape him. "Mrs. Steele," he said seriously, "I have waited to introduce myself to you until the time seemed appropriate. I have heard that you fly to Tulsa every other weekend to visit your children in Ballard. Is that right?"

"Why, yes. Yes, it is."

"As a fellow Oklahoman, then, please let me offer you the use of my company jet. We use it to transport Cameron planners and taxmen who have to be in Washington for weeks at a time, but want to spend the weekends with their families, so it's scheduled to fly out from Washington to Tulsa every Friday night and to return to Washington late Sunday. You might find it more convenient than the commercial airlines."

The memory of her last trip to Ballard flashed into Cassie's mind. She could not get a reservation for Friday night, so she arrived in Oklahoma at noon and had to leave Ballard at noon Sunday to get back. On top of that, mechanical problems kept the plane on the ground in Oklahoma so long that she had reached the house on R Street hours late and exhausted.

"If I could pay for the—"

"No," Cameron said. "My jet is not licensed to carry paid passengers, and the plane is never full anyway, so it won't cost us a cent."

Nothing came free in Cassie's world, however, and she suspected that the free flight might cost her far more than the price of a coach ticket on a commercial jet. Cameron was sure to expect political favors or, even worse, personal ones. But when she considered the extra time it would give her with Taylor and Martha, she knew that she had to chance it. Even as she gratefully accepted his offer, she resolved that she would keep meticulous records for her own protection, and that at the first sign of hanky-panky she would get out of the deal. There had to be a lack of moral fiber in a man who would wear that polyester suit.

Providentially Cully appeared just then, and Cassie thanked Mack Cameron and promised to call his secretary for instructions about the Tulsa flights.

In the car she told Cully what she suspected.

"Oh, come on, Cassie," he said as he shifted gears for the climb to R Street. "Mack's a good ole boy. Sure, he's got a lot of money, but he worked for every cent of it. Started out with nothing but a drilling rig and a big debt. That's when he got his nose broke, pulling one of his roustabouts out of a gyp joint. He won't want much, maybe just for you to hear his ideas, the independent's side on the next oil bill to come to the floor. What's so bad about that? After all, they all do it, all the representatives and senators, too: a free plane ride, a weekend of sailing, the congressional baseball game in Daytona Beach, maybe a country club membership. It's not like you're selling out, you know."

" 'They all do it' doesn't sound like much of a recommendation to me," Cassie said thoughtfully, "but I'll give it a try. Just don't be surprised later if I back out."

Cully chuckled. "Honey, I've been in politics seventeen years. There's not much of anything that surprises me." He pulled the car to a stop. "Look, Cassie, I'm going to Oklahoma tomorrow. How about you coming out Friday and spending Saturday seeing some folks in your district?"

Cassie's heart lifted, not at the thought of seeing constituents but at that of seeing her children. "Yes! I'll do it, Cully!"

That week Cassie took a break from studying in order to make plans for meeting with her constituents. On Thursday night she tucked a file folder into her briefcase and straightened her tired shoulders. She knew that she had accomplished almost nothing during the few months she had been in office, but that week she had begun to see some light. She had designed a structure for her work, one that would allow her to do what she had been appointed to do: to serve the people of her district as their representative in Washington.

Mackenzie Cameron was not on the Learjet Friday night, but according to the crew members, he seldom was. Cassie was relieved and oddly disappointed by his absence. There were only four other

passengers, an accountant and three technicians, and Cassie was
able to spread out her papers and spend the flight time fine-tuning
her plans for her district.

She had a joyous reunion with Taylor and Martha, who had
been allowed to stay up late, and they did not complain about her
spending Saturday on business.

Cully came to the house Saturday morning and Cassie took him
to James Steele's study for a talk.

She leaned back in James's leather desk chair. "Cully, what
precisely did you do for Dix? What were your duties?"

They were not that easy to define, but Cassie began to see that
Cully had served Dix in a variety of undertakings, some less appealing than others. He had been someone to lean on a company
president for a cash contribution, someone to soothe party bigwigs
with ruffled feathers, to tinker here and apply oil there until Dix's
political machine appeared to run on ball bearings. In short, he
had been essential.

When he finished, Cassie turned her chair and stared out through
the March drizzle at the tall buildings of downtown Ballard. After
a few moments, she turned back to him. "Cully," she said finally,
"will you work for me as you did for Dix? Will you do the same
job for me?"

Cully smiled at her, a grin as narrow as a fox's. "I already am,
Cassie. I been working for you right along. You just never did
notice it." He paused. "And never paid me for it."

Cassie remembered suddenly that the car was always there when
she needed it, that an excellent secretary, a young graduate student
from Sallisaw, had simply appeared in her office one morning, that
Cully himself had been available to her at any time of day or night.
"My God, Cully! I'm sorry."

He waved away her apology. "It ain't nothin', Cassie. I figured,
when you really got at the job—"

"Well, that's where I am now. Look, I'll pay you what Dix did,
with your salary retroactive to the last one he paid, and with a
bonus. Is that satisfactory?"

"It sure as hell is!" He leaned forward. "Now, what are these big plans you got?"

Two weeks later Cassie called Cully Meecham and that very night they sat in her house and began the process of putting her plans for the future into present action.

They took the first step when they flew to Oklahoma a week later. In the larger towns of her district they talked to the local politicians who would organize the creation of offices where volunteers and, frequently, Cassie herself would hold "Saturday Clinics." A constituent, she announced, was a constituent whether he had supported Dix or not, whether Democrat, Republican, Independent or just someone with a problem. He could bring that problem to the clinic, and it would be forwarded to her Washington office. Her own reports on solutions or failures would in turn be relayed back through the same network.

In each town they visited that day, Cassie made an impromptu speech to explain the concept of the clinics. Again and again she found herself ending with the same message. That evening as Cully drove them back to Ballard she realized that she had defined for herself as well as for her constituents the purpose of her job.

"When the governor appointed me to fulfill my husband's term," she told them, "when he sent me to Washington, it was not to do what I wanted but what you wanted. So use these clinics to tell me what you want me to do in Congress and I will try my very best to do it. I am in Congress only to do your work, to state your opinions and to deliver your messages to your fellow Americans. With your thoughtful advice and support, with your help, I can do that job. I will be your good and faithful servant."

Chapter 24

Blair Fuller and Joe Howe were married in May 1963. To her parents' delight and her aunts' dismay, Blair chose to have the ceremony take place in the somewhat overgrown garden of her parents' house.

Muffy Fuller, Blair's sister-in-law, huddled in conference with the aunts. Her mouth, like theirs, was twisted into a disapproving pout. "You'd think that at the very least Bobby would have had the shrubbery trimmed back!" an aunt said.

"Oh, no!" Margaret Fuller was passing just then, but she stopped and clasped her hands as if in prayer. "Destroy the birds' habitat? Bobby would never, never do so despicable a thing!"

The mother of the bride, Cassie thought, might have been wearing slightly runover heels, but her mantle of love for every living creature was cut from the cloth of glory.

Cassie's eyes filled with tears, however, as she approached the ragged reception line and took both of Blair's hands in hers. Blair and Joe would have their honeymoon en route to Africa for a two-year stint in the Peace Corps. "I am so happy for you, dear, but I'm going to miss you dreadfully."

Blair's eyes filled, too. "And I'll miss you, Cassie. You've done so much for me. But it won't be forever! We must remember that."

"For you to be in Africa for two years sounds like forever to me, damn it!" Cassie turned to Joe Howe, but he obviously could see no one but Blair. "Take care of her, Joe. She's very precious to us all."

"Isn't she just?" He beamed at his bride. "You take care of yourself, too, Cassie."

Her eyes filled and Cassie withdrew to the edge of the crowd, wishing she could join the birds in their leafy sanctuary. Someone handed her a glass of champagne, though, and someone else thrust a plate of hors d'oeuvres at her and she was trapped, juggling her handbag and unable to set anything down or, for that matter, to consume either the wine or the food. Just as she began to despair of leaving the reception unencumbered, a light baritone voice spoke behind her.

"Let me give you a hand with those." A long hand inserted itself into her welter of objects and removed the most awkward one, the plate.

"Oh, thank you!" she said, and turned to face her rescuer.

He was tall and slender, with a long narrow head and pale gray eyes. His clothes were conservative and his dark suit announced not in a shout but a whisper that it was the product of a bespoke tailor. He balanced her plate and his and a champagne glass with great aplomb. "I don't have to carry a handbag," he said, defending himself against her unspoken comment. "May I introduce myself, Congresswoman Steele? I am Eliot Peabody, an old friend of Blair's family."

"You know my name."

"Of course. Everyone knows your name." His firm mouth softened. "May I extend my sympathy for your loss?"

Cassie ducked her head. "Thank you," she said softly. She looked up to find his eyes surveying her from head to toe.

"Television does not do you justice, Congresswoman."

"Please call me 'Cassie.' "

"Of course. I see a small table free now. Shall we—"

"Yes. I'd like that."

At the table, however, Cassie was at a loss for conversation. Eliot Peabody was not one to encourage small talk.

"Are you in government, Eliot?" Cassie thought that was a safe enough question.

"Yes."

She waited for him to continue, to explain his job as most Washington men did, in terms that made it sound more important than it was. The lengthening silence made her uncomfortable. "I'll bet you're in State," she said finally.

"One could say that." He smiled at her and his pale eyes warmed. "I have admired the way you have handled yourself in the House."

"But I haven't done anything," she said. "I've hardly opened my mouth!"

"Perhaps that is what I find admirable. There were some who expected you to stand on your husband's murder to rant and rave about segregation."

"And I haven't done that, have I?" she said thoughtfully. "I've never once spoken out."

"A wise move, don't you think?"

"Wise, maybe, but—" She hesitated. There was a reason, after all, for her accepting the governor's request and taking Dix's seat in Congress.

"What are your committee assignments, Cassie?"

"The speaker was kind enough to pass along my husband's appointments. I'm on Rules and Judiciary."

"That is quite impressive."

"I'm very junior, believe me. I haven't yet spoken up in committee, either."

He looked at her as if he were reading her like a book. "You will," he said. "You will."

Cassie left the party shortly, but she kept thinking about Eliot Peabody. He was charming and obviously well-educated, a rather typical result of the melding of proper breeding and old money. Behind his impeccable manners, however, she had sensed a private man, someone untouchable. The outer man was pleasing, there was no doubt about that, but it was the inner, secret one who intrigued her.

She was not at all surprised to hear from Eliot Peabody a week later and after only a moment's hesitation she accepted his invitation to dinner. She was pleased by the restaurant he chose. It had a reputation for good food, but it was not a haunt of fashionable Washington. They could have a quiet dinner without it being reported in the gossip columns.

"You said you were in State, didn't you, Eliot? What does the department think of President Kennedy's increasing the number of advisors in Vietnam?"

"I believe you were the one who suggested a connection with State, Cassie. At any rate, I am more interested in your background than mine. I believe I know the bare bones of your story, but I would appreciate your fleshing it out for me."

It was a pleasant dinner but as they left the restaurant, Cassie realized that Eliot Peabody knew a great deal about her while she knew very little about him.

"Eliot," she said as he drove her home, "you aren't a native of Washington, are you?"

"No, Cassie. I am from Boston."

"How do you know the Fullers, then?"

"I was in school with their nephew William."

Cassie did not pursue the question because it was no longer necessary. The son of one of Blair's aunts would hardly have attended P.S. 59. She should have caught Eliot's slightly flattened "a," she thought. That, with the Fuller connection, would have told her all she wanted to know about his background. Groton, probably, then Harvard and Harvard Law, then the inevitable public service in—what? He was reluctant to identify his job, or even his government department. It dawned on her then: intelligence, of course! He was an offspring of the Dulles brothers and of the English-inspired tradition of intelligence work as an upper-class game.

She smiled to herself. She was not bad at intelligence herself. She had deciphered the code and placed Eliot Peabody in the proper niche. Her smile faded as she realized that there was much, much more that she wanted to know about him, about Eliot the man.

"Eliot," she said abruptly, "what did you do in the summers? I mean, when you were a little boy?"

He hesitated and it seemed to Cassie that as he shifted gears from the now to the then, he softened, as if his adult shell had cracked.

"Ah," he said finally, "we spent our summers on the coast in Maine, near Kennebunkport. My mother and father played at life during the summer. We had a little house, only a beach cottage. My father objected, but in some ways my mother was rather odd. She insisted on leaving the servants in Boston and doing the work at the cottage herself, the cooking and washing and of course we had our chores, too, making the beds and so forth."

"We?"

"My brother and sister and I." He was looking past the Washington traffic to a quieter, happier time. "We sailed every day. A little catboat—"

He steered the car into R Street and himself, it seemed, into the present. With his usual punctilious manners he escorted Cassie to her door.

Cassie found herself wanting to know more about the boy in the catboat. "Would you like a brandy, Eliot?"

"Not tonight, Cassie, thank you." He smiled. "I would like very much to repeat this evening. May I call you?"

"Yes," she said softly. "Please do."

One week later, on a Friday afternoon when the damp heat could almost be cut with a knife, Cassie received the telephone call that ripped through her life like an Oklahoma tornado.

"Mrs. Steele? Congresswoman? This is Tom Pearson, with the FBI."

Tom Pearson, who had been with her in Alabama, who had taken her to Dix's body.

"I told you someone would crack, didn't I? Well, we've got the suspects in your husband's death. We have them in custody."

Cassie gripped the receiver. "Finally! I thought they'd never be—the trial. When will the case come up?"

"The U.S. attorney is pushing for a speedy trial. I think he's trying for August."

August, she thought. In August she would see them face to face: the men who had murdered her husband. "I'll be there, Mr. Pearson. I'll be down there. And tell the U.S. attorney I will help him in any way I can."

There was a brief silence. "That question came up, Mrs. Steele. You are welcome to come and watch the trial, of course, but your participation might harm our case."

Cassie shook her head as if to shake some comprehension into it. "Is there some Alabama law against—he was my husband! I want to help convict the men who killed him!"

"Look, Mrs. Steele, folks down here don't much like having a woman in what is traditionally a man's job." He sounded embarrassed. "And you have a reputation as a civil rights activist. The thing is, the people don't like for Yankees to come down here and tell them how to run their business."

"Business?" Cassie laughed bitterly. "Beating people, killing them, that's their business?" She forced herself to regain her equilibrium. "Mr. Pearson, I'm sorry. I realize this has nothing to do with you. I will come, but I promise that I won't interfere. Tell the U.S. attorney that I will be the soul of discretion."

In August, Martin Luther King led the March on Washington. A quarter of a million Americans marched, black and white together, to ask that a one-hundred-year-old promise of equality be kept.

Cassie sat at home, watching the televised reports and wishing that Dix were there to see it. Masses of people gathered on the Mall to hear Reverend Martin Luther King, Jr., make a speech that would provide the strongest slogan of the integrationists' campaign: "I have a dream . . ."

If only, she thought, if only Dix were alive. He would be there, too, standing shoulder to shoulder with Martin King, singing "We Shall Overcome." And if that were so, then why was she, Dix's replacement in the House, huddled in front of the television in the safety of her own library?

Knowing that she would have a long visit with her children Cassie had put off trips to Oklahoma for almost six weeks in order to finish her congressional work. When the House rose, she left the place on R Street in Angelina's care and flew west.

The morning after she arrived, she reminded herself that Temple and the children had been on their summer vacation for five of those six weeks. She tried to reassure herself that the changes she saw in them resulted from their idleness rather than her neglect.

It started at breakfast that first morning. Cassie hugged her son, hungry for the feel of his thin seven-year-old body in her arms, then guided him to his chair. "Eat your breakfast, darling," she said. "I have a wonderful day planned for us."

He scowled at her. "Don't have to. Don't want no breakfast."

"*Any* breakfast," she said absently. "And yes, you do have to."

"Says who?" he said, pronouncing it "sezzoo."

"Says your mother, that's who. Sezzeye."

He folded his arms across his narrow chest and raised his chin to confront her. "Won't!"

Cassie glanced at the Steeles. Amelia was trying to smile but not succeeding and James was openly glowering at the boy. Neither of them had said a word. So it was all up to her, she thought. All right then. All right.

"Taylor," she said gently but firmly. "You are excused. Go to your room and do not come back down until you are ready to behave yourself."

He looked stricken for an instant and then got up so abruptly that he knocked over his chair. Without picking it up and without looking back he ran out of the room and thundered up the stairs.

Luella clicked her tongue in disapproval, set Taylor's chair in place and cleared away his dishes.

"Mama." Martha smiled at her mother, a smile so saccharine that it set Cassie's teeth on edge. "Mama, Taylor is *naughty!* I'm not naughty, am I, Gammy?"

Amelia smiled and held out her arms. "Indeed you are *not!*" Martha snuggled up to her. "You're Gammy's darling girl, honey, and just as sweet as pie."

Behind Cassie a loud sniff stated Luella's opinion of that.

"Where's Temple?" Cassie said. "Isn't she coming to breakfast?"

Amelia looked up from Martha. "I don't know."

"Asleep, probably," James said gruffly. "She sleeps late most mornings."

"James," Cassie said, but James put his napkin on the table and stood up.

"I have an appointment downtown. I will see you later."

"Come with Gammy, sweetie, and we'll wash the egg off your face."

Amelia and Martha left, giggling together, and Luella began to clear the table.

"Luella," Cassie said, "sit down."

Luella stopped, a plate in her hands. "Here? You mean you want me to sit down here?"

"That's exactly what I mean."

Luella edged her narrow hips onto Taylor's chair as nervously as if she suspected it to be a trick chair that would fall apart and drop her to the floor.

"Luella, what in God's name is going on around here?"

Luella's dark eyes narrowed. "What you sayin', Miz Cassie! What you askin' me?"

Cassie shook her head impatiently. "Don't play dumb with me,

Luella. You can damn well see it as much as I can: Taylor being stubborn and smart-aleck, Temple sleeping late like she owns the place, and Martha—well, a tattletale and so sicky-sweet I want to throw up. I need your help, Luella! Amelia can't tell me what's wrong, and James won't."

Luella relaxed enough to set the plate on the table and look straight at Cassie. "Then I reckon it's up to me. I tell you, Miz Cassie, since school let out, them three has been a sight to see. Taylor, he don't pay no never-mind to nobody. At the first, Temple, she tried screamin' at him, but she too busy with her own things to fool with him. Mist' James, he get red in the face and he yell a lot, but he ain't gettin' no place with that boy, no place at all. He know it, too, Mist' James, and it make him madder than a old wet hen. And Miz Amelia, she all bound up in little Martha, dressin' her, doin' her hair, playin' with her like she a dolly, not no six-year-old."

"And Temple? What's Temple up to?"

"No good. That's what that girl's up to: no good. Po' white trash if I ever seen it. Oh, I kin tell you 'bout Temple and that wild bunch she hangs out with. Sleepin' half the day, then down there at the juke joint, drinkin' beer, and I don't know what-all."

"Don't Amelia and James talk to her about it?"

"Yessum, but you think she gonna listen?"

Cassie put her head in her hands. "Oh, Lord, what on earth am I going to do?"

Luella leaned forward and took Cassie's hand in hers. "Miz Cassie, I ain't never been uppity, you know that. And I never thought on settin' here like this, tellin' a white lady—but Mist' Dix, he was *somebody*, you know?"

"Yes." His absence hung like a weight in Cassie's chest. "He was somebody all right."

"They ain't tried them yet, I reckon, the trash that—that killed Mist' Dix?"

Cassie sighed. "No, they haven't. The trial will be late this month. But, Luella, about the children—"

"I got to tell you, I reckon. Mist' James and Miz Amelia, they too old, Miz Cassie. They just flat too old to be raisin' little children and doin' with trash like that Temple. They cain't do it no more."

"Yes," Cassie said. "I can see that now. I never should have left my children with—"

"You had to! You didn't have no choice then! But you strong again now, I kin tell."

Cassie shook her head, but then she stopped and looked into Luella's dark eyes. "Why, Luella, I think you're right. I think I am strong, now. I am!"

Cassie felt strong when she marched into Temple's room and saw her sound asleep with mascara so smeared around her eyes that she looked to be fifty instead of nineteen.

"Wake up, Temple, right now! Get out of that bed and clean your face, you hear? Then get your things and the children's packed and ready to go. We're leaving for the farm in three hours."

She felt strong when she told the children her plans and when she tactfully explained to Amelia and James that she needed some time alone with the children. The relief in Amelia's eyes gave her even more confidence in her decision.

She felt strong as she chivvied all of them into action. Even James was affected by the momentum generated by her self-confidence. Without argument he chauffeured her to the automobile dealership and stood by while she wrote a check and took immediate delivery of a new Buick station wagon.

Her strength ebbed away, however, as she drove the station wagon down the red clay road to the farm. What had she done in taking full responsibility for the children and Temple? Was she capable of handling such a commitment?

Something changed, though, as they bumped along the rutted road past the overgrown track to the hill where the tenant house had been. The children fell silent and even Temple stopped grousing about being hauled off to the country. Cassie drove more slowly through the woods, through summer-dry post oaks and blue-black cedars. The station wagon emerged into the clearing and there it was before them, the old house with tall narrow windows and a shaded veranda.

It was home. The house had become once more the sanctuary Cassie had thought was gone, lost on the day that she saw Dixon Steele lying still and cold on that other red clay, in a landfill in Alabama.

When she switched off the engine it was as if she had switched on the children.

"I got to find Henry!" Taylor was running when he hit the ground. "And Rags!"

Martha was close behind him. "Mama, are there kitties this time?"

Temple sulked in the back seat and returned to her litany of complaints. "Stuck down here in the boondocks, nobody to run around with, no stores, no—"

"That's enough, Temple!" Cassie's eyes flashed with anger. "I don't know why I even bother with you! I should have put you on the bus for San Bois and sent you straight home to your parents."

"Wouldn't stay," the girl muttered. "Nobody could make me."

"And I couldn't care less whether you stayed with them or left. Temple, I will say this once, and never again. You can work for me and I will see that you get a good education and a start in life. Or you can go home to your parents' farm and fend for yourself. It's your choice. Just remember one thing. If you stay with me, you will abide by my rules."

Temple jumped out of the car and slammed the door. "Okay, *be* that way, Cassie! I can be just as hard-headed as you can! I don't need you and your fancy car and your fancy house in Washington, you hear? I don't need—" The cascade of words slowed and then stopped, as if only at that moment had she heard what she was saying.

Cassie fought back a laugh. At nineteen, Temple was angry and rebellious and, as people said, no better than she should be, but she was smart, too. She could see the difference between living with her slovenly mother in a sharecropper's house and living with a congresswoman in Georgetown. And she could clearly see the advantages in choosing Washington over San Bois, Oklahoma.

"Well," Temple said more calmly. "Well, I reckon I'd like to stay with you, Cassie, and with the kids."

Cassie frowned at her. "And with my rules."

Temple gritted her teeth. "Yessum. With your rules."

"All right, then. All right." Cassie frowned again but the frown became a grin and she gripped Temple in a bear hug. "Oh, Temple!" The girl was a damn nuisance, but there was life in her. She was a feisty one!

They had been at the ranch only three days when Tom Pearson called. "Mrs. Steele, the trial will begin next week."

"I'll be there, Mr. Pearson. Don't you worry. I'll be there."

Her family was settled at the farm by the time Cassie left for Alabama. With Henry Starr to ride herd on them, she knew they would be all right. On the plane, however, she wished that she had not agreed to go South, fearing the emotional drain of the trial. She knew, though, that she had to be there for Dix's sake, and for her own.

The two ceiling fans in the old courtroom managed only to circulate air that was heavy with heat and acrid with the odor of unwashed bodies. At the assistant U.S. attorney's invitation, Cassie took a seat at the prosecution table. She knew that she could not speak but at least she was not wedged between two hot bodies. There was not a black face in the courtroom, a fact which did not surprise Cassie. She knew that at such a time Southern Negroes would stay as far as they could from the edgy white crowds.

She could see the men at the defense table clearly, however. The one in the pale blue suit was obviously the defense attorney. The other three men were more appropriately dressed for a hot Southern day, in short-sleeved sport shirts and khaki pants. That they were farmers could be seen by their faces, tanned to halfway up the forehead where the tan changed to the fish-belly white of skin ordinarily protected from the sun by straw hats or baseball caps.

One of them, a sharp-nosed man with eyes the washed-out blue of a summer sky, saw Cassie watching them and turned away to mutter something to his neighbor.

Cassie looked through the papers on the table and made a mental note to ask the prosecutor why he had linked an apparently minor charge with murder by charging the men not only with killing Dixon Steele but also with violating his civil rights.

The judge looked like Hollywood's version of a jurist. He was tall and lean, with smooth white hair, a nose like the prow of a ship and deep-set intelligent eyes.

When the prosecutor rose to enter his physical evidence, however, the judge relaxed and sat back in his leather chair. The U.S. attorney presented a photograph of a tire as the first link in a chain of evidence that would place a defendant's truck at the place where Dixon Steele's body was found.

"Objection," the defense attorney said, and the judge, his eyes half-closed, said, "Sustained."

The exchange became a litany: the prosecution presenting evidence, the defense objecting and the judge supporting the objection.

Cassie felt sick. She had gone over the evidence with the U.S. attorney and she knew what was being suppressed. There was the tire tread that matched a track found on the red clay bank of the road. There were fibers from the truck bed and identical fibers from the shirt Dix was wearing. There was even a gun that the FBI had found in a defendant's house: a gun that would be identified as the one that had fired two bullets into Dixon Steele's body. The FBI's carefully erected structure of evidence collapsed like a card house. Finally the state's attorney sat down, defeated, while the defendants grinned at him.

"I call my first witness," the prosecutor said in a tired voice, and there was no objection.

As the U.S. attorney questioned his witnesses Cassie understood the rationale behind the civil rights charge. The defense lawyers and the judge could block the physical evidence that proved the charge of murder, but they could not stop witnesses from testifying that the defendants had violated Dixon Steele's civil rights.

In disgust, Cassie stalked out of the courtroom before the jury delivered its verdict. Reporters flocked around her on the courthouse steps but she did not answer their questions. To tell them that she had just witnessed a travesty of justice would only serve to antagonize the judge and make the prosecutor's job more difficult in future trials. And there would be more trials, she was sure. There would be many more trials before the whites accepted the fact that they were responsible for their actions, not just to the South but to America.

She was back in Oklahoma, back at the ranch, when she heard the final results of the trial. The three rednecks were acquitted of murder by a jury of their peers. They were found guilty, however, of violating Dixon Steele's civil rights. The bench, that Hollywood judge, sentenced each of them to one year's work on the county farm.

One year, she thought bitterly. In the South the life of a man like Dixon Steele could be precisely valued. It was worth one year on the county farm. With time off, of course, for good behavior.

Unsatisfactory as the verdict in the case might be, the fact that it came up for trial was some comfort to Cassie. It provided some structure for Dix's life, a beginning, a middle and, finally, an end. She clutched at that straw, trying to stay above water, but it did not help, not when the trial had revived the pain of his death.

She reached out, in her grief, and found help in her informal family.

*   *   *

Six weeks at the farm drew them together, Cassie, the children, Temple and Henry Starr. It shaped them into a family of sorts, one that had room for spats and resentments, for laughter, and even for love. Cassie worked with Henry in the daytime, seeing to the cattle, checking fences, usually trailed by a child, Martha clutching one of the most recent crop of barn kittens to her chest or Taylor, dressed on alternative days as a cowboy with chaps and hat and cap pistol or an Indian equipped with a feathered headdress and a bow with suction-cup tipped arrows. Temple more than kept the rules. She worked at being a member of the group, only disappearing into her room occasionally for a bracing shot of music from a Tulsa radio station.

At night, when the children were in bed and Temple had re-treated to her room and her music, the farmhouse became larger, and emptier. Cassie immersed herself in work, reading and making notes on the papers she had brought to Oklahoma and the others Cully Meecham forwarded to her. She often became restless, though, as the evening wore on, and got up from her desk to straighten a picture here or move a book there. One night she wandered out to the veranda and sat in a wicker chair to listen to the night sounds of the land and to stare up at countless stars in a blue-black sky. The stars blurred as tears welled in her eyes. Her loneliness for Dix ate at her heart like acid. She clenched her fists and pounded softly on her own knees as her pain built within her till she was certain it would emerge in an animal scream of agony. She closed her eyes to block out the stars, the pain, the past and, finally, was able to push herself up from the chair, to stand up and take deep, shaking breaths of the heavy, humid night air.

She did not scream. She did not cry, even, and after a few minutes she was able to turn away from the stars, to go back inside, to sit at her desk and bury her sorrow in work.

Every Saturday, Cassie tucked the applicable documents into her briefcase and drove herself to one of the Saturday clinics in her congressional district.

Some of her constituents required only an interpreter capable of translating Washington legalese into a variety of English understandable in Eastern Oklahoma. Others needed only to have a request sent on to Cassie's secretary in Washington to be retyped under a congressional letterhead and mailed to the appropriate bureaucrat over the magic signature of a member of Congress.

Other constituents, however, had problems that tore at Cassie's heart because there was absolutely nothing that she or anyone else could do to alleviate them. An old Indian came in one morning, a Cherokee with a poor grasp of English. He was, it seemed, the only living relative of his grandson, a private in the Green Berets in Vietnam. Mutely, he handed Cassie two telegrams that were flimsy from being folded and refolded. One regretted to inform him that Private John Deerkiller was a prisoner of war and the other that Private Deerkiller was missing in action.

Cassie put her hand over her eyes for a moment. We are all prisoners of war, she thought but did not say. She looked again at the telegrams. Which was correct? Were both correct? She would send copies to Washington, to Cully Meecham, who might or might not be able to find an answer, even though no answer could give the old man any reason to rejoice or even to hope. "Mr. Deerkiller, I will do my best to find out. I will do my very best."

Among the requests for intervention with the Department of Agriculture or Social Security were other questions in regard to sons or husbands or brothers in Vietnam. Cassie began to wonder about that. If there were that many men and boys from one congressional district, then how many Americans were in Vietnam? According to newspaper reports, the number was small, but were the newspapers telling the truth? For that matter, was the Department of Defense telling the truth? Cassie resolved to investigate the matter when she returned to Washington.

By the end of the summer Taylor and Martha were ready, even eager, to get back to their schools in Ballard. Temple went around the house purring like a cat, which made Cassie very nervous.

During the summer the girl had been miraculously well-behaved, but who knew how she would act when she wasn't under Cassie's eye? Nevertheless, Cassie decided to risk it. With Amelia and James's approval she would leave the children in Ballard on a trial basis, checking on them often.

The homework Cassie had done at the farm paid off when she was back in Washington. After six months in office, she was beginning to understand the processes of the House of Representatives. It was only in the fall that she realized, too, how gently the members of the House had treated her during that first six months, because of Dix, and because of the manner of his dying. During the summer her colleagues' attitudes appeared to have undergone a sea change. She was one of them now, and she was expected to stand or fall on her own.

Off the floor of the House, however, she was not fully a member. It was one thing, she discovered, to be a poor, weak widow filling her husband's congressional seat. It was quite another to be a woman playing on what was traditionally the men's field. The truth of this was made crystal-clear to her when she walked out of a committee room and overheard a brief exchange between two congressmen.

"Where do you think the Oklahoma broad will stand on this?"

"Who the hell cares?"

Cassie's stride broke, but with an effort of will, she walked past them and down the corridor, her high heels clicking on the marble floor. Her first reaction was fury. How dare they! She was a member of Congress, too, a colleague of theirs, even though she had been appointed rather than elected. She had been insulted, practically to her face. She hesitated. No. Not to her face. The two men had not seen her, but when did they ever see her? She was invisible, a woman in a man's job.

Cassie finished her work at the House as if nothing untoward had happened, but she sat up late that night, staring at the flames in the library fireplace, thinking about her future and analyzing her present. Too many unknowns, she thought. There were too many imponderables in the equation to allow for definite answers.

Only one decision could she make. It was for the present and near-future, not for the long term, but nevertheless, it was a definite decision and one to which she would commit herself wholly.

They, those men of Congress, would soon find out where she stood and what she stood for. They would learn it because she would tell them again and again until it infiltrated even their thick, prejudiced skulls. There would be no doubt where one congress-woman stood: U.S. Representative Cassandra Steele, "the Oklahoma broad."

Chapter 25

The house on R Street was quiet, too quiet, after the six weeks on the farm, but Cassie worked late most nights, returning from the House or a committee meeting to read, to think and to plan. She spent an occasional evening with Eliot Peabody, with whom she was developing a casual, undemanding relationship.

By late October, in fact, she felt comfortable enough with Eliot to ask him to escort her to a congressional cocktail party. She felt vaguely disloyal to Dix as she dressed, but she admitted to herself that it was exciting to be dressing once more for a Washington party. She wore a short dress, a crepe de Chine as blue as her eyes and cut to float with her movements. In defiance of the Jackie Kennedy look-alikes in Washington, she had kept her blond hair long and for that evening she secured it into a chignon. When she was ready, she took several practice turns in front of the full-length mirror in her dressing room. She liked what she saw.

Eliot's reaction was even better than her mirror's. His eyes widened noticeably, and he had to clear his throat before he spoke. "You are lovely tonight, Cassie."

The reaction of their fellow guests at the party affirmed Eliot's, to the point that Cassie was embarrassed by the men's fulsome compliments and the women's ill-concealed sniffs of disapproval. She was uncomfortably aware that she would be the subject for dissection at a number of luncheons the next day.

Eliot excused himself to get fresh drinks, and as she watched him move through the crowd a big hand suddenly gripped her upper arm and a deep voice sounded behind her.

"Cassie Steele! Never thought I'd see you here!"

She turned and looked into Mackenzie Cameron's grinning face. She almost laughed aloud. She should have spotted that shiny blue polyester suit clear across the room. Remembering the number of times she had flown on his company jet, she was tactful about removing her arm from his grip. "Mack Cameron," she said, distancing herself. "How nice to see you."

"And you're a sight for sore eyes, Cassie." He surveyed her from head to toe. "You look like a million bucks tonight."

"I owe you thanks for letting me ride on your company jet. It has been—"

"Hell, Cassie, forget it. You don't owe me anything at all."

Eliot returned with a glass of champagne in each hand.

"Eliot, this is—Eliot Peabody, Mackenzie Cameron."

Eliot smiled coolly. "We've met. How are you, Cameron?"

Mack looked from Eliot to Cassie, obviously adding one and one and coming up with two. "Yeah. Nice to see you, Peabody."

Cassie quickly raised her glass to cover a smile. They were like two strange dogs circling for an opening. Her smile disappeared, however, as she realized that it was she who was the bone of contention.

"Eliot, shall we go now?" she said.

"Of course," he said. "Let me take your glass."

He turned away to set their glasses on a table and Cassie offered her hand to Mack. He looked vulnerable just then, like a lost boy. "Good-bye, Mack."

Eliot nodded his farewell. "Cameron."

"Yeah," Mack said. "Well, good-bye." As the two of them walked away into the crowd, he said, "Cassie! I'll call you, hear? I'll call you soon."

Cassie nodded in acknowledgment, but as Eliot helped her with her coat she could not help comparing Mack Cameron to him. In the light of Eliot's impeccable manners, Mack appeared crude. He could call, if he wanted, but she was not interested in him. He was too crude, too much the Oklahoma oil man. He was too loud, too rich and too big. He was simply too much of everything.

Cassie invited Eliot to come in for a brandy, and when they were settled in front of the fireplace in the library she asked him the question that had been bothering her since August. "Eliot, you are probably someone who knows what I can't seem to find out. Why does President Kennedy keep sending more Americans into South Vietnam?"

Eliot looked at her quickly. "Why do you think that I would know?"

"Why, it's just that you're so well informed and—I thought maybe you had heard something about it."

He relaxed. "No more than anyone else, of course."

"Of course."

"You must keep it in a global perspective, Cassie. You remember the Bay of Pigs."

"Yes. It was a terrible CIA blunder—"

Eliot scowled. "It was a Kennedy blunder, too, you know. And then Kennedy met Khrushchev at Vienna and Khrushchev took the upper hand from the first. In fact, that meeting convinced Khrushchev that he was dealing with a weak President and that there would be only ineffectual opposition to his setting up missile bases in Cuba."

"But the President made him back down!"

"Yes, he did, but Kennedy was afraid that even that was not enough to convince the Russians that America and its President are strong and ready to fight. He still thinks he has to make it clear that he will stand up in a fight."

"But why South Vietnam, Eliot? A tiny country thousands of miles from here. I'm reasonably well read, but until Eisenhower sent in a few military advisors, I'd never even heard of South Vietnam. What has it to do with us?"

Eliot leaned back in his chair. For once his pale eyes were warm with amusement. "My father used to tell a story about an old gambler who played in a weekly poker game, and lost money every week. Someone asked him, 'Why do you keep playing with those guys? You know they cheat you.' 'Well,' the gambler said, 'the game may be crooked, but it's the only game in town.' See what I mean?"

"No, Eliot. I don't see."

"Look, how do countries, and Presidents, prove that they are strong? By winning wars. The war in South Vietnam may be a long way from us, a dirty little war in a dirty little country, but it's the only war in town."

Cassie swirled her brandy thoughtfully. "That's a pretty cynical view of things, Eliot."

He grimaced. "There aren't many Pollyannas in my job."

She looked straight at him. "Just exactly what is your job?"

He turned away. "I can't tell you, Cassie, and anyway, you don't want to know."

Cassie had a sudden insight. "You've been there! You've been to Vietnam, haven't you?"

Eliot drank off the last of his brandy and stood up. "I have an early appointment tomorrow."

Cassie stood up, too. "But you didn't answer my question!"

"No." He smiled coolly. "No, I didn't. Good night, Cassie. I'll call you soon."

Cassie prepared carefully to fight the image of "the Oklahoma broad." Her first opportunity came during a session of Judiciary, a committee made up wholly of lawyers. She was the only woman on the committee. The point under discussion was a small one, but she felt that it warranted further scrutiny.

"Mr. Chairman."

The chairman looked startled, as if he had never noticed that a woman sat on his committee. "The Chair recognizes the congresswoman from—" He consulted a list. "From Oklahoma."

"This paragraph is worded so vaguely as to be worthless. I doubt that it—"

"Congresswoman," a man interrupted, "surely it is both clear and concise. If you will yield the floor I will be happy to explain it to you and to add my interpretation."

Cassie gritted her teeth. "No, Congressman, I will not yield. I will say, however, that you have made my point nicely. As it stands, the paragraph is indeed open to interpretation, and that is not what we are trying to achieve here. What we want is a bill written in clear, precise language which will stand on its own merits."

The congressman smiled at her kindly. "I can see that a layman might feel that way, but a practicing attorney can—"

"I have been a practicing attorney, sir, and what I want is a straightforward law upon which I can build a solid case. I do not want a law subject to interpretation, one which will automatically kick my client's case into appeal. Mr. Chairman, I suggest that we send this bill back to the subcommittee for revision."

"Does the congresswoman so move?"

"I so move."

To her surprise, her motion was seconded and passed. It was a tiny victory, Cassie knew, but it was a victory, not just for herself but for every woman who was fighting to achieve stature in a man's world.

No important bills would come up in the House that Friday, so Cassie took time away from the House to shop for gifts to take to her children when she went to Ballard that week for Thanksgiving. She finished her shopping and, driving home to R Street, she switched on the car radio. Anthony Newley was singing "What Kind of Fool Am I?" Cassie hummed along but her thoughts were of Taylor and Martha and how eager she was to see them. According to James Steele's rather formal reports, the six weeks at the farm had made a difference in the children's behavior and in Temple's, too. Cassie herself had seen changes during her visits to Oklahoma. Taylor was calmer, Martha less prissy, and Temple, for a wonder, was bringing good grades home from junior college, instead of scruffy boyfriends.

Anthony Newley's voice was suddenly replaced by that of an announcer. "As we reported a few minutes ago, shots were fired at President Kennedy's limousine as his motorcade passed through downtown Dallas. We have now been informed that the President was seriously wounded and has been rushed to Parkland Hospital. Stay tuned to this station for further developments."

Cassie's hands gripped the steering wheel and the scene before her imprinted itself on her mind: the corner of R Street, a stoplight a red disk in the November haze, a blue car stopped in front of her, license plate 343-175, a woman hurrying up the hill, hunched against the cold.

The red disk changed to green but Cassie, frozen in the immediacy of the moment, did not press the accelerator until the driver behind her honked impatiently. She drove forward then, turning the corner to R Street and speeding up the hill. Her car squealed to a stop in front of the house and she ran in the front door and to the television set in the library.

Walter Cronkite's face appeared on the screen. For once he appeared shaken, so appalled at the news he was reading that it was difficult for him to maintain his professionalism.

Cassie sank down on the couch, still wearing her coat.

"—has been rushed to Parkland Hospital. Mrs. Kennedy is riding with her—with the President. To repeat, the nature of the President's wounds is not—"

Cassie jumped up from the couch. "Angelina!" She ran toward the kitchen, but stopped in the hall when she remembered that she had given Angelina a few days off so that she could visit her daughter in Baltimore.

That's what she would do, too, Cassie thought. She would call and reserve a ticket and fly to Oklahoma that very night. Her children might need her. Just as she returned to the library, however, the telephone rang.

"I'm calling for Speaker McCormack's office, Congresswoman." Cassie recognized the Boston accent of one of the speaker's aides. "The speaker is asking that the members of the House stay in Washington until further notice."

"Of course, I'll—why?"

"In case the speaker needs a quorum. We don't know yet what we're dealing with. Apparently it's some kind of right-wing conspiracy, but it could be the Communists, thinking the assassination would draw our attention away from an attack. Until the FBI knows more—"

"You mean 'assassination attempt,' don't you?" Even as she asked the question she became aware that in her heart she knew the answer. "Walter Cronkite just said, 'seriously wounded.'"

"Walter Cronkite doesn't know yet, Congresswoman." The young man's voice broke and made a shaky recovery. "The President's wounds may well be fatal."

"No," Cassie whispered. "Oh, no. But who would—why would anyone—"

"You will stay in Washington, then?"

"Yes. Yes, of course." Slowly Cassie replaced the receiver, only to pick it up again. She tried to place a call to Ballard, but the dial tone disappeared before she could get an operator. She clicked the receiver several times, but it was no use. The telephone was out of order. She hurried to the kitchen to check the phone there, because it was on a different circuit. It was dead, too. She stood in the kitchen, her hand at her mouth. Why would all the phones be dead? Was it sabotage, perhaps part of a larger plot against the United States? Maybe it was the Communists. Russia.

She hurried back to the library and the television set just in time to see Walter Cronkite, his face tense and a muscle in his jaw jumping uncontrollably. Even before he said the words, she knew what they would be. The President was dead.

Cassie put her hands over her eyes as if to hide from the dreadful news, but there was no place to hide. The facts were there and they could not be erased: someone or some group, for whatever reason, had shot John Fitzgerald Kennedy. The President was dead, and Camelot had come to an end.

It was after four when the Georgetown office of the Chesapeake and Potomac Telephone Company returned to full service, but Cassie had already learned from a local TV report that the lines had been blocked by overload. Everyone in Washington, it seemed, had tried to call everyone else. The phone breakdown was caused not by sabotage but by the very human need to discuss bad news with someone close.

Cassie got through to Ballard finally, but the conversation was unsatisfactory. James wanted the inside story and would not believe that Cassie knew no more than he did: they had watched the same TV reports. She talked to both of her children, but she could not share her grief with them. It was too much of a burden for them.

"No, darling," she told Taylor. "I can't come to Oklahoma this weekend. The speaker has asked members of Congress to stay in Washington in case—"

"In case what, Mama?"

"Oh, nothing. But I'll be there next week, I promise."

Cassie hung up the phone then, hoping she could keep that promise. She sat with her hand on the receiver, reluctant to break even that tenuous connection with the outside world.

There was someone she could call, she realized. She did not have to be alone. She dialed Eliot Peabody's office number.

"Mr. Peabody's office." It was the voice of a young man. "Who is calling?"

"Why, it's—is Mr. Peabody in?"

The voice became suspicious. "I asked, who's calling?"

"Congresswoman Steele. I want to talk to—"

"Mr. Peabody is not available."

Cassie eventually extracted the information that Mr. Peabody was out of town, and that neither his location nor his time of return could be revealed.

She slammed down the receiver. "Where is the man?" she asked herself pointlessly. "And why is it such a big damn secret?" When she thought more calmly, she knew the answer. He was where his duties took him. She was ashamed of her burst of irritation. It was not a day to be annoyed by an officious aide: not on the day that the President of the United States had been assassinated.

In a daze she went upstairs, from the television in the library to that in the sitting room. She watched in spurts while she changed from the suit she had worn all day to black flannel slacks and a black cashmere pullover.

"—Lee Harvey Oswald, aged twenty-four," the announcer said, and Cassie realized with a start that the President's killer had been captured and identified.

The television commentators appeared to be at a loss as they tried to make a smooth transition from suspicions of a right-wing plot to ones of a Communist plot. According to the reports, the city fathers of Dallas had breathed a collective sigh of relief, but it was not to be that easy for them. The reporters still hinted that the virulent hatreds in Dallas had created a climate for assassination.

Cassie dropped into an armchair and listened to further details. The oath of office had been administered by Judge Sarah T. Hughes, and now "Mr. President" no longer meant a tall young man with a vision for a greater America. "Mr. President" was a lanky Texan, a wheeler-dealer, a man who was first and foremost a canny politician.

The doorbell rang and Cassie rose to answer it, still wondering about the man who would be going into the White House. To her surprise, the visitor was Mackenzie Cameron, the Oklahoma oil man.

He looked embarrassed. "I hope you don't mind my coming over like this. I tried to call you earlier, but the phones were out."

"I know. They're working again now."

"The thing is, I sent all my people to Oklahoma so they could be with their families, and I—oh, hell, Cassie, it's a rough time to be alone."

Until that moment she had fought to control it, but his words undid her and her own sense of loneliness hit her like a hard blow to the stomach. "Oh, I know, I know! Do come in!"

She had thought Mack Cameron crude in comparison to Eliot Peabody but he was as sensitive that evening, she realized, as she herself was. Both of them were like raw nerve endings.

He joined her on the couch in front of the television and together they watched as bits of news began to create a picture in the way pieces of a jigsaw puzzle come together to depict a scene. Walter Cronkite displayed the still photograph that was taken on Air Force One, the picture of Lyndon Johnson being sworn in as the thirty-sixth President of the United States.

"She's still wearing that suit," Cassie said brokenly. "Jackie was wearing that suit when they landed in Dallas this morning."

"And the bloodstains are—"

"The blood. Yes."

They ate the chili Angelina had left in the refrigerator, taking trays to the library because they could not leave the television while the sad story unrolled. Again and again they saw the film of the motorcade dissolving into confusion, of stricken faces outside Parkland Hospital, of the white ambulance carrying the President's coffin from the hospital toward Love Field and Air Force One.

Finally they watched as the coffin was unloaded from an elevating platform at Andrews Air Force Base and was manhandled into an ambulance for transfer to Bethesda Naval Hospital. They saw Jacqueline Kennedy lifted down from that same platform and helped to a seat in the ambulance with Robert Kennedy.

Cassie switched off the television and Mack Cameron stood up. "I'd better go now."

"Yes."

"Look, would it be all right if—I don't want to be a nuisance, but can I come back tomorrow morning?"

"Yes!" Cassie did not hide her relief. She knew that there would be more on television on Saturday and that she could no more ignore it than she could fly. To be with another person would make the pain a little easier to bear.

On Saturday morning Mack Cameron had changed from his polyester suit to khaki pants and a plaid flannel shirt.

"You look more comfortable," Cassie said.

He looked down at himself. "Yeah. Guess I belong in khaki work pants and field boots. I go in one of those 'Big Men' places to buy a suit and I don't know what the hell to buy."

"You could have your suits made, Mack, you know. Tailored to fit you."

"Guess I could, but I never get the time to fool with it."

Mack was there when the television reported that Lee Harvey Oswald had been charged with shooting the President and a Dallas police officer, and when Oswald's Russian-born wife, carrying her baby, shyly tried to get through the crowd of reporters and policemen to see her husband. National leaders were interviewed but they said no more than Cassie and Mack had already said to each other. What more was there to say?

Sunday, a cold windy day, Mack was in corduroy pants and a heavy wool sweater. They watched television as the presidential coffin was loaded onto an artillery caisson to be transferred to the Capitol, where the late President would lie in state. The caisson rolled and the drums began to play in a sad, solemn beat that entered Cassie's body and mind and set a cadence for the events of the next two days.

Mack was there beside her when the television cut from a shot of people waiting on the Capitol plaza to one of the jail in Dallas. Lee Oswald was about to be transferred to the county jail.

They watched the Dallas plainclothesmen come out by twos and threes and they saw Oswald's face for an instant just as a bulky man in a dark hat pushed forward into the crowd surrounding Oswald. There was a pop of sound and a brief glimpse of Oswald's face as his mouth flew open in an unheard cry of surprise or pain.

"Mack!" Cassie cried, but he gripped her hand, warning her to silence. The information came in bits and pieces. Oswald was dead at Parkland Hospital, in the emergency room across the hall from the one where John F. Kennedy had died on Friday. The killer was a Dallas night-club owner named Jack Ruby. He was well known among Dallas police and a frequent visitor to the jail.

The television cut back to the scene in the Capitol. Mrs. Kennedy went to the coffin, with Caroline, and knelt and kissed the flag covering it. Various dignitaries walked past, showing their respect for the dead, and then ordinary citizens passed through to honor their fallen chief, a crowd of Americans later estimated at 400,000 people.

When Cassie switched off the television that night there was no need to discuss Mack's coming back the next day. At some point during that long, sad weekend it had been silently agreed that they two would see it through together. She dreaded his leaving, though. She hated the idea of being alone in the house.

"Mack," she said hesitantly. "It's late, and—would you like to stay here tonight? The children's rooms are both free."

He looked startled. "Well, I suppose it would be—yes, Cassie, I would like to stay. I would like that just fine."

Later, when she was in bed, Cassie hoped that he would not draw any inferences from her spur-of-the-moment invitation. But what if he did, she thought, what would it matter? Just knowing that she was not alone in the house was worth almost any amount of trouble. In spite of her sorrow, she slept better that night than she had in weeks.

On Monday morning, Mack went out and brought in fresh cinnamon rolls. They ate them and drank their coffee sitting, as before, on the couch in front of the television in the library.

They watched Jacqueline Kennedy in the Capitol, wearing deep mourning, including a heavy black veil. With Robert and Edward Kennedy, both in morning suits, she knelt by the coffin. Then, as the military band played "Hail to the Chief," the coffin was carried down the long steps of the Capitol and lifted onto an artillery caisson drawn by six white horses. It was followed by a riderless horse with empty artillery boots in the stirrups. And the drums began to play.

The drums played their slow, sad beat while the caisson moved toward St. Matthew's Cathedral. Following it on foot were the bereaved widow, the family and representatives of almost every foreign country.

After the mass, the drums played again as the caisson, now followed by limousines, was pulled across the Memorial Bridge and, finally, into Arlington National Cemetery. At the sight of row on row of white stones, Cassie clenched her fists so hard that her nails cut into her palms. Mack turned to her as if he would say something, but after looking at her he sat back, quiet.

The bagpipers played and the cardinal finished the ceremony. There was a jet fly-over, an artillery salute, a rifle salute, and then Mrs. Kennedy and the two brothers in turn applied a torch to light the eternal flame. The military pallbearers took the flag from the coffin and folded it into a neat triangle. Cassie found her own hands reaching out to accept it, as they had accepted the flag from Dixon Steele's coffin. Her hands closed, feeling the rough texture of the cotton cloth. "Taps" rang out, the bugle's tones clean and sure in the cold air, rising and falling with notes of utter finality, just as they had done at that other funeral, at Dix's funeral. It is over, they said, it is all over now. This is the end.

Even though she knew it was not the end, and never would be, any more than her deep sense of loss for Dix would ever end, it was a point at which some equilibrium was achieved, when a balance was struck. "It is over," she whispered. "The end." She felt herself shrinking into the couch, forgetting the television, forgetting the dead President, sinking into relived emotions, into a memory of Dixon Steele.

She felt Mack's big hand enfold hers and she was deeply moved, not because of her loss, but because one person was aware of the enormity of that loss. It was the touch of Mack's hand, the unspoken and unobtrusive kindness of his gesture, that set off her explosion into tears.

"Oh, Mack!" She put her face against his shoulder, against the rough wool of his sweater, and tears ran down her cheeks.

He put his arms around her and patted her sobbing back. "It's all right, Cassie. Go on and cry it out. Cry it all out."

She cried until she had saturated the white linen handkerchief he gave her, until her eyes were sore and aching, until she cried herself empty of tears and there was nothing left. With the last of the tears came a sort of peace, as if then, and only then, was she ready to hear the message of the bugle at Dix's funeral. It is over now. This is the end.

Her first feeling was one of joy, of happiness for Dix because he was at peace, and for herself because she was free of the obsessive need to pick and probe at the ulcer of her loss, free to let the wound heal.

"Mack," she said softly. "Thank you."

"It's okay," he said as gently. "I thought you needed to get it out."

"I did need to, but I didn't know it. How did you know?"

"I remember my mother, when my dad died—oh, hell, Cassie, it helped me, too. I wanted to cry, too, but men don't learn how to cry."

"Oh, Mack, I'm so sorry. I've been terribly self-centered."

"Don't apologize. What the hell, you probably thought that an old Republican like me wouldn't care that much about Jack Kennedy anyway."

"A Republican!" she said in mock horror. "What's a Republican doing in my house, on my sofa—"

"In your arms."

She pulled away from him, covering her embarrassment with a laugh, then looked at him carefully. "But you do care, don't you? I mean about President—"

"What man, what American would not? He was our President, and he was shot. Besides that—" He hesitated. "Hell, even a Republican can believe in Camelot."

"Yes. Oh, yes, Mack." Cassie sank back on the couch, careful to stay at her own end of it. "I suppose the House will sit tomorrow."

"Yeah. Business as usual." He laughed, a deep-voiced rumble. "I was thinking about that. Our President is assassinated on Friday and by Tuesday it's all over and we get back to work."

"Is that so bad? Government has to go on, and business, too."

"I didn't say it was bad, Cassie. In fact, I think it's pretty damn good. There are countries in the world where an assassination would mean that the government would fall, and others where the citizens would be in open revolt tomorrow instead of catching the bus to work."

At the front door they shook hands, formally, but Cassie stood in the open door as Mack left, and he paused at the end of the walk to look back at her. They were still for a moment and then he started walking toward his car and she closed the door and went to the telephone to find out if her secretary had returned. She paused for a minute before she dialed the number. No matter what happened in the future, either to Mack or to her, she would always remember and she knew that he would remember, too, that they had spent this long sad weekend together. The time stood as a recognition of death, it was true, but she knew that it had been, also, an affirmation of life.

Chapter 26

Cassie Steele, like most Americans, spent the next few weeks fighting for stability. After the shock of the assassination and with fears of a conspiracy still in the wind, she needed desperately to find solid ground.

To her relief and delight Eliot Peabody called to say he was back in Washington and would like to see her. She dressed with extra care for their dinner date, turning this way and that to see herself in the mirror, admiring the swirl of her purple skirt. It was not until she was anxiously smoothing a torn fingernail that she realized what she was doing.

She giggled and was startled by the sound and by the insight that had given rise to it. She was acting like a teenaged girl, nervously preparing herself for a big date. How ridiculous, she thought. She was thirty-eight years old, a congresswoman, the mother of two children. But it had been so long, so very long since she had dressed to please a man.

The miserable weekend of the assassination and its aftermath, that was different. She and Mack were not a woman and a man but two children clinging to each other in the dark. For her it had been a time of great sorrow but it had also had a cathartic effect. It had not taken away her grief for Dix, but it had loosened the bonds. She was like a flower enclosed in ice, but within the ice, it appeared, there was life in the flower even though she had neither recognized nor acknowledged it. It was only when the President was buried that the ice began to melt and the bud to open.

The evening was delightful. Eliot talked very little about where he had been or what he was doing. He preferred, he said, to concentrate on her.

"You've changed, Cassie. Has something happened? Some good news, perhaps?"

"Not really, Eliot. It's just that—" She looked down at her plate. "I suppose my mourning period is ending." She did not have to explain that she meant her mourning as a widow, not as an American.

"Good," he said quietly, and she looked up to find him watching her carefully. "I'm glad to hear that. Look, my dear, I don't want to push you, but I do want you to be aware that I'll help you in any way I can."

"Oh, Eliot! You are so—thank you. Thank you very, very much."

He reached across the table and took her hand as gently as if he were checking her vital signs. "After dinner, Cassie, would you like to go dancing?"

"Why, I hardly think that would be—" He was still holding her hand. "Yes," she said suddenly, "yes, I would like that."

Eliot took her to the new night club that was, he said, very much the "in" place in Washington. Cassie knew she was all too visible as the tallest woman there, one of the best-dressed and, possibly, the oldest. She lost her self-consciousness in the driving beat of the music, for once using her body as freely as it was meant to be used.

Eliot danced more sedately, but not as sedately as she would have expected of a cool Bostonian. The crowd shifted and while Eliot was lost, Cassie found herself partnered temporarily by a swarthy man three inches shorter than she and at least fifteen years younger. Their differences disappeared in his quick smouldering look at her: a look of hot desire. He grinned and she found herself grinning back in complicity. We can't have each other, their eyes agreed, but it's there, the desire is there.

Shaken, she turned away, dancing, and found herself facing Eliot again.

"Eliot," she said breathlessly. "Eliot, I think I should go home now."

He looked at her, a question in his eyes, but he snapped to as briskly as a toy soldier and punctiliously escorted her out of the club.

He had little to say during the drive to Georgetown, but then she hardly spoke at all. She had been surprised by the self she had found at the night club and by that pure animal lust for a man, a stranger who would remain a stranger.

Eliot would have come in, but she pled fatigue. She had to define her feelings before she was ready to deal with them. She undressed, and in her gown and robe sank into an armchair in the upstairs sitting room. She was thirty-eight years old and gray hairs appeared among her blond ones with appalling regularity. She was a United States Congresswoman. The mother of two children. A widow. Surely that was enough. Surely desire belonged to the past and could safely be left there, in the past.

But she had enjoyed the dancing that night, she had enjoyed her body, dancing, and she had enjoyed the surge of lust she had exchanged with a swarthy boy. Even if it lasted only for a few seconds, she wanted. Oh, how she wanted!

She shifted uncomfortably in the armchair. What had changed? What had awakened that wanton woman within her? Even as she asked the question, she knew the answer.

It was the weekend with Mack Cameron, the weekend when they shared the pain of a whole country, when John Fitzgerald Kennedy was murdered, was mourned, was buried. As she lived through that weekend she had relived the time when Dix Steele was murdered, was mourned, was buried. She relived her feelings that weekend, from day to day, she relived her tremendous grief.

And as she sat with Mack and listened to the slow inexorable beat of the drums, for the first time she accepted the truth. Dix was dead. Dix was gone and would not, could not come back to her.

She accepted the fact that he was dead, and at the night club she accepted the fact that she was alive.

Cassie stood up abruptly and began to pace back and forth, the length of the sitting room.

"Yes!" she said aloud. "Yes!" She was alive and it was all right for her to experience the feelings of a living woman: sorrow, anger, joy, yes, even lust. She stopped dead in the center of the room. She could even love again, sometime, be in love again. She could marry again.

Who? Whom could she love, she wondered and then she saw that the question was both premature and pointless. Dix had been dead less than a year. When he died, everyone had said time heals. She needed to let time work, to let it complete the job. The question of "who" was pointless because as she herself knew, love did not necessarily follow rational paths. Love appeared where and when it did and it was up to the love-struck to try to explain it, to rationalize it after the fact.

With her new understanding of herself and her needs, it was difficult for Cassie to concentrate on congressional matters but it became increasingly important that she do so.

No matter how people had rallied to the flag when the three shots rang out in Dallas, in the next weeks Washington was a churning sea of confusion. Lyndon Johnson had asked most of the Kennedy appointees to stay on but even those who did made no secret of their distaste for the new President, the crude lanky Texan who had, they felt, usurped the presidency.

Nevertheless Johnson held the country together even if it sometimes seemed that he did it by sheer momentum. He persuaded and dealt and cajoled, fighting constantly to wrest power from Congress and give it to the executive branch of government. His main line of attack was through congressional committees chaired by old Southerners, conservatives who were even farther removed from the Kennedy New Frontier than Johnson himself. Cassie found herself being called upon by Kennedy people for clarification of Johnson's attitudes, his motives and his actions, as if the southwestern United States was an area as politically cohesive as a one-party township in Vermont. She tried to help, but she could neither explain nor support the man's decision to commit the United States to send even more men to South Vietnam than the 16,900 Americans John Kennedy had invested there.

Cassie was relieved when the House rose for the Christmas break. She was exhausted, but more than that, she longed to be with her children.

Taylor and Martha appeared to be as delighted to see their mother as she was to see them. As she had planned, she spent only one night with the Steeles in Ballard before loading the children and Temple into the car and heading for the farm.

When Cassie walked into the farmhouse, she knew that she was home. The hickory smell of the welcoming wood fire Henry Starr had built blended with a slight scent of mildew to create the odor she had always associated with the farmhouse in winter. She and Temple went to the kitchen to stow away the groceries while Taylor and Martha explored the places where they had played during the summer.

"How are your grades, Temple?"

The girl muttered an answer into the cabinet where she was putting the canned goods.

"What's that? I couldn't hear you."

"That's one dumb school, that's what I said."

Cassie was instantly alert. "But how are your grades?"

"Not so hot. It's real boring there."

Be patient, Cassie warned herself. Tread lightly here. She turned around, but Temple would not look at her. "How bad are they? Are you failing?"

"Only history and English."

Cassie sighed. "Let's put the percolator on. I could do with a cup of coffee, couldn't you?"

When they were seated at the kitchen table, Cassie said, "Will you be able to pass your courses?"

"No," the girl said sullenly.

"What's gone wrong?" Cassie asked, but with a sudden insight she answered her own question. "You've been cutting class, haven't you?"

Temple blushed. "So what if I have?"

"How much?"

"Kind of a lot."

"Why? A boy. That's the problem, isn't it? You've cut classes to be with a boy."

Temple ducked her chin and let her red hair fall forward to shield her face. "I reckon so."

"But how could he—he isn't in college, is he? You had to meet him somewhere to—"

"No!" Temple raised her chin and her eyes snapped with anger. "I know what you're thinking, but we don't—well, not much anyway. He works at the Texaco station, if you got to know."

"How old is he?"

"Twenty-eight." She saw the look on Cassie's face. "The boys at the junior college, they're just kids. Randy's a man."

"You're just a kid yourself, Temple."

The girl smiled with foxlike self-satisfaction. "Randy don't think so. And you know I ain't no kid. You know it yourself."

Cassie stood up and stared at the sly redhead across the table, trying to control her fury. "After all I've done for you, Temple! After all Mr. and Mrs. Steele have—"

"Throw it in my face!" Temple pushed back her chair and jumped to her feet. "You can't just leave it lay, you got to throw it in my face like some rich lady bringin' in a Christmas basket! You want me to get down in the dirt and thank you? I never asked you to take me off my folks' place!"

Cassie looked at her coolly, unmoved by her histrionics. "No, you didn't ask, but you were quick enough to go, weren't you? I'm going outside to see to my children now. You finish putting these things away and I'll talk to you later, you hear me?"

"Yeah," Temple said sullenly. "I hear you, all right."

Cassie pulled on her sheepskin jacket and thrust her hands deep in the pockets to stop their trembling. She was shaking with anger, but also with the fear that there had been a grain of truth in the girl's ranting. Cassie had thrown it in her face, all right. Maybe it was not fair, but the fact remained that she had rescued Temple from a sharecropper's life and had given her an opportunity to rise in the world. She had paid for a private school in Washington, she was paying for junior college, and even the grammar the girl had learned was quickly forgotten when she was under stress. Were her only thanks to be accused, to be vilified? She would have to do something about Shirley Temple Vance and she would have to do it right away, during the Christmas break.

Hunching her shoulders over her problem she went around the corner of the toolshed and was confronted with another problem. Taylor was taunting Martha, holding her favorite doll above his head, just out of her reach.

"Taylor, you give me my baby!" Martha cried shrilly. "You give me her right now or I'll tell!"

"Taylor Steele!" Cassie called out. "Give your sister her doll, you hear?"

At the sound of his mother's voice Taylor whirled around and threw the doll on the frozen ground. "Well, take it then, crybaby! I don't want your damn old doll anyways!"

"Taylor! Don't you swear at your sister!"

He turned to face Cassie, standing four-square on sturdy seven-year-old legs. "Why not? You swear, I've heard you. And Temple swears, and Grandad."

Cassie wanted to smack her son. "But you don't!" She knelt by Martha. "Are you all right now, darling?"

The sympathy in her voice called forth a river of self-pity. "Mean old Taylor," Martha whined, "he was going to throw my baby in the creek. He picks on me, he always picks on—"

"That's enough, Martha." Now Cassie wanted to smack her daughter, but she managed to keep her voice level. "You two run on now, and play nicely. Did you see if there are any new kittens in the barn?"

"Kitties!" Martha brightened.

Taylor looked sideways at Martha. "I could throw a kitty in the creek and see if it could swim."

"Mama!"

"Stop it, Taylor," Cassie said through clenched teeth. "Stop teasing your sister. Now you two run play, hear?"

As the children disappeared around the corner of the barn, Cassie looked up at the lowering December sky. What had happened to her vision of a warm family Christmas? Just then the vacation stretched out before her as an interminable time crammed with problems to solve and decisions to make.

It was going to be a long, long Christmas.

At least Henry Starr had not changed. That evening he perched on a chair in the living room to discuss farm matters with Cassie.

"So I reckon we ought to add on to our herd and get out of the feedin' business, Cassie."

Cassie jotted some figures on a yellow legal pad. "It makes sense to me, Henry, if you're sure you can find men to do the work. I want you to remember that you're the farm manager and that you're not to ride herd on every last steer."

He laughed, a dry little cackle. "A feller don't get many bosses that tell him not to work so hard. Don't fret yourself, Cassie. I can get me the men if you can come up with the money for the herd."

She added a few figures on her yellow pad and did some mental calculation. "I can, Henry. I've got the money."

He shifted on his chair. "Did you know Ruby Keeler—well, she calls herself 'Ruby' now—that she's goin' to graduate college come spring?"

"Already? She writes to me, but I didn't realize that."

"She doubled up on some classes, I reckon. She's a smart girl, that Ruby, and a hard worker." He glanced at Cassie from the corner of his eye. "Wisht I could say the same thing for her little sister."

"I know." Cassie nodded, dejected at the thought of Temple's rebellious attitude. Something clicked in her mind, then, and she looked directly at Henry Starr. "What are you saying? Are you trying to tell me something?"

Henry straightened his shoulders. "Well, Cassie, I'll tell you. Mr. Steele come down here last month, just for a few hours, and me and him had a long talk. He didn't lay no blame on me for her bein' my grandkid, or on you, either, but the old man's right upset about Shirley Temple."

"Upset? Why?"

"Well, much as I hate to say it of my own kin, that girl ain't no better than she should be. She's been missin' her classes at that there college, hangin' around with some gas jockey up there in Ballard, and when Mrs. Steele tells her to cut it out, Temple gets downright smart-aleck about it."

Cassie sank back in her chair. "Oh, God. I heard about the boy, but I didn't realize she was—"

"You been gone, that's all. You ain't been here to see it and hear it."

"That's right, I've been gone," she said, but she knew that was not a valid excuse. When she had visited Ballard that fall, she had seen only what she wanted to see, but now she had to look, to see what she herself had done. She had unloaded her children onto their grandparents and what's more, the girl she paid to help with the children was more hindrance than help. She had been unfair to the Steeles, terribly unfair. "And they're too old," she said aloud.

"The Steeles are too old to cope with—" She hesitated, but honesty compelled her to continue. "With an insolent seven-year-old, a whiney six-year-old and, to boot, a surly college girl."

Henry looked embarrassed. "Reckon you're right, Cassie."

"But what am I going to do, Henry? I could take them back to Washington but most evenings I'm in committee meetings or the House sits late or—"

"Reckon they'd be better off in Ballard, then. It's only for a year. You finish up in Congress next December, don't you?"

Cassie was startled. "Why, yes, Henry. I was appointed to fulfill Dix's term and you're right, it will end in December, 1964."

"Ain't all that much can go wrong in a year."

Henry Starr left and Cassie changed into a flannel nightgown and a woolen robe. She went back to the living room to bank the fire but instead, she poured a brandy and sat down to stare into the flames.

Not much can go wrong in a year, Henry said, but he was wrong, so wrong. In that one year that was dragging to a close, in 1963, Dixon Steele was murdered and their life together ended. President Kennedy was murdered, too, and the American dream was shattered. What could, what would go wrong during the year to come, during 1964? Already she could see the sprouting of a vine that could strangle America in its evil grasp: South Vietnam. And closer to home, she could see nothing but trouble with her children and Temple Vance.

Only one more year, Henry said. One year until she would finish her commitment in Washington and, presumably, return to Oklahoma to concentrate on bringing up her children.

What would she do then, at the end of that year? Would she live here at the farm and be a country lawyer? Would she move her family to Tulsa and become what Dix had once teased her about: the first female wheeler-dealer in Oklahoma? She had loved creating deals when she was a Dallas lawyer, but could that compare with creating laws? And never could the give and take of courtroom argument be compared with a debate on the floor of the House of Representatives, a debate that would shape the future course of a nation.

And suddenly a picture appeared in her mind, a picture as clear and precise as a photograph and Cassie knew what she wanted. She knew exactly what she wanted to do.

She sat back, looking at the fire but seeing that picture, examining it from every side, focusing on the details and then widening her eyes to see the whole thing at once. She nodded once, briskly. "Yes," she said aloud. "That's the way it will be."

Cassie leaned down to poke up the fire then crossed the room to replenish her brandy and pick up the telephone.

"James? I hope I didn't wake you."

"No, I'm working in my study. Is something wrong, Cassie?"

"Oh, no, James. And we're still expecting you and Amelia to come down for Christmas Eve and Christmas Day. It's just that I want to tell you—I want you to be the first to know that I have decided to run for Congress on my own, for Dix's seat in the House."

There was a long silence. "I thought you might come to that conclusion eventually. It won't be easy, Cassie."

"You mean, beating some lackluster Republican hack? I'm the incumbent, James."

"It won't be a party hack you have to beat. The Republicans have been building strength all over the state, Cassie, and especially in your district. They call it 'Green Country' now that the new lakes have filled. There's a new kind of landowner: the retired fellow with a nice house overlooking a lake. These aren't the poor dirt farmers we have known, but comfortably fixed people who have a strong interest in maintaining the status quo. You haven't kept up with political changes the way you should have, Cassie."

"I've kept up with my constituents," she said defensively. "I've done a good job for them."

"But have you done a good job for the party leaders? I've heard it said that you went off to Washington and forgot all about the local party. You haven't kept in touch."

"Oh, sure," she said in disgust. "The glad-handing, the back-slapping, the dirty jokes. That's not my style, James."

There was only silence at his end of the telephone. Finally he spoke. "You'd better make it your style if you want the party's support in the primary and the election. I was reading one of little Martha's books to her last week, a thing called "The Cat That Walked by Himself." Now, that's all well and good for a cat, but you're old enough and smart enough to know that a politician can never walk alone."

Cassie's talk with James Steele gave her some idea of the opposition she would meet from the state party leaders, but neither his warning nor the words she heard during the meeting in Oklahoma could explain the depth of hostility she encountered.

After thirty minutes of heated discussion of her proposal that she be chosen the party candidate, the state party chairman pushed back his chair, glaring at Cassie, and lit a fresh cigar. "All right, all right! It's not really your business, Mrs. Steele—"

"Congresswoman Steele," she snapped.

"*Congresswoman* Steele. It's not your business, but I'll tell you just to get you off my back. We've already got a candidate for your district, a fine man."

Cassie was stunned. "Who? Who in my district can—"

"Harry White."

The name instantly brought to her mind a face she had seen at all too many political gatherings. Harry White was a county commissioner, a man who worked in the fringes of the power structure. His face was pudgy and clean-shaven, the face of a middle-aged man with an air of down-home affability. They wanted a Harry White in a seat that had been held by a Dixon Steele, that was held even now by his widow.

She wanted to scream at their low expectations, at their readiness to fob off a political hack on the people of her district, but she forced herself to relax, to sit back in her chair and smile to cover her dismay. Behind the smile, her mind churned madly as she tried to find a form for her chaotic feelings, to shape them into a logical summation that would win this case irrevocably for her client— herself.

"I find that difficult to believe," she said quietly. "I know Harry is popular with the party and I've heard that he's a fine companion in a duck blind, but a United States Representative? You gentlemen must be pulling my leg."

Her calm seemed to relax the men around the table. Someone said, "Sure as hell would like to pull a leg as pretty as that," but she ignored the remark as she surveyed the faces across the table from her. Two men looked embarrassed, so she directed her next words to them.

"Claude, Jim, you know Harry White better than I do. What kind of opposition do you think he'll be for a strong Republican candidate?"

"Ain't no such thing, not in Oklahoma." It was the same voice which had made a remark about pulling her leg.

Cassie faced the man, a fat, self-satisfied redneck with small piggy eyes. "If you believe that, Bill, you aren't keeping up with current politics. Jim? Claude? I asked you a question."

"Aw, now, Cassie," Claude Rich said. "Harry's a pretty good old boy."

"Yeah." Jim Perkins was from Eastern Oklahoma, too. "He's a man you can count on, Harry is. Folks like him."

"What folks are those, Jim? Other capitol cowboys? The gang in the all-night poker games at the Skirvin Hotel? Is he going to glad-hand my constituents into voting for him? The Republicans will put up their best, you can believe that. Someone like George Smathers, who has paid his dues to the voters of that district rather than to statehouse hangers-on."

"Hold on there, Cassie," Claude Rich said. "Harry's a good fund-raiser, too, and the Republicans are going to put a lot of cash into that race."

"And what makes you think that I'm not a good fund-raiser?"

Jim Perkins patted the air as if to gentle a skittish mare. "Cassie, Cassie. You know as well as we do that women running for public office can't get the financial support that men do."

Cassie forced herself to smile warmly as she looked around the table and saw that knowledge reflected in their faces. She had seen it before, that look. She had seen it in court in Dallas when the opposing lawyers looked at her and then away, discounting her because she was a woman. She had seen it in Washington when as a bona fide member of the House she had not been allowed to attend congressional social gatherings that were held at men-only clubs, because she was a woman. She had seen it in congressional committees when other committee members had ignored her because she was a woman, "the Oklahoma broad."

And now, here in her home state, here among her fellow Democrats, she was told that she could not run for the office she had held for a year, because she was a woman. She realized then what was at the root of their bitter opposition toward her. It was opposition that had nothing to do with her congressional record, with her relationship with her constituents or, for that matter, with the question of whether or not she could beat a Republican in the election of 1964. They thought she should be at home with her children, baking cookies and doing the wash, probably in a cast-iron pot with a washboard hooked over the side. They thought she should accept her two years in Congress as they had intended it: an honor extended to her dead husband, a feather she could tuck into her hat when she gathered with her peers for bridge or volunteer work or a ladies' luncheon at the country club. Because she was a woman.

What they did not understand was that Cassie herself looked upon the past year neither as a posthumous honor for Dix nor a friendly pat on the cheek for the little widow. She looked at it as a hands-on course in the business of legislation, as training for a job which she was now prepared to do.

Still smiling, she pushed back her chair and got to her feet. "Gentlemen," she said quietly, "I think that sometimes we forget those who came before us, those people who pushed off from the civilization of the East and headed West, always West, those fore-bears of ours who settled in the Indian Territory to the east and the Oklahoma Territory to the west. They fought the soil and the weather to bring forth their crops, to make their mark on a barren land. It was not 'men only' then, gentlemen. Every time I see that strong sculpture 'Pioneer Woman' over in Ponca City I am re-minded that men and women who created this state were partners in work and joy and sorrow and pain. Most of you have had the good fortune to have a grandmother or grandfather or even an elderly cousin who could tell you what it was like back then when a woman had to be as ready and as able as a man to fire a rifle, when there were outlaws roaming the country, and panthers in the woods and droughts and early freezes and late winters." Several men nodded, as if to say, yes, I have heard about the panthers, and the outlaws, and about the winter of '92.

Cassie went to the table and leaned over it to look each man in turn directly in the eyes.

"Are we to forget that, my friends?" she said softly, then she let her voice rise with the level of her emotions. "Are we to forget the pioneers, the men and the pioneer women, too, women who worked in full partnership with their men to create this place, this state of Oklahoma? Are those women's daughters and grand-daughters to be denied full participation in the running of their state? Am I to lose my right to run for public office not because I am a felon or a patient in a mental institution or even, for that matter, unqualified for the job, but for one reason and one reason only: because I am a woman?"

Cassie took a step back from the table, but no one said a word.

In a businesslike manner, with no trace of emotion in her voice, she said, "There are three points I would like to make in regard to my ability to win the election in November.

"First, even though I was appointed to the job, I am the incumbent. None of you, I think, will discount that fact.

"Second, my name recognition is high because of my husband, because of his—his murder, and because of my own person-to-person contact with my constituents at my bi-weekly clinics.

"Third, my fund-raising abilities have been questioned. I undertake to raise twenty-five percent, that is, one fourth of the campaign budget by April first, purely by my own efforts."

"Cassie," Jim Perkins said, "as far as I'm concerned you don't have to raise any money. You make a few speeches like the one you just gave us and you're a shoo-in in November."

The state chairman pursed his lips. "I'd like to see her raise that money."

"How much are you talking about?" Cassie said.

"We're calculating a hundred-thousand-dollar race." He watched her carefully, but Cassie covered her sudden nervousness.

"Dix's campaign only cost forty-two thousand dollars," she said.

"Sure, but that was against a weak opponent and we didn't do much with TV then."

"Oh," she said. "Television. Of course."

"John Kennedy taught us a lot about using TV in a campaign."

Jim Perkins laughed. "And Cassie's sure as hell prettier than any Republican."

The chairman turned to Cassie. "Let me make sure I got this straight, Congresswoman. If you don't get in twenty-five thousand dollars by the first of April, you'll withdraw your name?"

Twenty-five thousand dollars, Cassie thought, but she lifted her chin. "That's right. You have my word on it."

The chairman pushed back his chair. "Then I don't see how the party can lose on this. If she does it, we'll know she's a worker.

If she can't, we'll still have a head start on financing the campaign, and since we won't have to announce a candidate till April first, we'll still have Harry White waiting in the wings."

Cassie managed a light laugh. "I hope old Harry likes the wings. He's going to be waiting there long after I've won the election and gone back to Washington."

Chapter 27

After careful consideration, Cassie decided not to take the children and Temple back to Washington with her. To meet her fund-raising commitment, she would have to fly back to Oklahoma almost every weekend. She could not entrust her children to Temple alone, and the constant travel would be both too exhausting and too disruptive for them. She did her best, instead, to ameliorate the situation in Ballard. She had long talks with the children, with Amelia and James about the need for more discipline for Taylor and Martha, and the longest talk of all with Temple in regard to her need for more self-discipline. She used a carrot and stick approach with Temple, the carrot being the promise that the girl's good behavior would earn her a return to Washington in the fall. The stick was a clear statement that bad behavior would mean an instant return to the bosom of her sharecropper family.

It was back to Washington, then, for the opening of the Eighty-eighth Congress. Cassie's fund-raising efforts curtailed her time in the House, but she was careful to keep up with her committee work and she was meticulous about handling problems for her constituents.

Fund-raising proved to be more difficult than she had expected. She had her Oklahoma aides set up coffees and luncheons with the ladies of the district and at each appearance she gave a little talk, skillfully interweaving the latest news and gossip of Washington with pleas for financial contributions to her campaign. After a few of the meetings, however, she began to think that they were part of the problem rather than the solution. Little remarks were made. "I just don't see how you manage, dear. I mean, trying to be a good mother and a career gal, too. Oh, but I just remembered. Your children live with their grandparents, don't they?" Cassie realized that it was not just men but women, too, who resented her success in a man's world.

The other half of the problem was the fact that she was spending too much time to raise too little money. The contributions from even her wholehearted supporters were too small to do much good. One weekend, she spent half of Saturday at a well-attended meeting only to hear the organizer announce, at the end, "And I'm happy to say that today we have raised money for Congresswoman Steele's campaign, a total of one hundred eighty-seven dollars and fifty cents!"

That night Cassie got out her legal pad and made some calculations. At her current average of $125 per outing, she would have to make two hundred appearances to raise the $25,000 she had guaranteed, perhaps foolishly, to the state committee. Even if she could handle four meetings a week, it would take a year to raise the money she had promised to deliver and April first was just ten weeks away. She threw down her pencil. April Fool's Day, she thought, and it will be easy to name the fool.

Maybe she was looking for money in the wrong place. Oklahoma women *had* money, there was no question about that, but how they spent it was not always up to them. A Tulsa husband probably would not mind his wife's buying a thousand dollars' worth of dresses at Miss Jackson's shop, but he would object strenuously to her spending the same amount in the male world of politics.

Cassie's money was her own and she would spend it as she saw fit. She was tight for cash just then because of her commitment to Henry Starr to increase the size of their herd, but she had planned to sell stock to raise $5,000 for her campaign. All right, she thought, so she would sell more stock, more than she really could afford to sell, in fact, and contribute $10,000 to the campaign. That would leave $15,000 to raise. One hundred and twenty fund-raising appearances. Thirty weekends. Too many.

There had to be a better way, she thought, there had to! She could keep her coffee and luncheon schedule, but she had to go after the big money. And that meant she would have to go to the men who had control of it.

She took up her address book and made a list of names, each with the dollar amount she would ask for. The men whose names she put down were good Democrats and were people who had the money to back their political beliefs. Many of them, too, were happier with an old-fashioned Southern Democrat like Lyndon Johnson than they had been with the lofty idealists of Camelot.

When her first four telephone calls brought her compliments and good wishes but no cash, she realized that simply asking for a contribution was not enough. She had to approach these men not with a feminine plea but as another man would approach them, cocksure and demanding. She had to make them *want* to contribute to her campaign.

"So you see, Leroy," she said into the phone ten minutes later, "Lyndon is going to need a Democratic Congress to vote his ideas into legislation." Leroy owned several small-town banks, but an expanding herd of pure-blooded Hereford cattle was his pride and joy. "You know he's a friend to the bankers, and I don't have to tell *you* that Lyndon Johnson holds ranching close to his Texas heart." She glanced at her list. "So, I'd like to see you contribute thirty-five hundred dollars to my campaign."

"Hell, Cassie," he sputtered, "you can buy a damn Oldsmobile for that!"

"I know, but you don't want to put your money in an Oldsmobile, not with two Cadillacs in your driveway. Invest it in me, instead."

He chuckled. "You do your homework, don't you, girl? What's in it for me?"

"Well, Leroy, for one thing, you can step up to Lyndon when he's elected and you can say, 'Mr. President, I helped hold my Oklahoma congressional district for the Democrats, for you.' "

Dead silence on the other end of the line.

"Oh," Cassie said, trying not to sound desperate, "and you can expect a great big thank-you kiss from me!"

He laughed. "Cassie, I swear, you know the way to a man's heart, and to his pocketbook, too. Tell you what, will you settle for one of those Volkswagens instead of an Oldsmobile? That would come to about seventeen hundred dollars."

"Leroy, do I look like a woman who'd drive a Volkswagen?"

"Anybody looks like you ought to be driving a Cadillac."

She laughed lightly. "Then aren't you glad I only asked for an Oldsmobile?"

"Hell's bells, Cassie, you got me coming and going. Okay, okay, I'll send you a check for thirty-five hundred. But don't you think for a minute I'm going to forget that kiss you promised me!"

When Cassie hung up, she wiped her lips with her hand as if she had already delivered on her distasteful promise. She pushed back her mental picture of Leroy's fat face and large damp mouth, and although it demanded a big effort, she picked up the phone and dialed again.

She had some successes and some failures, and when she returned to Washington on Monday she called Cully Meecham into her office. "Cully, I'm going to run for the House on my own hook."

"Yeah. I know."

"Who told you?"

"Cassie, sometimes I think I keep a hell of a lot closer eye on Oklahoma politics than you do. Some of the good ole boys back there are pretty mad at you, you know."

"But surely they know I'm raising money for the party and—"

"They say it's for you, not for the party."

"I've told all my supporters how important it is for Lyndon Johnson to have a Democratic Congress."

Cully's dry little laugh sounded like a fox's cough. "Listen, when a politician starts believing what he tells his supporters, he's in deep shit. No, Cassie, don't try to kid old Cully. I've seen it too many times. You've gone and got yourself bit by the Washington bug. It swells you right up, that bite, makes you think you're the best thing since sliced bread, lets you see that without you in office the poor old U.S. of A. is going right down the drain. No, Cassie, that money ain't for the party. It's for you."

Cassie sat back in the big leather swivel chair that had come with the office, a chair with built-in importance. It fitted her. "So what?" she said coolly. "Maybe I'm no better than the other members of Congress but I'm no worse, either. Whoever or whatever the money is for, the question is, how do we raise it?"

Cully's eyes opened wide, then he laughed. "Okay, then. Tell me where you stand now and what you got in mind."

They put their heads together over her notes and they refined her approach. Cassie began to believe again that she could raise the money by April. Cully was not as sure.

"We're going to have to get us a miracle or two," he said.

The campaign fund built nicely through February. The ladies' money kept coming in during March, but the businessmen's contributions dried up. The men blamed it on the IRS, but whatever the cause the result was the same.

"I swear to God, Cassie, I've seen it before. It ain't you, it's taxes. These old boys feel like their backs are to the wall."

"But they knew how much tax they would have to pay. They expected it."

"Sure they did, but it's like you expect old age. You can expect it but that don't make you feel any better when you get it."

"Cully, I've come up with every cent I can from my own money and, damn it all to hell, we're still twenty-five hundred dollars short, with just two weeks to go. We need one of your miracles now."

"We do, Cassie. We sure as hell do."

Cassie was at home that night and staring glumly at the fire when the telephone rang.

"Congresswoman Steele, please. Mackenzie Cameron is calling."

"Mack?" she said. "This is me—I mean—she, oh, you know what I mean!"

His laugh was a deep rumble of amusement. "Cassie? I thought congressmen, I mean, congresswomen, had people to answer the phone for them."

"Well, this one doesn't. Mack, I haven't seen you in months. How have you been?"

"Fine. Busy. I've seen you a few times, at parties, but you're always with that tall thin guy."

"Eliot Peabody." She had nothing to hide from Mack Cameron.

"Well, you're looking great. Are you feeling better about—well—things?"

Cassie could translate that and Mack deserved an answer. It was with him, on that terrible weekend of Kennedy's assassination, that she had finally found the release of tears.

"Yes, Mack. I am feeling much, much better about—things."

"I'm glad to hear it." She heard the relief in his voice. "Cassie, maybe we could go out to dinner some night, maybe talk now that we're not as torn up as we were then."

"I'd like that, but I'm pretty much tied up just now."

"With this Eliot Peabody?"

"No!" There was more irritation in her voice than she had intended. "With my campaign for the House."

"Yeah," he said, "I've heard about that. In fact, that's why I called you. Cassie, I want to make a contribution to your campaign."

"Mack, that's very kind of you, but I know you're a Republican."

"What difference does that make? Look, if I lived in your district you'd have my vote because I know what you are and what you stand for. Since I can't cast a vote, I want to send a little of my money to do my voting for me. I mailed a check to your office this afternoon, for three thousand dollars. I wish I could do more but—"

"Mack! Did you say three thousand dollars?"

"Well, yes, but if you need more from me—"

"Stop! Wait a minute." Cassie tried to figure it out. He wasn't in her district, he was not even a Democrat. "Why so much, Mack?" She tried to keep the suspicion out of her voice, but she did not do very well at it. "What do you expect to get for it? Support in Congress for the oil and gas industry? Or is it more personal? Do you expect something of me, as a woman?"

There was a long silence. "Cassie," he said formally, "I have never tried to bribe anyone, least of all a member of Congress, and I am not trying to do so now. As far as you personally are concerned, you insult both yourself and me by implying that I would offer you money for—what do you take me for, Cassie Steele? Worse, what do you take yourself for, some kind of Washington courtesan? Back in Oklahoma, life is simpler. There's only one word for a woman who sells herself: prostitute."

"Mack! I'm sorry! I didn't mean that you were—or that I was—"

"Well, I'm sorry, too. I'm sorry I mailed that goddamn check. You go ahead and cash it, though, and use it. A Cameron doesn't go back on his word."

"Let me explain, Mack! Please!"

"What is there to explain, damn it? You've made it real clear what you think of me."

His receiver went down with a bang that reverberated in Cassie's ear.

Mack Cameron's check came the next day. Cassie sat at her

desk, holding it, but her big chair felt less comfortable and a good deal less important.

With the party's full endorsement of her candidacy, the Democratic primary was a runaway. Shortly after her thirty-ninth birthday, Cassie Steele became her party's candidate for the House of Representatives. With the Republicans fighting tooth and nail for Dixon Steele's seat, however, receiving the official nomination only meant that she had to work harder than ever. She was well aware of the cost of her constant round of speaking engagements and fund-raisers. Her constituents saw more and more of her even as they received less and less service. It was the ever-present problem for first and second term congressmen: the necessity of spending almost half of a two-year term on an effort to be reelected. Cassie's conscience pricked her, even though it was necessity that made her a politician rather than a representative of the people.

There was much to concern the people's representatives that spring. The "Freedom Summer" of 1964 began in June with the murder of three civil rights workers, two white and one black, near Philadelphia, Mississippi. For the first time, racial violence spread to the North, where Southern Negroes had immigrated in search of work and freedom to find waiting for them instead poverty and crime and the bitter hatred of Northern whites.

Cassie could take no active role that summer because of the necessity of making frequent appearances in Oklahoma. On the other hand, the trips west did mean that she could see more of her children. Taylor turned eight in March and that summer Martha was almost seven. The atmosphere in the Steeles' house in Ballard was more relaxed, perhaps because of her frequent visits. The problems arose when she had to leave to make a speech or show up at a town picnic. She took something of her children with her, though, some of their love and, that particular summer, the maddening rhymes and rhythms of "Puff, the Magic Dragon" tinkling in her mind.

There were other events that summer as shocking as racial violence in the North. In July, Lyndon Johnson dumped Robert Kennedy as a running mate in the presidential election. What was more, the President called in a few reporters and made fun of Bobby Kennedy's reaction to the news.

Cassie was incensed. She was no member of the "Irish Mafia" but she had great respect for Robert Kennedy as well as a deep personal gratitude for his actions regarding Dix's murder.

That news was followed within a week by reports that President Johnson had ordered the bombing of North Vietnam in reprisal for abortive attacks on an American destroyer. Only afterward did the President ask Congress to approve his actions in expanding American involvement in South Vietnam.

Cassie flew to Washington prepared to debate and to vote against the resolution, but the canny politician in the White House had forestalled a congressional defeat. He had gone on television to get the support of the American people, and no politician was going to vote against supporting American boys in battle—especially not in an election year.

On her first night in Georgetown, Cassie was surprised to receive a telephone call from Mack Cameron.

"I called to apologize," he said.

"Oh, Mack!" Cassie said in a gush of relief. "I'm the one who owes *you* an apology!"

He chuckled. "I guess our apologies cancel each other out, then, don't they? How about making the truce official by going out to dinner with me?"

"Mack, I can't," she said, dismayed. "Eliot is—"

"Eliot." His voice was flat. "I guess you'll be out late, then."

"No, it can't be a late night. I have to do some reading before tomorrow's vote."

"The Tonkin Gulf thing? I thought that a yes-vote was a foregone conclusion."

"It probably is but—oh, Mack, I don't know how to vote! I

think Johnson is pulling the wool over our eyes, using a crisis to push us into something we'll regret later, but—"

"Why don't you vote 'no' if you feel that way?"

"It's not that easy. This is an election year, remember? How am I going to defend such a vote back home? It would make my constituents think that I didn't care if American warships were attacked on the high seas, if American boys were killed."

"The way I heard it, Cassie, nobody got killed and the *Maddox* was likely in North Vietnamese waters anyway."

"You didn't hear the President speak on television, then. I can't vote for it in good conscience, Mack, I can't! I don't trust the President, not after what he did to Robert Kennedy." She tried to laugh. "But why am I telling you all of this? Washing the Democrats' dirty linen in front of a dyed-in-the-wool Republican."

There was a moment of silence. "I'm not all that damn sure political parties matter just now, Cassie. Look at the Republicans. We've got Barry Goldwater running for President—"

"And he sounds like he wants to blow all of Vietnam off the map!"

The phone was silent for a moment. "I don't think that is exactly what he says, Cassie. But listen, this Tonkin thing. You say it's a matter of conscience? Tell me something. Will your one vote pass or defeat the resolution?"

"Of course not. Johnson has all the votes in Congress he needs, and then some."

"Then to hell with it, vote for the damn resolution!"

"Mack, I told you, in good conscience—"

"Hell, Cassie, forget your conscience for a minute, will you? I'm not even sure politicians are entitled to have consciences. You oppose Johnson's methods, right? Okay, can you do more to influence the course of events as a private citizen or as a congresswoman?"

"In Congress, of course, but—"

"But me no buts, woman. Vote for the damn thing and get

elected and hang in there. Your next vote might be a tie-breaker. You might be able to accomplish something important."

Cassie sat back in her chair and the tightness in her shoulders relaxed. "Mack, thank you. You've helped me more than—I wish I didn't have a date tonight."

"So do I," he said softly.

"Maybe tomorrow night—"

"I've got to go to Dallas tomorrow. But when I get back, well, may I call you then?"

"Yes! Of course!"

Cassie hung up slowly, thinking of the pragmatic approach Mack suggested. She wrestled with her conscience, but then she repeated Mack's words: "To hell with it!" She would vote "yea," knowing that her vote would change nothing, and she would get herself elected and be prepared to oppose the President's tactics in committee and on the floor of the House, where her opposition might just do some good.

Eliot Peabody was as charming as always that evening, but his thoughts seemed to be a thousand miles away. "Have you been terribly busy, Eliot?" Cassie asked sympathetically.

"God, yes. This Plan Thirty-four-A has kept me—" He stopped abruptly.

"Yes? What is that?"

"Oh, nothing. Tell me, what are they saying in the House about the Tonkin resolution?"

Cassie chatted about the ins and outs of the debate, but her mind was busy, trying to connect the phrase he had mentioned to something she had heard in the House. Surely, she thought, Plan 34-A was tied up with McGeorge Bundy's idea of using South Vietnamese PT boats for commando raids on Communist shore installations. Could that possibly have anything to do with the attacks on the American ship, the *Maddox?* She wanted to ask Eliot, but she knew he would not tell her anything.

As always, too, he appeared to be much more interested in her life than in his own. "How do you think the Tonkin vote will go?"

Cassie explained her qualms about it.

"Who else is against it, Cassie? Does the President have enemies in the House?"

"Of course! What President hasn't? What worries me is the power we will give him if we pass this resolution."

Eliot looked thoughtful. "I can see that, but nevertheless—"

But nevertheless Cassie Steele gave the President what he wanted. Against her better judgement, she gave Lyndon Johnson her support. She voted in favor of the Tonkin resolution.

As the campaign came down to the wire, Cassie worked harder than she would have thought possible, speeding from fund-raiser to speaking engagement with Cully driving the station wagon and coaching her on local politicians and local problems.

She spent election night gathered with other Democrats in a hotel ballroom in Oklahoma City. President Johnson won his election early, but Cassie's race seesawed as the vote from different precincts came in. It was late when the trend became clear. The Republican candidate came to her for a brief exchange of graceful compliments and to concede the election.

The party faithful broke into applause and Cassie rose to accept their cheers for the first woman of her district to be elected to national office: Cassandra Taylor Steele. Congresswoman Steele, in her own right and by her own efforts elected a member of the United States House of Representatives.

The Washington scene changed when Lyndon Baines Johnson became President-elect of the United States. In spite of the lingering influence of the Kennedys—Robert, a senator from New York, and Edward, who had held his seat as a Massachusetts senator by 900,000 votes—Washington began to dance to Lyndon Johnson's tunes: "Hello, Lyndon" and "The Yellow Rose of Texas." Ten-gallon hats appeared in the halls of Congress and high-heeled cowboy boots added illusory stature to many men in government.

President Johnson himself seemed to be caught up in the Texas legend. Using troops and planes instead of fists, like John Wayne he rode into Vietnam, bombing the Viet Cong and increasing the American commitment there.

There were, however, a few bright spots on Cassie's personal horizon. For one thing, she discovered that a U.S. Representative who has been elected rather than appointed has considerably more clout. Not a lot of clout, Cassie realized, as only a second-term congresswoman, but enough to make a difference. People remembered her name and returned her telephone calls. Her requests to various government departments were not, as she had suspected before, buried at the bottom of the stack, but received relatively prompt action. If nothing else, those wheels of government which had seemed till then to be jammed with molasses and sand were lubricated by her election. She had evidently become someone who mattered.

Most pleasant of all, however, was the fact that she could spend more time with her children. She had brought them to Washington in September, Taylor and Martha to reenter their old school and Temple to enroll in a local junior college where she had a fair chance of getting her grades up by January. During the campaign, Cassie had been able to spend very little time with them. It was only when she saw them daily that she was able to see how they were growing and changing. Taylor was eight and a half and very much involved with cowboys and trucks and doing as little homework as was possible. Martha had turned seven in September and moved through the house in a covey of Barbie dolls and pigtailed friends.

Cassie promised herself that she would take Taylor, Martha and Temple somewhere for Christmas, to a place where they could be together and where she could become reacquainted with her children.

The solution to Cassie's problem came when she overheard a

conversation at a cocktail party. A couple was describing a trip they had enjoyed, to a place called Puerto Vallarta, in Mexico. It was a resort on the Pacific, the husband said.

Instantly Cassie could feel warm sand under her feet and smell a fresh ocean breeze.

"Well, not really a resort yet," his wife said, "because it hasn't been developed." Puerto Vallarta. The couple went on to say that the place was becoming well known since Elizabeth Taylor and Richard Burton had been there the year before to film *The Night of the Iguana*. It sounded less glamorous than Acapulco, and perhaps more suitable for her family. The Washington wife kept talking about it. "We virtually lived on the beach! Can you imagine, on the twelfth of November the water temperature was ninety-five degrees!"

The taut muscles in Cassie's neck relaxed at the very idea. Christmas, she thought. Christmas! She would take the children and Temple down there when the House rose. Perhaps Eliot could spend some time with them.

Eliot Peabody, always correct, always sedate. How would warm nights and a tropical moon affect him? For once, she would take a chance. She felt a quiver of excitement. For once, she was willing to let the moment decide.

Cassie called a travel agent the next morning. "It's too late, Mrs. Steele," the man said. "Too late for flight reservations and too late to get hotel rooms. I'm sorry."

After a moment's hesitation, Cassie identified herself more fully.

The man's voice rose. "*Congresswoman* Steele? You should have told me. Let me see what I can do, ma'am."

Cassie grinned as she hung up. To be a second-term representative might not carry much weight in politics, but it seemed to help outside the House. She was not surprised when the travel agent called back and said that all of the arrangements were made.

Eliot, it turned out, could indeed get away for a week, and something in his voice told her that he, too, was open to new

experiences. He could not get away in time to travel with Cassie
and her family, but he would arrive in Puerto Vallarta a few days
later. The children and Temple were entranced with the idea of
going to the beach in winter, and the Steeles agreed to celebrate
a late Christmas when Cassie next brought her family to Ballard.

Christmas shopping, added to her duties as a representative,
kept Cassie running almost until flight time, but when the Mexi-
cana Airways plane circled over the Pacific and then bounced to
an abrupt halt just before running into the jungle at the end of
the short runway, she knew it was worth all the hurry. Even in
the battered taxi she could feel herself relaxing, and by the time
they checked into the hotel the damp heat and the slower pace of
Mexico was soaking into her bones.

Cassie had reserved adjoining rooms, one for Temple and the
children and one for herself. The door between the two was open
and she could hear the excitement in Taylor and Martha's voices
as they changed to their swimming suits, but their chatter soon
faded in her ears. She went out on the balcony where the warm
moist air enveloped her and an ocean-fresh breeze from the Pacific
ruffled her hair. Below her were the impossibly green grounds of
the hotel, the blue-tiled swimming pool and beyond them, a golden
beach dotted with natural umbrellas, tree trunks supporting
thatched circles of sun-browned coconut leaves. The vacationers
on the beach moved in slow-motion, dabbling in the ebbing waves
at the water's edge, strolling along the sand or not moving at all,
stretched out on straw mats, their bodies glistening in the hot sun,
or sat in deck chairs in the shade and limply turned the pages of
a paperback book.

"Mama!" Martha exploded into Cassie's room. "Hurry *up!*"

"All right, dear, I'll hurry." Even the hurrying was different,
though, in Puerto Vallarta. Pulling on her bathing suit, she remembered the rush to the floor of the House for a vote and the
frantic haste to stamp out a small political fire before it could
become a conflagration. She slipped her feet into thong sandals

and just had time to snatch up a beach towel and a paperback book before Martha and Taylor pushed her into the hall like busy little tugboats urging a passenger liner out to sea.

On the beach she filed claim on a convenient umbrella by depositing her things in a deck chair. Holding her children's hands tightly she ran to the water, but she stopped them when they were ankle-deep in the first fringe of waves. "Wait here, right here, while I check the depth of the water."

Cassie plunged into an on-coming breaker and swam strongly through it to the calmer water beyond, which turned out to be too deep for the children. She tried to catch a ride on the next breaker, but she missed the moment and was sucked under the wave, abraded by the sand suspended in the whirling water, churned around like a carrot in a blender, and finally cast out into the shallows a good ten yards from the children. For a moment she lay still, catching her breath and regaining her equilibrium, then she stood up and walked shakily back to Martha, Taylor and Temple, who were running toward her.

"You all right, Cassie?" Cassie was surprised to see that concern had temporarily washed the sulkiness from Temple's face.

"Yes, I'm all right. Now." Martha took her hand and as they walked back to their umbrella, Cassie described the action on the breakers. "So you must stay well back from the waves, hear?"

Taylor would have argued, of course, but just then a man was cast out of the breakers, a strong young man. He got to his feet slowly and they all saw the raw patch on his arm and shoulder caused by the wave scraping him against the sand of the ocean floor. Taylor closed his mouth without a word of argument.

Cassie collapsed into a deck chair and scrubbed at her wet hair with her beach towel. She watched the children carefully, but even Taylor had been frightened by the way Cassie looked when she emerged from the breaker. Temple stayed as close to Martha and Taylor as a mother hen hovering over her chicks when a hawk circles a clearing.

Only then did Cassie realize how tired she was in both body and mind. From fighting the sea, she thought, but her fatigue was more than that. It touched the inner depths of being, her very soul. The campaign had taken more out of her than she suspected. A few days on the beach would—no. It ran deeper than the campaign. Her exhaustion resulted from her trying to be too many people: member of Congress, supervisor of family finances, politician, head of a congressional campaign and, most of all, both mother and father to her children. Her spirits lifted when she remembered that Eliot Peabody was coming in a few days. She could surrender a few of her responsibilities to him, at least temporarily. She sighed and leaned back in her chair. For once she would be able to relax and let someone else take care of her.

Cassie opened her book and read a few pages. A dark-eyed charmer named Felicity was apparently in the highly infelicitous clutches of Sir Randal, the local squire. Cassie turned one page and then another, but she no longer comprehended the words. She smiled. A beach book, after all, was to be dreamed over, not read.

It was Friday and Eliot Peabody would arrive in Puerto Vallarta at noon on Tuesday. That was surely something worth dreaming about. The influence of proper Boston might reach as far south as Washington, but she doubted that even Boston's long arm could extend its clutch to the Pacific coast of Mexico. In the tropics, in the hot Mexican night, what would happen to a Bostonian? Would he go mad like Somerset Maugham's pent-up preacher or would he merely relax, like Cassie herself, and absorb the sights and sounds of a Mexican Eden? Cassie found herself giggling like an impish schoolgirl. Maybe, with Eliot there, Puerto Vallarta would become that earthly Paradise.

Cassie sat up straight when she realized that Temple Vance had emitted her usual unconscious—or conscious—pheromone and entrapped the young males in the vicinity: a very large young man with white-blond hair and a sunburned face, and a smaller man, swarthy, who was rattling away in Spanish.

Sighing, Cassie rose and strolled to the water's edge.

"Cassie! Pepe's going to show me how to ride the breakers! Oh. Pepe, this is Cong-ress-wo-man Steele."

"Does Pepe speak English?" Cassie said.

"Only to say 'Coca-Cola.' "

"And the other one?"

"He knows some English," Temple said disparagingly. "He's German or something."

"No German," the red-faced boy said. "Norske!"

"He's a Norwegian, Temple."

"Oh, well. Cassie, will you keep an eye on the kids while I swim with Pepe?"

At the sound of his name, Pepe grinned at Cassie, a flash of white against his perfectly tanned skin. It was the sort of grin that made Cassie think that she'd better keep an eye on Pepe, too.

"Yes, of course," she said. "I'd like to get the children out of the sun for a while anyway. Come on, Taylor, Martha, let's get in the shade and build a sand castle."

They ran ahead of her and Cassie paused for a moment to drink in the tropical scene: the blue ocean, the sand, the nodding coconut trees around the white hotel.

And Eliot Peabody was coming on Tuesday.

Chapter 28

 During the next few days each of them found something very special in Puerto Vallarta. Temple acquired a polyglot group of admirers and learned to swim the breakers. Taylor found a friend, a nine-year-old California boy who was delighted to build sand castles over and over, because it was so much fun to smash them down again. Martha's friend spoke no English and Martha no Spanish, but evidently language was no problem to seven-year-old girls. They were happy to converse entirely in giggles. Cassie could at last relax: the problems of the House of Representatives were far, far away. While Temple swam and flirted with Pepe, Cassie and her children enjoyed the beach or explored the town.

Puerto Vallarta was gradually evolving from a sleepy town into a resort. Until the Americans had come to make their film, Cassie learned, the place had been a fishing village of no more than two thousand people. The movie people brought prosperity with them, filling hotels that had catered only to a few wanderers in the past. The stars had occupied private houses in an area called "Gringo Gulch." The publicity and the American money provided the impetus for expansion. There were two new hotels on the beach, foundations laid for three more, and even talk of a future Hilton.

But as they walked through the town Cassie wondered, were they really foundations? It was true that there was scaffolding and there were a few workmen around, but no progress was made. The excavations could have been archaeological sites as easily as construction sites. To Cassie it appeared that everything in town was either half built or half demolished.

Martha was the one who discovered that the old and new existed in harmony. They were on the narrow concrete causeway that took them across the river from the hotel and into town when she skipped ahead of Cassie and Taylor. "Mama!" she cried. "Look at those ladies!"

Cassie caught up with her and looked upstream past the fringe of trees. Eight or ten peasant women were standing knee-deep in the stream, chatting in Spanish and laughing together as they slapped wet cloth against the boulders, dipped it in the river, wrung it out and slapped it against the stones once more.

"They're washing, Martha. Look, Taylor, the women are doing their laundry!"

She felt as if she had entered the pages of *National Geographic* instead of taking a short stroll from a luxury hotel.

"Why don't they use their washing machines?" Taylor said.

So much for a good private education, Cassie thought. "Because they don't have washing machines, that's why."

Martha's smile disappeared. "Mama, are they poor? Are they real poor?"

Cassie watched the women for a few minutes. The Americans' presence put a stop to their chatter, but their dark eyes twinkled as they sneaked looks at the tourists on the causeway and then at each other. She thought she knew what they would talk about when she and her children moved on. "Yes, Martha," she said. "By our standards, they are very poor."

Martha cupped her hands around her mouth. *"Hola!"* she called. *"Gracias! Adiós!"*

The women's laughter cascaded down the river. Cassie smiled at them but she snatched Martha's hand and hurried across the causeway. Behind them the giggles rose again to laughter interspersed with quick conversation. "Where on earth did you learn that, Martha?"

"From Pepe. *'Hola'* is hello and *'gracias'* is—"

"I know, I know. So now you speak Spanish. Good for you!"

Tuesday finally arrived, and the evening flight from Guadalajara, and Eliot Peabody. Planning that she and Eliot could dine alone that first night, Cassie left the children to have their dinner with Temple. She was waiting when Eliot's plane stopped just short of the jungle and turned to taxi back to the little terminal.

Eliot looked pale as he descended the steps, but so did the other passengers. Cassie could sympathize, remembering the heart-stopping moment when it appeared that her plane was sure to use up the runway and plow into the jungle beyond.

Once he was on the ground Eliot looked as cool and self-possessed in his gray tropical suit as if he were strolling into a Washington restaurant.

"Eliot!" Cassie called. "I'm over here."

He turned and gave her one of his rare smiles. "Cassie, my dear." He set down his flight bag and put his arms around her. Looking down into her eyes he whispered, "I've missed you, Cassie." He kissed her.

Cassie responded to his kiss, hesitantly at first and then eagerly. Shaken, she stepped back. "There's a—I have a taxi waiting. I thought we could have dinner at the hotel, just the two of us."

They rode to the hotel almost without speaking, carefully separated, each to his own side of the back seat, alone with his own thoughts.

When Eliot had checked in, however, he turned to her and smiled. "Will you come up with me while I change, Cassie?"

She gave one quick thought to her children, but she knew they were safe. She nodded, although she knew well that her gesture agreed to far more than had been said. "Yes, Eliot. Yes."

While he tipped the bellboy, Cassie crossed Eliot's room to the window. His view, like her own, was of the beach and the blue Pacific spread out across the horizon. An on-shore breeze cooled the soft air and made the sheer white curtains billow around her. She was only half aware of Eliot's brief exchange of Spanish with the boy and of his closing and locking the door of the room.

Then his hands were on her shoulders, quiet for a moment and then gripping her shoulders and gently turning her body to face his.

He kissed her, a long sensuous kiss of exploration, and Cassie found herself responding, putting her arms around him, drawing her body close to his. From deep within her a moan rose as her body reacted to urges ignored but never forgotten.

Without speaking he eased her down onto the limp, cool sheets. He caressed her body gently, as if he were on a voyage of discovery, and Cassie's body awoke to his as his kisses rekindled fires she had thought to be dead. The fires had not gone out, it appeared, but were only banked, and the smallest spark could set them to roaring again.

He unbuttoned her dress and pulled it from her slowly and then raised himself on one arm to fumble with her bra. She helped him pull away the bra and then her slip and panties. He looked down at her, searching her eyes and then her naked body. She reached up to undo his necktie and he stood up to tear away his clothes. He paused, standing beside the bed, as naked as she, and then lay down next to her and pulled her close.

"Cassie," he said, his voice low and urgent. "Cassie." He bore her down onto the bed and covered her body with his.

Cassie's own body remembered, reacted, and pushed itself up to his, raising her pelvis until it ground itself against him, demanding.

He pulled back for a moment. "Are you protected?"

"No," she said, surprised that he would think so. "No."

He reached down to the floor beside the bed and fumbled at his clothing. She closed her eyes for a moment that seemed to be all eternity and then was electrified when his hand touched her most secret parts. She cried out, a wordless cry of wanting, of needing, He entered her, slowly at first, gently, but then with a surge of demand that overpowered her.

Cassie exploded instantly, but it was not enough. "More," she cried. "More!"

He rammed himself into her, into another explosion and another and yet another.

"Now!" he cried and in one last thrust he drove his own explosion into hers.

Cassie's back arched until it felt that she was supporting him, lifting him with all of her strength, with all of her body.

Eliot moaned, a long sigh of repletion, and sank down with her onto sheets that were no longer cool but hot and rumpled.

"Eliot," she whispered, but his eyes were closed. He put his arms around her and rolled onto his side, taking her with him. She lay wrapped in his arms, satisfied, content, and only gradually did she become aware of the room, the white curtains billowing at the window against the sudden darkness of a tropical night.

The children, she thought. I must see to the children. She opened her mouth to speak but closed it instantly. She had almost called him "Dix." She felt shaken suddenly and in desperate need to be alone.

"Eliot," she whispered. "I must go."

Half asleep, he muttered something.

"At the beach tomorrow, Eliot. We'll see you on the beach."

She disengaged her body from his and dressed quickly. More than anything, she wanted to be away from there, away from him. How could I? she asked herself. How could I sleep with him, with Dix under ground not even a year yet? Oh, God, how could I like it so much?

By the time she had returned to her own room, had showered and was in bed, she managed to get it into perspective. Self-castigation would do no good. She was even able to rationalize her actions to some degree. She was a normal woman, that was all. She had the desires and the physical needs of any other woman of thirty-nine. And it had been almost a year. Surely that was long enough to ignore a part of her that had brought her great joy through the years. She suddenly remembered her first husband, Jimmy Steele, and her poor aborted baby. Great joy, yes. And great pain.

Cassie was on the beach with Taylor and Martha by the time Eliot had breakfast and came in search of her.

"Where's your—what's her name, Temple?"

"Sleeping in," Cassie said. "I gave her the morning off."

"But I thought we would—" He stopped, but his look at her spelled out the rest of his sentence.

"No," she said. "Look, Taylor, Martha, your friends just came to the beach. Are you going to build a sand castle with them?"

Martha jumped up. "A castle with a moat!"

"No, I get to dig the moat," Taylor said.

"I thought of it first!"

"I'm bigger!"

"Mama! Taylor says he gets to—"

"I know, I know." Cassie kissed Martha and gave Taylor a pat on his firm little seat. "You'll need two moats, won't you? Taylor can dig one and Martha, the other. Run on now."

When the children were running to meet their friends, Eliot said, "Thanks."

"Thanks for what?"

"For getting rid of them. I want to be alone with you. Cassie, last night was—"

Cassie felt the heat in her face as she blushed. "I think last night was a mistake."

He dropped to the sand next to her. "My God, Cassie, what are you afraid of? You trust me, don't you? No one will ever know."

"But I know, don't I, Eliot? I know, and that's enough."

"You disappoint me. I thought you were above such trivial morality." He stood up and brushed the sand from his legs. "And after all, isn't it a bit late for this conversation? I'm going for a swim now, and then to my room to do some reading." He looked down at her with cold gray eyes. "Perhaps you need some time, too, to think about how you really feel."

Cassie watched him walking away from her, down the beach, and she felt bereft. Wasn't he right, after all? A woman of thirty-nine should take pleasure where she could find it. And she had found it with Eliot Peabody, in a room in a Mexican hotel. She straightened her shoulders. Yes, she had sinned, but she was unrepentant. She was happier, in fact, and more alive than she had been for a year, and she was certain that no act that provided so much joy could be truly sinful. What was more, she realized, she firmly intended to repeat that act as soon and as often as possible.

She took the children up from the beach that afternoon to bathe and dress, she helped them, laughing with them, teasing them as she had not done for almost a year. When they were ready to go down to the dining room, Cassie straightened her shoulders and stepped into the corridor briskly.

Except for one conspiratorial grin at Cassie, Eliot was cool at dinner, and his manners were as perfect as ever. In fact, he made it clear that he expected the same sort of manners from his dinner table companions. Nothing was said, and Cassie understood it no better than her son did, but Taylor found himself seating Martha before he climbed onto his own chair.

Something was said, however, when the children took up their incessant bickering.

Eliot looked at Cassie several times but she knew that at one word from her the bickering would escalate into tears and sulkiness.

"Taylor," Eliot said. "Martha. That is enough of that."

They ignored him, of course.

"Temple," he said tightly, "I see that you have finished your dinner. Please take Taylor and Martha upstairs and get them ready for bed."

Temple looked to Cassie, who had opened her mouth to protest his high-handed dealing with her children. One glance at Eliot changed her mind. "You heard Mr. Peabody, Temple," she said.

"Mama, I don't want to—"

"Go, Taylor," she said firmly. "Right now."

"Mama!" Martha was gearing herself up for a good cry.

"Martha, stop this instant!" In a softer voice, she said, "You two get into your pajamas and I'll come up to read you a story."

When Temple shepherded them away from the table, Taylor and Martha were sulking, but they sulked in silence.

Eliot reached across the table and took Cassie's hand. "There will be dancing later," he said.

Cassie looked into his eyes. They were not cool and distant then, but hot with desire. Deep within her, a pulse began to beat. "Yes," she said. "Yes."

Later she tucked the children into bed and hesitated to check her appearance in the tall dresser mirror. She adjusted the spaghetti straps of her black linen dress. It was low-cut, with a cool A-line skirt that moved with her body. For once she was wearing her blond hair down, instead of pulled into a chignon, and in the humid night air it floated around her bare shoulders.

Eliot was in the bar when she went downstairs. She paused a moment, admiring the way he looked in his beautifully cut blue blazer and white trousers. His appearance defined him: a handsome man, cultured and of old-world sensibilities. He was a man who could give a woman great pleasure.

Did she love him? Was she in love with him? That she did not know. She was not close enough to him to know. Then what, she thought uncomfortably, did that make her? A woman who went to bed with a man not for love but for lust. She brushed at her hair as if to sweep away a cobweb. It was not fair, she thought. Men had fulfilled their lust since history began but it was not deemed proper for a woman even to confess to such a feeling. But then, women had not been members of Congress for all that long, either. The idea made her smile to herself. First the freedom to vote and now the freedom to—why not?

With a secret smile she crossed the lobby to Eliot. He turned and stood up slowly, watching her.

"Tonight you bear a closer resemblance to the woman I know in Washington," he said, "to Congresswoman Steele."

She twisted her body to make her skirt swirl around her knees. "You like the dress?"

Unsmiling, he said, "I like what's in it. You wore the same dress at dinner but you looked more like the old woman in the shoe."

" 'Who had so many children she didn't know what to do'? I'm sorry the children acted so—you really didn't get to know them at all."

"Do your children always behave that way? Bickering and interrupting and—"

Cassie laughed. "Their behavior is fairly typical of their age, Eliot. I don't think you've had much experience with children."

"No. Very little experience, and no desire for more."

Well, Cassie thought, at least he was honest about it. To avoid looking at him just then, she surveyed the dance floor where tourists in tropical clothes and raw sunburns circled to the music of a five-piece band that added a touch of the mariachi to every number it played.

Eliot took her hand. "I've arranged for a table on the ocean side."

As he helped her to her chair, Cassie looked around. The room was not large, but with two walls missing, it seemed to become part of the tropical night. Only a low balustrade separated their table from the beach. Beyond the beach a full moon lit the crests of waves that rolled in from the Pacific, one after another, to crash on the beach.

Eliot took her arm and they joined the other couples on the dance floor while the band played the syncopated rhythms of "The Girl from Ipanema." Eliot was a superb dancer, but he seemed to be distracted, as if his body automatically went through the measures of the dance while his mind occupied itself with weightier matters.

Cassie was puzzled. Their lovemaking the night before seemed to be forgotten as they became no more than casual acquaintances. They knew each other intimately but—a thought stopped her. They knew each other's *bodies* intimately.

When they went back to their table, she said, "Eliot, tell me more about yourself, what you do, what you like and don't like, how you—"

"I'd rather talk about you, Cassie. You look glorious tonight."

Cassie blushed, flattered, but she was not drawn away from her goal. "You're in some kind of intelligence service, aren't you, Eliot? Is it the CIA?"

He frowned. "Do you think you can read me so easily? Surely an intelligence agent would not be so open about his work."

Cassie sighed. He was not going to tell her anything, not anything at all.

He stood up then and smiled stiffly. "Come on. Let's dance."

"Yes. Of course."

Eliot pulled her close to him as the band played "Call Me Irresponsible." She smiled to herself. "Irresponsible" was not the precise word she would have chosen for Eliot Peabody. The band segued into a second chorus, however, and she became aware that his hands were engaged in activities inappropriate even to a tropical resort. It was as if the proper Bostonian had been reborn in the tropics. The cool gentleman with impeccable manners had become a sensualist who cared nothing for what people saw or thought.

"Eliot!" she whispered.

"Let's go upstairs."

"But you—yes. Oh, yes!"

In the elevator he touched her again, secretly, and again, and

Cassie began to be afraid that she would make a public spectacle of herself before they reached his floor.

In the hall outside his room, she said, "Really, Eliot! I'm a member of the United States Congress! You can't just—"

"Yes, I can." He pushed her into his room and locked the door behind him. He put his arms round her then and kissed her deeply, at the same time pushing her body with his, back, back, until she felt the edge of the bed pressing against her legs.

"Eliot," she cried. "Eliot!"

If Cassie was less driven that night than she had been in the afternoon, Eliot was more so. The self-contained man was replaced by a man who demanded everything she would give him, and more. His hands played over her body like a musician stroking an instrument, calling forth extraordinary vibrations, giving immense pleasure and then capriciously withholding that pleasure to the knife-edge of pain.

When, at last, he took her it was not in shared climax. He reared above her like a stallion, in absolute mastery.

He collapsed onto her then, panting, and Cassie was pinned to the bed like a butterfly on display, a moth dispatched by a collector. She lay stunned until his breathing became even and steady and she knew that he had dozed off to sleep on her body, in her body.

"Eliot," she said, and again, more loudly, "Eliot." He stirred and she wriggled from beneath him and stood up beside the bed. The light in the room was dim, but not so dim that it hid his look of smug satisfaction. He opened his eyes and looked up at her. "Cassie, get back in bed."

"No. I must go."

"But I want you here. I want you to—"

"Not now."

He grinned at the implied promise in her words, but she turned away from him and dressed quickly. Without another word she slipped out of his room, closing the door firmly behind her.

In her own room, she stripped off her clothes and took a stinging hot shower, scrubbing herself from head to toe as she tried to wash away her sense of degradation.

As the warm water played on her she saw that her anger was not just at Eliot's easy assumption of control over her but also at her own acquiescence.

After all, she thought, what could she expect of him? The over-eager welcome she gave him the evening before, her easy acceptance of his suggestion that they leave the dance floor and go to his room, her half-hearted objections to his public fondling of her body, all of it had served to define her as a woman no better than a slut. An easy lay.

She stepped out of the shower and toweled her body until her sunburn was stinging, but self-flagellation did not ease her conscience.

She knew what she had to do.

Temple and the children were down the beach, making plans with Pepe, when Eliot came out to join Cassie by the pool. He leaned down to kiss her and was obviously surprised when she did not look up to receive his kiss. "Last night, Cassie, you were—terrific. Is there another place we can go to for dinner this evening? We can leave your children here with the girl."

Cassie pulled a bare toe across the sand, drawing a line between them. "Eliot, I think you should leave Puerto Vallarta."

"Leave?" He dropped into a deck chair and stared at her. "Just when you and I are—"

"When you and I are—what?" She tried to find a kind way to say it. "When we're getting out of control, Eliot."

"Now, wait a minute, Cassie. Your behavior when I arrived would seem to indicate that—would hardly—"

"I know all about my behavior." She blushed. "It was—an aberration, that's all."

"And last night, damn it! You loved every minute of it!"

She closed her eyes against the bright sunlight. Every minute, he said. Did I? "Another aberration, I suppose."

Eliot stood up abruptly. "My God, woman! You all but threw yourself at me! You call that an aberration?"

She tried to explain it to herself as well as to him. "It had been so long, you know, so long since Dix and I—" His face went red and her voice trailed away. It was the truth, she knew, but perhaps it was the wrong truth to tell Eliot Peabody.

"I see," he said, obviously fighting to regain his composure. "You needed a man—or did it even have to be a man? Wouldn't a vibrator have served you as well, or one of those dildo things the sex shops sell?"

Cassie blushed. "Eliot, you're twisting it all around. I wanted to be loved, that's all, to be held, to be—"

"To be fucked, that's what you wanted!" He loomed over her. "Well, you got what you wanted last night, didn't you? I fucked the hell out of you. And don't you try to tell me that you didn't love it!" He stepped back from her and grinned unpleasantly. "That's right, isn't it? Last night I fucked Congresswoman Cassandra Steele within an inch of her life and she loved every goddamn minute of it." In a sudden change of mood, however, he glared down at her and clenched his fists. "You used me, Cassie. By God, you used me!"

Cassie's laugh was shaky. "Isn't that usually the woman's line? Anyway, Eliot, you have used me, too. I didn't realize it until last night, but now I know. All those questions you asked about what's going on in the House—you have used me from the day we met."

He raised his chin. "It's my job."

Cassie started to speak, but she realized that it would be futile. Instead she looked down at the sand and waved one hand at him, helplessly. She no longer cared what he said to her, what he thought of her. All she wanted was for him to go away.

And he did. Without another word he stalked off across the

sand. She did not need to ask because she knew that he was leaving. He was leaving the hotel, and Puerto Vallarta, and her.

Cassie found relief from her brief bitter entanglement with Eliot Peabody in an incongruent attack of silliness of the sort which she had not even shared with Dix during the last year of his life. The children caught the virus, as did Temple when she returned from her adventures with Pepe. They all ended by giggling their way through the afternoon on the beach, through dinner and even through the two-hundredth reading of *Babar*.

It was only when Martha and Taylor were asleep and Temple was reading Cassie's book about poor Felicity and Sir Randal that Cassie was able to go out on the balcony alone.

It was a lovely night, warm and humid, with a steady salt breeze blowing in from the ocean. From her balcony a glaze of silver stretched out before her to the full moon, an iridescent path across the constantly churning waves of the dark Pacific.

She had not been able to explain to Eliot what it was that she wanted. It was not just a father for her children, and not just a man to be seen with in public, and it was most certainly not just sex.

Instead, it was all of those and so much more. She wanted, she needed a man in her bed not for constant sex but for comfort, for the security of waking with a bare foot planted on a hairy leg. She needed a man in her life to enhance its pleasures and ameliorate its problems. Perhaps most of all she needed a man who needed her.

The man she needed, however, was not Eliot, self-centered and secretive. The man she needed was Dix. And she could not have him.

Her loneliness for him was physical, a sharp pain deep within her body. Dix, she thought, oh, my beloved Dix, how am I to play out this charade for years and years? How am I to live without you?

But I must do it, she thought sadly. Even if there is no way, I must do it. For the children. For Dix, yes. And for myself as well. She raised her tear-wet face and looked out at the moon, the huge white disk sinking into the dark sea. She felt the soft breeze on her skin and smelled the salt sea air and heard laughter and music drift up from the streets below. It was life, with all its clutter, with its confusions of sounds and scents and sights. It was life and whether she wanted it or not, she was part of it. She was involved with life.

A bell tolled from the cathedral, calling out a deep hollow summons to ceremony, and Cassie turned and went back to her room, back to her life, and back to loneliness.

Part Four

The little hills shall rejoice on every side.

The folds shall be full of sheep;

The valleys also shall stand so thick with corn,

that they shall laugh and sing.

—Psalm 65, The Book of Common Prayer

Chapter 29

Congresswoman Cassandra Taylor Steele was a wealthy woman in January of 1965, wealth that came from her canny investments in oil and gas exploration and production, and her thriving ranch near San Bois, Oklahoma. As a second term member of the House of Representatives she was beginning to have some political clout and, moreover, she was beautiful. At almost forty, her face had refined itself to its strong bone structure. Her high cheekbones and square jaw hinted at her inner strength of character, and her obvious intelligence gave meaning to a tall shapely figure she kept supple with a regime of regular exercise.

She was never without escorts to Washington parties. She was in demand with older men who liked to flaunt her beauty as well as the young ambitious men who wanted to flaunt her power.

She immediately identified young Dean Clarkson as one of the latter. As Cassie said of herself, "I may have been born in Oklahoma but I wasn't born yesterday." He was high up in the Justice Department, but not yet high up enough to suit him. He was also very smart, bright enough to understand that to climb the Washington ladder to Number Three in the department, or Number Two, required more than intelligence and a good education and even unwavering allegiance to the party. He needed a mentor, someone in politics who could and would make sure that his name was mentioned favorably and, moreover, that it was mentioned

where it would do the most good. Since Dean was also a dedicated
ladies' man, a beautiful woman who was a member of the Judiciary
Committee in the House was the perfect choice. In his opinion the
fact that he was seven years younger than Congresswoman Cassandra Steele did not make her less attractive and could even prove
to be a bonus, since her rise in the political hierarchy would take
place that much earlier.

Cassie could understand her usefulness to him and still enjoy
Dean Clarkson immensely. He was tall, with quick, dark eyes, and
as swarthy as she was fair. She had to appreciate the fact that
together they made an extremely handsome couple. Moreover,
Dean's iconoclastic approach to political life was a breath of fresh
air in a smoke-filled room. He was able to play the political game
without forgetting for one moment that it was, after all, a game.

He was equally open about his attempts to get Cassie to sleep
with him.

"Cassie, Cassie, come on! It won't hurt anything if we—"

"Only my conscience."

"Your conscience! Hell, lady, you know as well as I do that
nobody who's been in politics for over fifteen minutes has such a
thing. Consciences are like most organs that don't get much use.
By the time they arrive in Washington they have atrophied."

In spite of his eagerness, Cassie had no trouble blocking his
advances and she found herself spending more and more time with
Dean. It was not so much that she wanted to be with him, she
realized, as it was that she became a different person when they
were together. She could be giddy with Dean, she could make silly
remarks. She knew that in some ways she was acting like a teenager, but she had spent her real teenage years fighting to survive.
There was never time, back then, to be giddy.

Dean took her dancing that winter. He took her to the zoo. He
took her to bars and to parties where she was accepted as one of
the group of protesters who railed against "Johnson's War" and
read Allen Ginsberg and talked about dropping out and going to

Haight-Ashbury. There were drugs at the parties and although Cassie refused to try them, no one seemed to be concerned about turning on in the presence of a congresswoman. And Dean's constant advances were not entirely unwelcome. Cassie admitted to herself that his obvious desire for her was extremely flattering.

Occasionally she saw old friends at Washington parties. She saw Eliot Peabody a number of times, and all the women he was with had one thing in common: each of them could be Eliot's sister. It seemed that with Cassie, Eliot had found all he wanted of adventure and that now he was ready to settle for a wife who would be equally at home at the better sort of Washington parties and in Back Bay dining rooms. She would bear him children who would be intelligent enough to go into the proper schools but not so intelligent that they would make intellectual waves. And they would all settle down together in what an archeologist of the future might label "the Upper Bostonian."

Cassie was less comfortable about running into Mackenzie Cameron. He was never alone, and the women he squired all appeared to be cut from the same pattern: beautiful and Western and youthful. She was glad for Mack, of course, because he had been so lonely. It was just that the women were all so damned young.

Mack's polyester double-knits seemed to fit right in that winter, as Washington hostesses packed away the last trappings of Kennedy elegance and changed over to the Texas look. Cassie's friend Fran Jordan, as one of Dallas's leading interior designers, was suddenly in great demand in the capital.

Cassie insisted that Fran use the house on R Street as her home base in Washington, and on her first night in town, arranged an evening with Dean Clarkson and a friend of his from Defense. The four of them had a night on the town, going from party to club to party. Cassie thought that Fran was uncharacteristically quiet, especially in the latter part of the evening, but she thought it was because of the long, tiring flight from Dallas.

When Dean and his friend left, reluctantly, Cassie and Fran

changed to their robes and flopped down in the library for a brandy nightcap.

Cassie dropped her left slipper and rubbed her foot. "I knew I shouldn't have worn those patent sandals tonight, Fran. They look great, but they're no good for dancing."

"Dumb," Fran said flatly.

"How right you are! But they're such pretty shoes."

"I didn't mean the shoes."

Cassie waited, rubbing her instep, but when Fran did not continue she looked up. "Okay, Fran, okay. What is dumb?"

"You. The way you're acting."

Cassie sat up straight. "Now listen here—"

"No, *you* listen. Dating a kid who's all over you, running around with that gang of juvenile delinquents, being seen all over Washington with a bunch of potheads—just what in God's name do you think you're doing?"

Cassie looked down at her slipper. "Having fun. Is it so awful for a woman to have some fun?"

Fran's voice was edged with irritation. "A woman? No, it's not awful at all. But the kind of fun you're having—for a mature woman, a mother, a member of Congress—it's beyond awful, Cassie, and you know it. It's just plain dumb."

Cassie stood up to replenish their brandy. She wanted to tell Fran how ridiculous, how wrong her accusations were, but the words would not come. "You're crazy," she said finally, but her voice lacked conviction.

Fran looked at her closely. "You know that I'm right, don't you?"

Cassie shook her head, slowly, but for once she was looking at herself as dispassionately as she might look at Temple Vance. She did not like what she saw: a woman who was all too ready to throw away her hard-won stature for transitory pleasure.

"All right," she snapped. "Suppose it's so, that what you say is right. I don't have to like it, do I?"

Fran smiled. "Don't hate me, Cassie. Don't kill the messenger."

"No," Cassie said. "I won't. I can see it now. I've made a complete fool of myself."

"Hey, now, don't be so quick to beat up on yourself!" Fran tossed off the last of her brandy. "You always have been one to go to extremes, Cassie. Remember when old James Steele told you to buy yourself a wardrobe appropriate to Jimmy Steele's bride and you were so stingy with his money that you would have been happy to go down and outfit yourself at Woolworth's?"

"Yes, I remember." Cassie laughed in spite of herself. "But you told me James had plenty of money and that I should spend enough to be well-dressed."

"Sure, I told you that. But you were the one who went to extremes. You damn near bought out Tulsa."

"You're making that up!" Cassie refilled their glasses, laughing. "That's not the way I remember it at all!"

Suddenly serious, Fran said, "We do go back a long time, don't we?"

Cassie sat down on the couch. "Look, I appreciate your being so honest with me about Dean Clarkson and—but then you always have been pretty blunt."

"Blunt? I suppose so. I try to be honest, that's all. But look, Cassie, I meant what I said. Don't go to extremes, hear? Don't think you have to be a nun. Just be more discreet, that's all."

Cassie laughed shortly. "And play with children my own age?"

"I suppose maybe—"

"There's no 'maybe' about it, Fran. Look, can we drop it now? Let's talk about you for a while. Any interesting men in your life?"

"There are *always* interesting men in my life, Cassie. Married men. Unsuitable men. I wish to hell—look, it's my turn to ask for a change of subject."

Cassie glanced at her and said quickly, "What do people in Dallas say about the war, about South Vietnam?"

"The war? Is it really a war?"

"Fran, people are killing each other with guns and bombs. In my book, that's a war. And as of last month there were twenty-five thousand Americans over there."

"That many?"

"And more going every day. It's a war, all right."

Fran laughed uncomfortably. "Last week a friend of mine said something I can't get out of my mind. He said, 'They warned me last fall that if I voted for Goldwater in November we'd be at war in six months. They were right. I did, and we are.' "

"We are. Yes." In a flash of recall Cassie saw the young widow at Arlington Cemetery. "I voted for Lyndon Johnson because he said he wouldn't send American boys to die in a foreign land. And now the political campaigner who said he would never send American boys to die in Vietnam has become the President who is doing just that."

At the end of January, the children's schools had a semester break and Cassie took Martha and Taylor to Ballard to visit their grandparents. The weather in Eastern Oklahoma was unseasonably warm and after one night at the Steeles' house Cassie took advantage of the weather to drive Martha, Taylor and Temple down to the ranch near San Bois.

On Friday, the children reacquainted themselves with Henry Starr and the farm animals while Cassie, planning to go to San Bois later to confer with her San Bois staff, glanced through the stack of letters that had accumulated on her desk.

One letter caught her eye immediately, a wrinkled envelope addressed in spidery handwriting.

Dear Miz Congressman,

Went in to town to talk to them people in your office on Saturday week, but they was reel bizzy. It was 2 hrs. wen my ride came and had to go. Wood not bother you, but need the social sec. money real bad and no more ride for 1 mon. Pleze help if can.

Yr. obt. svt.,
Mrs. Mary Ellen Landsaw.

As always, the four members of her San Bois staff flocked to Cassie that afternoon with a flurry of greetings and complaints about the Washington bureaucracy. Cassie made notes about whom she had to contact about what. "First I want to go out in the country and find this Mrs. Landsaw."

Allie MacIntyre, her chief aide in Oklahoma said, "*What* Mrs. Landsaw?"

"A woman who waited here for two hours and never even got to talk to anyone."

A voice in the back rank said, "Uh-oh."

Cassie looked directly at the speaker. "Uh-oh, indeed. Let me go see her and get the facts, and then we'll see what we need to do about it."

Finding Mrs. Mary Ellen Landsaw's house was not easy, but with the aid of a map sketched by an RFD letter carrier, Cassie did it. It was almost two when she parked the station wagon and stumbled up a rocky path through the oak woods.

She stopped when she saw the house because it was so much like the sharecropper's place where she had spent her childhood. The house was built of rough wooden planks, unpainted and grayed by years of cold damp winters and burning summers. A fieldstone chimney stood at one end of the house and an open porch ran across the front of the house. On the porch an old woman sat and rocked while the thin January sunshine soaked into her bones. Cassie stood in the fringe of the woods, waiting for the old lady to speak, waiting for her to call out in Granny's voice, "You, Cassie! Fetch me water from the spring."

Instead, the old woman raised a trembling hand to shade her eyes. "Who's there?" she called. "Who's that coming?"

"It's me, Mrs. Landsaw. Cassie Steele, your congresswoman. I got your letter."

The woman was silent for a minute, apparently working it out in her mind. "You come all the way out here from Washington?"

"No, ma'am. Just from San Bois. I was sorry that my staff didn't help you, so I came to see what I can do."

"For land's sake! Just to see me? You get up on this porch and sit down, you hear?"

Cassie climbed the rotting steps and pulled a handhewn oak straight chair close to Mrs. Landsaw's rocker.

The old lady looked embarrassed. "They ain't no coffee or I'd—"

"It doesn't matter," Cassie said quickly. "My, what a beautiful view you have!"

Mrs. Landsaw turned her head to look with Cassie at the low hills and the blue haze of the Ozark Mountains in the distance. "Yessum." She smiled with contentment. "Ernest—he was my husband, he got killed in the war—when we first come to work this place on the shares, Ernest said it was the prettiest view on the mountain."

"How can I help you, Mrs. Landsaw?"

The woman looked away. "Shames me to say it, but I got to get holt of some eatin' money. Me and Ernest, we never did hold with takin' charity, but I went and got too old to work."

"May I ask your age?"

"Sixty-eight come March."

Sixty-eight, thought Cassie, sixty-eight and she looked to be eighty. She was worn out, as Granny had been, by hard work and a poverty diet.

"They done laid me off at the mill when I was sixty-three, my rheumatism got so bad."

"With no pension, I suppose. You were an hourly worker?"

"Yessum."

"Do you have children?"

"Me and Ernest never was blest."

"Let's see, Mrs. Landsaw. I assume you get your social security and a widow's pension from the Veteran's Administration. Other than those, do you have any income?"

"Land's sake, honey, I don't get no government money! My neighbor lady, she says I ought to, so that's why I come in the office that day, but they was real busy and I had to—me and Ernest, we had us some savin's, but they's all used up now."

"It's going to take some time to get the paperwork together, Mrs. Landsaw, but you're going to get a regular income from now on."

"Glory be!" She hesitated. "I don't know. Like I say, me and Ernest, we never did hold with takin' charity."

Cassie took a deep breath. "I'm not talking about charity, Mrs. Landsaw, but entitlements. Do you know what that means?"

"No'm, don't reckon I do."

"It means you are entitled to this money. An amount was taken from every check you received from the mill and it was put into the social security fund to be returned to you when you were old. I'm surprised your social worker or visiting nurse hasn't explained that."

"Ain't got any of them, Miz Steele."

"We'll see about *that*, too!" Cassie said grimly.

As she drove back toward town, Cassie gritted her teeth, railing internally at bureaucracy. And my staff, she thought, my well-fed comfortable staff that was too busy shuffling papers to notice that this poor woman had fallen through a tear in the social fabric. How could a country come to a place where the numbers were more important than the people they represented?

Cassie gathered her staff in the back office. "You were all griping about the Washington bureaucracy, but it seems that we must deal with the San Bois bureaucracy before we take on Washington."

There was a general movement to disperse, but Allie MacIntyre stood her ground. "Is something wrong, Cassie?"

"I'm not sure yet. How many constituents came to the clinic Saturday before last?"

A junior staffer hurried to check a list. "Nine, Cassie. Nine people came in."

Cassie looked at them, one at a time. "And one of them, according to her letter, was Mrs. Landsaw. Look, there are four of you here. Will someone please explain why that old lady had to wait for two hours and then leave without having been helped with her problem?"

"The old woman with the liver spots," Allie said. "She did say something about having to catch her ride home, but—"

"But what? Why were you all too busy to help her?"

"The month-end report, Cassie," Allie said reproachfully. "You know it has to be mailed on the last day of the month."

Cassie turned a swivel chair and sat down to look up at them pleasantly. "So last Saturday, two weeks before it was due, you were working on the report?"

"Well, sure. I mean, there are all those figures to—"

"You're a full-time federal employee, aren't you, Allie? A GS-Twelve, as I remember. And you're paid overtime to work on Saturday because that's when the country people can get to town."

"Well, yes, but most congressional offices close on Saturday. If people really need help, they can take off work and get here some way or other."

Cassie heard the edge in her own voice. "This is not 'most congressional offices.' This is my office."

Allie flushed. "Well, it seems to me that—"

"It seems to *me* that you should do your paperwork during the week and reserve Saturday for seeing constituents! You seem to have forgotten, all of you, that you were not hired to be paper shufflers or petty dictators. You and I alike, we are the servants of the people, and we must remember that always."

"I suppose you're right," Allie said.

"And I suppose you had better start serving the people right now, you hear? Starting tomorrow, I want everyone in this office to see people, not papers, on Saturdays. Is that understood?"

The four staff members looked embarrassed, even angry, but they muttered an affirmative. "What about that old woman?" Allie said. "Is she coming back?"

Cassie stood up. "No, we—or rather, *you* will go to her. It's the least she deserves after the treatment she received here."

On the way home, Cassie stopped several times for social calls on local farmers and ranchers. Such calls served two purposes: they let the local voters see, in the flesh, their representative in Washington and at the same time they gave Cassie a chance to find out what was important to the people of her district.

At the ranch, she discovered that Temple had already fed the children and put them to bed. Cassie went into the dimly lit bedroom they shared. Awake they might act like devils, but asleep they looked like angels. She had not done too bad a job as their only parent for the last two years.

Two years, Cassie thought. She went into the living room and sat down to stare into the fire. It had been two years since that other January when Dix was killed and her life shattered like a crystal goblet. What had she accomplished in two years? She had held herself together, which was no mean feat. She had held the family together, the children and the elder Steeles and even Temple Vance. She had served her country by filling out Dix's term in the House and she had won election to Congress in her own right.

She stretched, soaking in the warmth of the room. She was doing all right as a mother and as a member of Congress, she thought, but her batting average as a woman was not as good. There were the brief abortive affair with Eliot Peabody and then lately the not-quite-innocent flirtation with Dean Clarkson: what had gone wrong? Perhaps, she thought, perhaps she had wanted too much, too soon. Or then perhaps—it was a dismal realization—perhaps she was fated to go it alone for the rest of her life.

Cassie shook her head as if to rid her mind of the sentence of life in solitary freedom. Sometime, she thought, surely someday when my life is not so much in the public eye, someday there will be someone for me.

She realized that she was slumped in the armchair, unloving and unloved, the personification of defeat. She forced herself to sit up straight, stiffening her spine, and chided herself. No matter what the future brings or does not bring, for the present I must do what I do and I must do it well. I will make sure that the Mrs. Landsaws of this world are not forgotten, but I will speak out on the bigger issues, too, when it is necessary. I will do my best to fulfill my duties as a member of Congress.

Returning to the damp cold of Washington in February, Cassie settled in for the winter's work. As a member of Lyndon Johnson's "Xerox Congress" she voted as reliably as her fellow congressmen, keeping her own counsel as she watched the changes in Johnson's approach as an elected President instead of an inheritor of the office. The President's reputation with the people was very high that February. A Harris poll, in fact, measured his popularity at an astounding 71 percent.

Also in February, however, there was a change of direction in military activity in South Vietnam: Americans became familiar with the name and the actions of the guerrilla army known as the Viet Cong. In an early attack, the Viet Cong surprised Americans at the Vietnamese mountain town of Pleiku, and in Qui Nhon three days later, the guerrillas blew up a hotel used as an American barracks. In both cases President Johnson, over the objections of advisors such as Vice President Hubert Humphrey, responded by sending Navy planes to bomb Viet Cong territory.

Some Washington analysts suggested that Johnson should get the United States out of Vietnam entirely, even though it would mean sacrificing the anti-Communist government in Saigon, but the President seemed to feel that he had to prove to the new Soviet leaders Brezhnev and Kosygin that he was tough and ready to fight. It was an eerie repetition of John Kennedy's need to prove his strength to Khrushchev after their Vienna confrontation, a decision which led to a greatly increased American presence in Vietnam.

In March, Taylor Steele had his ninth birthday and Cassie had a small home war to fight.

Taylor's teacher was a weedy young man who wore a tweed jacket, smoked a bull-dog pipe and affected a slight English accent to match his costume.

"We're having a bit of a problem with young Taylor," he said.

"A problem, Mr. Peters?" Cassie asked nervously. "What kind of problem?"

"One of attitude, actually. The boy's a bit of a rebel, I'm afraid."

So were all Americans, back in 1776, Cassie thought, but she did not say it, not to an American who was so obviously clinging to Britannia's apron strings. "He's a rebel, is he?"

"Taylor rather interferes with classroom discipline, you see. He questions everything I say."

"You mean he argues about how to spell a word or do a math problem?"

"No, not at all. One might accept that, actually, as the sign of a questioning mind. He demands that I provide the rationale behind my classroom rules and even my commands to the pupils. One can find little justification for that sort of behavior, Mrs. Steele. Actually, one feels it results purely from a desire to disrupt the class."

Or, Cassie thought, one might consider it a natural response of a normal, spunky boy to an affected, insecure teacher.

"I've taken it upon myself to discuss Taylor's misbehavior with our school psychiatrist and—"

"Without getting my permission? Without Taylor's?"

The young man blushed, not becomingly, but in large splotches of color on his cheeks and neck. "I did not mention Taylor's name. One felt that taking this approach was fully warranted."

"We'll see about that," Cassie said, but then she smiled, and her smile made the young man blush even more.

"The psychiatrist wonders if—well, if the boy is getting conflicting signals about—the masculine role, and acting out, as it were, his need to enhance his male self-esteem."

"Male! He's only nine years old, Mr. Peters!"

"But with no father and a dominant mother—tell me, Mrs. Steele, does the boy lack for masculine role models?"

Cassie sagged in fatigue. Whatever happened, she wondered to plain old report cards that stated grades clearly? A boy who got an F in Conduct took it home, got a spanking, and went back to school a sadder but presumably wiser boy. She could deal with an F in Conduct. She could certainly deal with it better than she could with the psychiatric gobbledegook summoned up to justify the current idea that any problem of any kid could be laid squarely at the door of the mother. She knew there was no point, however, in saying that to Taylor's teacher. It would only serve to confirm the ideas he had obviously swallowed hook, line and sinker. God only knew what *his* mother had done to *him*.

She smiled once more, sweetly. "Mr. Peters, I'm inclined to doubt that our discussing Taylor's potential role models would accomplish much, but I promise you that I will give your comments my full attention. You have given me much to think about."

He beamed at her. "One is always delighted to help the pupils' parents, especially with—ah—problems of some complexity."

Which one knows full well are far beyond the comprehension of mere congresswomen, Cassie thought as she pulled on her gloves. "Thank you so much for calling me in." She smiled.

Under her smile he expanded like a balloon attached to a fresh tank of helium. "One knows how important it is to maintain an open line of communication with the parents."

Cassie repressed a laugh. In this war against a nine-year-old? Oh, yes, very important. Perhaps we should encode our messages.

Her message to Taylor that afternoon was not in code but in clear basic English. "And there will be no more of that smart-aleck stuff, Taylor Steele, none at all! Do you hear me?"

"Yeah." He kicked a chair. "That Peters guy finked on me."

"Finked?"

"He's a fink, you know, like a squealer."

Cassie resolved to monitor his television-watching more carefully. "No, Taylor, he is not a fink." She was tempted to tell the boy what she thought of his teacher but she did not want to undermine discipline completely. "It's his duty to keep me informed, Taylor. And anyway, it's your behavior we're talking about, not his." So her son was a rebel, but he had rebelled against "one" which showed very good taste. She wondered if he would receive what the psychiatrist called conflicting signals if she—oh, the hell with it, she thought. Taylor's teacher had as much as said that she was a bad mother. If she had the name she might as well have the game. "Taylor, if we hurry we can spend an hour at the Smithsonian before they close!"

"Neat! Can we see the toy soldiers, Mom?"

"You bet!"

Chapter 30

That spring of 1965, Martha, who would be eight in September, became a social being. Cassie found herself wading through gaggles of second-grade girls who apparently existed only to play out elaborate stories with their Barbie dolls. Cassie felt vaguely guilty at allowing Martha even to possess the long-legged, bosomed creatures. To her they were ubiquitous reminders of the kind of person she could not abide: the girl-woman who lived to spend. Would Martha grow up to believe that life revolved around clothes glittering with sequins, and possessions, plastic accouterments for a life frittered away in shopping centers? Surely not. Surely the child had too much sense for that. After all, Martha was doing well at school and had outgrown being a tattletale. What was the word Taylor had used? A fink.

In April, Cassie received the best birthday present ever: Blair Fuller and her husband Joe Howe came home from Africa and the Peace Corps.

"We're going back, you know," Blair said on the first day she was free from her family and Joe's and could have lunch with Cassie. "We were able to accomplish a lot, but there is so much more to do."

Blair was tanned and fit and self-confident. She was far removed from the Blair Fuller Cassie had first met: the bored little rich girl tooling around Washington in a Mercedes sports car while she tried to figure out what to do with her life.

"Oh, Cassie, we have so much to give! Teaching the natives simple farming methods, for instance, and how a few ditches can drain stagnant ponds and cut down on fevers. But we have so much to learn, too, from people that close to nature. They know things about listening and seeing that we've long since forgotten."

"And you really did live like the natives? In grass huts?"

"In mud huts actually. And we slept on straw mats laid on the ground." She laughed. "I'm still having trouble getting used to an innerspring mattress, but Joe is ecstatic."

Cassie laughed with her but she thought that she herself would hate to sleep on a straw mat. For a moment then, on her fortieth birthday, she felt like an old woman. She envied Blair her youth, her adaptability and—yes—her Joe.

"I'm completely out of touch, after two years in the jungle. You'll have to tell me. What's the state of the union?"

Cassie told her, briefly, and the laughter went out of both of them.

"Please, Cassie, don't talk to Joe about Vietnam."

"I won't, if you say so. But why not?"

"In the Peace Corps he's exempt from the draft, of course, and away from it all, but his conscience bothers him. He thinks that either he should join the Army and fight for his country or join the protesters and fight against his country."

"He wouldn't be fighting for his country, Blair, not in Vietnam. I'm not sure he'd be fighting for anything at all, and he couldn't win by protesting. Tell him to stay in the Peace Corps. At least that has some meaning."

"I have told him that, Cassie. I do tell him! He's fluent in the language now, and what is more important, the village elders accept him and trust him. He's doing much more for his country than he could in Vietnam."

"Of course he is. Let me talk to him."

"I wish you would." Blair smiled in complicity. "Now, what's all this about you and that good-looking Dean Clarkson?"

"How did you hear about—oh. Muffy." Blair's brother's wife was addicted to Washington gossip.

"Muffy. Of course."

"Well, you can tell dear Muffy that it is all over with Dean. I haven't seen him or talked to him in weeks."

Blair looked concerned. "How do you feel about that, Cassie?"

Cassie grinned broadly. "Relieved! You don't have to tell Muffy this, but I managed to get myself into a situation that I almost couldn't handle."

Blair laughed. "Then I'm relieved, too, but I had hoped—"

"So had I." They laughed together then, and moved on to other subjects.

Cassie enjoyed, too, the chance to become reacquainted with the elder Fullers and to watch their acquaintance ripen into friendship. Her children began to be included in the Fullers' birdwatching expeditions and Cassie was delighted when Taylor came home all agog at the sighting of a lesser grebe.

As a member of the House Judiciary Committee Cassie helped to hammer out the new civil rights bills and saw the evidence that such laws were needed. The Ku Klux Klan increased its membership at an appalling rate that year. Negroes, or blacks, the appellation they had come to prefer, were split into many groups and their leaders were at odds with each other. At one extreme was Martin Luther King, Jr., who preached nonviolence and who spoke of lighting the torch of freedom metaphorically. At the other extreme it was, "Burn, baby, burn!" The separation even within those factions led to the assassination of Malcolm X by blacks of a group opposing the black Muslims.

The last big civil rights bill to go through the Judiciary Committee was the Voting Rights Act. Cassie spoke out in strong support of it, both in committee and in the well of the House. "Surely," she told her colleagues, "surely, Bloody Sunday has illustrated the need for this act. On March seventh, a group of blacks and their white sympathizers, in an attempt to draw attention to the need for blacks to register to vote, set out to march the fifty-four miles from Selma, Alabama, to Montgomery. Their reception was unbelievable. Sheriff's men on horseback, one hundred state troopers—at Pettus Bridge, they used tear gas on the marchers, they beat them with billy clubs and bullwhips until the blacks had to retreat, had to crawl back to the sanctuary of their church. They had been attacked not only by the Ku Klux Klan, but by the law-and-order forces of their own state as well. Martin Luther King arrived and, with the national government, arranged for a symbolic march back and forth across the bridge."

Cassie spoke in the well of the House. "Abraham Lincoln, as we all know, freed the slaves. Are you as appalled as I that today, one hundred years later, we are still trying to implement Lincoln's wise decision? My friends, I urge you to pass this act, to emancipate our black citizens once again by guaranteeing to them the opportunity that every citizen of a democracy enjoys: the right to vote."

To her surprise, Cassie's speech was reported in the national press and received much favorable comment, along with her work for civil rights in general.

The New York Times called her "the Okie realist," and *Newsweek* said, "Congresswoman Steele is in the finest tradition of American government. Neither an idealist nor a pragmatist, she simply wants to make the system work for all Americans."

Cassie's work for civil rights had to take a back seat, however, to her concern about Lyndon Johnson's rapid expansion of America's involvement in Vietnam. In January of 1965, there were 25,000 Americans in Southeast Asia but by the end of that spring the number had increased to 75,000.

The Xerox Congress was no longer monolithic. Cassie was one of a small but growing group that spoke out against the President's policies in Vietnam.

"We are allowing ourselves to be sucked into another Korea," she said in the House. "Into another war that cannot be won. I implore the President, put a stop to it now, while you still can and before more Americans die in this meaningless war."

At lunch one day Cully Meecham reported to Cassie that the word was out. Congresswoman Steele of Oklahoma was becoming thoroughly disliked by the White House. Moreover, the publicity given to her views of the Vietnam war was a thorn in the President's side.

As they walked back to the office, he pleaded with her. "Can't you lay off for a while, Cassie?"

"No, I can't. You know I can't, Cully. If I don't say it, who will?"

He shook his head wonderingly. "And you're not worried about what LBJ can do to you politically?"

"Look, Cully, I'm not a fool. Of course, I'm worried. But I have to do what I think is right."

"Oh, my God," he said. "You're beginning to sound like Dix."

Cassie stopped dead on the sidewalk. "I hope so. Oh, Cully, I do hope so."

Nevertheless, Cassie did ease off on her Vietnam speeches, not from expediency but because President Johnson's civil rights policy was under debate. Cassie supported his program and felt that he had done more to advance the black cause than any President since Lincoln.

It was an issue, however, too large for even Lyndon Johnson to manage. He could "reason with" Southern Democrats, the conservatives of the party, and he could do some effective arm-twisting with northern Democrats, but none of them had reckoned on the Watts riots. When it began that August, Cassie was all too aware that each new report of violence or looting meant a loss of ground for the civil rights movement.

At the same time, the American public was becoming more sharply divided on the issue of the United States involvement in Vietnam. The feelings of a country, Cassie thought, was often revealed in popular music, and two songs heard frequently that year were "The Ballad of the Green Berets" and "Eleanor Rigby." It became evident that the representatives of the disparate points of view had themselves become causes of the antagonism.

In the House, Cassie saw the supporters of the war in Vietnam: well-dressed citizens who had exchanged the fire of youth for the comfortable warmth of middle age, citizens whose history was a long one. They were the people who throughout American history had stayed home and turned a profit on the accouterments of war while the young men went off to bleed and die on the battlefields.

The young men of the sixties, however, in Dylan Thomas's words, did not "go gentle into that good night." Many of them came through Cassie's own house. At Cassie's insistence, Temple was registered in night classes to bring her grades up to a level acceptable to her junior college. Her new college friends were in the house day and night, eating, playing their music and smoking cigarette after cigarette. It was not so much a single event that pushed Cassie over the threshold of tolerance as much as an accumulation: girls in tie-dyed skirts ironing their hair in the bedroom while the kitchen was full of young men who wore long hair and beards and obviously were not even on speaking terms with soap and water. There was also a suspiciously sweet smell to their cigarettes that made it obvious that they would not be on sale in the corner tobacco shop.

There was a last straw, however: Bill Mackey, Temple's constant companion and the son of a New York dermatologist, appeared one afternoon in his usual torn, patched jeans and on that day, they were patched with a piece of an American flag. When Cassie protested, he sneered.

"You're quite a hypocrite, aren't you? You vote for Johnson's imperialistic policies in Vietnam, you send Americans over there to die and to soak this flag in blood. Well, check it out, lady. You're just like my father. You bring a hell of a lot more dishonor on the flag than I do!"

Cassie's angry look raked the boy from head to toe. A scruffy beard, ragged clothes. Living, no doubt on an allowance from the father he scorned, leaning against Cassie's refrigerator to eat a sandwich made from her ham and drink a beer paid for by her labor. She could argue with him. She could point to her voting record to prove to him that she did not support Johnson's policy in Vietnam, that she did not vote to send American boys to the battlefields. She could do that, but what was the point? She was over thirty and therefore, by his definition, a warmonger. Why should she bother to defend herself?

"Out," she said so softly that he had to bend down to hear her. "Out!" she said more loudly. "I want you out of this house right now, you hear? And I don't want you to come back, ever."

"Cassie!" Temple hurried across the kitchen. "You can't just throw him out like that!"

"The hell I can't," Cassie said calmly. "This is my house and I will not have trash like him within my walls."

"Your house!" Temple's eyes narrowed and she spat out the words like venom. "You mean the house you got by marrying Dix Steele! You weren't anything but poor white trash till you married him, and now you think you're so high and mighty! You got you a big fine house and some fancy Eastern friends, and you think you're pretty hot stuff!"

Cassie flushed at the girl's attack. She wanted to defend herself, to tell Temple that she had bought the house in Georgetown with money she had earned as an attorney not just for rich Dallas oil men but for battered wives, for the unfortunate as well as the fortunate. She could have explained but she did not, because at that instant she realized what lay behind Temple's vicious accusations. She was jealous. The silly girl was jealous. "I'm sorry you feel that way, Temple," she said mildly.

"Trash!" Bill said belatedly. "Are you calling me trash? Now you listen to me, you can't—"

"No, you listen to me, boy." Cassie turned to face him. She

owed nothing to Bill Mackey. "I am a representative of the people of Oklahoma and I will not allow you to dishonor the flag that they believe in. Get out of here, right now, and don't you come back until you know what it is to love your country, to love anything or anyone on earth more than you love yourself!"

Temple drew back. "I'll go, too."

Cassie took a long breath. How could she square such a thing with her conscience? For God's sake, how could she tell Henry Starr that his granddaughter had left with a hippy? But she could not stop Temple from leaving. Temple was a woman now, an adult. She was not sure that she even wanted to stop her. For once, she thought, a principle was more important than a person.

She forced herself to control her temper and to speak softly. "I wish you would stay, Temple. I will miss you and so will the children, but if you feel that you must go, then of course you must."

Temple looked from Bill Mackey's angry face to hers. "I'm going," she snarled, "and I'm not coming back."

During the next week, Cassie's mind returned to Temple again and again. Could she blame the girl? What were her alternatives? She could go with Bill Mackey, the romantic rebel who offered an aimless life and freedom both of mind and body. Or she could stay with Cassie, doing a job and subject to constant chivvying to work harder at college, to improve herself.

Cassie had to admit it: at Temple's age, she would have chosen Bill, too. She would have gone with him like a shot. It was something she had never realized about herself, but she knew the truth when she saw it. At forty, she should be ready to settle down, but like Temple she had a wild Oklahoma streak and she, too, wanted to vote for adventure.

That winter she had to be more of a responsible person, more of a mother, than she had ever been.

Angelina was willing to fill in to help with the children, but it could be for only a few weeks. After three weeks of interviewing everyone from an immigrant with a sketchy command of the language to a highly educated English debutante, Cassie despaired of finding a mother's-helper. It was then that she received a letter from Norman, Oklahoma:

Dear Mrs. Steele,

It's been a long time since I wrote you, but I graduated from Northeastern Oklahoma at Tahlequah and now I'm in graduate school in Norman, at the University of Oklahoma, working toward a master's degree in political science.

Granddad says you are having a hard time finding someone to help out with your children. I have a proposition for you. I need to do research at the Library of Congress. I could work there and still be home when the children came home from school. I've saved every cent I've made for graduate school, so all I would ask for would be room and board.

Respectfully yours,
Ruby (Keeler) Vance

Cassie called Ruby Keeler that night. "It's the perfect solution! But I insist on paying you a salary, because I have to spend a lot of evenings in the House or in committee meetings."

"That's fine, Mrs. Steele, if you're sure you—"

" 'Cassie.' "

"Cassie, yes, ma'am. Thank you."

"Thank *you*, Ruby Keeler! I do appreciate your—"

" 'Ruby.' "

"Of course. Ruby, this takes a big weight off my shoulders!"

Martha and Taylor were happy with Ruby from the start. Compared to Temple and her flamboyant good looks, Ruby was plain, but an inner honesty lighted her face. Martha liked the way Ruby identified plants and birds when they walked along the canal, and

Taylor loved her stories of Georgetown and the days when it was a seaport.

The only word of Temple was one postcard to Ruby. "She's in Haight-Ashbury, Cassie."

"Oh, Lord, that means drugs and—"

"I reckon so."

"Ruby, I never should have taken her away from your parents' farm!"

"It wouldn't have made any difference with Temple," Ruby said. "She would have found some other way, that's all. She's like Mama, living in some crazy dreamworld full of movie stars and Presidents. You can't blame yourself for that."

With Ruby there and her homelife stable Cassie could concentrate on her work as a representative. It took meticulous planning to balance her responsibility to her constituents with a role that was becoming increasingly national in scope. She made quick trips around the country to speak out against the war and to explain that it was possible to be antiwar and patriotic at the same time. When the House rose for Christmas she intensified her speaking schedule.

Just after Christmas, Cully Meecham dropped by her house.

"I'm glad you found me in, Cully!"

"Yeah, me too," he said, shifting his half-smoked cigar from one corner of his mouth to the other.

"Well, it's good to see you."

"May not be, when you hear why I come in. Cassie, the White House ain't exactly crazy about all these speeches you been making."

"So what? The White House isn't America."

"Might just as well be, in your case." He shifted his cigar again. "They can read polls, you know, just like you and me."

Cassie waved her hand in the air. "I haven't read them lately."

"Reckon maybe you should. Reckon you ought to give them a thought now and again, that is, if you're wanting to get yourself elected to the House again this fall."

"I do want it, Cully, believe me. I've just now begun to get to a place where I have some clout on the Hill."

"Then you better listen to old Cully. Next time you're back in Oklahoma you ask around, hear? And listen to the folks. Find out what your constituents are thinking, not what you want them to be thinking."

After considering what Cully said, Cassie decided to make a trip to Eastern Oklahoma as he recommended. She sent Ruby and the children on a Friday afternoon flight, calling Henry to meet their plane, and she herself took advantage of Mackenzie Cameron's standing offer to take Cameron Oil's dawn flight to Oklahoma.

Cassie spent all of Saturday at her office in San Bois, seeing her constituents and, as Lyndon Johnson said, "pressing the flesh." Her staff was on its best behavior, and Allie was obviously pleased to be able to report that Mrs. Landsaw, after a year, was still doing quite well.

It was almost dark when Cassie parked the station wagon in front of her house and trudged up the path to the veranda. A rising wind had dropped the temperature perceptibly. Inside, Martha and Taylor were on the floor, stretched out in front of a blazing fire while Ruby read *Charlotte's Web* to them. Cassie paused in the doorway, thankful to come home to peace rather than to bickering.

Ruby looked up from the book. "I found some stew in the freezer, Cassie, and got it out to thaw. I figured I'd make corn-bread, too."

"That sounds delicious, dear," Cassie said. Once again she thanked her lucky stars for Ruby Keeler Vance. She poured herself a drink of bourbon and water and eased off her shoes as she sank into one of the armchairs by the fireplace.

It was a quiet, homely scene, the fair-haired children huddled up to Ruby and hanging on her every word. The blazing fire on the hearth held at bay the January wind that wailed around the old house.

Just as she sank back, sighing in relief, someone knocked at the door. All of them sat up at the sound. Henry Starr always came and went by the back door, without knocking, and no one dropped in at the ranch without calling first, not at a house at the end of a bumpy dirt road, not on a dark January night.

In her stocking feet, Cassie switched on the porchlight and opened the door.

A large man stood in the circle of light. A very large man.

"Mack?" Cassie said. "Mack Cameron? What on earth are you doing here?"

Mackenzie Cameron's laugh was a deep rumble, like thunder on a summer day. "I was in the neighborhood and thought I'd drop in and cadge a drink. May I come in?"

Cassie was still surprised at the sight of him, but she pushed open the screen. "Yes. Of course! But I don't—"

He grinned and walked past her, bringing into the room a current of cold air and a faint scent of hickory smoke. "Hi, kids."

Cassie introduced Ruby Vance, but Martha and Taylor hung back as if they were overwhelmed by the sheer size of the visitor. When he took off his trench coat Cassie was pleased to see that he wore tan corduroy pants and a wool sweater rather than his usual double-knit polyester.

"A drink, Mack?" Cassie said.

"Sure. What are you having, bourbon? Sounds like a good Oklahoma drink to me."

Cassie handed him a glass, frowning suspiciously. "You said you were in the neighborhood, but there's no neighborhood to be in, Mack, not down here."

He grinned at her like a mischievous boy "Well, I was sort of in the neighborhood. I was in Oklahoma City."

She laughed. "Sure. Only three hours' drive. That's some neighborhood. How did you know I was here at the ranch?"

"My pilot told me you flew into Tulsa this morning, so I called the Steeles' house in Ballard. Talked to a lady there. She was sort of vague about things, but she said you were here and gave me directions that were almost correct. Fellow at the gas station in San Bois finally put me on the right track."

Cassie could feel a smile starting up within her, rising and expanding until her face felt crinkled with pleasure. "My God!" she said. "What some people will go through for a free drink!"

Mack laughed, an infectious rumble that took in Taylor and Martha, who laughed until they were rolling on the hearth rug. Even Ruby was giggling, hiding her mouth with her hand but not concealing her sparkling eyes. Watching them, Cassie began to giggle, too, and finally exploded in laughter that was more release than amusement.

Still laughing, Mack pulled her up from her armchair and into a bear-hug that took in Taylor and Martha, too, until Cassie and her children were all three encompassed in the safety of his arms. A subtle change occurred, however, and Cassie withdrew, putting some distance between herself and Mack Cameron.

"Mr. Cameron?" Ruby's voice was unusually soft.

"Yes, Ruby?"

"We got stew warming and I'm fixing to make up some cornbread. You want to eat dinner with us?"

"I'd like that." He glanced at Cassie. "If it's all right."

"Of course."

Ruby headed for the kitchen and Mack made himself at home on the couch. He made himself so much at home, in fact, that within a few minutes Martha was snuggled against one side of him and Taylor was on the other.

"Ruby was reading to us," Martha said hopefully, "from *Charlotte's Web*."

"She was reading to Martha," Taylor said firmly. "It's a little kid's book. I was just sort of—listening."

"Yeah," Mack said. "I know what you mean. How about I read

it to Martha and if you want to, you can just sort of—listen."

His maturity affirmed, Taylor moved closer to Mack and listened wholeheartedly.

Mack's rough voice softened and took on a serious note appropriate to the problems of a sensitive pig.

Cassie watched them, sipping her drink from time to time. She was even more confused than she was when Mack knocked on her door. To all appearances he had tracked her from Washington and halfway across the state of Oklahoma for the sole purpose of reading to her children.

"Taylor and Martha," Ruby called from the kitchen. "You kids wash up for dinner now."

When they were alone, Cassie smiled at Mack. "I was just thinking, you went to a lot of trouble to come out here and read to my children."

His eyes twinkled as he picked up his glass. "It looks that way, but I have to confess, Cassie, I have an ulterior motive."

"Oh, do you?"

"Yes. I think it's time for me to put my cards on the table." He grinned. "Okay. I will be forty-five next month. I am healthy, wealthy and not very wise. I have a few bad habits, but not many and they aren't terribly bad." He stopped and looked at her measuringly.

"I am divorced, Cassie. I married at twenty-three, a girl of nineteen. I say a girl, because she was too young to be a woman and too young to be a wife. We worked at it, both of us, but there were no children and when we couldn't make a go of it in six years, we agreed on divorce. I supported her well, of course, but she went home to Bartlesville and within a year married a Phillips petroleum executive, which ended my responsibility. We still exchange Christmas cards."

He paused for a sip of his drink. "To continue, I am an only child and both of my parents died some years ago. I am generally considered to be an honest, hard-working oil man, but I do have some quirks."

Cassie stared at him, astounded. "Why are you telling me all this?"

"Ulterior motive, remember?"

"Oh? So what is this ulterior motive of yours?"

"You."

Cassie did not speak. She knew that. She had known it since she first saw his face in the half-light of the veranda.

"I hope you will get so used to having me around that you won't want me to leave. But don't worry," he said quickly. "I'm not asking you for anything now. No promises, no commitments. I just want to see you now and again, if it's all right."

"I suppose—of course, it's all right." She laughed. "You're very honest about it, aren't you?"

"Honest as the day is long! See why you need me in your life?"

"Oh, Mack, you're such a nut!" She could tell, though, that he was more serious than he was ready to admit. In effect, he had issued a challenge: You may not want me now, but you will eventually because I will make you want me. And Cassie had been dealing with challenges all her life. Because of her training as an attorney, she could see that he had put them in an adversarial relationship, and whether he realized it or not, between adversaries there could be only one winner. All right, Mackenzie Cameron, she thought. Okay. Let's see what kind of case you can present.

He set down her glass and looked at her closely. "Are you still seeing that boy Dean Clarkson?"

Cassie pulled her sweater tight across her chest. "Why do you want to know?"

"Because he's a rotten kid, Cassie, and being seen with him isn't doing your reputation any good at all."

Cassie's temper flared. First Fran and now Mack Cameron. "And just why is it any of your business?"

His face was red. "I'm your friend, damn it! I care about you!"

She lifted her chin. "You're probably jealous of him."

"Me? Jealous of a pipsqueak that has to take dope to get along in the world? Don't make me laugh."

They were at sword points when Ruby called them for dinner, but the children's chatter eased the tension. Cassie welcomed the release from her fury at Mack's attempt to interfere with her life. His anger seemed to ebb, too, during Martha's interminable explanation of the familial relationships of the cats and kitties who lived in the barn.

Everyone, including Mack, pitched in to clean up the kitchen, and for once the children went off to bed giggling instead of protesting every inch of the way.

Cassie took her time tucking Martha into bed and giving Taylor the one good-night kiss that he permitted. She realized that she was purposefully delaying her return to the living room and to Mack, because she dreaded a continuation of their angry confrontation.

There was no confrontation. She was surprised to find Mack putting on his coat when she returned. Surprised, and oddly sorry.

"I have a long drive ahead of me," he said.

"I know." She leaned over the fireplace and poked up the coals so that he would not see the disappointment in her face.

"Cassie?" he said behind her.

She did not turn around. "Yes?"

"May I see you again? In Washington?"

She did turn then to look at him. He was as big as a bear and he was as gentle a man as she had ever known. He was as blunt as a sledge hammer, yes, but open and honest. He was not a man who would compromise his values, ever, and neither would he ask her to compromise her own. As he had said of himself, he had some quirks.

She hesitated before answering his question, even though he had asked for no commitments, no promises. All that he appeared to want of her was what she wanted of herself: an open mind. "Yes," she said. "I would like that."

He started to go outside.

"Mack."

"Yes?"

"I haven't seen Dean Clarkson for almost a year, and I don't intend to see him again."

He grinned at her and then he patted her arm awkwardly and disappeared into the cold dark night.

Chapter 31

The first call waiting when Cassie returned to Washington was not from Mackenzie Cameron but from three board members of the national Freedom for Women Coalition. It was a call she expected, and dreaded, because she knew what they would ask of her. She would see them, though. She owed them that.

"No," she said. "I can't do it."

"Now, look," their leader said, "all we are asking is that you give us your public support. Is that so much to ask?"

"No. And yes."

"And what's that supposed to mean?"

Cassie swiveled her chair to look out at her restricted view of Washington. "Oklahoma is pretty conservative."

"We're aware of that, Congresswoman Steele. And we know that you're the only woman in the Oklahoma congressional delegation. That is one reason why it is so important that we have your support."

Cassie turned her chair to face them. "Let me ask you this. Which would be better for the women's movement, my support or my existence as a congresswoman?"

"I don't know what you mean."

"As I said before, Oklahomans are conservative by nature and are becoming more conservative politically. The Republicans have made big gains there in the last few years. You have to understand that many of our women are of pioneer stock. Their grandmothers and mothers fought for what they have, fought shoulder to shoulder with their men. You see them as second-class citizens but that's not the way they see themselves. They can't make a common cause with the strident women they see on television. They just can't see any justification for the bra-burnings, the unshaved legs, the—"

"The dykes?"

"That's your word, not mine, but you're right. Lesbians down there are in the closet. And marriage as slavery or legalized rape, the way Ti-Grace Atkinson defines it, well, it just won't fly in Oklahoma. What's more, I am sworn to represent the *people* of my district, not just the women."

"So?"

"So to support the FWC manifesto would very likely cost me this year's election and my seat in Congress. I could give you all the support you want, but it would be the public support of a private person. Wouldn't it be better for the cause to have the private support of a public person?"

The three visitors conferred with glances and the leader nodded. "I suppose you're right," she said reluctantly. "But what support could you give us?"

Cassie leaned forward and confronted the woman grimly. "First, I can give you some advice. Before you approach anyone else in Congress, female or male, for God's sake do your homework! Find out where they stand before you start pressuring them. Find out how they voted on women's issues and who they appointed to their staffs. If you had checked my record you would not have needed to ask how I would support you. I intend to continue supporting the movement in the same way that I have, not by screeching about trivial issues but by working quietly to gather votes that matter and, above all, by working to keep my seat in the House, to be living proof that a woman can succeed in what has always been considered a man's world."

"If you win the election," the leader said tartly.

"Win or lose. If I lose, I will have plenty of time to work with you, and I will be representing only my own views and not those of my congressional district."

In early February, Cassie received a note from Mack Cameron. "Have to be in Scotland for four or five weeks on a big deal. Will get in touch as soon as I get back."

He signed it, "Love, Mack."

Cassie found herself folding the note neatly and tucking it into her jewelry box like a high school girl stowing away a souvenir. She laughed at herself, a forty-year-old swooning like a teenager over a boy's note. That she was no teenager was clear, however, because her second reaction to the note was to analyze it. "A big deal" in Scotland could mean only one thing: North Sea oil. She whistled, more impressed than she would have expected. If Mack had worked out participation in the offshore drilling, it would be a very big deal indeed. She tucked that bit of information into her mind as she had put the note into her jewelry box. To reveal such a bombshell, Mack must trust her, and she would not betray his trust, but even secret knowledge of his plans could be invaluable in the House.

Being a member of Congress was not easy during the spring of 1966. It was a time of tumult in the civil rights movement. The divisions in black leadership were polarizing the forces pushing for integration. White Americans who had been supportive of the progression toward racial equality were driven into defensive positions by the excesses of the militant factions and, at the same time, blacks who worked with whites and spoke out for nonviolence were labeled "Uncle Toms" by their fellows.

Increasingly, however, the nation's attention was focused on Vietnam, where some 400,000 Americans were fighting—and dying. Antiwar protests, as yet unorganized, had begun the year before with a trickle of draft-card burnings. The trickle became a river in 1966 and Congress imposed a penalty of $10,000 or five years in prison for young men convicted of destroying their cards.

Although she was guaranteed the Democratic party's support in the April primary, Cassie flew to Oklahoma frequently, speaking wherever she could gather an audience and dealing with small problems in her district before they could become big ones.

She used the trips, also, to prepare the ground for her candidacy in the November election. Like many other Democratic candidates that spring, she knew that she was on shaky ground. The war in Vietnam was even more unpopular than Lyndon Johnson's war on poverty. And the cost of the two was enormous. In 1965, the President had asked Congress to appropriate $4 billion for war and $3 billion for social spending.

Cassie could stand on her record of opposition to the war in Vietnam, but even though many of her constituents received federal aid in one form or another, it was difficult to handle what became known as the welfare issue. Like most Americans, the people of Eastern Oklahoma wanted to help the needy. Like most Americans, they would say, "Yes, I *am* my brother's keeper." But, again like most Americans, what they really wanted was to find another brother or even a sister who would pay the bill.

The retired people who had bought land around the new lakes in Cassie's district tended more and more to turn away from the Democratic party, especially from its welfare programs. She could not really blame them. Theirs was a generation who had made it through the Depression and had fought for their country in World War II. It appeared to them that the President and Congress had turned on them by voting to spend their hard-won savings to support the rebellious students they saw on television, young people who appeared to have rejected all of America's values. Many of them were from well-to-do families, but they wore ragged clothing and long hair and beards. They cut up the American flag to patch their jeans and they burned their draft cards and swore that they would never fight for their country. Every invasion of a college library, every failure of a youth assistance program was seen by older Americans as another attack on all that they had worked for and fought for, on everything that they believed.

Another polarization was taking place in America, one that pitted the young and the old against each other: the generation gap.

Cassie had been too busy to worry about her forty-first birthday coming up. Ruby Vance remembered it, though, and reminded Martha and Taylor. Although she could not really spare the time that close to the primary, Cassie made a point of being at home in Georgetown that evening to receive her children's gifts and to listen to their off-key rendition of "Happy Birthday." She had just kissed them good-night and tucked them into bed when one more gift was delivered to the door by a young man from Cameron Oil's Washington office.

"Mr. Cameron sent it in our courier pouch," he said. "It had a note with it, saying to deliver it at nine o'clock tonight."

Cassie thanked him and went into the library to open the gift wrapping. It was a brooch, a gold thistle that was just the right size to wear on the lapel of a suit. How thoughtful he was, she thought, to send her a gift that was both delightful and noncommittal. The telephone rang and, still holding the brooch, she picked up the receiver.

"Happy birthday, Cassie."

"Mack! Mack Cameron! Did you get back to Washington after all?"

"No, I'm calling from Aberdeen. Did you get the little souvenir of Scotland?"

"Yes. Oh, yes, Mack. I did, and I love it. You were so kind to think of me."

He laughed, a deep rumble that reverberated over the miles. "Hey, that's not hard. I think about you all the time."

"Mack, when are you coming home?"

There was a short pause. "I like the sound of that, Cassie. 'Coming home,' maybe to you."

"I didn't exactly mean—" She stuttered in confusion. "All I meant was—"

He laughed again, softly. "It's okay, Cassie, I'm not going to try to pin you down. Listen, I don't know when I'll be back. Dealing with all these bureaucrats takes forever. Hell, Cassie, it may be fall before I can get away from here."

"Fall? But Mack—"

"Think about me once in a while, will you? Don't forget all about me."

"Oh, Mack, I won't! And I do think about you, more than you—" She stopped abruptly.

"Good," he said. "I'm glad."

When they hung up, Cassie stayed on the couch in the library for a long time, holding the gold thistle in her hand and thinking about Mack Cameron.

The next morning Cassie flew to Oklahoma for another round of speaking engagements and to vote in the Democratic primary. As the plane took off she thanked her stars once again for sending Ruby Vance back into her life. The children would be safe and happy with Ruby and she knew that Ruby could deal with an emergency as effectively as she herself could.

Ruby's presence was invaluable that summer and even more so in the fall. Cassie won the primary handily, but she had a major fight on her hands with her Republican opposition. In-state polls showed Cassie ahead one week and the Republican ahead the next. Just when Cassie thought that she had shaken every hand and kissed every baby in her district, Allie MacIntyre or another staffer would come up with one more kaffee klatsch. By the time the polls closed on Election Day, Cassie was exhausted mentally and physically. It was not much comfort to know that her opponent was in much the same state.

Ruby Vance had brought the children out from Washington, so

it was in an Oklahoma City hotel suite with them and with Amelia and James Steele that Cassie watched the televised election results. Just as it had done in the polls, the lead went back and forth with each new batch of precincts reporting.

The children had dozed off on the couch and been carried to bed, Amelia and James had gone to their own room, Ruby was asleep, and even Cully Meecham was sound asleep in a chair before the final results came in.

"And in Eastern Oklahoma—"

Cassie raised her head, expecting the announcer to say that the race was still too close to call.

"—it is clear now that the race has been decided. Mrs. Cassandra Steele, the incumbent, has won by a margin of about ten percent."

Cully snorted and Cassie thought that he was waking up, but the snort turned into another snore and he slept on. She would wake him soon, and tell him, and she would go to bed herself, but for a few moments she would keep the news of her victory to herself.

She went to the window and pulled back the curtains to look at the black night and the sparse lights of the city. It was not that she wanted to keep the news to herself, she realized. She was tremendously excited, and she was proud. She had worked for this one, she had given her all, and she had won. It was not that she did not want to tell Cully the good news that kept her from waking him, but rather the fact that he was the wrong person to tell.

Dix, she thought, conjuring up his shadow, but the shadow was of the wrong man. Her hazy vision was not of Dixon Steele but of a big man, a huge man with wide-set eyes and a broad, easy grin.

She wanted to share the victory, she realized, she wanted to share the celebration with Mack Cameron.

As 1966 passed into 1967, Cassie felt that America was sinking into a waking nightmare in which the government no longer was leading the people but instead was following them down into insanity. Groups committed to the same goals, such as the antiwar protesters, fought bitter battles over processes while opposing factions banded together in unholy alliances such as that of wealthy New York liberals with the Black Panthers in what journalist Tom Wolfe called "radical chic."

In Vietnam, the casualty count grew from week to week as U.S. troops fought bravely but pointlessly. Even more than most wars, the conflict in Vietnam appeared to be run by demented schoolboys. The President berated members of Congress who raised even a mild protest over the conduct of the war. The protests increased, however, and apparently so did his feeling that any attack on his policies in Vietnam was a personal attack on Lyndon Baines Johnson.

In early December of 1966, however, Cassie had a pressing problem of her own. The first indication that Mackenzie Cameron had returned from Scotland was the arrival of a florist to deliver two dozen red roses. A note was tucked into the foliage.

> I'm home and eager to see you. Will telephone later. Dinner tonight?
>
> Love, Mack.

Cassie touched the card with one forefinger, tracing the words "Love, Mack." To her surprise she found that the one little word "Love" threw her off balance. Did "Love" mean love, or was it no more than a conventional closing for a brief note? Which was it? Which, she asked herself, did she want it to be?

She lifted the flowers and buried her face in their sweet fresh smell. That was the problem, she thought. It was not the flowers, or the note, or even that one ambiguous word. She was off balance because she could not define her own feelings. She felt steadier when she remembered what Mack had said on that cold January night at the ranch: "No promises, no commitments."

What he had said was unequivocal and to the point. She did not need to sift through and define her feelings about Mack, because he would expect of her no more than she could freely and happily give. Whatever else he might be—too big, perhaps, and too crude and wrong-headed politically—whatever else, he was clearly an honorable man. Mackenzie Cameron was a man of his word.

She took the roses into the kitchen and arranged them in a tall crystal vase. She was blessed, for once, with a free afternoon and an evening with no committee meetings. She waited for his call with eagerness and a great deal of curiosity. They had not seen each other for ten months. How would he feel about her now? And how would she feel about him?

Cassie opened the front door and there he was, even bigger than she remembered, and grinning like a Cheshire cat. She held the door open and he came in, bringing into her house the crisp cold of the December night.

"Cassie," he said softly and before she could say a word he folded her into his arms. "Oh, Cassie, I've missed you so damn—"

"Mack!" Taylor jumped up at him before he could finish his sentence. Right behind Taylor was Martha, raising her arms for a hug, and behind her, Ruby Vance, beaming on everyone in general.

The children took Mack's overcoat and Cassie purposely ignored his blue polyester suit. They tugged him in to sit on the couch in the library, with one of them plastered against each side. Ruby Vance made a drink for him and Cassie poked up the fire.

"Hey," he said, "this is a great welcome home! Thank you. Thank you all!" He spoke to all of them, but he looked only at Cassie.

Suddenly embarrassed she sat down in an armchair near the fireplace. He talked to the children, but still he watched her.

"I found Scotland on the map, Mack. Did you like it?" Taylor, at ten and (as he always pointed out) three quarters, was insatiably curious. "What's it like there? Do all the men wear skirts?"

"Kilts, not skirts. And they call it 'the kilt.' Yes, Taylor, I liked it a lot, but at this time of year it's colder than a witch's—broom-stick." He grinned apologetically at Cassie. "You ought to go see for yourself sometime. The castle at Edinburgh is—"

"Can we, Mom?" Taylor cried. "Can we go to Scotland?"

"I want to go to England, Mama," Martha said. "I want to see the Queen and all the princesses."

Cassie smiled as she imagined Martha's idea of the royal family. In the girl's nine-year-old mind they all probably resembled Barbie dolls, Barbies dressed in ball gowns and ensconced in royal coaches, twisting from one side to the other as, with unbending arms, they acknowledged the applause of their subjects.

Mack hugged Martha to his side.

> "Pussy cat, pussy cat, where have you been?
> I've been to London to look at the Queen."

He laughed. "Never did know how to make an Oklahoma 'bin' rhyme with 'queen,' but in England they do say 'bean.' "

Ruby giggled. " 'I've bean workin' on the railroad,' " she sang and giggled again, self-consciously.

As the children tried "bin" and "bean" in different songs, Cassie and Mack got into their coats and out of the door. In the car, however, their conversation was polite to the point of being rigid. It was not until they were seated on opposite sides of a table that Cassie relaxed enough to ask Mack a few questions.

"What's the political climate in Great Britain now, Mack?"

"The Labor Party is in control, but you know that."

"Yes. And Harold Wilson is Prime Minister. Are the people happy with what he's doing?"

"Some are, of course, but I'm not." He took a sip of his drink. "He's nationalized industry and instead of independent labor, men who can and will take pride in their work, they've got nothing but bureaucrats from top to bottom, right down to the assembly-line worker whose job is to tighten one hex-nut on an automobile's steering gear. He's a hell of a lot more interested in his tea break than in the quality of work he turns out, which means that steering gear may not hold in an emergency. Hell, even the Brits can see that British Leyland is going down the tube, but all they do is throw in some more inspectors or social scientists or something: another layer of bureaucrats to gum up the works. I have seen the future, Cassie, and it doesn't work."

"But you didn't have to deal with all that, not in the oil business." She laughed. "I had enough experience with oil interests in Texas to know that any good oil man is about half pirate."

Mack grinned. "That's right." He sighed nostalgically. "You're right about Texas, but believe me, Scotland ain't Texas. They've nationalized North Sea oil and it looks to me like it will take more oil than they've got just to run the presses that print out the bureaucrats' memos to each other." He signaled to the waiter to bring drinks. "The thing is, Cassie, the Brits have this idea—this fantasy, I call it—that North Sea oil is going to solve all of their economic problems. They think it's going to get their nationalized industries out of the red, retool their manufacturing plants, pay the tab for the army in Northern Ireland and—hell, for all I know, it's supposed to grow hair on bald men, too."

"You obviously don't believe the fantasy will become reality."

"Oh, it will, sure. When pigs can fly! Hey, that's enough griping. Just blame it on my being mired knee-deep in British bureaucracy for most of a year. Tell me, what's going on here in God's country?"

She shook her head sadly. "Sometimes I think He has disowned us."

Mack had little to say after her depressing recital of the state of the nation. She was glad that the waiter brought their dinners then, and Mack cheered up with his first bite of rare T-bone steak.

"American beef, genuine corn-fed Kansas City beef. That's more like it!" By the time he had described the British penchant for puddings and some of their names, they were both laughing.

"Not 'Spotted Dick,' Mack! You're making that up!"

"I swear. And then there's my favorite, 'Toad in a Hole.' "

The talk moved on to other matters and Mack's impressions of Scotland. The look of the Hebrides in a winter storm. The way the Highlands crofters reminded him of the hill people of Eastern Oklahoma. Cassie told him about her tough fight to defeat the Republican candidate in her district and about her confrontation with Taylor's teacher. Over coffee and liqueurs they touched on the vagaries of English and American speech.

"I like the way Churchill put it, Cassie, that our countries were separated only by a common language."

Cassie laughed but when she looked into Mack's blue eyes, no longer merry but dead serious, she fell silent.

"Does something separate us, Cassie? It can't be a common language, with both of us speaking fluent Oklahoman. And not children. I like kids, you have kids. Politics, maybe?"

"No!" she said. "We have the right to our own political beliefs."

"Then can't we—be together?"

Cassie became aware that she was letting go of something, softening like an ice cream cone in summer sunshine. Why couldn't they be together, after all? Why couldn't they—she took hold of herself and of her emotions. What did he mean, "be together"? Was it a proposal or a proposition? It occurred to her suddenly that his promise not to pin her down, to seek no commitments could be meant to protect him, not her.

"Why can't we be together" was a question as poorly defined as it was noncommittal. How could she answer it? Was this just one more case of a man's attempt to dominate her? Mack had once again put her in the position of an adversary. If she agreed to "be together," he could pull the rug from under her feet so that she would take a prat fall while he, the winner, stood by and laughed. But if she told him no, if she refused him, wouldn't she have to justify her answer to herself as well as to him?

Her only escape, she thought, lay in refusing to answer, in being as noncommittal as he himself had been. She took up her handbag and gloves. "Mack, I would like to go home now."

He stared at her. "But you haven't answered my question."

She allowed herself one direct look into his blue eyes. "You haven't asked it, Mack."

At the house on R Street, he offered his arm to help her up the icy front steps and she accepted it, but at the door she took her hand off of his arm and coolly told him good night. Inside the front door, alone, she had to lean against the wall and fight to control her shaking body. Her heart pounded madly, like that of a woman who has narrowly avoided a fatal accident.

As her pulse slowed, however, and her body stopped shaking, a strange sadness permeated her soul. He was gone, and not just for this night. He was gone. Mack Cameron was out of her life.

During the spring, Cassie dealt with her family and her job. Taylor and Mr. Youngblood, his teacher, had several run-ins that had to be settled by high-level diplomacy. The family of Martha's best friend was transferred to the American Embassy in France. Dealing with an intransigent son and a disconsolate daughter exhausted Cassie. Ruby tried to help, but with both her feet planted firmly and somewhat flatly on the ground she was better at handling the children's physical needs than their psychological ones. From time to time Cassie found herself wishing that Temple would return. Temple's flamboyance caught the children's attention, at least, and her constant problems with school, with her wild friends and with Cassie, made Taylor and Martha's difficulties appear small and unimportant. But no one had heard from Temple since that one postcard from San Francisco.

Fran Jordan flew in to Washington in February and brought a breath of fresh Texas air into Cassie's locked-in Washington life. Fran was in the house on R Street for two days before she and Cassie were able to get away for a dinner together.

The festivity went out of the evening when Cassie realized that the restaurant Fran chose was the one where Mackenzie Cameron had asked, or rather, had not asked his question. She had to force herself to listen to Fran rather than to the words she remembered from December.

"So I don't expect to get much business in Washington on this trip. LBJ is losing popularity and I'm afraid that means that Texas designers will follow him down."

"He's losing it because of the war, you mean? Because so many families have boys in Vietnam?"

Fran laughed harshly. "Cassie, love, families who deal with interior designers have their sons tucked safely away in college. The war is unpopular with my sort of client, but it's unpopular because of the sheer cost of the excursion. Well, it was twenty-seven billion dollars last year, wasn't it? And when it turned out that Johnson had been using phoney figures to make his estimates about the cost, that in effect he was lying, then the you-know-what really hit the fan." She took a long pull at her Scotch and water. "Oh, hell, Cassie. I've had it up to here with the war. Let's talk about more pleasant things." She flashed a quick smile at Cassie. "I want to hear all about your thing with that Oklahoma millionaire. How's Mack Cameron?"

Cassie looked down at her hands. "He's fine, as far as I know."

"And just what does *that* mean exactly?"

Cassie did not have to look at Fran to be aware of the increase in tension. She heard it in the sudden sharpness in Fran's voice. "It means, I suppose he's all right, but I haven't seen him since before Christmas."

"But I heard—" Fran broke off abruptly.

Then Cassie did look at her. "What did you hear, Fran? And where did you hear it?"

Fran had the grace to blush. "Oh, a fellow I know, a Texas oil man, just happened to mention Mack Cameron. He seemed to think Mack was getting pretty serious about you."

Cassie laughed bitterly. "Serious? I don't think so, Fran, not unless you can call a roll in the hay serious."

"You mean that you two—"

"No, I do not! I mean, that's all Mack Cameron seemed to want of me."

Fran's eyes narrowed. "So what's wrong with that? You're a grown woman, Cassie. You're free to do what you want."

"Maybe that's just not what I want, did you consider that? Look, I'm forty-one years old, Fran. I'm tired of playing games, of having some—some stud who thinks he's God's gift to women maneuver me into his bed."

"Tired of games like the one you played with Eliot Peabody?"

"You mean the one Eliot played with me."

Fran snickered. "It takes two to tango."

"I know, I know." Cassie turned her wineglass around and around. "Fran, why do men have to be that way? It's all wham, bam—"

"Thank you, ma'am. Damned if I know." She grinned. "And damned if I care. I like to play the field, Cassie. I've never made any secret of it."

"But you don't have children, Fran. And you don't have to go public for an election every two years."

"Okay, okay, and I'm not the marrying kind, but you are. I'm a realist, you know. The newspapers call you a realist, too, but they don't know you the way I do. You are a romantic to the core, Cassie. You don't want a real man, with all his snoring and belching and hair in his ears. You want a knight in shining armor to gallop up and sweep you off your feet."

Cassie could not keep from laughing. "Maybe you're right! But I'll tell you, Fran, you just would not believe how few knights in shining armor gallop through the streets of Georgetown."

Their dinner arrived then and they talked of other things, mutual friends, the latest gossip in Dallas, and Fran's design business, but the insights of their conversation stayed with Cassie long after Fran had gone back to Texas.

Chapter 32

In May of 1967, there were 480,000 U.S. troops in Vietnam and the number of Americans killed there passed 10,000. Ten thousand Americans had died pointlessly in a war that had no specific beginning and showed no signs of ever ending. On the home front, protests against the war had widened into protests against the establishment itself. Drugs, everything from marijuana to speed to LSD, permeated the society as more and more young Americans were taking Timothy Leary's advice to turn on, tune in and drop out.

Various militant factions of the civil rights movement were calling Martin Luther King "a black honky" and demanding an end to nonviolent protest.

Faced in the House and at home with unsolvable problems, Cassie grew more and more restless. She heard nothing from or about Mack Cameron that spring, but after all, she did not expect to. She had no interest in him. She began to think that a change of scene, a change of input was what she needed and might be what they all needed.

She gathered the children and Ruby in the library one afternoon, a few weeks shortly after her forty-second birthday. "Taylor, you're eleven now, aren't you, and Martha, you're nine."

"Going on ten!"

"Of course. And Ruby and I are—well, we don't need to go into that. Anyway, you kids are old enough to travel abroad now. What do you say to three weeks in England this summer?"

"And Scotland?" the two children said as one.

"Oh," Cassie said, "that's right. Mack told you all about Scotland, didn't he? Well, yes, I should think that three weeks would give us time to see something of Scotland, too."

"Hooray!" Taylor yelled, and Martha whirled around the room in excitement.

"We'll see the Queen!" she cried.

"I'm not sure we can—" Cassie stopped herself. Why pour cold water on Martha's dream? "We'll try," she said. "We'll do our very best."

"Cassie?" Ruby looked worried. "You're really nice to ask me too, but would you mind if I don't go? In that three weeks I could finish the first draft of my master's thesis."

Cassie was startled. She could take care of the children without Ruby, but she could not believe that the girl would give up a trip abroad to stay home and write footnotes. She started to protest, but she realized that what made her happy did not need to enrapture Ruby Vance. "Of course, Ruby. It is your decision to make. But do take a few days to think about it. If you decide not to go, by the way, I'll pay your regular salary in return for your being my house-sitter."

The travel agent was both knowledgeable and efficient. She was also confused and slightly offended by Cassie's insistence on traveling as an attorney rather than a member of Congress.

"But everyone in Congress travels semi-officially. I can arrange for red-carpet treatment everywhere."

"Which is precisely what I don't want," Cassie said. "This is my first trip abroad and I want to go as just one more American tourist."

*   *   *

Considering the length of the flight to London from Dulles and the wear and tear on her children and herself, Cassie invested in first-class seats. Nevertheless, the Steele family had to spend their first day and night in London getting over jet lag before they could take the train north to Scotland.

"But the Queen!" Martha protested. "I want to see the Queen."

"We're coming back to London, remember? We'll only be in Scotland for a week."

As they traveled north, Cassie realized that she was indeed just one more American tourist. She was enthralled, as were her children, with the lush green countryside where sheep grazed in white clusters that might have been arranged by the British Tourist Authority to point up the rich greens of the grass and the towering elms on the hills. Each fold in the terrain had its village with a Romanesque or Norman church tower, a cluster of houses and sometimes, to Taylor's delight, the battlements of a castle. The railroad tracks bisected many of the villages, showing them a view of the workings of the place that was frozen in the instant, like a snapshot. Taylor noticed that there was always a small store, Martha saw the fat-cheeked babies tucked into prams, but Cassie looked at the individual people they passed: an old man on a bicycle, a boy in his school blazer, a woman with a shopping basket hung on her arm.

It was dark when they reached Edinburgh and their hotel, and all three of them, exhausted from traveling, fell into bed. The next morning was crisp and cool even though it was August, and they walked the Royal Mile in bright sunshine. They toured Holyrood Palace. Martha was much taken with the bed of Mary, Queen of Scots, and Taylor was equally fascinated by the secret door to the bedchamber, the one Rizzio had known.

Good sightseers, they tramped back the length of the Mile, past shops that sold bagpipes and tartans and cheaper souvenirs of Edinburgh and Scotland. They climbed up to the castle so that Taylor could see the soldiers in kilts who marched and counter-marched on the ramparts. Cassie, the dutiful tourist, bought tickets for the evening performance of the Edinburgh Tattoo even though she was not quite sure what a Tattoo was.

After dinner at the hotel, they trudged once more up the hill to the castle and found their seats on open bleachers. With sunset a cold wind had come up and Cassie was glad they were all dressed warmly.

The Tattoo was a fine show, from the demonstrations of commando attacks to "The Lone Piper" who stood high on the battlements of the castle and played on his bagpipe the Tattoo, the British equivalent of "Taps." It was a moving experience.

As they walked back to the hotel the children chattered about the show. This, Cassie thought, is what travel is about. We've had an experience we could not have imagined if we had stayed at home in Washington. She became aware that Taylor and Martha had stopped talking and were giggling.

"What's so funny?" she said.

Martha nodded her head vigorously, signaling that Cassie should look behind them.

Cassie looked back, one quick glance, and saw that a man in a kilt was behind them, a large man with broad shoulders.

"Martha!" she said softly but firmly, "It is not polite to point and it's downright rude to laugh at a stranger."

"I didn't point," Martha protested. "I just sort of waggled my head a little, like this."

Cassie pulled her close to her side. "Don't do that," she whispered. "The poor man will see you."

"But he's not a poor man," Taylor said with the inexorable logic of an eleven-year-old. "And he's not a stranger, either. Didn't you look at him? It's Mack, and that's why we were laughing."

"Don't be silly, Taylor. The man could not possibly be Mack Cameron."

"But he is, Mama!" Martha tugged at her hand. "Look at him, you'll see!"

Cassie stopped and turned around. The man in the kilt hesitated but came toward her with long, free strides. He was a huge man and within his well-cut tweed jacket his shoulders were broad. Under his velvet, ribbon-trimmed cap his hair was blond. And his twinkling eyes, of course, were very blue, because it was Mack. It was Mackenzie Cameron.

"Mack?" she said tentatively, still expecting it to be no more than a trick of the light. "Is that you, Mack?"

The man laughed, a familiar laugh. "In the flesh."

Taylor snickered and Mack looked down at his bare knees. "Some of which you can see for yourself."

It was Cassie's turn to laugh. "I'm not all that familiar with your bare knees, you know. Why are you wearing a kilt?"

"*The* kilt, they say here. Och, woman, I'm a Cameron, and of Clan Mackenzie, too."

"And what are you doing here, on the Royal Mile?"

"What do you think? Looking for you." He grinned at Martha and Taylor. "And you two house-apes, too, of course. I'll walk you back to your hotel."

Taylor ran ahead with Martha, as always, close behind him. Mack looked down at Cassie. "I hope you don't mind."

"Mind?"

"I mean, my hunting you up like this."

They crossed a side street before Cassie answered him. It was not that she minded, she thought. It was just that she wanted to know why. Why had he hunted for her? To ask again the question that was not a question? To make demands of her? This time, perhaps, if he asked the question she would not walk away from it. This time she might just say "Forget it" and get on with her life. Or then, she might say "Yes." But she did not ask him why he was in Edinburgh. Instead, she asked him how he had found her.

"In Aberdeen I heard you were coming to Scotland and I—"

"Heard? Who told you?"

"Oh, a kid in my Washington office. Before I left the United

States I gave him—" He chuckled. "I guess the spies would call it a watching brief."

"To watch me, you mean? To keep you up to date on me?"

"Don't worry. He's not watching every little move you make, Cassie, but when he heard you were coming here he found your travel agent and found out the details."

Cassie made a mental note to find herself a more discreet travel agent. "So you came to Edinburgh to see me."

"So I came to Edinburgh to see you." They were at the door of her hotel. "Look, when you've got the children to bed will you come back down? I'll order coffee."

"I had British coffee in London this morning."

"Right. I'll order tea."

Cassie tucked the children into their beds. After the long chilly evening they would undoubtedly be asleep before the antiquated elevator got her down to the lobby.

Mack led her to the hotel lounge where a tray with tea and warm scones was waiting. She felt unusually light-hearted as she poured tea and passed a cup to Mack. In the light she could see him more clearly. His tweed jacket was gray with a fleck of heather that picked out the heather thread running through the tartan of his kilt. "That's a handsome outfit," she said. She reached over to feel the tartan. "Why, Mack!" she said in mock surprise. "It's not polyester! It's wool. And your jacket is wool, too."

He blushed. "I don't think they make the kilt in polyester."

She smiled wickedly. "My, don't the Scotch have good taste?"

"The Scots." He recovered his aplomb. "The people are Scots and the adjective for them is not Scotch, but Scottish."

"Then what do you call the whiskey? Scottish?"

He looked down his nose at her. "You call it whiskey. The other sorts have to be defined as Irish whiskey or bourbon whiskey, but you can't get bourbon anyway, except at a few places in London."

"Or in my luggage. I bought two bottles at the duty-free shop at Dulles."

He grinned broadly. "I knew you were a woman of good sense."

He crossed his legs and gave his kilt a quick tug. "I don't have this kilt business down pat yet. A good ole boy from Oklahoma don't get much practice wearing a skirt."

"Now, look, you can wear a kilt or you can talk with an Oklahoma twang, but to do both just doesn't work at all."

He laughed. "Come to think about it, Ah reckon h'it don't."

"Oh, Mack!" She laughed at the incongruity of his accent and his historic clothing, but mostly in pleasure at sharing an Oklahoma in-joke with someone. She stopped laughing as abruptly as she started, however, because she realized it was not just "someone" she enjoyed. It was Mack Cameron himself.

"Look, Cassie, I've got a proposition for you."

Her breath caught. Here it came, his nonquestion. He had suckered her into it again. She hardened herself as she waited.

"I think I told you how much I like Scotland. Well, I'd like to show you and the kids some of it. So if it's okay with you, I'll rent a car and drive us around for a few days."

Her surprise that his proposition was not the one she expected opened her eyes to how much she would enjoy such a trip. And the children, she knew, would love it. "Mack, I—we would love it, I know!"

"Great! Drink up your tea then, and I'll make arrangements at the desk for a car. We'll want to get an early start tomorrow."

"At the desk?" Cassie stood up. "You're staying here?"

"Why, yes. Your travel agent might be a little too talkative about her clients' itineraries, but she does know her stuff. This is the most comfortable hotel in Edinburgh."

Cassie might be suspicious, but she could not argue the point. And Mack had not asked her any difficult questions, at least, not so far. "Fine," she said. "Maybe you can arrange for an early breakfast, too."

Edinburgh had its morning rush hour, but it was primarily confined to trams and buses. Mack drove their rented Jaguar to Dunfermline, pointing out the Firth of Forth to the south. Martha and Cassie, too, were so entranced with the name that they ignored the facts about the tides and Cassie was able to forget for a while the unnerving sensations caused by Mack driving on what felt like the wrong side of the road.

They went north then, through Perth and Dundee to drive up the North Sea coast to Aberdeen. Mack pointed out changes in the town, the new construction, the new life, in fact, that was a result of exploration for off-shore oil and of preparations to pump that oil. North of Aberdeen they went, then west, following the narrow coastal road through hamlets that had none of the lush greens of England. These Scottish towns were gray, with houses huddled together against the Arctic winter winds. The people looked gray, too, and thin, with the pinched faces of the chronically poor. Only the village stores and the pubs showed signs of life.

Without explaining, Mack turned off the main road at a sign that said CULLODEN MOOR.

"Is it time for lunch?" Taylor said hopefully.

"No." For once Mack was serious. "It's a place every Scot should see."

"But we aren't Scots," Cassie said.

Mack's voice picked up a hint of a Scottish accent. "I'd not be too sure of that. Most hill people in America, if their forebears came from the Appalachians, have a bit of Scottish blood."

"Even sharecroppers' children?" Cassie said.

"As a matter of fact, the Scottish peasantry were sharecroppers themselves. They had a saying: 'Ane to gnaw, and ane to saw, and ane to pay the laird witha.' "

Taylor was perched on the edge of the back seat so that he would not miss a word. "What does that mean, Mack?"

"One share to eat, one to plant and one to pay the landlord." Mack glanced at Cassie. "Sound familiar?"

The Jaguar emerged from the woods then and Culloden Moor appeared. The sky was dark with a storm moving in from the west and beneath it the wind swept acres of ripe wheat until it tossed like waves in a golden sea. Mack pulled the car to a stop near a low building set into a fold in the hill.

They sat for a moment, silent. Even the children appeared to be awed by the strong sense of history that lay over the place like a mist of memory.

"It was the last great battle of Bonnie Prince Charlie," Mack said softly. "On the sixth of April in 1746, he gathered the clans here, he summoned the Highlanders to do battle with the English. The Sassenach army lost three hundred men, but Prince Charlie's forces were crushed. Twelve hundred Scots fell that day, died here on the moor, and here they remain. Do you see the markers?"

Cassie saw them, simple headstones set here and there on the moor.

"Those are the Graves of the Clans," Mack said. "The dead were buried with their kin, each clan lying dead together as it stood in life."

Two hundred years ago, Cassie thought, but she felt that it could have been only two hours. She had a strange feeling that there were presences on Culloden Moor, memories too restless to sink to a peaceful rest in the golden fields.

Martha sucked in her breath and Cassie looked back at her fearfully. It was, perhaps, too much of death for a girl of not-quite-ten to handle. "Mack?" Martha asked. "What happened to those men's children, to their little kids?"

"Ah, yes. Their mothers took them home, Martha, and taught them to work and to honor the cause for which their fathers died."

"Like Mama told us about our daddy," Martha said.

Cassie turned in surprise to look at her daughter. She had not harped on Dix's death nor had she drummed into her children's heads knowledge about the cause of civil rights. Or had she? At any rate, it was obvious that they knew all about it.

She turned back to the front and saw that Mack was watching

her. "Yes," he said, ostensibly to Martha. "Yes, they were brave, like your mama, and true to what they believed."

Taylor had obviously had all that he could manage of subtleties. "Did they kill Prince Charlie, too?"

"No, he escaped and had other adventures all over Scotland. Some of the stories about him are true and some are legends, but I'll tell you about them later."

Taylor was persistent. "Mack, what's in that little house?"

"It's a museum of the battle, Taylor. There are weapons and armor and that sort of thing."

"Wow! That's what I want to see. Can we go in there now?"

They had left the museum and were almost to Inverness before Cassie could shake off the sadness she felt when she looked at the Graves of Clans.

Inverness, however, was crammed with the living, Scottish and English and American tourists. Fortunately Mack had phoned ahead for reservations so they had good rooms in the town's best hotel.

Mack was wearing a striped shirt and chinos at breakfast the next morning and all trace of the Scot had disappeared. "Kids, I hope you're brave today, and tough. We're going monster-hunting!"

Martha looked anything but tough. Her voice trembled. "Monsters?"

Cassie said, "It's all right, honey, it's just a—" But Mack had already picked up on the child's fear.

"Nessie," he said, "is a lady monster and *very* well-behaved."

Taylor looked disappointed but Martha was somewhat reassured. "A lady monster? Does she eat people?"

"Never!" Mack said. "She lives in a lake and eats nothing but weeds. Anyway, we might not see her, you know. She's pretty shy."

Martha smiled and patted Cassie's hand. "See, Mama? You don't have to be scared."

*　　*　　*

Loch Ness was a long narrow lake lying within low hills. It was larger than Cassie had expected and was dotted with power boats, including some large cabin cruisers.

"How on earth did they get all those boats here, Mack? And why?"

"They cruise down the Caledonian Canal from Inverness," he said, "and they're here, of course, to look for the monster."

Mack stopped at a souvenir shop so they could see copies of photographs that purported to be of the monster. From what Cassie could see, if Nessie existed she looked like a large fishing worm. Martha was happy enough with that version of a monster to squander her spending money on a Nessie coloring book.

On the way to the car Cassie hung back to say a few words to Mack. "I think the Loch Ness monster is mostly just plain old good business."

Mack laughed. "Hey, you Okie, where's your sense of awe? Aren't you amazed at the possible existence of a present-day hold-over of the dinosaurs?"

In her strongest Oklahoma twang she said, "Not so's you'd notice."

He took her arm as if to help her and she liked the feeling of his large warm hand. He chuckled. "But the scientists say—"

"Scientists? In a pig's eye!"

Mack was still laughing when they got in the car. Taylor was glued to the window, watching the water, but Martha was coloring in her book, content enough with cartoon monsters without needing to see a real one.

From Loch Ness, Mack drove the Jaguar south to Fort Augustus where, he told them, the Duke of Cumberland had made his headquarters after the victory at Culloden, and then on to Oban, a thriving town where they would spend the night.

They checked in early enough to have a walk before dinner. Cassie was fascinated by the slightly surrealistic look of the place and of the people who looked like Americans but wore clothes that were completely different. The laborers, for instance, wore flat tweed caps and old suit jackets with mismatched pants instead of the Cat-hats, shiny team jackets and blue jeans of American workmen.

When the children were in bed Cassie met Mack in the lounge for a brandy. She felt strangely shy of him that night, as shy as the Loch Ness monster.

"I wish we had more time," he said. "We could go to Mull tomorrow and cross over to Iona."

"Iona? I must have missed that in my reading for the trip."

"It's an island off the tip of Mull. Supposedly the first Christian contact with the Britons came when St. Columba landed there, in 563 A.D. Also, for centuries Iona was the burial place for Scottish kings and clan chieftans. I'm sure the kids would like it."

Cassie sipped her brandy. "Mack, you are terribly good to Martha and Taylor."

He smiled. "It's not hard. They're good kids."

"Taylor good? His teacher, Mr. Youngblood, would call that an oxymoron."

Mack whistled. "Oxymoron! Is this the girl who never even finished high school?"

Cassie flushed. "I can read and write, you know. And there's no law against using an unabridged dictionary." She took another sip of brandy. "By the way, Mack, I don't think you've ever said where you went to college for your degree in petroleum engineering. Was it OU or Oklahoma A & M?"

"Neither. I worked my way through the University of Tulsa. Didn't learn all that much about engineering, but I can always hire excellent engineers."

"And Tulsa is where you learned to wear those damn polyester suits."

"What the hell, they travel well, and in my business, too, I deal with a lot of small-town bankers."

"Protective coloring? Is that it?"

He grinned. "Sure. Don't forget, Cassie, I've seen you in action, too. Sometimes you sound like a Dallas debutante and sometimes I'd swear you never left that sharecropper's shack."

Cassie sat back and relaxed. "I guess you're right, Mack. I'll confess, though, that sometimes I feel like a phoney when I remember that my family didn't have a pot or a window."

Mack laughed so loudly that the proper British tourists in the lounge gave him a fishy eye. "A pot to piss in or a window to throw it out of. I haven't heard that one in years!"

Cassie blushed. Maybe Mack was right, and half the time she was still in a sharecropper's shack.

He looked at her closely. "Hey, now, don't apologize for what you were, Cassie, not to me or to anyone else. With what you've done with your life, for your children, you should be damn proud."

She straightened her shoulders. She *was* proud, damn proud. She looked across the coffee table at Mack. She was also proud that she did not need anyone's permission to feel that pride. Where did he get off, telling her what she should feel? What was it about men, anyway? Jimmy had bossed her around, Eliot Peabody had tried, even Dix, during that last year of his life, Dix had wanted to dominate her. She was not interested in playing a role assigned to her by a man, any man, no matter how nice he was or how good to her children.

"Mack, don't tell me what I should or should not be," she said quietly. "I do not need a man to tell me how to feel." She got to her feet. "Since you rented the car, I will act as you wish in this one matter. Would you prefer that we part company tomorrow? The children and I can return to London by train."

"No." He stood up too and looked down at her. "I would *prefer* that we complete our tour as planned. I would also *prefer* that you would not be so goddamned touchy. You're as taut as a guitar string."

The other tourists, she saw, were watching them with poorly concealed interest. She settled for lifting her chin and saying one cold "Good night."

Chapter 33

The atmosphere at breakfast was chilly but Martha and Taylor were impervious to cold, chattering away about the children they had seen in school uniforms, especially the girls who began rolling their modest uniform skirts up at the waist to become fashionably miniskirted within seconds of the time they left their school building. They talked about the shops, too, where sweets meant candy and biscuits were cookies and lollies were suckers.

After breakfast they all packed their gear and Mack drove the Jaguar away from the sea. The moors were gray-green in the drizzling rain, and the steady beat of the windshield wiper lulled the children into dozing on the back seat. Cassie and Mack were quiet too, their thoughts going their separate ways. Cassie realized that in spite of her irritation at Mack the night before, she was comfortable with him. Whatever their relationship might be, there seemed to be room in it even for disagreement. She relaxed in the comfortable seat.

"All this green, green grass. Mack, just think what this sort of rainfall would do for ranching in Eastern Oklahoma."

Mack was quiet, as if he too were visualizing the long days of August in Oklahoma and the pastures withering under a baking sun. He grunted agreement. "Irrigation. There has to be more irrigation, even in areas that by Oklahoma standards have normal rainfall."

"I already irrigate my high pastures."

"I know, but it has to become more widespread."

Cassie shook her head. "There's no government money available for—"

"Government money!" Mack struck the steering wheel a hard blow. "That's the trouble with you damn Democrats. You think everything has to come from the government, from that big Santa Claus in Washington. Don't you realize that someone has to pay for it? You pay, and I pay—every last taxpayer has to pay the tab."

"And you damn Republicans refuse to see the truth, that not everyone can walk into a bank and get the money to irrigate or whatever. Just to keep your taxes down, you would abandon your fellow Americans to lives of deprivation."

To her surprise, Mack's rumbling laughter filled the car. "Well, Cassie, you can't say that we don't understand each other."

She laughed too. "No, Mack. No, you can't say that."

Mack stopped the car near Killin and roused the children. "Hey, kids, wake up. This is Finlarig Castle."

Martha, coming up from sleep, rubbed her eyes. "Is the Queen here?"

"No, love," Mack said, "but there is something else to see, something special."

"What, Mack?" Taylor asked eagerly. "What is it?"

"They say Finlarig Castle has the last beheading pit in Scotland."

"Oh, wow! Can we go in and see it?"

Martha crossed her arms and settled herself firmly on the car seat. "Not me. I don't want to look at it."

"Neither do I," Cassie said just as adamantly. "We'll wait in the car."

When Mack and Taylor were gone, Martha shook her head. "Mama, why do they want to see a place where people's heads got cut off?"

Cassie shuddered. "Darned if I know, honey. Men are just like that."

"And boys?"

"And boys, yes."

Martha pursed her lips. "But women are too smart for that, right? And girls."

"And girls. I like to think we are. You do understand, don't you, that this—this pit thing probably hasn't been used since medieval times."

"Then I guess men and boys are sort of middyval."

"Medieval," Cassie said, suppressing a giggle. "I suspect you're right, honey. They are far too interested in fighting—" Her mind skipped to the war in Vietnam and she made the effort to bring it back to peaceful Scotland. "In fighting and killing."

"But *we* aren't, are we, Mama?"

Cassie sat still, considering the possibilities. Had her nine-year-old daughter chanced upon the main difference between men and women? "No," she said slowly, "we aren't interested in fighting and killing, Martha. Nor in soldiering and uniforms and all the folderol that is attached to war." She continued her reflections in silence. And that is something, she thought, that we must keep in mind as we women liberate ourselves. To take positions of responsibility in a man's world did not mean that we should accept male values. The only valid position is one in which we can be sure that in government and business the values of women are of equal importance to men's values. We don't want to be men. Heaven forbid. We want to be women, but women whose values affect the future of our country.

Mack and Taylor returned, strutting a bit as if they personally had just beheaded a particularly unsavory highwayman.

The rain had stopped, so after lunch in Killin all four of them took a walk to stretch their legs before continuing their trip.

Cassie told Mack something of her conversation with Martha.

"That is one smart kid!" he said. "I think you have a Women's Libber on your hands though. I just hope she doesn't turn into one of those who want to be independent women but still want to have doors opened for them."

"Oh, Mack, that's such an awful cliché. It was old before the women's movement was even off the ground."

"Okay, okay. But you probably understand men as little as I understand women. I don't agree with you and Martha about men. Men like to play at being bloodthirsty, but they don't really want to kill anyone. Look at my kilt, for instance. I admit that I like dressing like a wild Highlander and wearing a dirk in my sock, but I can't imagine slashing away with a claymore at some poor guy."

"But don't you see, Mack, that to glamorize killing—" She stopped abruptly. How could she preach a nonviolent line when she herself had killed a man? It was true that it was in self-defense and in defense of her young son, but she had shot and killed her own half brother. What was more, she had hidden the body, she had covered up her crime.

Was it so far, after all, she wondered, from killing in what was perceived as defense of one's child to killing in what was perceived to be defense of one's country?

With Mack's next remarks he unwittingly drove the point home. "Even though we've left criminals out of the equation, I'm inclined to think that not just men find a need to kill. A mother would probably kill to defend her child."

"The mother-tiger syndrome?" she said absently.

Mack chuckled. "The mother-tiger syndrome. Say, we'd better round up the kids if we're going to drive to Perth."

In Perth they toured Scone Palace, a castle more to Martha's liking. There was no beheading pit.

"Scottish kings were crowned here at Mote Hill, over the Stone of Scone, from the ninth century to the late thirteenth century," Mack told them. "To be precise, until 1296, when the English seized the Stone and took it to Westminster Abbey."

When they left the Palace, they drove to Branklyn Garden for a stroll. The rain had stopped again and the late sun threw a clear yellow cast across the two acres of plants. Cassie's spirits lifted and she was able to consign the night of Bo's death to the black hole of the mind, to be stored away as all memories were which could not be allowed to rise to the surface of the mind.

As usual Cassie and Mack met in the hotel lounge when the children were in bed, but on their last night together in Scotland their conversation was abortive. There were hints of what might happen when they met again in Washington, words said quietly, half heard and not repeated, parts of sentences and partially completed thoughts. Cassie went upstairs early, leaving Mack to finish his brandy alone.

In Edinburgh the next day, Mack took them to the train and settled them in their compartment for the long ride south to London.

When there was nothing more to do, he stood by awkwardly, his bulk half filling the compartment.

"So I guess I'll see you back in Washington, Cassie."

"I guess so," she said, too uncomfortable to look into his face. "Will it be long? I mean, before you come back to the States?"

"No. Not long now. A few more weeks, that's all."

"I'm going to London to look at the Queen," Martha said confidently.

"Oh, that reminds me." Mack fished a card from his pocket. "I called a friend in London after you'd gone up last night, Cassie, and he says your best chance will be at Buckingham Palace. The Royals will be returning there from Scotland." He tapped a scribbled map on a card. "This is the best place for a good view. You'll be on her side of the car."

"Mack. Oh, Mack." Cassie felt as if something within her that had been frozen solid was thawing, melting away. "For you to take the time to call, to go to the trouble of—"

"Hey, it wasn't all that tough. My friend is a Royals buff. He has all the routines down pat."

Mack left the train but waited on the platform as if to be there in case of any last-minute problems.

Martha and Taylor waved at him until the train jerked and began to move. Cassie stayed at the window, smiling down at him. The train sped up and he ran with it for a few yards, waving to her and mouthing words she could not hear. She waved back. She waved until he looked like a toy, a tiny man with one arm raised in farewell.

Cassie was never quite sure whether she and Martha and Taylor took London by storm or if it took them. However it went, they loved every bit of it. The Tower of London, for instance, was steeped in enough gore to satisfy even an eleven-year-old boy, but it also had the crown jewels, which delighted Martha. They toured all the educational sites—Westminster Abbey, the British Museum—that Cassie thought they should see and still had time for the noneducational ones—Billy Sunday's Circus and Madame Tussaud's Wax Museum—that the children thought they should see. They had a marvelously wild shopping spree at Harrod's and an even wilder one in the Portobello Road. And on the last day of their stay in London, they went to Buckingham Palace.

With the usual Londoners' fondness for children the crowd passed Martha forward until she was right at the tall bars surrounding the Palace. She was close enough to the drive to receive what appeared to be a personal smile and wave from the Queen. She was starry-eyed as the crowd passed her back to her mother.

"Mama," she whispered, "she smiled at me, and waved! Wait till I tell Mack!" She drew herself to her full height. "Wait till I tell him, I've been to London to look at the Queen!"

As they toured the sights of London, however, Cassie had become aware of a dichotomy of feelings. She wanted to be seeing London and sharing London with Mack Cameron. Looking through his eyes, seeing things from his viewpoint, she would have a different, fuller comprehension of what she saw. And it would be the same thing for him, she knew. For the two of them to see London together would do more than just double their pleasure.

At the same time, as she went with her children from one place to another, she felt that rather than three in their party, there were four, that Mack explored London with them whether he was present or not. Her mind was full of unspoken comments, of the sort of comments shared with adults but not with children. Her children would not understand the immense pleasure she felt when she saw that the Star of India had been replaced in the display of the crown jewels by a neatly hand-printed card that said IN USE. According to Mack's informant, the Queen was still in Scotland that day. Was she wearing the Star of India while she watched her horses run? Perhaps she wore the royal jewel while she gave the royal corgis a run on the moors. But Mack was not there to indulge in fantasies with her, and Cassie's idle thoughts faded away.

She wished that Mack, with his easy command of history, had been with them in the British Museum to fill out her sketchy half-remembered description of the finding of the Rosetta Stone by Napoleon's troops in Egypt.

And in the evenings, when her exhausted children sank into bed while the western sky slowly darkened in the last delicate shades of gray and pink, she paced her room restlessly, longing to recall the memories of the day with someone, with Mack, or better, to go out with him into the streets when, as another American in London, T. S. Eliot, had said, "the evening is spread out against the sky . . ."

But Mack Cameron was in Aberdeen finishing his deal with the British government, preparing to pump oil out of the North Sea to increase Great Britain's wealth and, incidentally, his own. He was not in London to walk the narrow streets that reeked of Dickens, and he would not be in Washington, either. Except for that one brief interlude in Scotland, Cassie Steele and her children would go on as they had gone for almost four years. They would travel alone.

Washington in September was hot and muggy. Cassie was tired after the long trip home, and dispirited. She longed to be back in the fresh crisp air of Scotland. In retrospect, her week there with Mackenzie Cameron was dreamlike, a light-hearted time that had nothing to do with her regular life.

Three weeks away from Washington had given her a sense of perspective that she had been lacking before. Earlier, she had seen the various incidents of moral breakdown, from the popularity of drugs to the proliferation of smut, as separate issues from the war in Vietnam. With her new perspective, however, she began to see as parts of the whole what previously had been isolated incidents: the strong connection between spurning the establishment and scorn for established rules of behavior.

The war, she thought, was the central issue, and the time had come when she could no longer maintain her silence. She called in Cully Meecham and told him what she intended to do. "I have to speak out, Cully. There is nothing else that I can do in good conscience. It is my duty."

"In good conscience!" Cully shook his head slowly. "Do you truly believe that one congresswoman from a backwoods district in Oklahoma can turn it all around?"

"I have to try."

"I guess you realize that it means the end of your political career."

"Cully, Cully, do you think for one minute that I don't know what I'm risking? But I have to do it. I must."

He shrugged. "It's your funeral."

"Yours, too," she said with sudden insight. "You tied yourself to my star, didn't you? And now that it will fall, you will fall, too."

"I'm a big boy now, Cassie. I took my chances."

"Oh, Cully, you are a good friend! Please, will you help me figure out how to get the best press exposure for a statement?"

"How about making a speech in a deep cave, to no audience. Would that ease that conscience of yours?"

Cassie laughed. "Be serious."

"Let's see, then. You've got a speaking date coming up with the Washington Business and Professional Women."

"Come on, Cully. A woman arguing national policy in front of a group of local women? We can do better than that."

He shuffled the pages of her desk calendar. "Well, there's—no, that's next Wednesday. You wouldn't have time to write your speech."

"What is it? A speaking engagement?"

"You're down for twenty minutes of debate time on the floor of the House."

Cassie tapped a yellow pencil against her lower teeth. "That's it," she said thoughtfully. "A speech given to my peers in the House. Can you get the leaderships to okay the change of topic?"

"Reckon I can, if you're sure you want to do it."

"I'm sure. Oh, yes, I'm sure. And alert the press, too, Cully. I don't want this to get buried in the Congressional Record.

Ruby Vance left the Library of Congress early that afternoon and came to stay with the children so that Cassie could seclude herself in her upstairs sitting room. Late Tuesday night she read the final draft of her speech and sighed. It was no oratorical prize and it did not cover every point she wanted to make, but it would have to do. It was the best she could come up with in such a short time.

On Wednesday her secretary, sworn to secrecy, typed a final draft and made photocopies for the press. Cassie prepared herself in front of a mirror in her office, checking out her navy blue suit, straightening the blue and white striped bow-necked blouse and making sure that her blue kid pumps were gleaming.

In the House, the Democratic leader approached the speaker and he announced the new subject of her speech: government policies in Vietnam.

Forewarned by the leadership, party members took their seats, and as word of her new topic spread through the building, Republicans, too, left their offices and committee meetings for their seats in the House.

"As a Democratic member of the House of Representatives," Cassie said, "I find myself in the embarrassing position of opposing the policies of our Democratic President. In all good conscience, I can do no less."

She reviewed the roles Presidents Eisenhower and Kennedy had played in regard to Vietnam, but she set the responsibility for the country's present plight in Vietnam solidly on the shoulders of Lyndon Baines Johnson.

"In order to gain our cooperation, the President has lied to us. He lied about the cost of the war in dollars, in casualties, in the effect our fighting has had on the enemy; and in regard to what may end by being the costliest result of the war, he has concealed knowledge of that other, less direct result of the war in Vietnam, the continuing erosion of the American moral fiber."

She looked up from her notes and surveyed both sides of the aisle. "It is obvious that a society riddled at the top with lies and dishonesty can not and will not maintain a sound moral commitment at its base."

She looked back to her typed speech. "We have spent, so far, almost sixteen thousand American lives in Vietnam. We are paying for the war at a cost of seventy-two billion dollars a year. And yet, all this enormous expense in human lives and in dollars has not helped the people we wanted to protect. We have not ameliorated the position of the Vietnamese people. They are dying in droves, trapped between warring armies."

"We," she said, smiling at her audience, "we are Democrats and Republicans, men and women, doves and hawks, but above all, we are Americans. Since the days of Benjamin Franklin, Americans have been blessed with a somewhat pragmatic view of life. If our car turns out to be a lemon, we don't pour good money after bad in a futile effort to repair it. Instead, we junk it, we write it off and we start again from scratch. Ladies and gentlemen, the war in Vietnam is a lemon and any effort to fix it will bear a horrific cost: the lives of our young men. There are the other costs of war, too: the dollar cost which will be paid by our children and their children, the criminalizing of dissent when we have fought for two hundred years to protect each citizen's freedom to say what he will, and that greatest cost of all—the breakdown of trust, of the government's faith in its people and the concurrent breakdown of the people's faith in their government."

She looked at a page of her speech to read. "I am reminded of the words William Butler Yeats wrote about the Russian revolution:

"The best lack all conviction, while the worst
Are full of passionate intensity."

Cassie squared the pages of her speech on the rostrum and looked out at her audience.

"I propose, therefore, that we, the members of the United States House of Representatives, as a body request that the President shall undertake in a speedy manner the withdrawal of all American personnel from Vietnam. I propose that we declare not that the Vietnam war is won or lost but, simply, that we no longer wish to participate in it.

"I ask that the leadership of this House bring this plan to the floor of this House as a resolution and I ask of you, the members, only that you vote your own consciences. Can we as a nation afford the loss of our young men? Can we afford to lose our national wealth? Most of all, can we afford to lose faith in one another, in the President and in the American people?

"I do not believe for one minute that the forces of communism— 'domino effect' or not—will defeat the forces of democracy in battle. We will be defeated only by being tricked into it, by wasting our people, our resources, and by putting aside our great sense of a common goal for all Americans."

The applause was tentative at first then grew, if not to a tumult to a respectable show of support. Cassie could not tell whether more applause came from her part or from the Republicans across the aisle. She hoped that it was bipartisan, because acceptance of her proposal would have to be bipartisan to succeed.

She need not have worried about her speech getting attention, however. It was all over the afternoon papers and the network news.

"LBJ is ready to shoot you and stake you out for the buzzards!" Cully Meecham reported. "He says you'll never be elected again, not even as dogcatcher."

Cassie flushed in anger. "Does he expect me to recant? I won't do it, Cully. Here I stand."

He chuckled. "You and Martin Luther, right? You goin' to nail a copy of your speech on a church door? Anyway, you can't back out now. You got to face it, Cassie, you made yourself some damn powerful enemies."

"Support for my views is building."

"The support, maybe, but not the votes in Congress. Folks will tell you what you want to hear, but when it comes down to it, they'll vote the party line."

Cassie made some new enemies and some new friends as well. Some of the compliments on her speech were surreptitious, quick words behind a pillar in the Capitol lobby, but some were open and were heard right across the country.

On the day after her speech, she received a cable from Scotland:

ABERDEEN REACTION FAVORABLE ALSO BBC STOP IF LOSE PRESENT JOB APPLY SOONEST CAMOIL STOP LOVE MACK

Cassie's speech was summarized in the next week's news magazines, and long quotations appeared in *Time:*

Cassandra, daughter of Priam and Hecuba, was cursed by Apollo to make prophecies which were always true but were never believed. Her namesake, Representative Cassandra Steele, Oklahoma (D), tried her own hand at prophecy this week, comparing the war in Vietnam to an automotive lemon and suggesting that we junk it before it destroys our national will. Representative Steele's attempt to lead her colleagues out of the bewilderness of Vietnam did not meet with approval in the White House.

The article in *Time* placed Cassie's views on the war firmly in the public eye. To push those views she participated in newspaper and TV interviews and made personal appearances when she could find the time.

There were several more cables from Mack in the next month, and a long letter explaining how the British bureaucracy had once more tossed a monkey wrench into the works and thereby delayed his return to Washington.

Cassie ran her fingertips over his letter, as if she were touching the man himself. Did she want him to return? She was not sure. All that she knew was that she did not have time for Mack Cameron during that particular period of her life. She simply did not have time for him.

Chapter 34

In December, Cassie flew her children to Ballard to spend Christmas with Amelia and James Steele. Martha, at ten, and Taylor, eleven, did not seem to notice how much their grandparents had aged, but Cassie saw it immediately. In her seventies, Amelia was shrinking, and she had developed a definite dowager's hump. James was thin, fit-looking for his age, but his cheeks were sunken until his nose emerged from his face like the prow of a four-master. They loved seeing the children. Taylor was at that rewarding, if brief, point of early puberty when he was content to spend hours with his grandfather's stories of Oklahoma's early days as a state. Martha was equally fascinated by Amelia's descriptions of the way she was dressed during the First World War: the quasimilitary, long-skirted suits and the white headwraps the ladies wore while they rolled bandages to be sent to the Front.

James broke away from Taylor to question Cassie about her antiwar stand in Congress. "It's not popular with the local party, but I must admit that I agree with you. I think Lyndon ought to bite the bullet and say, 'We can't win this one, boys, so let's pack up and go home.' "

Cassie nodded. "But how can we get the local people to understand this, James?"

He smiled. "Cassie, why don't you just leave that to me. My word still carries some weight around this state."

Cassie remembered how he used that weight in the old days. A phone call to an Oklahoma City bank, a personal note to an attorney, a private word in the ear of a union official. Yes, she thought, James Steele had been a powerful man in Oklahoma politics and it was very likely that he still was.

Mack Cameron had been back in the United States for a week before Cassie found out that he was home and immediately was thrown into emotional turmoil. One minute she longed to hear his voice, and the next she hoped she would never see him again. She heard that he was in Oklahoma.

He called her a few days later when he was back in Washington, but Cassie was not terribly cordial.

"Yes," she said. "I heard that you were back from Scotland."

"I would have called you but I needed to do something else first."

"Oh, did you?" she said distantly.

"Yep, sure did. Something that involves you." He ignored the coolness in her tone if, she thought, he had even noticed it. "Look, Cassie, are you free Saturday night?"

She checked her desk calendar. "I suppose I could be."

"Who will stay with the kids? Ruby?"

"No, she's spending all her time in the library. Probably Angelina."

"Okay, then. Let me pick you up at two that afternoon. And wear something that would be comfortable for long walks, will you?"

"Long walks? Mack, what on earth are you—"

A firm click on the receiver told her that he was gone.

Cassie worked hard that week to meet her responsibilities and those new challenges her speech to the House had brought her. Between appointments, however, she found her thoughts returning to Mack Cameron. She wondered what sort of crazy plans he had made for her. She knew she should have turned him down flat, but it was not his plans but he who appeared in her vision: his amused blue eyes, his tousled blond hair, the big grin he turned on her like a warm floodlight, his hand on her hand, touching it, covering it.

Cassie was ready long before he appeared at her Georgetown door. He came in the house to hug Martha, to shake hands with Taylor and, to Cassie's surprise, to exchange melodramatic winks with Angelina.

"They be fine, Mizteel. Me and the kids, we all be okay. You no worry, okay?"

"For heaven's sake, Angelina! I'll only be away for a few hours."

For some reason Angelina thought that was the funniest thing she had ever heard. She exploded with giggles, wiping her eyes with her apron. Mack tugged Cassie's arm, and after giving Martha and Taylor quick good-bye kisses she allowed herself to be hurried to his car.

"What's the rush, Mack? And where are we going?"

He immediately began to discuss her speech in the House. "What kind of reaction did you get in Congress?"

He kept to that topic and the related one of the progress of the war in Vietnam. Cassie was impressed by his clear understanding of an area made shadowy by claim and counterclaim. She was so interested in what he had to say that when she first looked around she realized that they were in Maryland. And still he had not answered her question about where they were going.

"Mack, you do know, don't you, that we're in Maryland. Where on earth are you taking me?"

"Just down to this next road to start with," he said. He turned the car and drove down a gravel road to stop next to a low tower with weather apparatus on its roof.

"What is this? A private airport?"

He looked around in mock surprise. "Why, I do believe it is! Wait in the car a minute, will you?"

She was too confused by the developments to do anything but

wait. At any rate, he reappeared in a few minutes and shepherded her toward a small plane waiting on the runway. He buckled her into the passenger seat and jogged around to get into the pilot's seat.

"Mack!" Her confusion had changed to alarm. "Where's the pilot? Where are we going? And what on earth are you doing?"

"I'm the pilot," he said absently as he ran his fingers over the banks of switches and checked the lights on the control panel. "And don't worry, Cassie, I've been flying for fifteen years and I'm checked out for multiengine aircraft, instrument flight, the works."

"But what are you—where are you—"

He turned in his seat to grin at her and put one long finger to his lips. "Shhh. I'm kidnapping you, Cassie Steele. And I warn you, don't mess with me. I've already broken one federal law, the Mann Act, by transporting you across the Maryland state line."

"No," Cassie said, the lawyer in her coming out, "the Mann Act is broken only when the woman is transported for immoral purposes and—" She swallowed. "Oh," she said in a small voice.

Mack leered at her in caricature of a dirty old man, and broke into a belly laugh. "Ah *ha*, me proud beauty—"

The radio crackled and he broke off to acknowledge the instructions, taxied the plane to the end of the runway and swung it into position for the take-off.

Cassie waited until they were successfully airborne before asking again, "Mack, where are we going?"

"Did you know you're beginning to sound like a broken record?"

"But I—"

"We're going to Hilton Head. I have a place down there."

Cassie took a deep breath. "Mack. Now, Mack. This is all terribly romantic and I might even like it under other circumstances, but I do have a job to do."

"It's not romantic," he said shortly. "It's business."

Cassie sat back, feeling diminished. She had been a fool to reveal herself to him like that. Still, the way he had acted in Scotland, his wisecrack about the Mann Act—had all that been no more than a line? He seemed to enjoy her company, but he had never made a pass at her. She did not understand Mack Cameron. She did not understand him at all.

It was almost dark when they landed, but a car was waiting and with it a black man wearing a chauffeur's cap. When he stopped the car, he darted ahead of them to conceal his cap and open the front door for them in the role of a houseman welcoming the lord of the manor and his lady. While Mack helped Cassie with her coat, he issued a stream of instructions. "Now, George," he said at the end, "we won't want a real dinner. Ask Minna to fix up a few trays of substantial snacks, then you and she can go on home."

"Yessuh, Mr. Cameron. Minna'll do that directly."

"Will that be all right with you, Cassie? I'm afraid that by the time we finish our business it will be too late to have dinner."

"Yes, of course," Cassie said. Behind him, she could see the living room, with its two-story-high ceiling and with huge windows that faced, presumably, the sea, although it was too dark to tell.

Two men were waiting in the living room with drinks in their hands, standing before a roaring fire in a fieldstone fireplace. As Cassie and Mack came through to the living room, one of them stepped forward.

"Why, I know you!" she said in surprise. "You're—"

"Yes. I'm Jim Weston, the vice chairman of the Republican National Committee, and this is Frank Kelly, an associate. We're here in Hilton Head for a conference and sneaked away to meet you. And let me assure you, Congresswoman Steele, that nothing that is said here will ever go beyond the four people present."

"Cassie, let me fix you a drink."

"No, thank you, Mack." She smiled at Weston. "If I'm to be in a room with three Republicans, I'd better keep a clear head."

"A wise woman," Jim Weston said, "and if you don't mind my

saying so, a highly attractive one, too. I can see that the reports I've received have not been exaggerated."

Mack made a drink for himself and sat next to Cassie on the couch.

George and Minna came in, each carrying a tray. Cassie spotted Virginia ham and beaten biscuits, and muttered to Mack, "This is hardly your blue plate special."

"Is there anything else, Mr. Cameron? Some ice maybe, or—"

"No, George, this is just fine. You two can take off now. Oh, I do want to say one thing. If there's anyone here you recognize, just forget he was here, okay?"

"Yessuh. We'll forget *she* was here. Miz Steele, me and Minna, we just want you to know that we're mighty proud to see you, ma'am."

"Why, thank you. I appreciate that."

"Yessum." Minna beamed at her. "But you wasn't never here, was you? No, *ma'am*."

Weston watched them leave. "As I said, the reports I've received appear to be true. Your recognition factor extends far beyond your congressional district in Oklahoma."

Cassie had no comment to make on that. They sat in silence for a few moments until they heard the back door close and a car start up behind the house.

"Well, gentlemen," Mack said, "Congresswoman Steele has made a long trip and has no idea why. I suggest that you get to the point."

Jim Weston set his drink on the table by his chair and went over to stand by the fireplace. "You're right, Mack. Mrs. Steele, we appreciate your coming with Mack here on faith and we hope that you'll consider our proposition in the same way."

Cassie nodded, indicating no more than a willingness to listen.

He watched her face closely. "Mrs. Steele, we propose that you cross the aisle, that you become a member of the Republican party."

Cassie was too surprised to make an intelligent comment. "What? You mean you want me to—why should I—"

"Let me make it clear from the start that we have no intention of using a hard sell on you." Weston smiled. "You are far too intelligent for that. We are inclined to think that there is a great future for you in the Republican party, but I will admit that we may need you more than you need us. We need a woman, and we need one whose opposition to Johnson is crystal clear."

"Mrs. Steele." Frank Kelly spoke for the first time. "Richard Nixon is going to win the 1968 election."

"You are certain of that?" she said.

"I am. He will win because he will promise to get our boys out of Vietnam."

Cassie laughed. "Mr. Kelly, I am sure you've been in politics long enough to know how much weight campaign promises carry. Remember, President Johnson said he would not send American boys *into* Vietnam."

"We remember," Jim Weston said. "And those words are coming home to haunt him." He looked down at Kelly. "I'll differ with you, Frank. Richard Nixon will win in '68, but it will be because Lyndon Johnson *can't* win."

To Cassie the discussion seemed pointless. "So?"

Weston grinned at her. "A lawyer's mind. *So,* Mrs. Steele, we are here to tell you that 1968 will be a Republican landslide. You will have to defend your seat in the House this year, and we want to ask you to cross the aisle. We want you to run—and to win—as a Republican."

"Look, my constituents like me. I've held that seat before and I will hold it again. To be frank, Mr. Weston, I don't need you."

Weston sat down and laughed. "My dear, my dear, do you really believe the vice chairman of the RNC has time to hassle with a congressional district in the hill country of Oklahoma? Mrs. Steele, we want you to run for that seat one more time in preparation, and then we want you to run again in 1970, not for the House but for the United States Senate."

The Senate. A thrill of excitement ran through Cassie. To be one of the few women who belonged to "the most exclusive men's club in the world." What couldn't she do with the power of a Senator, not just for Oklahoma but for the nation? Senator Steele. Senator Cassie Steele. The words had a sweet taste.

"What if I lost that election?"

"You wouldn't. That Senate seat is one of our targeted races for 1970, which means that you would get extra campaign funds and big-name speakers, probably even the President himself. But if by some crook of fate you lost, your name would still be well enough known to make a cabinet-level appointment a logical choice for the President."

"Do you mean a position actually in the cabinet?"

Weston chuckled. "Why not?"

"But why?"

He leaned forward. "Because we need you. And we need you badly enough to make it worth your while to cross the aisle in the House."

His answer did not satisfy Cassie. Why did they need her so much? Why Cassie Steele? But then she did understand and she saw the Republican's plan laid out as neatly as an architect's sketch, measured with calipers and drawn with a T square.

"Could I have that drink now, Mack?" she asked, not because she needed a drink but because she needed a few minutes to consider her assessment of the Republicans' plan.

Mack handed her a glass but she set it down, untouched, on the coffee table. Yes, she thought, she could see what they were doing. They needed her because they were afraid of her. They thought she could and would be elected to the Senate from Oklahoma, no matter which party sponsored her, and they wanted to enroll her as a Republican to pre-empt the Democrats. But what was she to do about it, now that she understood their plan?

They had done their maneuvering, she thought, getting Mack to deliver her to Hilton Head, arranging a secret meeting and confronting her with the possibility of a major change in her life. Now it was her turn to manipulate them.

"You gentlemen realize, I'm sure, that I can't give you a decision tonight."

Frank Kelly looked slightly disappointed, but Weston smiled. "Of course," he said smoothly. "We understand."

"I will promise as you did, however, that no word of this meeting will go beyond the four of us."

"Thank you. It could prove to be embarrassing," Weston said.

"To me, too." Cassie gave him a quick smile. "All I can say now is that I am honored by your proposition and that I appreciate the spirit in which it was made. I promise that I will give it careful thought."

Jim Weston stood up. "There is just one thing, Mrs. Steele, just to save us all from any future embarrassment. For a presidential appointment, an FBI check would be necessary. Is there any reason, any reason at all for you to suspect that you would not pass such an investigation?"

Cassie thought immediately of her half brother, Bo. She could just imagine their faces if she said, "Oh, no, other than that one little old murder." But Henry Starr was the only living soul who knew about that, and Henry would never tell anyone. Of that she was as sure as she was of her own name.

"Nothing, Mr. Weston."

"I did not think there would be anything. Tell me, when can we expect an answer from you, Mrs. Steele? I don't want to rush you, but—"

"I'm going to Oklahoma next week, Mr. Weston, to my ranch, and by the time I return I'll have an answer for you."

When Jim Weston and Frank Kelly left in their rented car, Cassie turned to Mack Cameron. "What do you think of *that?*"

"Crossing the aisle? Running for the Senate as a Republican?"

"No. About a sharecropper's daughter becoming a cabinet officer!"

Mack looked at her soberly. "I don't think that is exactly what Weston said. I believe he said 'cabinet level.' "

"Mack, come on!" Cassie was irritated. "He all but promised me a cabinet position."

" 'All but' are the operative words there, Cassie. He didn't make any promises, you know. It's not down in black and white."

Cassie laughed. "Are you telling me that the men in the upper levels of your party can't be trusted?"

"Can they be trusted in yours?"

Cassie paced the room nervously, only to stop suddenly and look at Mack. "How about that long walk you promised me?"

"The moon is up now. I think there'll be enough light."

Mack insisted that she add a windbreaker of his to the pantsuit and pea jacket she had worn from Washington. She felt like a child in her father's jacket, but when they reached the open beach she appreciated the protection his coat provided against the damp cold wind. She stumbled once and took Mack's arm.

"You seem to think I'm pretty naïve about politics, Mack."

His rumbling laugh was transmitted through his arm. "You, naïve, Cassie? Never! But you are human, you know, just like the rest of us. You believe what you want to believe."

She found herself laughing with him. "Yes. You are so right! Not that it matters, though, because I'm not going to change parties."

"Good."

She stopped and looked up at him in the white moonlight. "I thought you wanted me to become a Republican."

"I do want you to. You're quick and intelligent and able to break a big problem down to understandable terms, and you have a hell of a lot of stamina: all the attributes of a successful politician. But I don't want you to change affiliation for the wrong reasons."

"And what are the wrong reasons, Mack?"

"You know. For personal gain, for the possibility of a cabinet job. Because you've been romanced by the pros." He walked on a few steps, scuffing the sand. "Sure, I want you to join my party, but if you ever do, I want you to do it for your constituents, for the people of Oklahoma rather than your own personal gain. You have to live with yourself, Cassie."

Cassie laughed sharply. "What makes you think I'm so damn noble, Mack? What if I'm in it for me, for what I can get out of it?"

He stopped and for a moment all she heard was waves slapping on the beach as the tide came in. "You aren't, I know, because I believe in you, Cassie Steele. You are a good person."

She could not look at him. "Oh, Mack, if you knew more about me, if you knew the things I've done—"

"I don't need to know anything more. I know you as you are now, and that is enough for me."

Cassie took her hand from his arm. "Let's go back to the house."

"Are you cold?"

"Yes. And anyway, I have to get back to Washington."

"You can't."

"And just what do you mean by that?"

"Just what I said." He grinned at her. "The air strip closes at dark. We can go back tomorrow morning."

She felt a flash of anger. "And you did this to me, knowing that we couldn't—"

"I kidnapped you, remember?"

"But my children are—"

"Are safe with Angelina," he said. "I arranged it with her by phone this morning."

Cassie remembered the dramatic exchange of winks in her front hall. In spite of her irritation, she began to see the humor of it. "You—you—"

"Kidnapper?" He laughed. "You have to admit that I'm damned efficient. Not every kidnapper sets up a baby sitter for his victim."

She turned to face him and clutched her hands together like Lillian Gish in a silent movie. Weakly she cried, "And now you'll wreak your will on this poor unprotected girl!"

He grinned broadly. "Well, yes, I had considered that."

The game suddenly shifted gears. Deep within her body Cassie felt a flutter of emotion, and then a surge of desire. "No," she said flatly, denying both the game and her response to it.

Mack backed away from her, one step. "No?"

Without a word she turned and walked down the beach toward his house. She had been compliant with other men, she remembered. She had willingly allowed men to run her life, with Jimmy Steele and Eliot and even Dix, and it had led to nothing but grief in the long run. She would no longer play that game. She no longer needed to play it. She was in charge of herself, of her body, and she would not give over that control, not to any man.

In the house, their talk was limited to brief discussions of ways and means. Mack showed her to the guest room and a bathroom supplied with new toiletries. He opened a dresser drawer to reveal pajamas of champagne-colored silk, with a robe to match, still in their original folds. She followed him to the hall door and closed it firmly behind him.

Her anger at his easy assumption of her availability rode with her as she showered and put on the silk pajamas, as she climbed into bed and pulled the blanket up to her chin. The anger ebbed and was replaced by restlessness. She got up, slipped on the silk robe and went to the windows overlooking the beach.

The tide was coming in and moonlight topped each wave with white: crests of foam against the dark sky beyond, each wave building until it caught the light then falling, sliding down into the dark oblivion of the sea.

"Oh, hell," she said aloud because yes, she was in charge of her own life, and yes, she was in control, but there were emotions and desires that went far beyond that, far beyond her capacity for control. "Oh, hell."

Barefooted she slipped out of the guest room and down the hall to the master bedroom, which had been warmly lit and welcoming earlier, when Mack led her past it to the guest room. The door was open.

She hesitated in the doorway and when she spoke it was no more than a whisper against the crashing of the waves on the beach. Her voice was no louder than the silken shuffle of her robe. "Mack?"

"Yes?" his deep voice answered.

As her eyes grew accustomed to the dim light, she saw his over-sized bed, and on it in a splash of moonlight like the reverse of a shadow, Mack himself, watching her.

She crossed the room to stand above him, looking down. "Mack?" she said again. "Do you always take 'no' for an answer?"

Chapter 35

 Without a word Mack stretched both arms up to her and she sank down on the bed, into his arms, as if her whole life and his had been lived in preparation for this one moment. She let herself relax, let herself go limp in the safety of his arms and let her silken robe slide across his bare skin.

He laughed, a rumble that started somewhere deep within his body and welled up to sound. She felt it with her own body, a laugh that was like a trembling in solid earth. And she realized that she was laughing, too, a soft giggle at first that exploded with his rumble into a tumult of laughter that filled the darkest corners of the room.

He pulled her close, still laughing, but his mouth found hers and the laughter disappeared into a long deep kiss. "My God, Cassie," he whispered. "I've wanted you so. I need you so much."

"*You* need *me?*" she said but any answer he might have made was lost in another kiss. His hands explored her back, pulling her closer to him, always closer, until their bodies were sealed together. She pushed away to shrug off her robe but he stopped her.

"Wait." He reached out with one long arm to switch on the bedside lamp and then he eased off her robe. In the pale light of the moon, they both watched as his large blunt fingers worked at the tiny padded buttons of her pajama top. She slipped her hand under his and undid the buttons, leaving it to him to pull the

459

garment away. As they were exposed, he kissed her breasts, one and then the other.

She slipped away from him to stand up by the bed. She eased the elastic over her hips and let her pajama bottoms slide down to a pool of silk at her feet. She did not look down at her body. She did not need to look because his reaction to it was reflected in his eyes.

"Cassie," he said thickly. "Oh, God, Cassie!"

She went to his waiting arms, lying on top of his body with her bare skin pressed against his from her face to her toes. He wrapped his arms around her to hold her tight against him and adjusted his position so that he was between her legs, rubbing himself against the most sensitive area of her body. He raised his hips, pushing himself against her and at the same time clutching her buttocks with his big hands, until she could stand no more. She rolled off of him and instantly he was upon her, touching his sex against hers gently, then more demandingly, prolonging for both of them an exquisite agony.

"Mack!" she cried and with one sure thrust he entered her, probing the depths of her body as it raised itself to meet his. Cassie cried out again, "Mack!" and as if her cry were a signal, he gripped her body and drove himself into her, to the final depth. He sank down on her then, depleted.

"Cassie," he murmured. "Oh, my love, my Cassie."

She, too, was spent. She shifted her body slightly and Mack would have rolled off of her, would have relieved her of his weight, but she gripped his body. "No," she whispered. "Stay. Stay with me, darling."

They dozed together, rousing only to whisper "darling" and "love" and "dear," those words that have been battered and bruised by long usage but have never been replaced.

The first light of dawn was glowing in the east when Cassie nestled against Mack, then drew away to stretch hugely and laugh in delight. He laughed too, and put one arm around her as if to keep her from getting too far away from him.

"Mack, I wish you would explain one thing to me. We have known each other for a long time. We have even traveled together for a week. And you have never so much as made one little pass at me. Last night, even. Last night I damn near had to rape you to get your attention!"

He rolled on his side and looked at her with great interest. "You rape me? Now there's a new idea. Let's see, I suppose you could— or if I—"

"Mack! Answer my question! Why have you played hard to get?"

He sat up, pulling the sheet over his lower body. "I will answer it, Cassie. From the first time I ever saw you—it was at a Washington party, remember?"

But Cassie was looking at his body instead of remembering. My Lord, she thought, his chest is the size of a barrel. And how does he get shoulders that broad through a door? It became necessary for her to reach up and measure those shoulders. Mack laughed and caught her hands, kissing the palm of each in turn.

He glared at her with mock severity. "Have you heard a word I said?"

She grinned at him and caressed his stubbled chin. "Not a word."

"I was answering your question. I wanted you from the first minute I saw you. God, how I wanted you! But the more I knew you, the more I admired you. The way you do your job as congresswoman, your high ethical standards, the way you're bringing up your kids—you are some woman, Cassie Steele. And I knew right away that you are a woman who thinks for herself. I was afraid that if I made a pass, if I pushed you, you would dump me the way you dumped Eliot Peabody."

"I guess I did dump him at that, didn't I? Poor old Eliot."

"Well, I had no intention of becoming 'poor old Mack,' so I decided I had better wait until I became as important to you as you are to me."

"And now you are."

"Am I?" There was no longer any laughter in his eyes. They were dead serious. "Am I really so important to you, my dear?"

Cassie sat up too, but she did not bother to pull the sheet up. "Yes. Yes, Mack, you are." She tried to laugh but what she said was too serious and too important to joke about. "Where else could I find a man who knows me better than I know myself? And besides that—" She hesitated and with a deep sigh of trust, she cast aside her defenses. She looked directly into his blue eyes. "I love you, Mack Cameron."

He put his arms around her. "Do you? Do you really love me, Cassie? Because I love you so damn much I can hardly stand it."

"I do, Mack. Yes! I do!"

"Then prove it, will you?"

She laughed and waved a hand at the rumpled bed. "I thought I'd done that already."

"It came damn close." He grinned at her. "But I'm not just one of your good-time boys, you know. I'm not in this just for a roll in the hay, no matter how much I enjoy that." He started to get out of bed, but pulled at his sheet and sat back. "Look, I'd do this properly, on my knees and all that, but I think I'd look pretty damn silly when I'm naked as a jaybird. Cassie—" He cleared his throat. "Cassie Steele, will you do me the honor of becoming my wife?"

"Huh?" she said thickly.

Mack clicked his tongue in mock disbelief. "And I said you are intelligent! For God's sake, Cassie, marry me, will you?"

"Why I never thought—I don't know what to—Mack, I'm forty-two years old!"

"And I'm forty-six. Gosh, should we buy our burial plots now or do you think it's safe to wait a week or two? Cassie, what difference does age make?"

"Mack, I can't give you a baby, not at forty-two."

"Well, surprise, surprise, Cassie, I don't want a baby, not at forty-six. I do want to be sort of a father to Martha and Taylor, though. Do you think they'd mind?"

"Mind! They'd eat it up with a spoon!"

"Well, then."

"Well, then." Cassie climbed out of bed and stood up straight and proud to face him, ignoring the fact that she was stark naked. "Mr. Cameron, sir, the congresswoman from Oklahoma accepts your proposal, in full cognizance of the legalities thereby implied."

It was Mack's turn to say, "Huh?"

"Of course I'll marry you, you idiot. And listen, your proposing to me only beat out my proposing to you by about two minutes!"

Mack beamed at her and slid down into bed. He held his arms out. "Come here, woman. Let's seal it with a kiss."

She slipped back into bed. "Or whatever."

"Or whatever."

On the flight back to Maryland Sunday and in the car on the way to Washington, Cassie and Mack had a million decisions to make: The date for their wedding (summer, when the primary was over), the size (small), the make-up of the guest list (private). They agreed that they did not want to become involved in complicated plans.

The children had just returned from school when Cassie and Mack arrived in Georgetown. Both Taylor and Martha were delighted with the news that Mack was to be their new father, and Angelina looked so smug that Cassie knew that within a few days it would appear that their engagement to marry had been personally arranged by Angelina.

During the next week, Cassie glowed with happiness. She and Mack saw each other at every opportunity, but only when they could manage to be alone at Mack's hotel. It was difficult to be discreet in Washington, but it was not impossible.

When Blair Fuller Howe called her at home early on a Monday morning, Cassie was only sorry that she had not called her friend first.

"Blair! I've been planning to call to tell you that—"

"Cassie, I have only a minute, but I'm so worried about you that I had to call."

"Worried? Why on earth—"

"My brother mentioned it at a family dinner last night. He said it's going to be all over town that you had a secret meeting with some Republican bigwigs and that you'll probably switch parties."

"Damn! Did he say where he heard it, Blair?"

"No, he didn't, but you know his wife Muffy. She goes everywhere."

"Sees all, tells all."

"That's about it, Cassie. Listen, I told him there was nothing to it, but if you want to track down where he heard the rumor, you have his phone number."

Cassie hesitated, but Blair was a good, true friend. "The first part is true. I did meet with some Republicans, but I am definitely not going to cross the aisle."

For a moment, the telephone was silent. "I'm relieved to know the truth. I have to run now, Cassie."

"But I want to tell you about—"

"Later, Cassie, later!"

Cassie acted on her first impulse and called Mack. "Remember how your Republican friends insisted on our discretion? Well, it appears that they leaked it themselves, Mack. The word is out that I met with the Republicans and what's more, that I'm going to join them."

"They are no friends of mine, Cassie. It's true that I took you down there, but that was a favor for an old Oklahoma friend, a man I owe a lot to. Believe me, love, I had no idea they would let word of the meeting get out."

The "love" made her knees go weak. "Of course I believe you, darling. It's just that I don't quite know what to do about it."

"Go public, Cassie. That's what you'll have to do. Stand up in front of the press and tell them exactly what happened." He chuckled. "The truth and nothing but the truth, but it might be wise to avoid telling them the *whole* truth."

"Mack, darling. I can't wait to see you."

"How about my hotel after your committee meeting tonight? Will Angelina stay late?"

"Angelina will grow gills and become a fish if that's what it takes to get you into the family!"

"Then let's put the poor lady out of her misery. Tonight let's set a date for our wedding."

Cassie's heart pounded, but she forced herself to sound businesslike. "I'll bring my planning calendar."

"You do that, love, and don't forget to bring—" He lowered his voice to a sibilant whisper.

"Mack! Can you say that on the telephone?"

He laughed. "I just did, didn't I? See you tonight!"

She sat still for a moment, looking at the telephone. Go public, Mack said and he was probably right. She picked up the phone and rang her office for Cully Meecham.

"Cassie," he said, "what's all this about you meeting with the chairman of the Republican National Committee?"

"Vice chairman, Cully." Her laugh was shaky. "News spreads fast, doesn't it?"

"Yeah, but how come I'm about the last to hear it?"

Cassie gave him a brief rundown on her conversation with the Republicans. "Cully, I'm worried about all the rumors they've started of my changing parties. Don't you think we should call a press conference and nip the gossip in the bud?"

"Yeah," he said reluctantly, "but you know how press conferences are. They can get out of hand."

Cassie laughed. "Cully, I'm an old hand at fielding questions. You don't have to worry about me! And don't forget, the House will rise for Christmas in ten days. By January I'll be yesterday's news."

Eight or nine reporters gathered in Cassie Steele's office at two that afternoon. None of the big-name reporters was there and there was no television coverage. For once Cassie was glad that a

U.S. Congresswoman ranked low on the totem pole of newsworthy people. In a brief statement she walked carefully along the thin line of truth. She did not mention the Republican's suggestion that she run for the Senate, for instance, since the more she thought about it the more she felt that she might well be the Democratic candidate in 1970.

In effect she gave them only the news that the Republican party had invited her to cross the aisle and that she had rejected the idea. When the more experienced reporters realized that no hot news was going to come out of the press conference they relaxed and went on fishing expeditions.

"What about Cameron Oil? Is it true that Mack Cameron himself flew you down to Hilton Head?"

"Yes, it is. Mr. Cameron is an old and valued friend—and a Republican."

Another old hand, a man, grinned. "Just how valued a friend is he, Congresswoman?"

Cassie smiled at him. "I don't believe that lies within the purviews of this meeting, Robert."

After a few more idle questions, the reporters began to fold their notebooks away. Cassie relaxed and had begun to chat with a few of them when one more question was asked.

It came from a young woman in the back of the group, obviously a girl so new at her job that she did not understand the unspoken rules of the Washington game in regard to the private lives of the men and women in Congress. Either that or she was willing to break the rules to make a name for herself to jump-start her journalistic career.

"Congresswoman Steele!" Cassie turned at the sound of the woman's voice. "Congresswoman, will you comment on the recently revealed information about your past?"

Cassie stared at her. "I don't know what you're talking about."

The woman's voice became shrill with excitement. "Congresswoman, is it true that you have had an abortion?"

Cassie, Cully Meecham, everyone in the room turned to spot the questioner in the back row. Cassie saw that she was young, very young, and that her embarrassment at being the cynosure made her blush in two splotches of red that appeared on her cheeks like poorly blended cosmetics.

The room was silent as a tomb as slowly, slowly the faces of the reporters turned back to Cassie. They waited for her reply.

The problem, as only Cassie knew, was that she had no idea how to answer the girl's question. It was true that an abortion had taken place, but when? When was it? It was as if by dating the event she could strip the word "abortion" of its emotive burden and make it no more than one more paper to file away in a dusty cabinet. Nineteen forty-five. Yes, she thought, that was the year. Jimmy Steele and she had still been married in 1945. In an effort to salvage something from their marriage, she had slept with Jimmy while he campaigned for a political position. She had become pregnant, as she hoped she would, but the doctor had sent her to the hospital for what he called a routine examination and, she learned later, at the behest of Jimmy and James Steele, the doctor had performed a therapeutic abortion. Jimmy had given her more than a baby. He had given her gonorrhea. She left Jimmy Steele then, and Ballard, parlaying a promise of silence into a car and enough money to make a new start in Dallas.

But now, in a Capitol conference room, the abortion had come back to haunt her. And it must have come direct from Oklahoma, from someone who had access either to the doctor who performed the operation or to his records. From someone who hated her.

She stood silent before the reporters, desperate because so much depended on her next words. Denial of the accusation would be a lie and one that would probably be revealed as a lie. Acknowledgment of the truth, on the other hand, would open a box more crammed with evils than Pandora's own box. The conservative citizens of Oklahoma could accept an abortion only if it were therapeutic and for a reason that was beyond reproach. What would happen if Cassie defended herself, if she admitted to the abortion but revealed the cause? Jimmy would simply deny it and she was certain that nowhere, nowhere was it down in black and white that her own husband had given her a venereal disease. James might make a statement, but who would listen? People were always all too ready to heed rumor and ignore the truth.

As was all too common, not the man but the woman would bear the brunt of public disapproval. And to this particular woman, to Cassie Steele, it would mean the end of her political career.

Since she could neither deny nor acknowledge the abortion, she decided to try to ignore it.

Cassie straightened her shoulders and looked directly at the young reporter. "I will not answer that question," she said. "It has long been the opinion of the Washington press corps and, indeed, it is my own opinion, that the private lives of members of Congress should be precisely that: private."

With that, she took her briefcase from the table and left the room with Cully trailing close behind her. When she reached her offices her secretary told her Mack Cameron was on the telephone and she went immediately to her private office to take his call, signaling to Cully to wait in the outer office.

"Mack."

"Cassie, what the hell's going on down there? A reporter just called me and—"

"Wait. I'll explain tonight or better still—when are you going to your hotel?"

"I can leave right now. But you have a Judiciary Committee meeting at—"

"I'll have to duck that. I'll be at your hotel in fifteen minutes."

She opened the door of her office. "Lisa, ask them to bring my car around, will you? Right now!"

"Hold on there, Cassie," Cully said. "We've got to talk. I'm going to be getting calls and I have to know what to tell them."

She put her hand on his arm. "Just give everyone a 'no comment.'

It will be all right. And I'll tell you everything, I promise. I'll call you at home tonight. Right now, the less you know, the better."

"Now, I don't think that's a very good idea—" he started to say, but she was halfway out the door.

Cassie drove directly to Mack's hotel and turned her car over to the parking valet. Mack was waiting for her in his suite.

"For God's sake, Cassie! What the hell is—"

"Mack." She kissed him lightly and drew away to sit down in an armchair. "Will you fix me a drink first?"

"I will, and I'll get myself one, too. I need it!"

He brought their drinks and would have questioned her, but she said, "Please, Mack. It's hard enough to tell you this, so please let me do it my way."

He nodded encouragingly and she could finally make a start. She told him the whole sordid story, from agreeing to travel with Jimmy only because James said that Jimmy needed his wife to campaign with him, to Jimmy's infidelities, to her awaking in the hospital to learn that her baby had been taken from her infected body.

By the time she finished, tears were rolling down her face, unnoticed. Mack pulled her to her feet and held her close. "You poor kid. And you were only—what? Twenty years old?"

She brushed away the tears. "Don't feel too sorry for me, Mack. I got a car out of it and money, too. I got away from Ballard."

He held her shoulders and looked into her eyes. His blue eyes were sad. "At what cost, darling? Think what you had to pay."

"And I guess I still have to pay." She tried to smile. "For once I can't find a way out, Mack. There's no way out of this one, no way at all."

"There's always a way, Cassie, but you have to hunt for it. Look, go in the bathroom and wash off that mascara, will you, before I begin to think I'm in love with a damn raccoon."

"You mean that you still love me?"

"Of course!" He hugged her and swung her around twice before setting her back on her feet. "As I told you before, love, I'm not some kind of good-time Charlie. Like it or not, kid, you're stuck with me. Remember me? I'm in for the long haul."

Washing her face with cold water helped Cassie begin to climb out of her abyss of misery. It helped even more to have Mack waiting, holding out to her a white terry-cloth robe.

"Hang up your clothes, love, so they don't get all wrinkled. I want to hold you."

She went to his arms as if to a sanctuary, but their bodies were not those of a nun and a monk. Cassie pulled away.

"I have to figure out what I'm going to do, what to say to the press."

"Right. But remember that Mark Twain said that sex concentrates the mind wonderfully."

She giggled. "I think what he said was that *death* concentrates the mind—if it even *was* Mark Twain."

"It doesn't matter, does it? You're laughing."

Cassie was surprised. "I am! Mack, oh, Mack darling, what am I going to do with you?"

"Get those clothes off and I'll show you."

Chapter 36

Her short stay with Mack Cameron reaffirmed Cassie's belief in herself, but it did not make her problem disappear. During the drive to Georgetown, the two of them discussed it.

"It's going to depend on what the papers do with it tomorrow," she said.

"You mean, if it's in the back of the paper it's unlikely anyone will follow up on it?"

"I mean, that's what I hope. By the time the House rises, it should be a dead issue."

Angelina met them at the door. "Señor Meecham, he call you five, six times."

"Oh, dear," Cassie said. "I'd better go upstairs and call him back." She hesitated in the door of the library. "Mack, Angelina, please. Don't let the children watch the television news." She left Mack showing the children how to build a fire in the fireplace.

Cully was at home and answered on the second ring. "Cassie, where the hell have you been? I've been fielding calls from the press all afternoon!"

Cassie's heart sank. That did not sound like page 8 of the next day's papers. Nevertheless, she explained her strategy to Cully.

He was calmer when she finished. "You know, you may be right. It might be better just to ignore it. Any kind of big news could knock you right out of the papers."

Cassie twisted the phone cord in her fingers. Going on recent history, she was afraid that anything short of a cease-fire in Vietnam would not quiet a juicy Washington scandal.

"Cassie? Are you still there?"

"Yes. I'm sorry. I was just thinking—"

"Well, look, I had an idea that would fit right into your plan. What do you think of getting yourself right out of town until this blows over? A week or so maybe."

"But the House won't rise for four more days."

"I know. And seeing you go in and out every day is going to keep you right at the front of everyone's mind. With you out of town, there's no way the reporters can get fresh fuel for this little brush fire. I can just go right on saying 'no comment' until they get bored with asking. Anyway, it might not be a bad idea to see your constituents right now. They could be a little bit nervous about all this going on."

Cassie hated to leave Mack so soon, but she knew it was the right thing to do.

"I'll have to make arrangements for my children, Cully, so they won't miss school, but I can fly out by noon tomorrow."

"Good girl, Cassie. And don't worry about the office. I'll stay in touch."

"You do that, Cully. You stay in touch."

Cassie went down the stairs slowly, dreading Mack's reaction to the news that she was leaving for a week. To her surprise, he was relieved.

"I've been putting off telling you this, Cassie, but I've got to spend about six days in London, either now or very soon. The final contracts are being drawn up and I need to be there to make sure everything goes the way I want it."

"And maybe by the time I get back to Washington I'll be old stale news."

"God, let's hope so. I know this is terribly difficult for you."

"Just so I don't become front page news."

"Love, you'll always be front page news to me, no matter what."

An immediate problem was solved when Ruby Vance immediately agreed to stay with the children for a week. Cassie made meal plans with Angelina and had her house in order by the next morning, when she finally had time to pack her clothes.

The telephone rang just as she closed her suitcase. She answered eagerly, assuming it would be Mack.

"Mrs. Steele, this is James Weston." It was the vice chairman of the Republican National Committee, the man she had talked with at Hilton Head.

"Oh, yes, Mr. Weston. I promised to have an answer for you within a week, didn't I? Well, I can give you that answer now."

"That will no longer be necessary, Mrs. Steele. Not after the reports of your press conference Friday. Mr.—ah—someone near the top of our organization has become rather nervous about that, and we have been asked to withdraw the informal proposals we discussed with you."

Although Cassie had no intention of changing parties, she was infuriated by his summary dismissal of her. "Now, wait just a minute, Mr. Weston. One question was asked at that press conference, only one, and I refused to dignify it with an answer. Are you telling me that your party is no longer interested in me because of one question, a question based on unproved information, on rumor only?"

"I'm sorry, Mrs. Steele. It is not proof or lack of proof that matters in politics, a fact that you yourself must know. It is a matter of perceived truth, which might be totally unconnected to real truth. One word—especially a politically sensitive word like 'abortion'—can create a perceived truth whether or not it has anything to do with the facts involved."

"I am a politician, as you say, Mr. Weston, and I know how political parties arrive at decisions, but I must protest this line of action."

"I can understand your dismay, Mrs. Steele, and I am sorry that you feel so strongly about it, but the decision has been made. Good-bye."

Without another word, he hung up on her.

First the newspapers, then the Republican party. What next, Cassie wondered. Who would be the next to drop her?

At Dulles Airport, Cassie saw that news of the Tet offensive occupied the front pages of America's leading newspapers. The story about her, in the two papers she bought to read on the plane, was no more than a page 5 squib. With no facts and no comment from her, she could begin to believe that James Weston was wrong and her own instincts were right. Uninformed gossip about her could indeed blow over within a week.

The Oklahomans of her district, however, were more interested in their representative than they were in "Johnson's war." She spent the afternoon talking to people at the San Bois clinic but drove to Ballard to spend the night with Amelia and James Steele.

After dinner, James asked Cassie to come into his study. She pulled a chair up to face him across his desk. The green glass shade of his desk lamp threw a reflection on his cheeks and gave his gray face a cold sheen of death.

"Cassie," he said. "I am ashamed to tell you this, but I feel that I owe you an explanation."

Cassie was startled. "Ashamed? Why, James?"

"I know the source of these new rumors about your abortion. I suspected they came from Jimmy, and it turned out that I was right, indirectly. It seems that a few years ago he was drunk, which is hardly surprising news, but at that time he told his wife Maggie about the—well, the abortion. He finally admitted to me that she had brought it up again quite recently and had nagged at him until he told her Dr. Mathers's name, everything. Mathers died seven or eight years ago, but Maggie made it her business to cajole Mrs. Mathers into letting her see his files. She took the records of your—

dealings with the doctor. Maggie's family, the Welleses, have friends whose daughter is a junior reporter with a Washington newspaper. It was Maggie who contacted the girl and gave her the information about you."

"But why, James? Why would Maggie do such a thing? I hardly know her!"

"According to my son—" He seemed to wince from an inner pain. "According to Jimmy, she has always envied you your position in Congress, and your children and, he says, your striking good looks. I'm afraid that time and alcohol have taken a toll on Maggie. And now that there are reported links between you and one of the richest men in Oklahoma, well, Jimmy says she has come to hate you."

"You don't mean Mack Cameron, surely."

"Mackenzie Cameron, yes. You must be aware that he is very wealthy, Cassie."

"Wealthy? I suppose so."

"Perhaps I chose the wrong word. Maggie's family, the Welleses, are wealthy. You, for that matter, are wealthy. Oil men like Mackenzie Cameron have spawned a new term entirely. Mack Cameron is what oil men call 'Big Rich.' "

"I've heard the phrase, James." She shook her head slowly. "I still don't understand Maggie's doing this to me. She must know what it will do to my political career. Oh, Lord, how she must hate me!"

"No, Cassie, I don't believe the woman has any conception of what this story can do to you. She is malicious, but she hasn't the intelligence to be truly evil."

Cassie rubbed her temples with her fingertips. "Mack thinks it will all blow over," she said without much hope.

James shook his big head slowly. "Then it's as well that Cameron is in oil and not politics. I don't mean to add to your depression, Cassie, but I think you should be prepared for the worst." He opened his desk drawer and withdrew three sheets of paper. "This is the original of Dr. Mathers's record and these are two photo-copies of it. I am sorry to say that I can't guarantee that there are no other copies."

Cassie took the papers without looking at them. She did not want to read those dreadful words. "What shall I do with them, James?"

"I don't know. I simply do not know. But there is a possibility that you should wait awhile before you do anything at all. If a reporter gets hold of Maggie, an experienced reporter, she might make the story sound even worse than it is. You might need the original records to refute it."

"How could it be made to sound worse than it is?" she asked bitterly. She glanced down at the doctor's record and a name caught her eye. She looked up in surprise. "James, your name is here. You are implicated."

"I know."

"And you are giving yourself, your reputation into my hands?"

"Yes. I am." He looked away. "I can only hope that you will protect me better than I protected you, Cassie." He turned back to her, obviously forcing himself to look directly into her eyes. "I am sorry, more sorry than I can ever say. I misjudged you and your motives from the start, Cassie, I misjudged you. I can only hope that someday, even if it is after I am gone from this earth, you can find it in your heart to forgive me."

Cassie stood up, holding the papers that would destroy her career, and looked down at James Steele. She remembered quite clearly the first day she ever saw him, a hot dry day when she was five years old and stood in the dusty yard of her father's share-cropper shack. She stood in the dust and looked up at the big heavy man who was a legend in her family, the very embodiment of wealth and power.

And now she looked down at him, at the age-thinned, rounded shoulders, the tired, lined face and the gray skin already tinged with death.

"I forgave you long ago, James," she said softly. "I had to forgive you because you are my children's grandfather, as Amelia is their grandmother. They are part of you, James. They carry your blood and your genes. And because you and Amelia have been my family, too, for these last years. You have to forgive your family, James. You must forgive them everything."

James ducked his head for a moment and then he stood up too, and with moist eyes looked across the desk at her. "Thank you," he said with great dignity. "I thank you, Cassie."

She turned away, taking the papers he had given her, and opened the door of the study. She paused in the doorway to look back at him.

"James," she said. "Next time little old Maggie comes by, you might just want to put a bug in her ear."

"What do you mean?"

"I just thought you might enjoy being the one to tell her the latest news, James. You know that Big Rich fellow, that Mackenzie Cameron? Well, the sharecropper's daughter, Cassandra Taylor Steele, is going to marry the man!"

During that week in Oklahoma, Cassie found more and more often that her constituents met her not with the usual smiles but with skeptical eyes and mouths tight with suspicion. Conservative Oklahomans did not hold much with abortion and they did not hold at all with having their representative hide her past from them.

Each night Cassie went home to the ranch to call the children and then, invariably, to call Cully Meecham and check the thermometer of her Washington support. It was well below zero, he reported, and there were no warming signs.

"You won't do any more harm here than you will out there, Cassie. If you're not winning friends in Oklahoma, or keeping old friends, then it's a sure bet that this damn thing isn't going to blow over."

"But why, Cully, why? Why should the private life of a congresswoman from the hills of Eastern Oklahoma interest so many people? Everyone in Washington knows that there are twenty congressmen sleeping with their secretaries and at least three sleeping with page boys, and nobody pays any attention to it at all! Why should I be the one who is belabored over something that happened twenty years ago?"

"Maybe because there aren't very many of you, Cassie, I mean, of women in Congress."

"But that's not fair!"

"Whoever said life was fair? I'll tell you something, though, the way this thing keeps developing, I got a hunch that maybe somebody's pushing it."

"I told you about Jimmy Steele's wife, Maggie."

"No, I mean somebody here in Washington. There are a few places where you aren't real popular, you know, like in the White House."

"Cully, you're really grasping at straws, now. That's ridiculous, and you know it. President Johnson has a war to run, and a country—"

"I didn't say Johnson, did I? There's lots of people up there that'll do something just on the chance that it will win them some brownie points."

"There can't possibly be anything to that, Cully."

"Well, I'll keep digging around. Maybe I'll come up with something—or somebody—by the time you get back here."

"I hope so! I have reservations for day after tomorrow. The state party bigwigs want me to come to Oklahoma City tomorrow for a meeting. I imagine it is to get wheels in motion for the primary election in April."

Bill Little, the state party chairman, was a soft-looking man in his fifties. He spoke for all of them, he said. "We can't back you in the primary, Cassie."

"Can't back me?" Cassie half-rose from her chair. "What on

earth are you talking about? I'm the incumbent, remember, a proven vote-getter and fund-raiser. Why on earth would you say such a thing?"

He patted the air with a pudgy hand as if to calm a skittish horse. Cassie reluctantly subsided into her chair.

"What we're talking about, Cassie, is this rumor that's going around. You know, about you having an—"

She waited, forcing him to say the word that offended everyone so much.

"An—ah—abortion. I'll tell you this, Cassie, you've put us in a real bind."

"*I've* put *you* in a bind?"

"Yeah. See, the thing is, an accusation was made and you haven't done anything to refute it, not one damn thing. So that leaves everybody thinking that it's true."

"What if it were true, Bill? A therapeutic abortion still wouldn't be illegal."

"Maybe not, I mean, not by the letter of the law, but to lots of folks it's breaking God's law."

Cassie took a deep breath. "God has nothing to do with deciding whom the party will support in the Democratic primary, Bill. That is your responsibility."

"Well, yes. Not just me, Cassie, all of us here. But I'm glad you brought up the subject of responsibility. That's what I'm aiming at. You see, it's our responsibility to support a primary candidate that can end up winning the general election in November. And you can't do that now, Cassie, and you know it as well as we do. There's no way you can win an election with this thing hanging over your head."

"Oh, come on, Bill. It will be forgotten by November. Water under the bridge."

"With a strong Republican candidate hitting on it every day from now till the election? Forget it, girl."

"The way you're forgetting me?"

"Cassie, that isn't it at all! I mean—"

"I can see what you mean. You mean that you are happy to support me when I'm on a roll but that you won't stand by me when I need your help."

"Now, you wait just a minute," another committee member said. "There's no call to talk that way."

"Look, Cassie," Bill Little said, "try to see it from the party's standpoint. We've got a tough fight coming up and we can't afford to take on somebody that's already got two strikes against her."

Cassie stood up, holding her briefcase and handbag. "I can see that your minds are made up, that they were made up long before this discussion began. Good-bye, gentlemen."

Bill raised his hand. "Wait a minute, Cassie. You aren't going to just walk out on us, are you, after all that the party's done for you? We know you'll support our candidate all the way and we hope you'll do your usual fine fund-raising."

"After all that the party's done for me," she said slowly. "I hope so, too, gentlemen. I hope so, too."

Mack Cameron came back from London the same day Cassie returned from Oklahoma. The next day the two of them met to confer with Cully Meecham.

"I'm damn sure somebody is pushing this thing," Cully told them, "but my sources have all dried up. I can't get the time of day out of anyone."

Mack leaned forward. "Cully, do you think it would help if I put some private investigators on it?"

"Oh, Mack!" Cassie protested. "This is not a matter of someone stealing plans for an invasion of Russia!"

"No," he said seriously, "it's stealing your reputation, and to me that's even worse."

After hours of talk they agreed on one thing. Cassie should not run in the Democratic primary. "I don't like backing down," she said, "but I'm afraid that my running would just intensify the thing. Let's face it. Without the party's support I wouldn't have the chance of a snowball in hell of winning, anyway."

The one bright spot that spring was the weekend that Cassie and Mack were able to get away to Hilton Head. George and Minna were delighted to have the house open and their total approval of Cassie was made obvious in the marvelously unobtrusive service they provided. There was delicious food available at all times of day and night. "It's like magic," Cassie said to Mack. "All this food just appears and we never even catch a glimpse of George and Minna. I think it's some kind of voodoo."

"Mmm," he said into her neck. "Voodoo, yeah, and you're the high priestess. Come, let us rise now to the second story and indulge ourselves in a few pagan rites."

"Will you be my love slave?"

"Eternally!" he swore.

"Zen come wiz me to ze Cazbah."

"Wrong movie," he complained but it did not keep him away from their private Casbah.

After the primary in Oklahoma was over, the rumors about Cassie faded away as suddenly as they had arisen.

"That confirms it, to me," Cully said. "Somebody someplace just plain wanted you *out!*"

"Then they should be happy now," she said morosely. "There is nothing quite as definitely, positively *out* as a lame-duck congresswoman."

As time wore on, even her Oklahoma constituents were more interested in their present than in Cassie's past. Lyndon Johnson's decision not to run again, Martin Luther King's assassination and that of Robert Kennedy, the riots at the Democratic national convention in Chicago, McGovern giving Eagleton the vice presidential candidacy and then taking it away because Eagleton had consulted psychiatrists, race riots everywhere, vicious fighting in

Vietnam, everything seemed to happen at once, as if on one endless terrible day. Finally, in 1968, American citizens realized that their country was sailing on dangerous seas.

Mack pushed her to set a date for their wedding but she did not want to start her new life in defeat. He could understand that, he said, and he would not press her. They were able to spend a lot of time with each other, and with the children. She appreciated Mack's patience and told him so.

"Well, I don't appreciate your stubbornness, but if you have to see it through, I'll just have to wait," he said, smiling.

Cassie went through the motions of her job, but she had a strong sense of futility. No one wanted her views, no one was interested, because politically she had become a nonperson. By the end of the year, she was keeping her office open only to deal with her constituents' problems.

Cully Meecham was getting other offers, she knew, but he evidently decided to stay with her to the end. He took on all sorts of minor jobs as her staff members peeled off, one by one, and headed for greener fields.

The day finally arrived when she could turn her keys over to a building custodian and close the door of her office for the last time. She paused to run her fingertips over the incised letters of the doorplate: Representative Cassandra Taylor Steele.

She walked slowly down the corridor and just as she turned the corner toward the elevators, a hand gripped her elbow.

"Is this former Representative Cassandra Taylor Steele?" a gruff voice asked.

She turned, laughing, to face him. "Soon to be former Representative Cassandra Taylor Steele Cameron," she said.

"Very soon," Mack said. "But that does solve one problem."

"What? What problem?"

"You can never divorce me, woman. There wouldn't be room on a nameplate for even one more husband."

"Now, you listen to me, Mack Cameron. You said that you

were in for the long haul. Well, I am too, so just don't you think for one minute that you can ever get away from me!"

"And if I ever get away from you I'll take you with me. I'll kidnap you! In fact, that's what I'm doing right now unless, of course, you have any objections."

"Mack. Will you please tell me what you're talking about?"

"Ruby and Angelina packed a bag for you, just a few things, because we can pick up the rest when we're there. They are all set to stay with the kids and there's a car waiting to drive us to the Supreme Court and—"

"Wait. Wait! The Supreme Court?"

"Yes. Justice White." He raised his wrist to look at his watch. "In fact, the good Justice will be ready for us in about ten minutes, so we'd better hit the road."

"I don't understand!"

He held her away from him. "My, you are thick today, dearie. He is going to marry us, what else?"

"But the children—"

"They are already at the Court, waiting, along with Ruby and Angelina and your friend Blair and her husband. Enough of an audience?"

"Yes! But why the suitcase, if we're to be—"

"Because I'm kidnapping you, the way I promised. We'll go right from the wedding ceremony to our plane."

"What plane? To where?"

"Questions, questions! Come on, we have to hurry."

"Mack," she said, pulling at his arm. "I am not going to take one step until you tell me where we're going."

"Sydney."

"Sydney, Australia?"

His blue eyes twinkled. "That's the only Sydney I'm aware of, but who knows? We could end up in Sydney, North Dakota, or Sydney, Oklahoma, for that matter. But all Sydneys are renowned, I've heard, as good places to think."

"To think?" Cassie's mind was still awhirl with Sydneys. "To think about what?"

"About what you're going to do next, of course. You can't go straight from the House of Representatives to watching soap operas, you know. You have to figure out what world to conquer next."

Cassie stared up at him and then she smiled, a smile that became wider with every second that passed. "Mack," she said, and that was all.

The elevator doors opened and Cassie tucked her hand into the crook of Mack's arm and marched in, singing loudly:

"Sydney, Oklahoma, here I come . . ."

Ignoring the open laughter of the other passengers, Mack joined her in song:

"Right back where I started from . . ."

As the doors closed, they finished together in a rousing chorus:

"Open up that elevator door,
Because, Sydney, here I come!"